Bullet for an Encore

Michael Litchfield

HALE
CRIME

ROBERT HALE · LONDON

ISBN 0 7090 7734 3

Robert Hale Limited
Clerkenwell House
Clerkenwell Green
London EC1R 0HT

2 4 6 8 10 9 7 5 3 1

Typeset in 10/12pt Palatino
Printed in Great Britain by St Edmundsbury Press,
Bury St Edmunds, Suffolk.
Bound by Woolnough Bookbinding Ltd.

For Michele, Luke and Savannah – three very special people

A special word of thanks to Gill Jackson for her eagle-eyed editing and helpful advice, without which this story would not have worked.

Chapter One

Elvis Presley received a standing ovation.

'More! More! Encore! Encore!'

The rhinestone suit glittered in the harsh, incandescent glare of the spotlight. He bowed extravagantly. He blew kisses theatrically. He gyrated his hips and worked his pelvis.

'How about that?' the leader of the small band demanded rhetorically into his mike, which was on the end of a long leash.

The nightclub audience of well-dressed diners stayed on their feet. Incitement was unnecessary. Elvis had been hot and the audience wasn't ready to let him go just yet.

'No! No! No!' they roared as Elvis loped awkwardly off the diminutive, circular dancefloor, his stage for the last forty minutes, the spotlight – now more of a searchlight – following him as if he were an escaping convict.

'You really want more?' boomed the bandleader, already prepared for the inevitable, prompted answer.

The unanimous response was returned with the speed of a ricochet, roistering but good-humoured.

'OK, let's have Elvis back one more time.'

On cue, Elvis reappeared, immediately beamed back to centre stage to another spontaneous outpouring of appreciation.

'Ladies and gentlemen, I truly thank you,' he said in his baritone, rich, though contrived, Deep South accent.

He treated them to four more favourites from his long-established repertoire, then finished with 'Love Me Tender'.

Still they didn't want to release him. It was the same every performance. The trick was always to leave them still hungry and lusting for more.

Before taking the final bow, he took from a trouser-pocket a pair of white silk boxer shorts, bearing the saucy, red-embroidered inscription, 'Elvis made it big in these!' and tossed them into the audience. They were caught by a middle-aged woman, whose reaction to her catch was that of a swooning teenage groupie. Her half-drunk escort, who may even have been her husband, clapped gleefully, not feeling the least threatened because it was all part of the show; all part of the past; living history.

In his closet-sized dressing-room, Elvis removed his wig and combed back his tacky, receding light-brown hair, flecked with premature grey strands, especially down the sideburns. Sitting in front of a horseshoe-shaped ensemble of mirrors, he winced at the image of a bald patch, which seemed to be expanding daily on his crown. Elvis wasn't happy. Still sweating profusely, he poured himself a generous whisky into a tumbler from the bottle he had placed strategically on the dressing-table, like a loaded syringe, all ready for a quick shot into the bloodstream. He drank like a man with a need, doing it for maintenance, rather than for social pleasure.

Five minutes later, he had wriggled out of his trademark white costume and was squeezing into faded jeans. After hanging the suit in the compact wardrobe and placing the brown cowboy boots underneath, he finished dressing – T-shirt, black leather jacket, suede calf-high boots and a thick woollen, dark-blue overcoat with a matching belt around the waist. He finished his tumbler of whisky, pushed the bottle into his overcoat pocket, left the wig on the dressing-table, switched off the light, and departed the nightclub via the rear fire exit, which opened into an alley, mainly frequented at that time of night by dealers, the *demimonde*, their pimps and potential punters.

A draught of frosty air, an unwelcome gift from Siberia, slapped him in the face, instantly freezing the pearls of sweat on his forehead. Burying his chin as deeply as possible into his overcoat to protect his face from the chafing mid-winter wind, he strode out purposefully for the nearest multi-storey car park, about 200 yards away towards Soho Square.

He had taken only a few slippery steps when his mobile vibrated in the left-hand pocket of his overcoat – the opposite side from the bottle of Scotch.

'Hello,' he said into the phone, his stride shortening only temporarily. It was too bitterly cold to dally.

'It's me. Where are you?'

'On my way to the car.'

'I won't delay you, then. Be careful. See you soon.'

'Half an hour.' With that, he killed the call and switched off his cell phone.

Hurrying on, he ignored the incessant, stereotype propositioning from the hookers who were lobbying for their last trick of the night before their pimps would free them from their pavement patrol.

Once out of the alleys, he could see the car-park sign ahead on the other side. He crossed the well-lit road, trotting a couple of paces to avoid being run over by a taxi. Sleet had turned to snow, which was settling. The forecast was for more of the same, with a severe, overnight frost. Roads would be treacherous in the morning. Winter really was kicking in with an ugly snarl.

On reaching the cover of the car park, he swore at the notice warning that both lifts were 'Out of Order'. *Doesn't anything ever work in this damned city?* He shivered and shook himself down as he climbed the echoing stone stairs to the third floor, consoling himself with the thought that he would have another swig of whisky from the bottle as soon as he was inside his Jaguar.

By the time he reached the third floor, he was out of breath. *God, thank goodness I won't be doing this for much longer! This is ridiculous.*

There were only five cars now on the third floor. His silver, four-door saloon was the furthest away from him, berthed next to a stone pillar and a red BMW. He rubbed his hands to massage away the numbness as he neared his Jag. The echoes ceased when he stopped. Now it was so deadly quiet as he ferreted in his trouser pockets for the key. *Come on, where are you? Gotcha!*

That was the moment he heard a movement, another footstep, amazingly close, catching him by surprise. He looked up.

'Grief! *You*! I never expected....'

'Of course you didn't, Elvis. That's the whole idea, right?'

Before Elvis could reply, the trigger was squeezed on his fragile life. Two more shots echoed.

Elvis lay dead amid the acrid smell of cordite. Running footsteps disappeared into the night.

The 'King's' reign, for what it was worth, was over.

Yet again.

Chapter Two

Detective Inspector Luke Templeman padded naked towards the large bay window where the bedroom telephone was bleating for instant attention, like a baby demanding to be picked up, cradled and fed. Having the telephone well away from the bed was deliberate strategy. He recognized his own foibles – well, some of them. He knew that if he was called out in the dead of night while still tucked-up cosily in bed, warm as fresh toast, the temptation would be to turn over and rejoin his dreams and nightmares after putting down the telephone, rather than doing what was demanded of him. Such an admission to himself was a source of comfort. He liked the equilibrium that came with the belief that he tussled with similar weaknesses to everyone else.

Charley, his wife, idly watched him silhouetted in the moonlight against the frosty window. When Luke spoke sleepily into the mouthpiece, his voice sounded to Charley like a TV set murmuring in the background.

Charley slithered out of bed and slipped into a silk robe, before migrating desultorily into the bathroom, where the mirror, harshly rude, told her stark truths she had no wish to know, especially at 2 a.m. Ignorance could be a consolatory ally. During the day she was able to delude herself, and the rest of the world, by papering over the cracks, but cosmetic repairs did nothing more than mask wear and tear. They didn't turn back the clock, which, in her case, had been ticking inexorably for thirty-five years; even faster, it seemed, during the last few months. Youth's bloom was well beyond full flush, but she was blessed with an intrinsic beauty which she couldn't see, thus making it all the more beguiling and appealing to others.

She fingered her prominent chin, cocked her head to the left, then to the right. 'Well, old girl, where are you going?' she chatted to herself in the manner of two old friends confiding in one another in a powder-room. The question was rhetorical, of course. She didn't expect much sense or compassion from her mirror. If *she* hadn't the answer, why should she anticipate one from her reflection?

Sleepily, she ran her spidery fingers through her dark, frizzy hair, pulling faces at herself, displaying perfectly arranged white teeth, playing chimp, then chump; always self-effacing and disarming, which made her a dangerous opponent. Here she was forlornly counting the cost of failure, while others counted their good fortune at having her on their payroll. Her talents were magnified by the fact that her self-esteem was so fragile. Her brilliance was in the eye of the beholder and not in any self-promotion.

Flattening her neat little snub-nose, as if pressing a lift button, she laughed at herself. 'Sorry, ugly duckling, it's too late to be dreaming of making the transmutation into a swan.' Self-deprecation suited her. Critically, she raised her breasts and fondled the nipples on which no child had ever weaned. 'Don't tell me you're becoming broody?' she asked herself aloud. 'Not me. Don't be so bloody silly!' Such doubts and questions disturbed her, so she walked away from them, back into the bedroom, where Luke was just finishing dressing.

'Who was it?' Charley asked needlessly. The question was merely a lawyer's way of initiating a gentle probe for more information.

'Old Nick.'

'Always Old Nick.'

Luke's job and his anti-social working hours were currently a sore point between them. *Old Nick* was their shorthand for Scotland Yard, Britain's nerve centre of law enforcement.

'It pays the mortgage.'

'It *contributes* to the mortgage,' she corrected him.

'Sorry. You're right, we're a partnership. You do your bit, which is bigger than mine. I'm appreciative.'

'Thanks, Bigheart!'

'This isn't the time for this.'

'No time ever is. Just for the record and not because I'm the least bit interested, where are you going?'

'Soho.'

'Very nice!' The sarcasm was nothing more than a throwaway line.

Their kiss, initiated by Luke, lacked passion and was nothing more intimate than an oral handshake – at best.

Just as he was at the bedroom door, Charley asked evenly, 'So, who's been killed?' She had been married long enough to a senior cop to realize that he wouldn't be summoned from his bed for anything less than murder.

'Elvis Presley,' he answered deadpan. 'Shot just minutes after completing a gig.'

'Not funny,' Charley berated him for his apparent bad taste.

'Wrongly accused, Counsellor,' Luke countered, in a manner that precluded further cross-examination. 'I must go. I'm sure you'll hear all about it on radio and TV.'

After Luke had gone, Charley switched on her bedside radio, which was tuned to an all-night music programme. Elvis, courtesy of the DJ, was crooning his famous ballad, 'Love Me Tender, Love Me Sweet'. He had already been dead for more than twenty-five years, but the legend had survived the grave, maturing annually. The 'King' transcended all generations, all genres. Little old ladies remembered with watery eyes the days when they rocked to his beat. Kids, who hadn't even been embryos when Elvis departed with so little warning, genuflected to the memory of the Nashville monarch. While alive, he had adoring fans. Now he had worshipping disciples.

So what did Luke mean? Charley wondered, genuinely intrigued.

Meanwhile, Elvis continued with his rendition, 'Love Me Tender ...' and explanations seemed a long way off.

Chapter Three

Templeman caught a glimpse of himself in the driving-mirror as he fired the engine of his black Ford Mondeo. He grimaced at what he saw and was pleased to focus on the road ahead. He hadn't shaved for thirty-six hours and what a few years ago would have been accepted as designer stubble would now be described as untended vegetation. His darkling, penetrating eyes seemed to be protesting against being bullied into opening for business at such an anti-social hour. The puffy pockets under his eyes accentuated his tiredness and dishevelled appearance. His short hair, which matched the colour of his eyes, had been combed back marginally with his fingers. His lean, hungry look worried his mother ('Doesn't that wife of yours ever feed you, or is she too busy gadding about doing a man's job?') but most women found him attractive, though dangerous. Silent and deep. Like Loch Ness. No one was quite sure what monsters lurked in the depths of those murky waters, in his soul. There were rumours, stories, that evoked both *frisson* and fascination, but also caution.

The West End was still busy, even at that hour. *Doesn't this city ever sleep?* Of course it didn't. The question to himself was rhetoric. This was London, a sister to New York, Paris, Chicago, Los Angeles, San Francisco, Miami – one of a large family of insomniacs. All of them with bad-blood. Bad people.

The volume of traffic was noticeably different from early in the day, though. For a start, it flowed freely and without the urgency and simmering rage under the surface, which so often flared, blowing off the lid. As he pulled up outside the car park in Soho, he confronted himself again in the mirror. *What a mess!* Many women, however, would have said, *How raffish!*

Detective Sergeant Simone Tandy, his partner, was waiting for him on the third floor. It was Tandy who had called him at home.

If he had told Charley that they had been woken by Tandy, that would have added an extra salty dimension to the friction.

'Who raised the alarm?' There was no preamble. Templeman's voice was laced with phlegm. They were standing about ten yards from the body and the Jaguar, where the scene-of-crime team was assembling its equipment. Yellow tape had already been used to seal-off the entire third floor to the public.

'Over there.' Tandy, a 33-year-old brunette who had given up teaching 9-year-olds to join the police for safer career prospects, pointed towards a pallid little man who was clearly in shock.

'What's his story?'

'He works as a waiter at the Society nightclub, just around the corner.'

'I know where the Society is,' Templeman said prickly. 'Has he a name?'

'Tony Peno. He's Italian. Well, Italian/English. His English is good. Perhaps not good, but better than ours.'

Templeman was in no mood for a side show. 'What was he doing here?'

'I was just about to tell you.' Templeman could overawe most people if so disposed, but not Tandy. In her, he had found his match. 'Harry Markham had left his wallet in his dressing-room.'

'Harry Markham?'

'The stiff. Alias Elvis Presley. He's a professional impersonator, along with half the world, it would seem. Markham had finished his performance and had left the club. The manager sent Mr Peno after him.'

'How did he know where to look?'

'Because Markham always parked here.'

'Always on the same floor?'

Tandy pulled a face that said, *You've stumped me there!* 'I haven't gone into detail,' she added quickly, defensively.

'You mean you didn't think of it.'

'No, I meant exactly what I said. Perhaps you should ask him yourself, Inspector.' *Inspector* was emphasized in such a way that it suggested it wasn't her customary style of addressing him.

'I intend to.' With that, he peeled away from the team.

Peno was still shivering, induced by a combination of shock and the bitterly cold night. Templeman introduced himself and proffered a hand for shaking, but very little registered with the waiter, who just stood rooted, staring with a sightless gaze.

Templeman withdrew his hand, not the least offended. His understanding came from empirical experience. The witness was blitzed and shell-shocked.

'Did you make the call to the police, sir?'

'No.' Peno's voice hardly rose above a whisper.

'Why not?'

'I hadn't my mobile on me. I ran back to the club.'

'So who did put in the call?'

'The boss.'

'The manager?'

'Yes.'

'And who might that be?'

'Mr Velatti.'

'How's that spelt?' Templeman took his black, leather-covered flip-over notebook from his overcoat pocket and removed the top from his ballpoint pen with his teeth.

Peno spelt out the manager's name, as requested, having to correct himself a couple of times as nerves impaired both tongue and brain.

'Does he have a first name?'

'Yes, of course.'

'Well?'

'Oh, sorry, yes, Joe.'

'So you were with Mr Velatti when he made the call?'

'No. He sent me back here. He said, "You go wait until the police show up and see nothing's touched."'

Good man, thought Templeman, nodding approvingly.

'What about you, Mr Peno, have you touched anything?'

The waiter's lips, blue with cold, quivered a little and his frightened eyes seemed to be jumping around for a place to hide. 'Only when I first got here, not the second time.'

'What did you touch, Mr Peno?'

'Him.' He pointed shakily towards the body, which was now the property of the coroner's office. Two coroner's officers fussed around the police doctor and the corps of scene-of-crime experts who were growing in number as more were dragooned from their beds. Peno couldn't bring himself to look at the body and pools of blood.

Templeman stopped writing. This was a time when observation was more important than anything else. He could catch up with paperwork when this interview was finished.

'Let's just run over some of the things you've probably already told my colleague. When you arrived initially with Mr Markham's wallet, did you come straight to the third floor?' It was a question with plenty of top spin.

'No,' Peno replied, without having to give the question much thought. 'I didn't know where his car was parked. I looked on the ground floor, then the first, second, and finally ...' He dried up momentarily, choking on an emotional lump. 'There's never many cars in here after midnight. It wasn't like looking for a needle in a haystack. But I did think I'd missed him. My boss expected me to return with the wallet, saying he'd gone. It was a long shot.' He blanched at his unfortunate choice of metaphor.

'Why do you suppose he parked on the third floor?'

'I beg your pardon?' Peno was confused.

'If the car park's virtually empty, why drive up three floors?'

Some colour reappeared in the waiter's cheeks and he shook his head, pleased to be tested with questions that kept his attention away from the macabre activity just a few yards away.

'Before midnight, the car park can be quite busy with the cars of theatregoers and late-night diners. It's after midnight when it thins out.'

'What about the clubbers, like your customers? Don't they use it?'

'Some. Mr Markham would have parked while the West End night-life was at its peak.'

'Did you see Mr Markham on the ground from the top of the stairs?'

'Not immediately. It was only when I looked towards the cars—'

'How many cars?' Templeman interrupted brusquely.

'I didn't count.' Peno seemed amazed by such a question. 'I saw him on the floor. I didn't go round counting cars.'

'You could tell who it was from all of thirty yards?'

'No, I just saw someone on the ground.'

'And then?'

'I went to him, of course, thinking it was someone who'd perhaps suffered a heart-attack.'

'When did you realize who it was?'

'As I approached. His head and shoulders were partly propped up against the bumper of his car.'

'How did you know it was *his* car?'

'I assumed. I assume ...'

'What else did you see?' Templeman had hit a rhythm and he was anxious not to slacken the tempo.

Peno's eyes rolled around in their puffy, shell-like lids. 'The blood,' he said with a shudder.

'He was still bleeding?'

'I don't know about that, but his T-shirt was soaked and there was blood on the concrete around him.'

'Did you move him?'

Peno hesitated. 'I don't think so,' the waiter finally said, uncertainly. 'I tried talking to him.'

'*Talking?*'

'He wasn't obviously dead. I said something like, "What's happened, Mr Markham? Are you all right?" I realize it sounds silly now; you know, asking if he was all right. But at the time I was in panic. My head was spinning; still is.'

Templeman slowed down. 'I'm not trying to confuse you or catch you out. However, the sequence of events and what you saw – or didn't see – are very important ... could turn out to be crucial. That's why I'm trying to draw out as much detail as possible while it's still fresh in your head. Follow?'

Peno relaxed a little. 'I think so.'

'Good. Now I assume Mr Markham didn't say anything in reply to your questions? He wasn't conscious?'

'His eyes were closed. He said nothing. His lips didn't move. Nothing moved. I guess I could tell he was dead, but it didn't register immediately. It was too unbelievable.'

'What next?'

'I felt for a pulse in his neck.'

'Was there one?'

'His head just plopped to one side. There was no pulse that I could find. After that, I sprinted to the club for help.'

'You had no further contact with the body?'

'That's right.'

'OK, let's return for a moment to your initial arrival here: did you hear anything?'

'Such as?' Peno's face became creased with doubt.

'Footsteps. Someone walking, running; people talking.'

'No, nothing.'

'You didn't see anybody else?'

'No, nobody.'

'No sound of a gun being fired, no shouts nor screams, no angry outburst?'

Peno was shaking his head vigorously throughout this last question. 'If I had, I'd have told you straight away – and that lady.' He looked for Tandy, but couldn't see her now.

'There's absolutely nothing you can think of that might be helpful?' Templeman pressed, well aware from experience that usually the most useful information had to be unlocked and prised out. Most witnesses of violent crime didn't deliberately try to withhold evidence, but it had to be siphoned out because trauma played havoc with spontaneous recall.

A flicker of recollection rippled over Peno's face. Templeman hoped that he had opened a door to a memory that had been shut away by shock.

'There was something ... the smell.'

'Smell? Like perfume, you mean? Or after-shave?'

'No, no, it was ... I can't think of the word. Sort of acrid and smoky. Yes, that is it. Smoky.'

'Gunsmoke?'

'Possibly. I wouldn't know.' Defensively, he added, 'I've never fired a gun. Never owned one. Never been around anyone using one.'

Templeman guessed that the waiter must have missed the murder only by a matter of seconds; a few minutes at the most. Yet he had heard nothing. Perhaps a silencer had been fitted to the weapon or the shots would certainly have echoed throughout the car-park and into surrounding streets. *In that case, we're looking at a professional hit.* Templeman was confident of being able to pinpoint the time of the killing to within five minutes, as long as the nightclub manager was clear about when he had despatched Peno in pursuit of Mr Markham. Continuity of thought led him to his next line of questioning.

'Fine. Well done. That's very useful. Now, you see the cars on this floor: is the number the same as when you found Mr Markham?'

Peno's face was suddenly empty of all expression.

'What I'm trying to establish is whether any vehicle left this car-park, from this floor in particular, while you were raising the alarm? Think hard, please.'

Peno's Latin temperament began to surface. 'I had other things on my mind other than counting cars.' He was wringing his hands and lacing his fingers in frustration now as he spoke. 'I wouldn't know. I can't see any change, but I couldn't swear to it.' He made exasperated gestures with his arms. 'Everything looks the same, but ...'

'You're not sure, that's OK,' Templeman calmed him.

'Can I go now?'

'We won't keep you much longer. Just wait here a moment.'

Templeman went hunting Tandy, finding her with Dr Harry Patterson, who was wearing his outdoor clothes over his pyjamas.

'Have you got Mr Peno's home address and phone number?' Templeman butted in.

'Not yet,' said Tandy, breaking away from the experienced physician. 'Have you finished with him?'

'For now. Get his personal details. Tell him we'll require a signed statement from him, later today or tomorrow. Then thank him and let him go. Keep him sweet.'

'Did you?'

'Just do it.'

'Aye, aye, Captain!' she teased him, throwing a mock salute as she left Templeman with the doctor, who was just snapping shut his black medical bag.

'There's nothing I can do for him and not much for you, either,' the bespectacled doctor said drily. 'He was shot a minimum of three times, from close range, I'd say. Hit in the chest, stomach and neck, so he'd have been facing the killer.'

'Death would have been immediate, huh?'

'Well, you don't stay healthy for long with those kind of wounds.'

'Any exit points?'

'Are you asking if the slugs went right through him?'

'I am.'

'I couldn't find any evidence of that.'

'So we probably won't be looking for a high-calibre weapon?'

'That's your department, Inspector. Now, if there's nothing else, I'll return to my bed and try to complete whatever's left of the night. I'll have a report knocked-out for you this afternoon.'

'Thank you, Doctor.'

Doctor Patterson was already heading for the stairs. Like everyone else in the scene-of-crime circus, he had been made to leave his car outside in the street.

Templeman was eager to interview the nightclub manager, Joe Velatti, before he went off duty. Before vacating the car park, he asked Tandy to 'hold the fort', explaining his intentions and estimating that he shouldn't be longer than an hour.

Although epicentres of nocturnal life, nightclubs are soulless graveyards outside of opening hours. The Society was no exception. The punters had gone. The metal shutters were down on the bar. The lights, which during business hours – 10 p.m. to 3 a.m. – would be subdued or turned off completely, now magnified all the blemishes that the gloom conveniently hid. An austere female cashier, wearing silver-rimmed reading glasses on a matching neck-chain, was auditing the night's bar takings. A wan young man steered a noisy vacuum-cleaner across the stained carpet, while a woman cleaner was polishing the dancefloor. Most of the black-tie waiters had already gone home, having first changed into civvies. For Templeman, catching this nightclub undressed and ungroomed was tantamount to encountering a movie goddess with a hangover, no make-up and in slobby gear. The glamour and glitz had been dimmed by the bright lights.

Velatti was still in his tuxedo and bow-tie. He was holding a brandy glass half full of cognac. He offered his visitor a drink, which Templeman declined.

'How about a coffee, then?'

That was different.

'Black with two sugars,' said Templeman, who was overdue for a caffeine shot. His sugar level also needed a lift.

Velatti led the way to a ringside table, on the perimeter of the dancefloor, where Elvis did his last spot.

As soon as they were seated, Velatti swallowed two mouthfuls of cognac in quick succession. 'This is my nightly tipple after work, my little treat. But tonight this is my third. It's treatment rather than a treat, you understand?'

'No problem,' Templeman sympathized.

Velatti was diminutive and dapper, a second generation British-Italian. His complexion was much duskier than Peno's and there was more of an Italian flavour to his voice. Templeman suspected that he had been brought up in London in a predominantly Italian-speaking family, which probably originated from the Naples region. It was just a hunch, but he had a good record at that kind of speculation.

'Is it true, that Mr Markham's dead?' Velatti's husky, rapid-fire voice quaked. Most of the talking, however, was coming from his smoky brown eyes, too large for his sharp-featured, leathery face. The eyes were jumping in their sunken sockets like twitchy toads.

'I'm afraid so,' Templeman said solemnly, not missing anything of Velatti's abstract telegraphy.

'My God!' Velatti drank some more, until there was only a small pool of cognac, which he swished around contemplatively, remaining in his glass.

'Why? Was he robbed? Was it a mugging?'

'It's too early for those kind of conclusions. It's possible, however, that you can provide me with vital clues.'

'Me?' His bewilderment represented an equal mixture of disquiet and curiosity.

A coffee was plonked in front of Templeman by one of the kitchen factotums whose expression was meant as a reminder to his boss that he had a bed and a wife waiting for him. The coffee slopped into the saucer and a few drops landed in Templeman's lap.

'I'm sorry. Good cheap kitchen labour is scarce in London these days,' Velatti commented on the times and his own specific problems. 'If I admonish him, he'll phone in sick later today, knowing I won't be able to get a replacement at short notice and there'll be extra pressure on the rest of the staff. There's no union, but they still have us by the balls.'

'You get what you pay for,' remarked Templeman, inadvertently leaking a little insight of his own political gravitation.

'Wrong. That's just what you don't get. If you did, I wouldn't be bleating.'

Templeman wished he hadn't introduced the diversion. It was always a mistake, once the ice had been broken. Never break a straight line, he'd tutored others. Detours threw up more chances of a derailment. *Get back on track*, he chided himself.

'I believe you sent one of your waiters, Mr Peno, to run after Mr Markham?' Templeman stirred his coffee methodically, appearing to be mesmerized by the ripples he was making, but this was a carefully crafted deception, a skill that had taken years to perfect, although he'd be the first to admit that much of his cunning had been inherited.

'That's correct. I went to the dressing-room to see if he wanted a drink. He'd gone, but his wallet was on the floor. It must have dropped out while he was changing. So I picked it up, went into the restaurant – here – and gave it to Tony.' He stopped as if that explained everything.

'What instructions did you give Mr Peno?'

'I said, "Quickly see if you can catch up with Mr Markham and tell him he dropped this". Off he went.'

'How did he know where to go?'

'Because all our cabaret acts park there. It's so convenient and it's the nearest off-street place.'

'Don't any of them come by cab?'

'Sure, but not him. On his first night we chatted in his dressing-room before he went on. He complained about the traffic, even so late at night. He lived out of town, so it would have been very costly, a two-way trip by taxi, I mean.'

'Did he say where he lived?'

'Yes, Bedford.'

'Was he married?'

'He never said. I never asked. We never got that personal.'

'Was Monday his first night?'

'It was.'

'How long was he booked for?'

'Just the week. That's routine with us. We have a lot of regular weekly customers. They want something different every time they come.'

'So this was his third night,' said Templeman, thinking aloud, and quickly adding, to help with bonding, 'Now I'm showing off my flair for counting on my fingers.'

Some of the gauntness was miraculously flushed from Velatti's face.

'That's right. He was booked through to Saturday.'

'How did you book him?'

'Through an agency.'

'Which one?'

'Abe Kline. He's hot in the trade. He doesn't have any real stars on his books; well, not that we can afford, but he's a perfect provider for the cabaret market. He's able to look after most of our needs at the right price.'

'Where's he based?'

'Just around the corner, in Wardour Street. Abe often drops in to catch the show, to have a drink and a gossip.'

'Was he in tonight?'

'Not that I saw.'

'And you would have seen him … if he had paid a visit?'

'No doubt about it. I'd have been tipped off the moment he came through the door.'

'Do you recollect when he last popped in?'

Velatti stroked his chin thoughtfully where the dark growth was coming up overnight as quickly as mushrooms. With his hands he sleeked back his raven-black hair. Templeman had him tagged as a lounge lizard; a staunch custodian of the comb, cologne and condom culture.

'Couple of weeks ago, maybe. But we've talked on the phone twice since then.'

'What about?'

'Nothing important. Small stuff. Just looking to the future. He was pushing a couple of fairly new performers. We were looking at some early summer dates.'

'OK, now let's return to tonight's sequence of events. What time did you open?'

'Ten o'clock for the public. Staff are here by nine.'

'That include you?'

'No, I arrive at eight. That's when I'm able to catch up with the admin., before everything begins to swing.'

'What about Mr Markham?'

'He went on at twelve-thirty. That's showtime here. Every night. It never varies. Six nights a week.'

'How long was he on for?'

'An hour. It should have been just forty minutes, but he took an encore. The same as he did on Monday and Tuesday. He was good. Special. A very talented copycat.'

'Were you busy?'

'The club was full.'

'What time did he get here?'

'Round about eleven-thirty.'

'Talk me through the procedure. You know, did he come through the front door?'

'Yes, just like everyone else.'

'And then?'

'I asked him if he wanted a drink. We always look after our entertainers well here. We're known for our hospitality.'

Templeman allowed the commercial to run uninterrupted.

'He asked for a Scotch, then said he'd like a bottle to take home with him and he'd pay for it. I called a waiter—'

'Mr Peno?'

'I think so, yes. I placed the order and told him it would be on the house and that I'd sign for it. We could bury that little loss in the night's profits. Mr Markham sat at a staff table at the rear for about twenty minutes, listening to the band and the resident singer. He wasn't drinking. Finally, he went to his dressing-room, the only one we have. We don't have a dancing troupe; it's not that kind of nightclub. So one dressing-room is sufficient.'

'What happened after the cabaret spot?'

'Nothing immediately, except that the band returned and dancing recommenced. I was chatting to a table of regular customers who were celebrating a birthday. After that, I went to see if Mr Markham fancied a drink before hitting the road.'

'Even though he'd be driving?'

Velatti looked sheepish and shrugged. 'Old habits die hard.'

'But you'd already given him a full bottle of whisky, you just said.'

'He'd said that was for taking home, not to drink here.'

'What did you find in the dressing-room?'

'I'll show you. Follow me.'

Velatti led the way. 'Mind the flex.' The cleaner was pushing the vacuum-cleaner up and down the floor as if he were mowing a lawn.

'Is this the way Mr Markham would have taken to the dressing-room?' Templeman enquired, as they threaded around the now bare tables and tipped up chairs.

'More or less, except he'd have gone around the outside of the room. A few couples were dancing. The others were dining and drinking. Lights were low. Candles were lit on every table. The tempo was lively. He wouldn't have been noticed.'

The dressing-room door was ajar. Velatti prodded it open with a pointed toecap and stepped aside for the detective.

'You must specialize in midget artistes,' commented Templeman, alluding to the puny-sized room.

'It's adequate,' Velatti retorted uncomfortably.

Templeman ferreted around without fingering too much. He noted the wig. He opened the wardrobe and felt the Elvis rhinestone suit. He lifted the boots and inspected the soles.

'Was this his own costume or was it provided by the club?'

'It was his own.'

'So he had every reason to believe he'd be back for another

performance.' Templeman was now talking to himself. 'No bottle of whisky.'

'He must have taken it with him, as he said he would. But he did have a drink from the bottle in here.'

'How do you know that?'

'Because Tony removed a glass after Mr Markham had gone.'

Templeman had almost run out of questions.

'He didn't say anything about anyone following him, someone who might have been a threat, someone who could have been in the audience?'

Velatti shook his head slowly but positively.

'Had he arrived with anyone on any of the previous nights?'

'No, definitely not.'

'And, as far as you're aware, no one followed him out of the club tonight?'

'As far as I'm aware, no.'

'One last question, Mr Velatti: was there anything unusual about tonight? Anything at all? Perhaps something that seemed insignificant at the time, but now strikes you as a little odd?'

Velatti deliberated for a few seconds before answering reflectively, 'Nothing comes to mind; nothing leaps out.'

'Well, if anything does occur to you, please call me.' He left a business card before shaking hands and forging, head bowed, back into the cutting-edge of winter.

He hurried only for the reason of trying to keep warm and not as a matter of urgency. Elvis would still be waiting for him, but no longer with a song in his heart, just a bullet.

Chapter Four

Templeman and Tandy adjourned to a twenty-four-hour café in Chinatown, just off Shaftesbury Avenue. Templeman drove. 'I'll drop you off at your car on the way back,' he said peremptorily. It was less than a five-minute hike.

The Shanghai Surprise Snack Bar was a greasy spoon joint that catered for junior office workers by day and the rootless during the night. Any surprises it served were mostly unwelcome.

An Arctic gust followed them, whistling and chanting, through the door. Instinctively, they made for a corner table next to the counter and the furthest point from the ill-fitting door. Without speaking, they scrolled their sore, red-rimmed eyes down a sticky, plastic menu. Tandy had her back to a glass sandwich-cabinet. Welcoming warm air wafted from the griddle behind the counter where an elderly, wizened Hong Kong-born cook was frying eggs and other fatty foods for a couple of breakfasts. Despite the name of the place and the culture of the staff, there wasn't much in the way of a Chinese flavour in the food or drink. The sandwiches on display looked as tired as the pock-faced man turning the eggs.

'I'll just have a coffee,' said Tandy, pushing the menu to one side, making a comment with her dismissive gesture.

'Me, too,' said Templeman, tilting back his hard chair and rising wearily from the table, which was covered with stained, patterned plastic.

It was self-service and a woman who was taking orders and the money, handling food and cash simultaneously, served Templeman with two mugs of black coffee.

'Sugar on the table,' she said in a snappy, heavy Far Eastern accent.

Templeman guessed that the server was the cook's wife, not that it was of any consequence. But, like most detectives,

Templeman hated incomplete pictures. Loose ends meant that something was missing. He couldn't rest until he had people and situations accurately labelled and pigeon-holed. Gauging ages, however, wasn't his métier, especially when it came to Asians, with whom he had been known to be as much as thirty years out. So many of them seemed to grow old without ageing. He wished that he could be privy to their secret, but this wasn't the time for such considerations.

Tandy was flicking roughly through her notebook when Templeman returned to the table. Anyone observing their behaviour would have noted that it hadn't been necessary for Templeman to ask his female sergeant how she liked her coffee.

For a while neither of them spoke. It was a comfortable hiatus. They wrapped their hands around their piping hot mugs of coffee, absorbing the heat. Introspectively, they watched the steam curling upwards like cigar-smoke rings. None of the other customers took any notice of the detectives. Two of them appeared to be truck drivers, the other two looked as if they were there for shelter, using the café as a refuge. An electric clock on a peeling wall showed that it was almost six o'clock. It would remain dark for at least another two hours.

'So, what do we have?' Templeman said eventually, massaging his prominent chin, conscious of the black stubble that pricked his fingers.

'You tell me, *Inspector*'. The smile was in her emerald eyes, not on her sallow, but not unattractive, face.

Their eyes met and locked. Their silent communication said a lot. Templeman broke the spell.

'Let's just run through the items you found on him.'

Tandy didn't need to refer to her notes for that.

'Car keys and others, presumably to his home. A bottle of whisky, opened. The bottle was by no means full. A handkerchief and some small change. Oh, and a silver Cross ballpoint pen.'

'What about the contents of the car?'

'What you'd expect. A road map of London, a national gazetteer, a packet of Extra Strong mints, car gloves, an RAC handbook and the Jaguar's service history.'

'Who has the wallet now?'

'Forensics … along with the other things I've just mentioned.'

'What was in it?'

'Eighty pounds in tenners. Two credit cards – American

Express and Visa. A bank cheque card – Barclays. Three store charge cards.'

'We still can't rule out robbery as the motive.'

'That's right; the killer wouldn't have known he'd left his wallet behind. Also in the wallet is the name and address of the person to be contacted in the event of an emergency, though I doubt whether anything like this was ever imagined.'

'You've listed everything?'

'Of course.'

'Any obvious clues?'

'Not so far.'

'So we have his home address and name of his wife … I assume his wife's the one he wanted contacted?'

Tandy's nod was almost indiscernible. The shorthand between them was fluent.

'Fifty-eight Embankment Close, Bedford, matches the computer data of vehicles; we had that checked out within ten minutes.' There was a hint of *please give me some credit* in her pleasantly cultured voice.

They continued to caress their coffees without drinking.

'Credit card transactions might help us to map out his movements during his final hours,' Templeman said, pondering.

'I'll see that the usual drill is followed,' Tandy said crisply.

Adrenalin was their antidote to mental exhaustion.

Templeman's next question had to be asked, though he already knew what the answer would be.

'There's nothing I should know about in the context of contaminated evidence?'

'Nothing I've mentioned has been touched by naked hands, rest assured,' Tandy confirmed confidently. 'The boys in blue from a cruiser knew their stuff. They were just a couple of minutes away, having dealt with an affray, when the call came in. They followed the book to the letter. Their prints won't be on anything. It's the A team out tonight – all vets, except you and me.'

She switched on one of her lethal smiles, against which there was no defence.

Templeman yearned to reach out to her, but restrained himself, conscious of the fact that he should be setting an example in professionalism.

'Good,' he said simply. 'Drink up. Your coffee will be cold.'

'Yours, too.'

Their eyes hooked up again and Templeman knew that this was all wrong, but he didn't have the will to offer even tentative resistance.

'What's the plan?'

Tandy didn't intend a double entendre, but Templeman wondered. Correctly, he dealt with the question at face value.

'We'll go back to the Yard. We'll evaluate what – if anything – is coming in. Then we go to Bedford on a death-knock.'

'*We*?'

'I haven't a clue how the wife is going to react to the news. I think you should be the one to break it to her. You know, woman to woman; the gentle-touch crap we hear so much about.'

'Thanks.'

'I'll be with you.'

Death-knocks breaking the news of tragedy to families – came with the territory and Tandy wasn't really complaining. She accepted that women officers tended to have more flair for overt compassion because, generally, they weren't inhibited or screwed up about emotion. This didn't mean that men failed to feel equally and deeply, but, as a generalization, they were intimidated by emotional expression. It was a macho handicap. 'Our Achilles' heel,' Templeman had admitted several times to Tandy. By *our*, he meant gender.

'These are always tricky,' Tandy said, almost absently, her look faraway, her gaze sightless, as if she was reliving another case.

'I know what you mean.' Templeman did, too. Although they had to assume that the wife had no idea that she was a widow, the spouse was always a suspect in these kind of murders until emphatically eliminated. Therefore a subtle and sensitive balance had to be struck between imparting information and eliciting it.

The door opened and winter pushed in behind an obvious hooker and her equally obvious pimp. Both of them had just come off duty. The whore appeared to be in her late thirties, but was probably no older than twenty-five. From her disarranged appearance, it seemed as if she'd had a hard shift. Her dead eyes reminded Templeman of the corpse they had just left.

Templeman was thinking about something that had been bothering him ever since Tandy had chronicled the items found on Markham and in his car.

'No mobile?' he finally said, starkly.

'What?' Tandy's bemusement was telegraphed graphically.

'Markham wasn't carrying a mobile. Neither was there one in the car, right?'

'Right.' Tandy was visualizing the contents of Markham's pockets as, wearing sterilized rubber gloves, she had examined each article. 'So?'

'Don't you think that's odd?'

She shrugged. 'Unusual, maybe. I'm not sure about *odd*.'

'Eighty per cent of the adult population owns a mobile.'

'That means twenty per cent don't – several million.'

'He was an entertainer, depending on agents, club managers and impresarios for a living. Like an actor, he'd always be living in anticipation that the next call would be the big one.'

'But he was already booked for this week. And who'd be phoning him at midnight, except his wife?'

'You're missing the point. I'm talking about habit, a way of life, a culture.'

'OK, maybe he just forgot it. Maybe it's at his home, in his bedroom, or just inside the front door, where he left it by mistake, but couldn't be bothered to return for it. I do think you're making something out of nothing.'

'That's where mountains and great oaks come from.'

'That's not the first time you've said that.'

'OK, so it lacks originality, but there must be some truth in it.'

Tandy thumbed through her notebook again until she came to a blank page and wrote, in capital letters, the one word MOBILE, followed by a question mark.

'Now it won't be forgotten,' she promised needlessly.

'Let's drink up and go,' said Templeman decisively.

The hooker had gone to sleep with her head propped against the damp stucco wall. Templeman was glad that the dead eyes were now closed. He was thinking about the girl, not Elvis. 'Love Me Tender' sprang to mind, something he was sure that had no relevance to this pathetic woman's life.

Chapter Five

The body was taken over the river to St Thomas's Hospital, where Sir James Hudson, one of the country's most eminent pathologists, scheduled the post-mortem for noon.

'Do you want to be here for a running commentary and all the gore?' he asked Templeman affably over the phone.

'No, I'll be out of town, thankfully. I'll catch up with you later in the day. I'd be grateful for the highlights ASAP, though. The rest you can let me have, at your convenience, in your written summary.'

'Very well. I assume that by at my *convenience* you don't mean at my *leisure*?'

Confirmation wasn't necessary. Templeman gave his mobile number and killed the conversation.

Commander Dick Lilleyman was at his desk in Scotland Yard by 7 a.m., as usual. An operations-room co-ordinator had briefed Lilleyman about the murder before the commander had left his suburban home.

Templeman was summoned to Lilleyman's office, up among the gods, before the commander's leather-upholstered swivel chair was even warm.

'Am I reading this one right?' Lilleyman began, opening a pristine buff folder, containing only two sheets of paper, which had been waiting for him on his desk.

Templeman, who hadn't been invited to sit, waited for Lilleyman to elaborate.

'I take it that this has all the makings of a professional hit?'

Only now did the bald-headed top brass acknowledge Templeman with his vulpine eyes.

'Too early to jump to that conclusion,' Templeman opined neutrally.

The commander, a tough Scot who would never have survived the first week in the Diplomatic Corps, was irritated by Templeman's reticence. Almost as much as he was irritated by Templeman himself.

'You're talking to someone who's broken down more doors in hairy busts than ...' His gruff Glaswegian voice tailed off when he couldn't think quickly enough of an original continuation. 'This isn't a press conference. You're not going to be held accountable for your opinion.'

Templeman wasn't alone in his dislike of Lilleyman. If there had been a World Cup competition for bullshitting, it was generally accepted at Scotland Yard that Lilleyman would be first choice for Britain.

'It could be a hit,' Templeman agreed patiently, refusing to bite either the bait or the bullet. 'All I'm saying is that we're not off the ground yet.' He was already too tired for internal aggravation. 'We know next to nothing about the victim.'

'We know he was Elvis Presley. That's a bloody good start.' Lilleyman kicked his feet on to his desk and crossed his legs at the ankles. Not only was he a control freak, he also had a fetish for uniform. His shoes had been so buffed that Templeman could see his own reflection in the toecaps. The commander's uniform was pressed every evening by his long-suffering wife, who also had to spit and polish his silver buttons. He bragged repeatedly that the sharpest weapons in his household – and indeed at Scotland Yard – were the creases down his trousers.

'A Presley impersonator,' Templeman corrected the commander prosaicly, aware that this would incite Lilleyman to further pugnacity.

'You're bad for my ulcer, Inspector. Pernickety people piss me off.'

'Evidence-gathering is a *pernickety* business.'

'Fuck *evidence*! I'm talking about public perception. The press are going to run with this one because of the Elvis Presley angle. If you can't see that, then you should be playing with the fairies at the bottom of your garden.'

'I understand what to expect from the media coverage.'

Lilleyman snorted. 'But I'm the one who'll have to field all the shit from the politicians.' His ulcer was in a spiteful mood, which made him lash out more than usual at Templeman. 'I've never been in favour of fast-tracking, you know that, don't you?'

'I've read your comments in magazines and newspapers many times.' He was going to say *ad nauseam*, but decided against it just in time to avert a major clash.

Fast-tracking was a Home Office initiative to attract university graduates into the police. They spent minimum time on the beat before promotion, often earmarked for chief constable status by the time they were forty. If they chose to take the CID route, as Templeman had, they could expect to become a detective inspector while most of their contemporaries were still competing for the first step up the ladder. Templeman had been recruited from Oxford University, where he had read law. By contrast, Lilleyman, known throughout the Yard without affection as Bulletbrain, had worked his way up through the ranks, after first having served in the army as a military policeman. Hence his instinctive antipathy towards Templeman, despite the detective inspector's impressive track-record.

Lilleyman dropped his elephantine feet to the floor and sprang forward with feline agility, despite his bulk. His boulder-shaped head came to rest on his clasped hands, about halfway across his shiny-topped desk.

'You reckon you're up to handling this one, do you?' he goaded Templeman, sneering overtly.

'The result will be the best answer to that question,' Templeman said equably.

'A good answer, Inspector. I'll hold you to that. Incidentally, I hear your wife is defending that sewer rat Carlos Petrelli at the Old Bailey next month.'

'So she tells me.'

'God, how I hate shysters. What's it like being married to one?'

'Charley's no *shyster*,' Templeman retorted loyally. 'She's a very gifted defence counsel, as you know well.'

'Good at getting vermin off, you mean. Good at deluding naive jurors. We take trash out of circulation. She puts it back on the streets. We clean, she pollutes. Whose side are you on, Inspector?'

Templeman side-stepped the question that was designed to compromise him, whatever his answer. 'What Charley does is test the case against her client to the best of her ability.'

The commander scowled contemptuously and made a dismissive wave with a massive hand.

'There are men and women in this building who've spent their entire careers trying to nail Petrelli. The murders he's been charged with are only the tip of the iceberg.'

'He'll go down; you know it, I know it. Then there'll be a week of partying.'

'If he doesn't ...'

'Yes?'

'I wouldn't like to be in your shoes.'

'Is there anything else you wish to speak to me about, Commander?'

'Not right now.' His steely eyes had hardened even further and their laser stare was drilling into Templeman's forehead. Templeman could even feel the burning intensity of those eyes penetrating the back of his head as he exited Lilleyman's sumptuous office.

Templeman and Tandy set out for Bedford just after 7.30. Dawn hadn't yet peeped through the night curtain. Heavily laden clouds, like bomber aircraft, were approaching fast, preparing to dump their load on London and the Home Counties. The snow-raids were forecast to continue sporadically throughout the next couple of days, at least. Biting winds from the east would cause drifting. This was the kind of day when Templeman wouldn't have complained about being tethered to his desk, bogged down with paperwork and computer chores.

'What did Bulletbrain want?'

'Trouble. A fight.'

'Did he get what he wanted?'

'No.'

'Someone back at the ranch will pay.'

'So, what's new?'

After that, Tandy said very little while Templeman massaged the Mondeo through the slushy morning gridlock. They stopped for breakfast at a service station on the M1 motorway just south of Luton. The first 'raid' from above had just begun.

'There's talk,' said Tandy, almost incidentally, looking up solicitously from her croissant.

Templeman put down his knife and fork. 'What talk?'

'About your wife?'

Templeman relaxed a little. 'Not about us?'

'I haven't heard anything like that, but I wouldn't, now, would

I? That sort of stuff would be said behind both our backs. No, the talk is about the Petrelli case.'

'I've just had that from Bulletbrain.'

'It's difficult for me.'

'How do you think it is for me?' Templeman pushed aside his half-finished cooked breakfast. 'Jesus! Charley's only doing her job.'

'I understand that; you understand that.'

'I sense a *but* in the air.'

'The *but* is that there are many of our colleagues who are too close to the Petrelli investigation to be objective.'

'That's *their* problem – not mine, not yours, and certainly not Charley's. If the case is as watertight as the team leader's been bragging, then Petrelli will go down for life. If there's a flaw, then it'll be ruthlessly explored and exploited by Charley. You can't condemn her for being professional.'

'She's not very popular among your brothers and my sisters.'

'Of course not, because she exposes their sloppy detective work.'

Tandy flushed. 'I don't think that's entirely fair.'

'What's she expected to do, deliberately throw a case, be the equivalent of a crooked cop? Would that make everyone happy?'

'Some, maybe, but that's not the point.'

'What *is* the point?'

'It's just that she's rather ahead of the odds. Even other barristers on the circuits call her The Magician.'

'That's because she's capable of performing miracles – and most prosecuting counsels can't.'

'You have to see it from our side.'

'*Your* side! I thought we were a partnership. I'd no idea you'd crossed over.'

'Of course I'm on your side.' She covered his hand with hers and although they were a long way from base, she automatically checked that they weren't being observed.

'The friction is because Charley's married to a cop. Not just *any old cop*, but a high-flying detective who's privy to a lot of sensitive operational detail.'

'You mean I'm suspected of leaking confidential information about investigations, such as weaknesses from the prosecution angle?'

'There's nothing as crystallized as that. Emotions are highly charged right now. Many reputations are riding on the outcome of the Petrelli case.'

'None less so than Charley's.'

'Sure. Look, I mentioned this only so that you were aware.'

'Now I'm aware.'

'I only wanted to help,' said Tandy, frustrated and smarting.

'OK, you've helped.'

'I don't believe so.'

Templeman's mobile came to the rescue. He recognized his own home number before answering.

'I've heard the news,' said Charley, before Luke could speak. 'Where are you?'

'Out of town.'

'That's a big place.'

'*En route* to Bedford.'

'That where he lived?'

'Yes. Where did you hear about it – on TV or radio?'

'TV.'

'Was he named?'

'No. The newscaster just said a man had been gunned down in a Soho car park and that he wouldn't be named until next of kin had been notified.'

'That's a relief.'

'I knew it had to be the job you were called out on. When do you expect to be home?'

'I couldn't even hazard a guess. What's your itinerary?'

'A case conference this morning that will almost certainly spill over into the afternoon. We have our monthly chambers' meeting at six which will maunder on until eight, followed by the mandatory adjournment to the Wig and Pen for booze and a bite. If you're not going to be home, I might as well dine properly there.'

'Is that Plan A or B?'

Charley tittered in a tremolo. 'B, I think.'

'I should go ahead with that. Chances are I'll be visiting home over the next week or so only to change clothes.'

'See you whenever, then.'

'Yeah, whenever.'

Tandy hadn't taken her searching eyes off Templeman's face throughout his brief and terse conversation with his wife.

'This is stressful,' she said.

Templeman knew exactly what she meant, but now wasn't the moment for an examination of their relationship.

He was done with his food. So, too, was Tandy.

'You drive,' he said, tossing the Mondeo's ignition key to her as they reached the car.

For the next forty minutes, Templeman slept in the front passenger seat, until Tandy nudged him awake.

'We're there,' she said, almost tenderly.

The fog of disorientation took its time clearing. A forty-minute catnap wasn't enough to refresh him. In fact, he felt more wretched than before nodding off. After rubbing the cobwebs from his itching eyes, he appraised himself critically in the vanity mirror above the windscreen.

Oh my God!' he muttered his self-deprecating verdict.

Both of them took a few seconds to compose themselves. Templeman fastened his shirt collar-button and slid up the knot of his silk yellow necktie so that it was centred and then ran a comb through his easily controlled hair. Simultaneously, Tandy applied a modicum of lilac lipstick to her small mouth and powdered her neat nose.

'Ready?' Templeman asked rhetorically.

'Ready.'

Although there was snow on the trees, hedges and rooftops, it had turned to mush on the slippery pavements. Embankment Close was a cul-de-sac comprising sixty detached houses, all built within the last twenty years: odd numbers one side, even numbers opposite. The Markhams' house was the last but one on the even side, constructed on the curve at the dead-end part of the close.

Tandy led the way through black wrought-iron gates which bore the warning sign, 'Beware of the dog'. They ignored the warning, aware that many people deployed those kind of notices to deter burglars and other unwanted callers. The odds favoured there being no dog and, if there was one, the chances were that it would be a neurotic poodle. The concrete drive, wide enough for a vehicle, went straight to a double garage, about thirty yards from the gate and alongside a mock Tudor residence. In front of the house and beside the drive was a medium lawn, rectangular in shape and surrounded by an herbaceous rockery. Tall sentinel trees, their spidery limbs now bare and exposed, paraded stiffly, despite the aggressive wind, inside the six-foot-high wall that afforded privacy to the residents of this property. The detectives had noticed that most of the houses in Embankment Close were of similar architecture, though the end four appeared to have considerably larger grounds than the others.

'Nice house,' remarked Tandy.

'Nice price,' said Templeman, as they peeled off the drive to join a gravel path that zig-zagged to a sturdy black front door.

The edge of a curtain twitched behind a window to the left of the door.

'I think we've been watched since we came through the gate,' said Tandy, deliberately averting her eyes from the window where there had been movement.

'Prime Neighbourhood Watch territory this,' said Templeman, sounding disparaging but without intent.

After Tandy had pressed the doorbell twice, they had to wait for what seemed an extended scrutiny under the microscope before they heard distant footsteps, seeming to start somewhere in the bowels of the house and quickly growing louder.

'No dog,' said Templeman, in the manner of a gambler who had just won a wager.

The door finally inched open on a safety-chain and a hawkish female face examined them disdainfully through the narrow gap.

'Yes?' Her voice was sharp and rasping, devoid of melody.

There is a dog, after all! mused Tandy, before saying as sweetly as possible, 'Mrs. Markham?'

'Who wants to know?'

Tandy produced her police ID, taking the opportunity to introduce Templeman.

Confusion crept across Audrey Markham's bird-like face.

'Police! What do you want with me?'

'This isn't something we can deal with on the doorstep,' Tandy said firmly, though without being too pushy.

'Oh, of course, come in, please.' Mrs Markham softened slightly as she unfastened the chain to let them in, then steering them to the lounge, which was furnished with a four-seater, black leather settee and matching armchairs. Mock oak beams perpetuated the Tudor theme.

The plan was for Tandy to conduct most of the early talking, with Templeman remaining on the periphery of the proceedings until the fact-gathering process gathered pace.

'I hope this isn't going to take long, only I have an appointment in town this morning,' said Mrs Markham, her voice not quite as serrated now.

'I think you should sit down, Mrs Markham.'

Mrs Markham looked apprehensively from Tandy to Templeman and back to the woman detective.

'Has something happened to Harry? Has he been in an accident?' The black pools in her eyes somehow seemed to flood her pallid face. She was wearing a flowered housecoat and only underwear beneath, which became apparent as she sat in one of the armchairs beside a fake log gas fire, which glowed sunset red and yellow, as if wood really was burning. The reflection from the fire helped to bring artificial colour to Mrs Markham's flat cheeks and thin lips. If she did use make-up, it hadn't yet been applied.

The detectives occupied the settee, Templeman taking the end furthest from the new widow.

'I have bad news for you Mrs Markham.'

'It *is* Harry, isn't it?'

Templeman didn't take his eyes off Mrs Markham's face, not for a split second.

'There's no easy way of saying this. Your husband has been killed.'

Tandy waited, not just out of respect and compassion. This was a watershed moment – always was in any murder investigation. Feigning shock, disbelief and grief was the most demanding screen test for any next of kin.

'An accident! Harry, dead! When? Where? How? It can't be!'

Her face was in tune with her words. Templeman listened and looked for any transparent trace of artificiality. So far, there was none. In an atom of time, she had metamorphosed from merely wan to a ghost.

'I didn't say it was an accident.'

Mrs Markham's mental disarray deepened. 'Not an accident? What then?' There was an appeal in her eyes that pleaded for clarification.

'Your husband has been shot.'

'Shot!' Her hands flew to her mouth, as if catching a scream. 'Are you telling me Harry's been murdered?'

'I'm afraid so. I'm sorry.'

Mrs Markham stood, turned her back on the detectives, took a tissue from a pocket and dabbed her watery eyes. She was standing on a shaggy white rug in front of the ornate carved fireplace. Centre stage on the mantelpiece was a framed photograph of Elvis Presley, alias Harry Markham, with his arm around a vivacious teenage girl. Above the mantelpiece was a large mirror, which reflected the devastation seeping from Audrey Markham's very soul.

The telepathy between Tandy and Templeman was so finely tuned that it signified something more deep-rooted than a professional partnership. Neither of them attempted to plug the silence with platitudes. What followed was the eyeballing strategy of poker players. Basically, they were saying, *It's your call, Mrs Markham.*

With her back still to them, Mrs Markham said, 'You're sure it's Harry?'

'Is that your husband, Mrs Markham? The man in the photograph on your mantelpiece?'

'Yes, that's Harry.'

'Then there's no doubt, I'm afraid.'

'How? I don't understand. This doesn't make any sense.' She wheeled to face them, almost angrily now, the tear-stains smudged on her desolate cheeks.

'He was shot in a London car park in the early hours of this morning, beside his Jaguar.'

'But why? Was it robbery?'

'That's something we're still trying to fathom. It's complicated by the fact that he'd left his wallet in the nightclub.'

'Not the car?'

'No.'

'Then why?' she repeated herself. 'This is unbelievable. I can't begin to take it in.'

Tandy turned to Templeman, who shook his head just the once, meaning he was content for her to continue to lead the expedition.

'What time did you expect your husband home?'

Mrs Markham seemed unprepared for this thematic question and her holding reply alerted the antennae of both detectives.

Tandy rephrased her question and Mrs Markham's expression persisted as she replied shakily, 'I wasn't expecting him back.'

Tandy tensed up, while Templeman continued to give the impression that he was just along for the ride.

'Are you saying that your husband no longer lived here?'

Shock of a different sort now shaped Mrs Markham's sharp

features and prickly cadence. 'Oh, no, I didn't mean that. I didn't expect him home because he was staying over in London.

'Just the night or all week?'

'All week. He'd often do that when on an out-of-town engagement.'

'Even though central London's only about an hour away at night?'

'Harry always needs a few drinks to control his nerves during a show, even after all this time.' She talked as if her husband was still alive, something else that the detectives immediately filed in their heads. 'Lots of other entertainers, including some really big names, are the same. He doesn't like driving too far after drinking.' She blushed, feeling guilty, as if she had been disloyal to her husband by discussing his law-breaking drinking habits with two strangers, both police officers.

'Where was he staying?'

'With his agent, Abe Kline. That was the advantage of London engagements. He didn't have to meet the cost of hotels or guest houses. He always used to complain that you needed to take out a mortgage just to stay a night even at a fleabag place in London. He and Abe were friends.' She had finally come to terms with the past tense, it seemed.

'Where does Mr Kline live?'

'Harry never said.'

'When did you last speak with your husband?'

Mrs Markham's hooded eyelids fluttered as she struggled to engage her brain in methodical recall.

'Yesterday afternoon, about four o'clock.'

'Did you call him?'

'Yes, on his mobile.'

'You rang his mobile from your land line here?'

'That's right. Is that important?'

The detectives exchanged non-committal glances. Mrs Markham couldn't help but be aware of the static in the air.

'Did he always have his mobile with him?'

'Always. It was his lifeline. In any form of showbusiness, you have to be instantly accessible these days.'

'What about when he was doing a gig?'

'That made no difference, though it would be left in the dressing-room while he was out front. Why these questions?'

'No mobile was found on him. Does that surprise you?'

Mrs Markham cocked her head sideways, puzzled. 'There must be some mistake.'

'What's the mobile number?'

Mrs Markham dictated it without the need to refer to her personal address and phone book. Tandy wrote it down and read it back to Mrs Markham to double-check that she had recorded it correctly.

Templeman took his mobile from his pocket and punched out the number as Tandy read it aloud from her notebook, with Mrs Markham nodding involuntarily.

A mechanical operator's voice informed Templeman that it was impossible to connect him, but invited him to leave a message.

'Which network did your husband subscribe to?'

Templeman allowed a thin smile of admiration to crease the corners of his mouth. Tandy was pressing all the right buttons and he was impressed.

'O_2,' replied Mrs Markham, after a moment's vacillation.

'This is a cliché question, Mrs Markham, but please give it careful consideration: did your husband have enemies?'

'Grief, no!' she answered with the speed of a ricochet, too spontaneously to have pondered the question adequately.

Templeman decided the moment had arrived for a change of pace and face. He took the baton from Tandy as smoothly as if they were Olympic athletes in a relay race.

'Your husband was a good-looking man.'

'So was Elvis.' This reply was returned on the volley; no time allowed for it to be bounced around. 'It's natural that Harry had a similar physical appeal or he wouldn't have been so successful and in such demand.'

'How about admirers?' This question was delivered with considerable undertow.

'I'm not sure that I follow.'

Templeman doubted that this was true. 'Elvis was idolized by millions.'

'Still is, Inspector.'

'And your husband was in his image, a point *you* made. It follows, doesn't it, that he must have attracted groupies?'

'It doesn't *follow* at all,' she contradicted him indignantly, a blade of sharpened steel glinting in her bird-of-prey eyes.

'But did he?' Templeman persisted.

'What?' she almost snapped, her grieving temporarily suspended.

'Have groupie followers?'

'Not at all,' she replied defiantly.

'You're very positive about that?'

'Absolutely.'

'Did you ever accompany him to his shows?'

'Not of late,' she sighed. Briefly she retreated into a world of her own, day-dreaming of a past that would now have to sustain her present and future. The metal in her eyes had been replaced by a mistiness that seemed to presage gathering precipitation.

'Yet you're confident he didn't have a personal following?'

'Harry was excellent at what he did, but he wasn't a star in his own right,' Mrs Markham explained patiently, as if talking to the uninitiated about a specialist subject or a foreigner who was unfamiliar with the nuances and quirks of the English language. 'If he'd been at all bothered by something untoward, he'd have told me.'

'Maybe he wasn't *bothered* by it. Maybe he enjoyed adulation.'

'There was never *adulation*, as you put it.' She worked her shoulders wearily. 'He was an impersonator. One of many. He helped to keep alive the memory of a legend. But he never pretended to be anything more than a facsimile. What are you *really* driving at, Inspector?' A perceptible change had come over her.

'I'm just wondering if there might have been a stalker?'

Mrs Markham, happy to be distracted from her grief, mulled over this proposition unhurriedly, evaluating it dispassionately, like weighing it on scales. 'If there was one, it would have been a woman.'

'What makes you say that?'

'It stands to reason. It was the women who went crazy over Elvis. But no one's daft enough to muddle up the superstar who died so many years ago with my husband, an imitator.'

'There are some very weird people on this planet, Mrs Markham, and I meet one or two of them most days of my working life. I'm wondering if someone was offended, outraged even?'

'*Offended*? Harry's gigs were always clean; fit for a vicarage garden party. In fact, in his early days on the road he did quite a few shows in church halls for charity.'

'I'm thinking about the possibility of a crackpot *offended* because he considered your husband was taking the *Kings*'s name in vain; similar to a religious nutter. A silent, invisible stalker who blamed your husband for desecrating the memory of an icon.'

'But Harry never did that,' she protested. 'He was perpetuating the memory. Every performance was an exhibition of hero-worship. When he took his bow, it was an act of genuflection to the man whose death made it possible for Harry to make a decent living doing what he loved most.'

'And maybe someone resented that fact.'

'Why should any such person pick on Harry when there are thousands of Elvis doubles? Why him? What made him so different from the others? Don't you see, that theory's skewed?'

Templeman diced with this. Audrey Markham had a point, though not much of one. Every person diagnosed with terminal cancer wails, *Why me?* None of us ever believes we deserve bad luck. And we don't, of course. The random strike has no regard for merit. Just like a serial killer with a fixation, it has to begin somewhere. Someone has to be first. Each victim is the result of a spin of a roulette wheel. Pure chance determines whose number comes up.

'To your knowledge, your husband never received any threatening phone calls or letters?'

'Not one,' she replied emphatically.

'Please bear with me, Mrs Markham, but I must exhaust this line which is nothing more than conjecture, a mere embryo theory, but did your husband have any enemies among other Elvis impersonators, who perhaps believed Mr Markham was encroaching on their patch, taking their business?'

'No one would kill just for that, surely? It's unthinkable. For it to have got that bad, there'd have been a history of arguments and a nasty atmosphere.'

'But there wasn't?'

'No, no, no.... How many times do I have to say it?' She was unshakeable.

An impasse had been reached. It was time for a fresh approach. Tandy was poised for a cue to retake the baton, but Templeman had hit a rhythm and stride that took him along with its own kinetic energy.

'How much do you know about your husband's past?'

She eyed him oddly, as if suspecting he was fishing in deep

and murky waters where he hoped for a big catch. 'What part of his *past*?'

'I'm thinking about his upbringing and childhood.'

Mrs Markham acted relieved, as if climbing out of a dentist's chair, thankful that the ordeal was over.

'Well,' she began, thoughtfully, pausing as she assembled her untidy memories into some kind of coherent order, 'he didn't get on with his father.' She stopped abruptly, as if fearing that she had divulged too much, but she was already over the Rubicon.

'Did he say why not?' A door had been unlocked, so Luke pushed it open.

Audrey Markham bit her lips, wishing she hadn't opened up, feeling that somehow she was being disloyal. 'He said his father was always jealous of him.'

'As a boy, or later in life?'

'Oh, as a boy. He believed his father was envious of all the attention he got from his mother. I think the truth is that Harry was a bit of a mummy's boy. What son isn't, though? His father must have had something of an immature personality, from the sound of things. Anyhow, his sister gravitated more towards her dad than her mother. His parents split up when he was thirteen or fourteen.'

'So he and his sister were brought up, from then, by their mother?'

'No. The father was granted custody of both children.'

'Not the usual distribution in divorce.'

'Times have changed.'

'Not then, they hadn't. You mentioned that Harry was closer to his mother, yet his father won custody – and for his daughter, too.'

'The court must have had its reasons,' Mrs Markham said vaguely, as if that was an adequate explanation. 'Anyhow, a few months later, Harry's father was killed in a road accident. Harry and his sister Emma were separated and placed with separate foster parents.'

She sniffed, mopped up a couple of tears and laced her fingers tightly in her lap, a damp tissue squashed between her hands.

'Are you up to continuing, Mrs Markham?' Templeman wasn't really offering her a choice. It was nothing more than an habitual ploy to project the humane face of the police and to win her confidence.

She answered with a tentative nod, but didn't look up.

'Where did all this happen?'

'On the south coast. Bournemouth.'

'Did Harry and Emma keep in touch?'

'No!' This was said with both force and economy, adding to its impact.

'Why was that?'

'He said she was trouble.'

'Did he elaborate?'

'Only to mention she was a muck-stirrer.'

'Did he give examples?'

'No ... and I didn't ask for any. Within our relationship, Emma and the rest of his family were Ice Age history. I've never met any of them. Never had the inclination. They are characters from a previous life of his, as distant and irrelevant as an out-of-print book. They didn't figure one jot in our framework of things.'

The reins of experience held him back from pressing on down this stony track. It was time for yet another digression.

'Tell me something about Harry, as a person opposed to the spotlight showman.'

Audrey Markham's sightless gaze focused towards a distant horizon in her many yesterdays, aware that, with Harry's death, their sun had set and would never rise again. Last sunsets eclipsed so much. It was goodbye, not just goodnight. Memories were cold comfort, painful reminders of so much unfinished business.

'He was a good husband and a loving father.' She balked at her own voice, which sounded so measured, like a priest in the pulpit delivering the homily at the funeral of an old codger who had kept his relatives waiting longer than was decent for their legacy.

'Is that your daughter?' Templeman pointed to the photograph on the mantelpiece in which Harry had his arm around a teenager.

'Yes, that's Chelsea. That was taken three years ago. She's eighteen now. We have a son, Richard. He's twenty-one. I don't know how they're going to take this.'

'Do they still live at home?'

'No. Richard's at Cambridge, reading economics. I think he'll end up in the City as a broker, that sort of thing. Chelsea's less prac-tical, but still very talented in her own way. She's taking a year out before going to Durham University to read English and modern history. What she'll do afterwards, I don't know, but I don't have any worries about either of them. They're both very clever.'

'You're very lucky.' Templeman couldn't believe he had said that. It just jumped out, a careless, crass remark that was designed to keep the wheels of the interview oiled and turning smoothly. Although he didn't take his eyes off Mrs Markham, he could sense Tandy stiffening perceptibly at his side. 'I'm sorry, that was a stupid thing to say,' he apologized hurriedly. 'What I meant—'

'It's all right,' Mrs Markham interceded. 'I know exactly what you meant. Yes, I am lucky to have such uncomplicated children. There's never been a problem with drugs or adolescent rebellion. Let's hope they're not late developers in those respects and that this isn't the trigger. Oh, my God! What am I saying?' Now it was her turn to cringe at her unfortunate choice of words. Her whole body shuddered as if she was in a spasm, but there were no more tears.

'Is Richard at Cambridge now?'

'Yes, he's been back only a few days.'

'And Chelsea?'

Mrs Markham hesitated, then, 'She shares a flat in London. I've hardly spoken to her since Christmas. She has so many friends. No time for Mum. You know how it is.' She shot them both a twitchy glance, made a brief connection, before dipping her eyes again.

'How did you first meet your husband?'

A dreamy half-smile made a cameo appearance. 'At a night-club. I was on holiday in Bournemouth with a girlfriend ... our first day there. We danced all night. He was full of rhythm. My friend was really miffed because she hardly saw me for the rest of the fortnight. He phoned me every day after I'd gone home.'

'Where was home?'

'Here in Bedford.'

'What was he doing for a living?'

'Not a lot; odd-jobbing mainly. But at nights he worked the pubs and small-time clubs.'

'As an Elvis impersonator?'

'That's right. During my holiday in Bournemouth, when we first met, he took me along to a couple of pub gigs. He was good. Outstanding. He was determined to make it professionally. Since he was a boy, he'd been doing Elvis impersonations. Today, it's big business.'

'Were *you* into Elvis mania?'

'Not really, but that didn't stop me recognizing flair. Within

six months of my two weeks in Bournemouth, he was making a living from his music. He invited me to stay with him on holiday the next summer. That's when he proposed. I accepted. My parents were livid. Usual thing. They wanted something better for their daughter. Didn't think he was grand enough. Objected to his unorthodox lifestyle. Thought he'd come to no good....'
For the second time she wished she had kept tighter control of her tongue.

Templeman popped his next question promptly to avoid her brooding and perhaps having misgivings over opening up about family conflicts. 'Nevertheless, your marriage worked?'

This time she reviewed her reply before releasing it. 'We had our rows, just like any other married couple, but we always made up and kissed before we went to sleep at night – when he was at home.' She privately scolded herself for disclosing the minutiae of her intimate moments with Harry, as if she was guilty of pillow-talk betrayal. But she went on, like the driver of a runaway truck, unable to apply the brakes. 'We've never been rich, but neither have we ever been poor. Harry was never going to be a star; that was something we both accepted. The star would always be Elvis Presley and Harry would never be more than a disciple. He worked in a crowded and competitive market. The number of performing disciples swells by the day. His agent, Abe, will tell you all about that. Even so, Harry was always in demand – never without an engagement. He'd send me and the kids on holiday but rarely came himself, superstitious about declining a booking, fearing he might never be offered another one. Entertainment folk are like that. He was a conscientious provider and worked all of God's hours to do it. Whatever his faults, a shyness of work wasn't one of them.'

Templeman's next question was shaped almost before Mrs Markham had completed her melodramatic outpouring.

'What *were* his faults?'

This really was inciting betrayal and Audrey Markham wrestled with her conscience. It was a close contest, but the need to talk prevailed. 'I didn't really have anything particular in mind. He drank more lately than I liked and that led to a few arguments. He'd been drinking more recently than ever before. It's difficult to do the nightclub circuit and not drink. It's all part of the scene.'

'But not your *scene*?'

'Not really. Not any more.'

Templeman had run out of questions. Now came the hardest bit of all.

'I'm afraid I'm going to have to ask you to return to London with us to officially identify your husband.'

'Do I have to?' She was making a plea to be spared.

'It has to be done, Mrs Markham. If you put it off, it'll only play on your mind. From my experience, although it's always going to be an ordeal, the sooner this formality is tackled, the easier it is to face the future. Strangely, shock seems to afford a cushion against the full impact of this harrowing responsibility. It won't take a minute and I mean that literally. Afterwards, I'll have you driven home.'

'Very well,' she said, suddenly resolved. 'First, however, I must make a call to postpone an appointment.'

Although Templeman and Tandy didn't exchange even fleeting glances, neither of them would have been the least surprised to learn that they were sharing a similar vagrant thought, albeit uncrystallized. How could someone who had just learned of the murder of a loved one retain such clarity of thought and mental orderliness as to remember an appointment and to feel sufficiently composed to make a call to cry off? Of course, delayed shock was frequently responsible for bizarre, aberrant behaviour; that was one possibility. Another explanation, however, could be that Audrey Markham wasn't grieving quite as much as she would have the detectives believe.

Interesting, thought Tandy.

A genuine widow, or a creative producer of crocodile tears? wondered Templeman, putting his judgement on ice.

Chapter Six

Identification was a formality.

'Yes,' lamented Mrs Markham as the white sheet was peeled back. As she reeled away, a hand shot to her mouth, as if she was about to vomit. Tandy was prepared for Mrs Markham losing the support of her legs.

'It's all over now,' the woman detective soothed, using an arm to comfort and control the distraught widow, steering her as quickly as was manageable out of the morgue and away from the antiseptic odours and everything they represented.

'No, it's only just beginning,' rejoined Mrs Markham, remarkably perceptive for someone so blitzed. 'Until now, I've been able to console myself with the delusion that you must be mistaken, that Harry would walk through the front door of our home and rock with laughter over his greatly exaggerated death. That would have appealed to his sense of theatre. But it's not going to happen. It isn't a dreadful mistake. It's just dreadful.' She was sobbing tears of the heart. Her eyes had run dry after the original flood. And then she contradicted herself. 'It must have been a mistake. He must have been mistaken for someone else. There can't be any other explanation.'

Mrs Markham had just echoed a theory that had been doing the rounds in Tandy's head for several hours.

Templeman was in his office speaking on the phone with pathologist Sir James Hudson.

'Pretty straightforward,' Sir James said laconically.

'Not pretty!' Templeman corrected the esteemed surgeon, waggish.

'Oh, don't be so pedantic, Inspector.'

'Look, I'm bushed, so just give me the headlines.'

'Oh, you poor, precious thing!' Sir James then changed gear

fluently, quickly leaving behind levity. 'Three gunshot wounds. Heart penetrated, rupturing an artery. Left lung and spleen shredded with separate shots. Any of them would have proved fatal.'

'I don't suppose you were able to determine in which order the shots were fired?'

'Of course not! Does it matter? He's dead as a result of the bullets in him.'

'At this stage I've no idea what matters and what doesn't. Have you recovered all the rounds?'

'I have. They've been preserved and packaged, according to protocol, and are currently winging their way by courier to Ballistics.'

'From what range would you say the shots were fired?'

'Very close. There was gunpowder residue on the clothes covering his torso and a lot of shattered bone. Extensive viscera damage. The bullets travelled around internally, making in laymen's language, a bloody mess.'

'But not one of the slugs passed through him?'

'As you correctly say, not one.'

'Sounds like .22s to me.'

'That's more your department than mine.'

'Anything else?'

'Only that the killer was an idiot.'

'Why?'

'He wasted his time and has gambled unnecessarily with his future. In a nutshell, he killed the walking dead. In addition to the bullets, I found tumours.'

'Cancer?'

'Cancers.' Sir James stressed the plural. 'The primary was in the prostate.'

'But he was only forty-five.'

'That *is* young for prostate cancer, I admit, but not unknown. The secondary was in his bones.'

'Malignant?'

'Undoubtedly. You don't have a secondary without the primary being malignant.'

'Was his condition terminal – before last night's shooting?' Templeman pre-empted any further facetiousness.

'Indubitably.'

'How long would he have lived?'

'Hard to say. There's no exact science for that kind of prog-nosis.'

'Minimum and maximums will do.'

'Six to eighteen months.'

'Would he have known?'

'Not necessarily. You'll need to speak with his GP about that.'

'Well, thanks for that, Sir James.'

'Now you can go to bed, eh?'

'If only!'

While Tandy made arrangements for Mrs Markham to be chauf-feured home, Templeman conferred with other senior members of his team. Forensics had little to report. Partial footprints had been lifted from Level Three of the car-park. Photographs had been taken and were being blown up. However, there wasn't much optimism on this front. Most likely the prints had been made by Harry Markham himself and any number of motorists who had used the car park legitimately during the day or evening prior to the shooting. Lots of latent fingerprints had been lifted from the Jaguar, but no one was becoming excited by them. They, too, probably belonged to Markham and his wife.

After that, Templeman went upstairs to update Bulletbrain Lilleyman.

'Solved it?' said the commander, provocatively, as the inspector encountered Lilleyman in the corridor.

Templeman ignored the sarcasm, briefing Lilleyman succinctly as they headed in single file for the commander's office, Templeman following, the pace brisk and purposeful.

'Leave the door,' Lilleyman ordered, stomping towards the other side of his desk, but not sitting. Instead, he remained standing with his fingers splayed on his desk, taking his weight, which was considerable. 'There aren't any great breakthrough secrets we need to keep from the ears of passers-by in the corridor, are there?' A sardonic smile didn't bring any cheer to his florid face.

'Not so far.'

'I didn't think so.' The sneer was fluorescent.

Templeman talked Bulletbrain equably through the patholo-gist's initial report and the commander asked if there was any news from Ballistics.

'Too early,' said Templeman. 'We won't have anything from them until the morning.'

Lilleyman was eager to hear all about the widow and Templeman treated him to a condensed version of the interview with Audrey Markham, which served only to whet the commander's appetite for more detail.

'Is she involved?'

'I'm certainly not ruling her out.'

Lilleyman was hoping for bar gossip and guessing, rather than diplomacy and measured assessments.

'What did your gut tell you?'

'Not much.'

Lilleyman was becoming exasperated. 'Every good detective gets a feel about someone they're interviewing,' he taunted.

'One thing I've learned, sir, is not to read too much into the behaviour of someone in shock. I've had a woman laugh her head off when I told her that her son had just been killed in a road accident. Two days later, she was hysterical. The fourth day, she committed suicide.'

'All right, Inspector, there's no need to lecture me. You're obviously intent on being bloody awkward. On this occasion, I'll give you the benefit of the doubt and put it down to fatigue. Let me approach this from another angle. In your opinion, with all your flair, do you think her shock was genuine or a sham?' This came with lashings of sarcasm.

Templeman was too enervated for combat, albeit verbal, but he was conscious of the fact that from day one of a murder inquiry Lilleyman liked to have a target. It gave him direction and focus. A sense, as he described it, of 'Being on the road, motoring, not just sitting in traffic with the engine idling and going nowhere'. The danger was that, given too much steer, he would head blindly down deadends. Finding the perfect balance was tricky when fully alert; virtually impossible when stultified.

'I have an open mind.'

'Brain-dead, you mean?'

'Not at all. I'm not being evasive, either. Like a juggler, I want to keep all balls in the air for as long as possible.'

'You're a tiresome bugger, Templeman.' Lilleyman retreated, finally flopping into his chair. 'I'll leave you to get on with it in your own inimitable way – for the time being. What and where next?'

'I'm going with Detective Sergeant Tandy to speak with Harry Markham's agent.'

'The hacks are screaming to be fed. I've called a press conference for five o'clock. I'll take it. Leave the limelight to me.'

'That's your prerogative. Has Markham's name been released
yet?'

'No, that's the first thing the jackals will want. You'd better
warn Mrs Markham to expect a press invasion. She should be
given the opportunity to go to ground for a few days.'

'I'll see to it.'

'On with it, then!' Just as Templeman was on the threshold of
the door, Lilleyman said, as if an afterthought, 'Only half an hour
ago I saw your wife, though she didn't see me. She was much too
occupied.'

'Oh, Templeman said, vacantly, hovering, waiting for a point
to be made.

'I was crossing the road behind her, near the Aldwych. She
seemed to be talking very animatedly to the man on whose arm
she was hanging. I didn't manage a look at his face, but he was a
lawyer type – a stuffy pinstriper. I expect it was strictly business,
something no doubt to do with concocting an alibi for that little
turd Petrelli. But you don't want to hear this, do you? You've got
more than enough on your plate here.'

The double meaning was unmistakable. He hadn't named
Tandy, but he might just as well have done. Templeman froze in
the door-frame. Seething, he demanded, 'What's that supposed to
mean?'

'Only that you're up to your eyeballs in a sticky murder investigation; nothing more, nothing less.' Lilleyman chortled,
delighted that he had touched a nerve. 'Carry on like this much
longer and you'll have me believing you're becoming too
neurotic and sensitive for your job.'

Templeman slammed the door behind him.

The sky ahead was greyish pink, like the face of an unhealthy old
man whose nurse had shown too much leg. The snow clouds had
been blown out to sea. What was left of the daylight canopy was
a spaghetti junction of fluffy jet-streams, the legacy of aircraft
approaching or departing Heathrow. Snow on rooftops, edifices
and monuments conspired to promulgate a lie about the city's
cleanliness. The contour of the skyline – the irregular highs and
lows of the buildings – somehow symbolized the variety and
versatility of the capital; a jumble of ancient and modern, of

pageantry and pallor, moulded into a plausible entity. *Anyone tired of London is tired of life – not true*, Templeman mused. *Anyone tired of London is tired of strife*. All around was mass murder; the strangulation of an over-loaded infrastructure. Not to mention the mass poisoning from pollution. Even the river craft seemed to be struggling against the tide of self-destruction.

Good old London, survived the Blitz only to get blown away by its own planners. This London hath made a shameful conquest of itself. Luke smiled cynically as he mixed a little adulterated Shakespeare with his own contempt for the desecration of *this blessed plot*.

Tandy brought the Mondeo to a halt on double yellow lines outside a strip club and a massage parlour. Passers-by gave the two detectives odd looks as Templeman and Tandy nonchalantly left their car illegally parked with a female traffic warden, who was busily writing a ticket, no more than thirty yards away.

Abe Kline's offices were on the first floor above the low-life premises. The entrance was via an electrically-operated sliding glass door, controlled by sensors, at ground level. Seated behind a reception desk was a poor imitation Marilyn Monroe, whose voice was as artificial as a ventriloquist's dummy.

'Is Mr Kline expecting you?' she trilled.

'Hard to tell,' retorted Templeman combatively, simultaneously flashing ID.

They were directed to a lift in a small, black and white art deco lobby. Kline's secretary, another blonde-out-of-a-bottle, met them at the first floor. Her voice was even more ridiculously tinny than that of her double downstairs.

Kline was a caricature showbusiness agent – short, bald, plump and smarmy, with ostentatious rings on six fingers. He was sucking a submarine cigar the way a baby would a dummy.

'This is a terrible day, terrible. Come in. We must talk. How about a drink? Coffee, tea, something packing more punch?'

Templeman declined on behalf of both of them. Before elbowing shut the door, Kline instructed his secretary to ensure that they weren't disturbed and not to put through any calls, 'not even from Elton John'.

The art deco theme was remorseless throughout. Kline pulled up two chairs, black and white with chrome frames, in front of his silver-grey, metallic desk. His own chair was in the grand fashion of a Hollywood studio boss's 'throne'.

'I get the distinct impression you know exactly why we're here,' Templeman began, picking up on Kline's preamble.

Kline sidelined his cigar in a silver ashtray and crossed his stunted legs at the ankles, revealing silk yellow socks. He flicked a speck of dust from the glossy trousers of his powder-blue mohair suit.

'Joe Velatti called me from the Society nightclub. I couldn't believe it. I'd heard on my car radio that a guy had been shot in a Soho car park, just around the corner from here. But no name was given. I didn't think any more of it until I got Joe's call. I'm in denial, absolute denial.'

Kline was as theatrical as his clients, while his voice was refined cockney; a poor East-End-boy-made-good; very, very good. 'What's the world coming to? Who would want to do such a thing?'

'That was one of the questions I was going to ask *you*,' said Templeman, seizing the chance to kick-start the business agenda.

Kline's expression was blank as he pinched the top of his fleshy nose, as if trying to squeeze out some sense of it all. He closed his piggy eyes and rolled his head, his sagging features appearing even more pendulous than on the detectives' arrival. 'I can't think of anybody. It couldn't have been personal. He must have been in the wrong place at the wrong time. Was he robbed?'

'It would appear not,' Templeman said flatly, while Tandy made notes.

'So mindless, so senseless,' muttered Kline, rubbing his eyes with the back of his hands.

'It's my understanding that you and he were close.'

Kline was alert to the nuances. 'I represented him for ten years. Of course we were close.'

'How close?'

Kline now reclined with his hands clasped behind his head, his paunch accentuated and one of his shiny pumps hoisted on to the desk.

'We had faith in one another. I had belief in him, as an entertainer. He was immensely marketable. He was never going to be in the charts or have his own TV show, but neither would he be out of work while he had his voice and looks.'

'Was he the only Presley impersonator on your books?'

'Currently, yes.'

'So at one time you had others?'

'One other.'

'When did that cease?'

'Approximately a year ago.'

'What happened to him?'

'He was dissatisfied. His bookings were drying up.'

'Why?'

'Because he was always in Harry's shadow here. He believed I was pushing Harry at his expense.'

'Was that true?'

'Of course not. I wanted them both in full-time work. After all, the more they raked in, the more for me. It's not uncommon for there to be a little jealousy and friction in a stable among those artistes competing in the same market-place.'

'Serious rivalry?'

'Nah! Petty stuff. Handbag warfare at worst. Margaret Thatcher would have broken both their heads with one swipe.'

'Who are we talking about here?'

'I was speaking generically about competition.'

'Not when you spoke of the other Presley you had on your books.'

Kline screwed up his face in a signal that suggested he was already regretting having introduced the subject. 'There was never any real aggro between them. Any ill-feeling was directed at me.'

'I hear what you say, but what's his name?'

'Do I have to? I mean, the poor sod's struggling to make a living. He has mouths to feed. The last thing he needs is to be dragged into something like this.'

'He's not being *dragged* into anything. Trust me.'

Kline capitulated uneasily. 'This really goes against the grain. His name is Marty Rosselli.'

'Did he find another agent?'

'Ben Graham acts for him. The change of stable's done him no good, though. Ben couldn't spot a star from the moon. If anything, Marty gets even fewer engagements now.'

'I'm intrigued by the whole Presley phenomenon.'

'So you should be; it's mind-blowing, a monster thing that's out of control and needs feeding more by the day,' Kline enthused, circumnavigating his desk, massaging his hairless chin as he endeavoured to articulate something about which he was clearly passionate. 'They refer to themselves as Elvii, you know that?'

'No, I didn't.' Templeman hoped that his ready confession of ignorance would help with bonding.

Kline stopped to straddle a corner of his desk, spreading his flesh. 'People tend to forget that the Elvii population wasn't born out of the death of Elvis. There were already one hundred and fifty Elvii around *before* Presley died. But by the time of the millennium, there were more than thirty-five thousand. And get this, if that number continues to grow at the same rate, a third of the world's population will be rhinestone replicas by the year two thousand and nineteen.'

'That's hard to take in.'

'Ain't it just! The market's flooded; more Pied Pipers than rats. Bad for business. Very bad. You can even take degree courses on Elvis. Harry did one years ago at the University of Tennessee – the Cultural Phenomenon of Elvis Presley: The Making of a Folk Hero. How about that? There are more courses than tutors to take 'em. A pal of mine studied the Hawaiian movies of Elvis at the University of Mississippi. There's even an Elvis religious cult.'

Templeman's focus was immediately sharpened.

'*Religious cult?*' he intoned.

'Yeah, the Elvis Gospel Ministries. They're an international network of evangelists, Presley disciples, who are devoted to praying for everyone in Elvis's world. Amen!'

'Extremists?'

'Everyone in the Elvis clan takes their adoration to the extreme or they wouldn't be what they are. They're defined by extremism, but they're as harmless as hamsters. They're gentle folk; never been noted for trouble-making. Remember, Elvis's origins were rooted in the days of flower power and make love, not war. When you go on an Elvis university course in the States, you live just like the King himself – on fried pickle chips, boiled chicken livers wrapped in bacon, and fried peanut butter sarnies. There is a whole series of Elvis cookery books on the market, containing literally hundreds of recipes, most of 'em lethally unhealthy, but that's the way he was. Harry used to get all of his gear from Memphis … at Lanksy Brothers, the official Elvis outfitters, clothiers to the King. A black velvet shirt would cost him two hundred bucks – or more, but it was worth it because it made him all the more authentic.'

'Just how talented was Mr Markham?'

'He was one of the best at what he did.'

'I've already spoken to his wife about how he got started. You say he was with your agency for the past ten years; that means he was on the circuit some years before he came to you.'

'That's right. He joined my outfit when he felt he wasn't getting anywhere. He was doing OK, making a modest living, but he was always only one bad week away from bankruptcy. That's really living on the edge, right? Especially when you're married and have young kids. He struck me as being very sensible and level-headed. He wanted an objective assessment. Was there a future in what he was doing, or should he start looking for a real man's job. To be honest, I wasn't that interested. Impersonators are more common than a cold in winter. Mostly I'm scouting for original turns. You know, a star of the future, the next Tina Turner or Cher. Anyhow, Harry was persistent, so I sent one of my scouts to catch his act when he had a gig in an outer London suburb. For the life of me I can't remember where that was.'

'That's not important. The feedback must have been encouraging?'

'Oh, it was. My scout reported that Harry had a great voice. Deep as a South American rainforest. Very rich. Very Elvis. In fact, he reckoned Harry was a better Elvis than the original. Now that's real heresy. What's more, he believed Harry was versatile enough to broaden his act and widen his appeal, extending his gospel, so to speak – the way Tommy Steele did and other survivors from rock an' roll.'

'Why didn't that ever happen?'

'Market forces. Club managers and concert producers only ever wanted him as Elvis. It was his niche, his gravy train. Why get off and maybe never make another connection? Many people specialize by accident. A general news hack deputizes for the showbiz correspondent who's off sick one day and next thing you know he's the newspaper's next entertainment expert. Life's like that. Things happen by chance.'

'Did he make a lot of money?'

'What's a *lot* these days? He made enough. He was earning far more than he'd ever have been without the promotion of my organization. Harry wasn't one of my mega earners, but he was clearing a hundred grand a year – that I can tell you.'

'After your cut?'

'After my percentage for services rendered, yes.'

'How many clients do you have on your books?'

Kline scratched his bald dome, as if trying to unearth statistics. 'One hundred and fifty as a round figure. That's a real guess, but it won't be far out. Is that of any relevance?'

Templeman ignored the question and asked his own. 'Out of all those, Harry became your friend? Is that correct?'

'I'm friendly with everyone I represent.'

'But Harry was a special friend?'

Kline steepled his fingers beneath his chin as his eyes mirrored glazed incomprehension. 'Where's this coming from? Where's it going?'

'It's my understanding that he'd stay with you whenever he was working a London nightclub,' Templeman explained himself.

'Who told you that?'

'Mrs Markham.'

'Well, it's not true. Sorry.'

'Are you saying that he wasn't sleeping at your home this week?'

'He most certainly *wasn't*. Not this week, not ever. Where did Audrey get that idea from?'

'Her husband, apparently.'

'Oh, dear. It would seem that there has been some domestic deception. I can only guess at the reason for that.'

'And what would your guess be?'

'The same as yours, Inspector, but in view of the circumstances I'd rather have respect for discretion and keep it to myself.'

'Do you know where Mr Markham had been staying this week?'

'I'm afraid I can't help you with that.'

'Can't or won't?'

'*Can't.*'

'Who would know?'

'I can't think of anyone except his wife and she … er … got it wrong, didn't she?'

'When did you last see Mr Markham?'

Kline tossed back his head in a demonstration of concentrated rumination. 'It has to be at least a couple of weeks ago.'

'Where was that?'

'Here. He dropped in for a chat. We talked over plans for his future, which, to be honest, didn't amount to much. Nearly all entertainers have insecurity hang-ups and Harry was no exception. He constantly needed to have his confidence pumped up.'

'He didn't mention anything that was troubling him, then?'

'Such as?'

'*Anything*, literally.'

'No, if anything, he was more positive than he'd been for months.'

As always, Templeman had saved the best until last. Without pausing for breath and avoiding telegraphing a change of tack, he asked abruptly, 'How did you spend last night – from about eleven o'clock?'

Kline's mental stride didn't miss a beat. 'The same as most weekdays, Inspector. I was in bed with my wife, Goldie, from about ten-thirty. I'm an early riser; always here in my office by seven sharp. Can't burn it both ends any more, so my nightlife is strictly confined to weekends.'

'No exceptions? Not even for Elvis?'

'For Elvis, I'd probably have broken my rule, but not for Harry Markham. Sorry, Harry!'

Now Templeman did take his time. 'How was his health?' He dropped the pebble in the pond as if indifferent to the ripples.

'Whose? Harry's?' Kline's staccato burst of counter-questions were rhetorical. 'Harry was as fit as a flea on a drinking spree. He had so much energy he made me exhausted just watching him.'

'So you didn't know he was dying.'

Kline's rat-eyes flicked between the two detectives like windscreen wipers gone mad. He grinned momentarily, the way people do when the emotions and physical elements of the body aren't co-ordinating, before his face became etched in haunting disbelief. 'What are you saying?' he said tremulously.

Templeman slowed down the tempo, hoping to catch a crack in Kline's mask – if that's what it was – but nothing artificial showed. 'Mr Markham had terminal cancer.'

It took Kline some time to compute this. 'Cancer? Harry? I don't believe it!'

'The autopsy was definitive. No margin for error. He had only months to live. It's possible he wasn't aware. Obviously it wasn't something he told you about.'

'My God! How could he possibly have kept on working the way he did, with such energy and panache? Such swagger. He didn't look as if he'd lost any weight.'

'Weight-loss isn't associated with all cancers.'

'Had he confided in Audrey?'

'That's something we still have to find out.'

Chapter Seven

They picked up a couple of pizzas on the way to Tandy's Kilburn flat. They both had difficulty staying awake long enough to eat their takeaway dinner, which they ate while sitting on the floor opposite the TV. In silence, like zombies, they watched the News. Top of the bill was a raid by American and British troops on a terrorist cell on one of the islands in the Indonesian chain. The Western allies had acted with the blessing of the Indonesian government, it was stressed. Second item was the 'Elvis Murder' as, inevitably, it had been labelled. It began with a report from outside the car park in Soho. The reporter, an intense young man, presented his bulletin with machine-gun rapidity, clearly schooled to believe that a breathless, staccato style would beef up any drama. Templeman yawned. Tandy's eyelids drooped. The next sequence was from the press conference with Lilleyman playing to the gallery, represented by cameras and microphones.

'No questions until I've completed my presentation,' he was saying pompously. A publicity photo of Markham, dressed as Elvis, was held to the cameras. The commander ran through the timetable of events from Markham's arrival at the nightclub. He appealed for witnesses to come forward; anyone in the vicinity of the car park at the 'material time' who might have heard the shots or 'seen something unusual, perhaps someone behaving suspiciously'. He sipped archly from a tumbler of water before continuing starchily, 'However trivial you may think your information is, please don't hesitate to contact the police. You can go to any police station to make a statement. It doesn't have to be Scotland Yard. You won't be wasting our time, whatever the outcome. What may seem like nothing to you could prove to be the big breakthrough for us; that's so often the way it happens.'

He was then asked who was in charge of the investigation.

Reluctantly, he named Templeman, with a sniff and in the tone of an apology, quickly qualifying that with, 'But I shall assume overall responsibility. Detective Inspector Templeman will be running the day-to-day operation ... for now.'

The *for now* wasn't missed by either Templeman or Tandy, despite their drowsiness.

Lilleyman finished bullishly. 'We shall catch this cold-blooded killer, I shall see to that. I shall never rest until we have this enemy of decent society locked away.' It was nothing more than self-promotional, egotistical rhetoric.

'Rah! Rah! Rah!' Templeman mocked, managing a slow hand-clap.

Tandy had fallen asleep with her head tilted on his shoulder. When she jerked awake just before midnight, Templeman also opened his eyes, stirred by Tandy's sudden movement.

'Are you staying tonight?' she asked sleepily.

'If I'm invited.'

'You're invited,' she intoned dreamily. 'I must take some tablets. Help me up.'

'Another headache?'

She nodded. 'Blame it on a combination of tension and fatigue.'

That night, they both slept fitfully. Tandy was entertained by a pastiche of dreams loosely based on her own family. Her grandmother, Eve Lautier, had been a prominent member of the French Resistance during World War II. In 1942, she had given shelter to a young, debonair Allied spy, who was on the run from the Germans. Denis Marchant had been captured, interrogated, tortured and sentenced to death by firing squad, but had escaped from a concentration camp with the help of the Resistance. Briefly, Eve and Denis had been lovers in France, but he had been eager to return to London. This was facilitated by Eve's underground network. They both survived the war and were reunited in 1946, marrying in an English village church, a short distance across the meadows from the spires of Oxford.

The Marchants had only one child, a daughter, who was christened Michele Rose. Michele married a Gregory Tandy and they, too, had only one child, Simone, though they adopted a boy, Sam, who was a little older than their daughter. Simone's childhood was very different from most of her contemporaries. For a start, she never really knew what her parents did for a living. All she was ever told was that they did 'mysterious things' for the military and the government, matters that were never discussed in the home. Gregory Tandy would be away for long spells, without phoning or writing, and then would suddenly, as if by magic, be sitting in his chair, beside the open fireplace in their country cottage, smoking his pipe and reading *The Times*, when Simone returned from school.

Despite her parents' long absences from home, on their return there would never be any explanations about their exploits or travels and for a long time Simone grew up believing that this was normal between married couples and within families. While her contemporaries had conventional children's bedtime stories read to them, Simone was weaned on her grandmother's true adventures with the Resistance.

Simone had matured with the self-induced belief that she was very different from her immediate forebears. She gravitated to teaching and taught English and History. By then, her adopted brother was training to become an airline pilot. Teaching for Simone was a blackboard jungle nightmare. She was attacked frequently in the classroom, but wasn't expected to defend herself. Soon she was having daily headaches. Her GP diagnosed migraine, speculating that classroom stress was the trigger. 'Change your job and I think you'll find the headaches will gradually become a part of your past,' her doctor prophesied. Simone took the advice. By then, however, she had begun to suspect that her inherited genes were having an increasing sway over her. She dropped out of teaching to join the police and immediately her chemistry and career were in harmony. Even so, her GP was wrong. The headaches didn't disappear. If anything, they were worse and more regular. She kept meaning to consult her doctor again, but it always seemed a low priority. She loved her job now and she was afraid of missing some action if she took off time for a medical check-up. In any case, over-the-counter painkillers usually worked, so there couldn't be too much wrong with her, she consoled herself.

She woke up in Luke's arms.

'You're sweating,' he said kindly. 'You were calling out, shouting. Are you all right?'

The nightmare was still vivid in Tandy's memory. Her grandmother had been standing over Harry 'Elvis' Markham with a smoking gun in her hand. Fragmented particles of her past and present had been sewn together into a crazy, surreal quilt of the mind.

'It was just a dream.'

'It must have been scary. Want to talk about it, flush it out of your system?'

'It's already fading. What's the time?'

It was 7 a.m. They had another hectic day ahead of them. Templeman had planned to be at his desk by eight, but that wouldn't happen.

They showered together and, while Templeman shaved, Tandy made coffee and toast. The fact that he had a razor and tooth-brush in permanent residence, plus a change of clothes, including a suit, corroborated the measure of their relationship.

They left the flat with a round of toast between their teeth. Most of the snow had gone, but another load was due to be dumped on them later in the day. The morning had broken grey and the weather forecasters were predicting that it would remain that way all day. 'Cold and damp,' a Met man was saying over his car radio. In a reflex response, Tandy turned up the heater. Templeman blew into his hands, a winter habit of his. 'What a crap time of year!' he scowled.

Before Tandy had a chance to comment, Templeman's mobile bleated. It was his sister, Rachel.

'Good morning, Brother,' she trilled. 'Just calling to alert you to the fact that we have two runners at Wincanton this afternoon, though I guess you've already noticed. Dad's surprised you haven't already called to find out the score.'

'I'm up to my ears in a new murder inquiry. I haven't looked at a racecard for a couple of days. Look, Sis, I'm in traffic, running late, breaking all the rules of the road trying to catch up on the clock, and adding to the danger considerably by trading small talk with you.'

'It may be *small talk* to you, Big Brother, but to your family it's a living – and don't you forget it.'

'No lectures, please. Not now. Just give me the punchline.'

'Ignore Lady Macbeth in the opener, a novice chase, but you can wager your life on Tombstone Caretaker in the three-fifteen, a maiden hurdle. Get your money on early, though, because the owner's intending to have a big punt. So, too, the stable – us – of course.'

'What do you reckon the odds will be?'

'You may get tens when they open in the ring.'

Templeman whistled. 'And it's hot, really hot?'

'Red-hot as a poker can get. Would I con my cop brother?'

'No comment. I take the Fifth Amendment, even though we don't have one.'

'Seriously, Luke, the market in the ring at Wincanton isn't strong, so getting on early is essential. The sort of dosh that'll be going on Tombstone will quickly knock it down through all fractions. I can even see him starting favourite. Next time you're home, you can take me out for a meal on your winnings. By the way, how's your trailblazing wife?'

'*Trailblazing.*'

'At who's expense?'

Templeman manufactured a processed laugh. 'Must go. The lights are changing. If I get the chance, I'll call you later, after the race.'

Tandy was leaning against the front passenger door, angled inwards towards Templeman.

'That was Rachel,' he explained unnecessarily.

'Obviously.'

'Dad has a fancied runner at Wincanton this afternoon.'

'I gathered that, too.'

'We can make enough for a winter break somewhere in the sun in one hit.'

'*We?*'

'There's no one else I want to go with and I've no intention of going anywhere on my own, if we can be together.'

'The horse has to win first.'

'They always do when it's carrying the family silver on its back.'

'Don't tell me your father's into fixing?'

'That's not funny, Simone,' he berated her. 'My dad is a maestro at preparing a horse for a particular race. He calls it targeting – the same way that we have targets to meet. Everything that horse does beforehand is merely a warm-up for the day of harvesting. The horse will run three or four times over a distance that doesn't suit it, creating the impression that it's a dog.'

'You mean your father cheats in a sanitized way?'

'I don't think we should be having this conversation, Simone.'

'Then let's not have it.'

Templeman gave her a quizzical sideways glance that posed the unspoken question, *What's eating you? Is this serious?*

Templeman was brought up with horses. His father, George, trained at an eighty-box stable in Wiltshire, not far from Swindon. His mother, Grace, had the business brain and was the stable manager, in charge of finances and general admin. Rachel, Templeman's sister, was the lead work rider and responsible for the pastoral care of the young staff. Luke was no less an accomplished rider than his parents and sister. By the age of four, he was telling all his friends that he was going to be champion jockey when he grew up, but even then George Templeman knew that his only son would be too heavy for professional race-riding.

Although George had secretly hoped that his son would go into the family business with him and keep the Templeman flag flying in horseracing, he was determined that Luke would have a solid education so that he would have a whole raft of career options. Luke was sent to a modest boarding-school, where he excelled, particularly at poker and punting – on horses rather than on the nearby river. He was combative to the core, and his housemaster wrote to the Templemans prophesying that their son was destined to be either 'a great advocate of the law courts or a lyrical orator on the floor of the House of Commons'. Not surprisingly, in view of such donnish testimony, Luke had little difficulty being accepted to read law at Oxford, where he met Charley Masters.

Charley was also reading law, but she came from a very different background. Her father was a long-distance truck driver. Her mother was a school dinner lady and their home was on a council housing estate. Charley had to burn the midnight oil for all of her achievements. The only way Charley's parents would be able to afford to send her to university, especially Oxford or Cambridge, was if she won a scholarship, which she duly did. So much had to be sacrificed for her that the determination to conquer had become her obsession.

Like opposite magnetic poles, Luke and Charley had been drawn to one another inexorably, seeing their coming together through their young, romantic eyes as preordained. Luke could pass exams without revising for them, much to the irritation of his peers, including Charley; *especially* Charley. While she would lie on her bed swotting for her finals into the dead of night, Luke played poker with his friends in an alcove of his favourite, spit and sawdust watering-hole.

It was during a weekend party – from Friday evening until the Monday morning – that they had become lovers. They were both drunk, of course, celebrating the completion of the finals. For Charley, it had been a case of sleeping with the enemy, but they had bonded. He invited her to stay a few weeks that summer at his parents' stables, where he taught her to ride.

During those halcyon days, they also discussed serious and social issues. Gradually it dawned on Charley that Luke was no different from any other clown. The mask was worn for protection. The jester was no joke. Inside was an angry young man. A fine match and catch for an angry young woman. Both were attracted to criminal law, but Luke was less patient than Charley. They joined chambers near one another in the Inner Temple, London, and by then they were living together in the kind of harmony Charley would never have imagined possible between them a couple of years earlier.

Charley was prepared to serve her pupillage shadowing other barristers and doubling as a glorified filing clerk, learning her trade, receiving a thorough grounding, just waiting for the break which she was confident would come her way with persistence. Luke's chemistry, however, had to be fed with quick-fix thrills. Within six months he had walked out of his chambers, hung up his wig and gown, and joined the police force – not telling Charley until he'd signed on.

Both Luke's and Charley's careers had been carried along on a tidal wave of high octane. Charley was the confident cynosure of every court in which she starred, yet her stardom was underpinned by insecurity. When you have been reared on secondhand clothes, then every shower you fear is the start of the rainy day against which you have been tutored to buttress yourself. No amount of money would ever reduce Charley's drive because she would be forever spurred by the spectre of retrogression to hardship, the wheel of fortune taking her full circle. Luke didn't have to live with such demons, from which he had always been cushioned. The initial divide between them had been bridged by a love that they had both believed permanently binding, but careers at their altitude allowed for little oxygen for anything or anyone else, except those on the same climb.

The report from ballistics was waiting for Templeman in his office.

'As I suspected,' he said, standing behind his desk reading, Tandy at his side. 'Two-two. Pros use them frequently because the soft-nosed slugs bounce around so much in the body that they get damaged and that often makes it impossible to match them to a weapon.'

'What's the verdict on these?'

'One is OK, apparently. If we come up with a piece, the lab team should be able to confirm whether or not it's the one.'

'Promising.'

'Only if we find the shooter.'

'Of course.'

They slipped smoothly into business-speak, having entered the building separately.

Together they joined the pool of detectives working the case under Templeman, who sought an update.

The owners of all the vehicles which had been in the Soho car-park at the time of the shooting had been identified.

'I want statements from all of them today,' Templeman said, turning to Tandy, who just nodded.

Harry Markham's sister, Emma Kemsley, had been traced to Bristol through routine police networking.

'I'll tackle the sister,' Templeman decreed peremptorily. Then to Tandy, 'I'll leave you to present the commander with our programme as *a fait accompli.*'

'*Muchas gracias!*'

'If he has any problem with it, he can get me on my mobile when I'm on the road.'

The team didn't need much leading. There was an intuitive cohesion that had matured through constructive familiarity.

Before setting off for the M4 and Bristol, Templeman called home. Charley picked up on the second ring.

'I was just about to go out of the door,' said Charley, meaning, *Make it short, I'm in a hurry.* 'I'm going to be late.'

'For what?'

'Work, what else!'

'Are you in court today?'

'No, I'm going to prison.' Charley paused for effect, as if in court, playing to the gallery, but it made zero impact on Luke, who was firing the engine of his car in Scotland Yard's underground lot. 'To take instructions from a client,' Charley finished her explanation.

'Not Petrelli?'

This time the heavy breathing sent a very different message. 'As a matter of fact, it is. A friend of yours?'

'Funny girl. Petrelli is a subject I want to talk to you about.'

'Not now.'

'No, not now,' Luke agreed.

'I hope you're not expecting me to breach client confidentiality?'

'I know my own wife better than that, for God's sake!'

'How was *your* day yesterday? Any score?'

'I'll answer the questions in the order of delivery: manic and no.'

'Oh, well! Are you coming home tonight?'

'Doubt it.'

'Look, I really must dash.'

'Bye, then.'

They blew each other kisses on air, more from habit than with any significance.

Despite the continuing wintry weather, Templeman was on Emma Kemsley's doorstep in Bristol in two and a half hours. The doorbell chimed somewhere in the building's bowels. He stamped his feet and punched one hand with the other to keep himself from freezing as he waited for a sign of human life from within. During the last few minutes of the drive he had focused on the neighbourhood: mostly Victorian semi-detached, three storeys; attics and some basements, a number of properties with railings in front and sweeping stone steps leading up to the front door, remarkably similar to many districts of London, such as Notting Hill and Paddington. Lowther Road had the look of a middle-class, salubrious tree-lined avenue; there was little external evidence of serious neglect or dilapidation. The cars parked both sides of the road were a far cry from the old bangers of districts just a few streets away. There were even a few BMWs and top-of-the-range Rovers, though the majority were two-door, town-sprinters, ideal for parking on a postage stamp. Most of the houses had been converted into flats; the pods of illuminated bells were the giveaway.

At last a dim, jaundiced light popped on somewhere in the distant interior. Then a human shadow became framed in the frosted pane that formed the upper half of the front door.

'Who is it?' The voice was female and not unpleasant.

'I'm here about your brother,' said Templeman, proffering his ID through the letter-box, but not letting go.

A chain rattled, a key was turned and a bolt was levered noisily, before the door finally creaked open. She didn't utter another word until they had passed along a dowdy corridor and into a large sitting-room of fading elegance. The lofty ceiling was peeling in places, the colours of the flowery wallpaper were flagging, there were threadbare patches in the carpet and the furniture, probably not cheap when bought new, was now shabby.

'Sit down,' she invited, gesturing amiably to one of the armchairs placed at angles beside the fireplace, which had been made for coal and logs but now accommodated a gas heater designed as a wood fire. Even before Templeman had taken the weight from his feet, she advised him dogmatically, 'There's nothing I can tell you about Harry's death. I haven't seen him for years. Neither shall I be going to his funeral – whenever that is.' Her speech was now laced with a certain triumph. Her features were pendulous, her manner melancholy, as if permanently that way and not because of the macabre events.

'How did you hear of your brother's death?' Templeman was determined not to be sidetracked.

'On TV, on the News.'

'Not from Harry's wife?'

'Definitely not! We had no contact, period; no exchanges of Christmas cards or birthday cards, no phone calls, no letters; nothing. We have always been separate islands in different oceans of life.' She used an arm in a guillotine motion to demonstrate how the two families had been cut off from one another.

'Since learning of Harry's death have you tried to make contact with Audrey Markham?'

'God, no! Why should I do such a thing?'

'Because that would be natural.'

Emma Kemsley contrived a hollow laugh that made her flesh wobble like pink blancmange. She was large, grossly overweight and unkempt. The interior of the house matched her appearance, but was at odds with Templeman's impression of the neighbourhood as a whole.

'There was nothing *natural* about us Markhams,' she said with overt, ugly self-deprecation. 'That has to be your starting point. Whatever else you've been told is moonshine, so forget it.'

Templeman noted the lack of self-esteem and also the aggression that was easily ignited.

'Have you talked to his wife?' she demanded keenly, her eyes suddenly sly and shifty.

'I interviewed her at length yesterday.'

'Did she speak about me?' Now she eyed him as if nailing a Judas to a post.

'You did get a mention.'

'*A mention!*' Mrs, Kemsley threw up her arms and her guffaw came from her substantial belly. 'I bet she *mentioned* me!'

'To be honest, you hardly figured in the conversation. She did, however, say there had been differences between you and your brother.'

'*Differences!*' Now she slapped her bloated upper legs. 'Forked tongues belong to serpents. And serpents are slippery creatures.'

Templeman was being hit by one surprise after another. The time had come to structure the interview, to keep it on a tight rein and restrict to a minimum the number of tangents.

'Can you think of anyone who might have wanted to kill your brother?'

'Yes.'

Once again Templeman found himself wrong-footed.

'Who and why?' *Keep it simple*, he briefed himself.

'Anyone he had dealings with. Because he was a rotten, shitty bastard.'

'I think we should start at the beginning, Mrs Kemsley.' Templeman banished all emotion from his voice and face.

'Where's *that?*'

'Your childhood. The roots. It's unusual for there to be such bad blood between brother and sister.'

Mrs Kemsley's eyes misted over. For a few seconds it was as if she was somewhere else, far away, in another time. She wanted to unload, it seemed to Templeman, yet at the same time there were forces within her pulling her towards the shrine of silence. Such ambivalence worked in Templeman's favour.

'We were never a normal family.'

'And that includes the relationship between you and Harry?'

'*Especially* between me and *him*.' This was said as if she was on the brink of performing an exhumation or about to open a cupboard in which she was aware that all the skeletons were kept. They were fencing and Templeman suspected that there must have been an apocalyptic event to have sustained hatred that even transcended the grave.

'When did it happen?'

'What?' she challenged sharply, jolted from her reverie.

'The *thing* that poisoned your relationship so irrevocably?'

Mrs Kemsley tossed a mental coin. Templeman realized that there was nothing more he could do except wait to see if the call went his way.

'What would you do if you walked into your parents' bedroom to discover your thirteen-year-old brother on top of your own mother?'

'*On top*?' Templeman echoed. Of all the possibilities and probabilities, this wasn't one for which he had been prepared.

'Yes, on top, as in fucking. Well?'

Shock, confusion or a mixture of both must have rearranged Templeman's expression because again there was something triumphal in Mrs Kemsley's voice as she quickly added, 'Now you see where I'm coming from, don't you?'

'I'm beginning to. I'm still absorbing the enormity of what I think you're saying.'

'There's no *think* about it. The dirty little sod! It was his birthday. That was his present from our mother.'

'Did you blame him?'

Momentarily, she was thrown by the question, as if she had never analysed the incident in that context.

'I suppose so. He had been my hero, my champ, how most brothers are at a certain age to their sisters and there he was spoiling everything. Nothing could ever be the same again. It was so damned selfish of him. Of both of them! They were both as bad as each other. She was a whore. He had her blood; suddenly that was so obvious to me.'

'And you didn't have her blood?'

'Oh, she was my biological mother, all right, more's the pity. I hadn't been adopted, nothing like that.'

'Yet you say Harry had your mother's blood, making an inference.'

Impatience flared. 'I thought it was obvious what I meant: mum and I were different, thank God! I took after my father.'

Such exhumations often proved to be a focal point of a healing catharsis and Templeman was hopeful that this might be one of those occasions.

'If this is too stressful for you, please say so and we'll leave it awhile.' The offer was more an artifice to ingratiate himself with her, rather than a genuine manifestation of benevolence and willingness to delay progress.

'I can bear it if you can,' she responded, as if throwing down the gauntlet in her first concession to self-effacing humour.

Templeman smiled wryly, as if saying, *I admire your style … if little else.*

'Describe to me what you did … after walking into the bedroom and finding them …' He hesitated over how to continue.

'Screwing,' she helped him out. 'There's no cause for you to be coy. I won't be offended; I'm past that, long ago. Yes, I stumbled on them screwing. To say they were making love would be an insult to the concept.'

Templeman nodded his understanding, his pace deliberately plodding because it was proving productive. 'So what did you do?'

Emma Kemsley assembled words carefully in her head before setting them free. 'I froze. To begin with, I didn't take it in. Even when I became aware of what was going on, I still didn't move. I was rooted. I couldn't take my eyes off them. There was a bedside photo of my parents taken on their wedding day. And there was my mother fucking my brother where, presumably, Harry and I had been conceived. Here was the woman who'd lectured me daily to beware of boys who would be trying every trick to get inside my pants; this was the keep-your-knickers-on-at-all-costs-and-times puritan. Despite the overwhelming nausea engulfing me, like rising sewage, I couldn't look away.'

Templeman was equally riveted.

'Suddenly my mother's eyes diverted to me. She shoved Harry off her, like he was a spent cartridge being ejected from a rifle just fired. He actually fell from the bed. There was a thud as he landed unceremoniously on the floor. "Emma!" she exclaimed, as if *I'd* been caught doing some dreadful wrong, not her. "What are you doing here?" I was speechless. My jaw quivered, but nothing came out of my mouth. I was determined not to cry. "Go to your room immediately!" she ordered, no doubt deciding that attack was the best form of defence. Harry ran past me, sheepish as you like, out of the bedroom, shielding his penis with his hands. He wasn't ashamed, though. He was smirking, like the smutty little rat he was. When I didn't retreat, my mother rolled off the bed and came towards me. "I'm not going to hurt you. I want to explain. We were just having a cuddle. Harry's got an emotional problem and I'm trying to help him."

'She took me for such an idiot. I roared with contemptuous laughter. That's when she smacked my face, a real belter, then burst into tears, blathering on about how sorry she was and how she'd never forgive herself. She tried to hug me, but I dashed from her and locked myself in my room. I remember everything about that day as if it were yesterday.'

'Did she follow you?' Templeman was anxious for the momentum to be maintained.

'No, she knew better than that. I never spoke to either of them again.'

'*Never?*'

'That's what I said; not a single word.'

'Not even when you and your brother went to live with your father, just the three of you?'

'Who told you about that?' she challenged.

'Your brother's wife.'

'What does she know, except Harry's lies. I didn't speak with Harry, even when we were living with Dad.'

'Life must have been very difficult, to put it mildly, at your age then?'

'There was *no* life.'

Templeman kept his voice measured. 'You were too young to leave home. Surely you had to interact within the family?'

Emma shook her head vigorously. 'I did no such thing. I shut them out … completely. I switched them off and unplugged them, so that no current flowed between us. They no longer existed.'

A psychologist's intensity overcame Templeman as he drilled ever deeper. 'Surely your mother tried to reach out to you?'

'Of course she did – because she wanted to buy me off. I rebuffed her every time. I shouted out that I was going to tell my father about everything I'd seen. I wasn't talking to *her*, you understand? I was shouting to the world.'

'How did she react to your threat?'

'Exactly the way I anticipated. She warned me I'd regret it, which only made me more determined.'

There was no stopping her now. She had a story to tell and it was going to come out, in a flurry of pulses; natural birth, no caesarean, no surgery, only the occasional pushing and prodding was required.

'So you told him?'

'My God, I did!'

The fires of old fury were being rekindled.

'What was the outcome?'

Her eyes clouded over as her memory escorted her on a voyage of torturous rediscovery.

'He was very calm, very rational. He wanted to know precisely what I'd witnessed.'

'That must have been very traumatic for you.'

'No, it was easy. I couldn't get it out fast enough.'

'Weren't you embarrassed?'

'*Embarrassed*! Me? Why should I have been? I was just the messenger. I related everything to him. I'll never forget the look on his face, the panic. He was in Hell. But he didn't react the way I anticipated.'

'What did you *anticipate*?'

'I thought he'd rant and rave, then confront my mother. Kill her even. And if he had, I'd have willingly covered for him, taking the blame myself or more likely trying to pin it on Harry.'

Templeman saw no mileage in fanning the flames, so he attempted to lower the temperature.

'Where were you at the time?'

'I'd gone to his office at lunchtime. He ran a small import and export business. After telling him everything, I said to him, "What are you going to do? Aren't you going to kick them both out?" '

'What did he say to that?'

'He said he'd have to think about it awhile. That was typical of him. He was always so damned unflappable and placid. Everything had to be evaluated. In contrast, my mother was volatile. My Dad would suck a pipe and hoped it soothed away all of life's wrinkles.'

'But there was a showdown?'

'Oh, yes!'

'When did that come?'

'Later that same day. I visited a school friend for tea. When I got home, my mother was screaming at him, like it was all his fault – or mine.'

'Where was Harry?'

'He'd been sent out to play. Soon as I walked in, she picked on me. "Now see what you've done with your malicious lies. Always fantasizing. Always jealous of your brother. You've got a dirty little mind, just like your father". Then she came rushing at me.'

'What did you do?'

'I stood my ground. She didn't scare me; never did, never could.'

Templeman didn't take his eyes off her, while she had latched on to a cobweb in the armpit of a wall and ceiling on which to focus lazily, as her brain searched into its old files, which were hardly ever opened these days.

'And your father?'

Emma's watery right eye began twitching. Templeman had hit a nerve. This didn't surprise him. The father was pivotal to the plot, he surmised.

'Dad grabbed her. That was the first and only time I saw him get physical. She punched his face. Even then he didn't retaliate. She taunted him, "Go on, hit me. Show me you're as much a man as your son. Where's your balls? You don't have any, do you? You're spunkless!" Dad turned to me and said very tenderly, "Leave me alone, please, Emma. You shouldn't be dragged into any of this". I never disputed anything he ever said. As I trudged upstairs, my mother yelled after me, "Just you wait, my girl! I'll fix you!" When I got to my room, I left my door ajar, so that I could hear everything that was being said downstairs. My father's speech remained very level. "This is the last straw", he said, almost formally. "I've taken all your flirting, all your affairs and one-night stands, but incest with our son is not just intolerable but also criminal. I want you out of the house within twenty-four hours or I go to the police".'

'Quite a performance, all things considered, by your father. How did she take it?'

Emma spread her masculine hands on her thick, woollen skirt at her knees and her eyes moistened. She didn't shed a tear, but she was crying inside. She had more heart than she wanted and she cursed her bad luck for being so human.

'My mother scoffed. "You haven't the guts", she provoked him again. "What's more, you haven't any proof – just the word of that dizzy daughter of *yours*", then added, "Well, she *might* be yours. I didn't think she was until now, but the way she's *acting* makes me begin to believe that, by some miracle, you must be the biological father after all". I wanted to rush downstairs to slit her throat.'

'What stopped you?'

'I didn't want anyone to suffer any further because of her. If I killed her, I'd go to gaol, whatever the provocation. Secretly, I suppose, I hoped someone else would do it for me.'

'Such as your father?'

'No, I didn't want him to get into trouble, either. Anyhow, she packed up and left. With my brother.'

'It's my understanding that you both stayed with your father.'

'Not to begin with.'

'When, then?'

Emma Kemsley was suddenly ill at ease. 'My father wasn't a weak man. It's just that he hated friction and waves.'

'I think you've already made that clear.' Templeman wondered where this was going.

'I couldn't believe he was allowing it to drop. OK, he was planning to divorce her, but not citing my brother. She admitted – no, bragged – about adultery with several other men and that was good enough for Dad. He intended keeping Harry out of it.'

Templeman was beginning to follow the drift. 'But that didn't satisfy you?'

'Damned right, it didn't!'

'So what did you do?'

'I had to be careful how I played it. The last thing I wanted was to drive a wedge between me and Dad.'

'So?'

Mischief sparked a blaze in her eyes. 'I wouldn't eat my school dinners. When I was asked at school if there was anything wrong, I said I wasn't sleeping at night because I was afraid of the nightmares I'd been having. The teachers kept a close watch on me and finally had me see the school doctor. It was then I pretended to break down, spilling the whole story, and the police were called. Next day, Mum was arrested. Dad was overcome with remorse for what he thought I'd been going through.' Triumph had blossomed again from ear to ear.

'You were quite a little machiavellian actress, weren't you? Manipulator extraordinaire.'

Mrs Kemsley reacted as if she had just been paid a compliment.

'She'd ruined my life. If I had failed to ruin hers, I couldn't have lived with myself. I also felt I owed it to Dad. It was important for Harry to have counselling, though that wasn't my motivation at the time.'

'What happened to your mother?'

'She pleaded guilty, so sparing Harry and myself having to give evidence against her in court. She went to gaol for eighteen months.'

'And that's when Harry rejoined you and your father?'

'No, he was already with us – from the day she was charged.'

'But still you wouldn't talk to him?'

'No, I refused, despite all the cajoling from Dad.'

'That must have made him sad?'

She reacted badly to that. 'I never did anything to make Dad unhappy. He understood me. We agreed to differ.'

'Even so, there must have been an uneasy atmosphere?'

'No more so than before.'

This last reply was snappy. Templeman didn't want to lose the rapport, so he backed off.

'There was an accident, wasn't there?'

The pleasure on her face was replaced with pain. 'Seven months later. Dad went to work and never came home. He was killed in a car crash. My world crashed, too. Harry and I were packed off to different foster families. We were too old to appeal to couples looking to adopt. They wanted babies.'

'Where did you go?'

'Up north.'

'*North* is a big area.'

'Ashton-under-Lyne in Greater Manchester. John and Josie Milburn, they were my foster parents. A lovely, down-to-earth, working-class couple. No airs nor graces, but they were good to me. I must confess, though, I didn't fully appreciate them at the time. I was still too devastated at the loss of Dad. No one could ever take his place in my life and I resented John trying to.'

'Where did Harry go?'

'He stayed in the south. He wrote to me a few times, but I burned the letters. I never replied. He was always bragging about how he'd gone to a rich home and was being spoiled rotten. Each time he wrote he had just returned from a foreign holiday, though he could have been lying, of course, knowing him. He said he'd been sent to a posh school and the old man owned a fancy car and a yacht. It was probably all bullshit. It made zero impression on me. As I said, I torched all the letters.'

'You never had any inclination to trace him? Not even years later, when you were grown up?'

'No. Not at any time. He was out of my life. Good riddance! – that was my sentiment.'

'And he never came looking for you?'

'If he did, he was singularly unsuccessful.'

'So, from the moment the pair of you were separated, you never saw Harry again?'

'Correct.'

'What of your mother?'

'Who knows? Who cares?'

'Surely she tried to win you back when she was released from gaol?'

'If she did, I was never told. Anyhow, she wouldn't have had a chance, not after what she'd done, and she knew it.'

'You wouldn't know, then, if Harry ever met up with her later?'

'That's right, I don't know.'

'Have you any idea if your mother is still alive?'

'No. I have no idea. No interest whatsoever.'

Templeman was almost finished.

'Where were you the night before last, let's say between eleven p.m. and three a.m.?'

'That's easy. I was where I am every night nowadays by ten thirty – in bed here until at least seven the next morning. Why? You don't think I'd waste my life on that dross, do you?'

Templeman smiled disarmingly. 'We detectives go about our work in a very similar fashion to doctors. We diagnose and detect to a large degree by a process of elimination, then seeing what we're left with.'

'Am I eliminated?'

'Most certainly, if what you've told me is the truth.'

'Ah! So it's a conditional yes?'

'I couldn't have put it better myself. Do you know, we've talked all this time and I haven't even asked you if you're married?'

'You have now. Is it relevant?'

'Well, I suppose the real question I'm asking is whether you were alone in the house on the night that your brother was shot?'

'Ah! Now I see; you're testing my alibi?'

Templeman didn't contradict her.

'I *was* married.'

'But no longer, eh?'

'We separated, then divorced. The marriage didn't have a chance; I should have realized that long before marrying him. I was always comparing him with my father and, of course, he never matched up. He resented the comparisons. We fought, naturally. It was a disaster. He took off with another woman. My life has been a mess. I live alone. I sleep alone. You have your answer.'

Templeman had exhausted his questions.

Before driving away from the house, he made two calls from his car. The first was to the bookmaker with whom he had a credit account. Without flinching, he placed £500 'on the nose' on Tombstone Caretaker in the three-fifteen at Wincanton, adding, 'I want first show.'

'First show, you've got, Mr Templeman,' he was assured.

The second call was to Tandy. 'Any progress?' he enquired succinctly.

'Negative progress. We've tracked down everyone who had a car parked in the multi-storey at the time Markham was gunned down and they all appear to be kosher. Most of them are staying at nearby hotels which don't have on-site parking space. They get tokens from the hotel, allowing them out of the multi-storey without having to pay. We're talking about families and couples – no chance of a connection with Markham, if you ask me. Nevertheless, I'm having statements taken from each one, just so we have them all in the system.'

'Good.'

'It's not *good* really. It's boring, frustrating and fruitless.'

'But essential.'

'Yeah, well … how's your day going?'

'I won't know until around three-thirty – after the race. Only then will I know if luck is riding with us.'

Chapter Eight

The return journey to London from Bristol was a nightmare. The traffic after Bath was solid, like debris, and its clearance was slow. A series of minor accidents made the ratchet progress even more pronounced. It was stop-start all the way.

Templeman replayed his Beethoven and Mozart tapes, over and over, helping him to keep his impatience manageable, but even soothing music couldn't smooth his passage back to the metropolis. Just after the two Swindon turn-offs, he pulled into a service area.

Once again his first call was to his bookmaker. Tombstone Caretaker had obliged at the ungenerous odds of five-to-two, but first show had been a thank-you-very-much ten-to-one. Templeman had just won himself £5,000 tax-free. One phone call had magicked him into a happy man. To hell with the fact that the world seemed to be grinding to a halt, polluting everything and everyone in the process. All irritations washed over him as he made his way jauntily to the small mall and self-service restaurant.

After queuing for fifteen minutes for a mediocre coffee and a tasteless ham and mustard sandwich, he found a vacant table in the non-smoking section beside a window overlooking snow-capped hills, which were barely visible in the blackness of late afternoon, despite the white topping. He left half of the sandwich, drank some coffee, which at least was hot, if bitter, then called Tandy. His good humour travelled well.

'You sound chirpy,' said Tandy, her tone enquiring.

'I've had a fruitful day.'

The telepathy between them was as reliable as ever.

'You mean you've won some money?'

'I mean I've won a *lot*. Enough for a holiday – for us. That's not all. It's been a profitable day workwise, too.'

'Well, I'm glad someone has something productive to report because this end it's been one gigantic yawn.'

'Any grief from Lilleyman?'

'Plenty, but nothing I couldn't handle.'

'Good. Now, I want you to do something for me. The way traffic and weather conditions are, I can't see myself being in central London before eight. I want to try to slot in a meet this evening with Marty Rosselli.'

'The Elvis impersonator who was marginalized and squeezed out by Markham?'

'That's him. Try to fix it for me.'

'Do you want him brought in?'

'No, that's unreasonable. I'll go to him. It may be that he has an out of town gig, in which case don't push it for today.'

'Leave it with me. I'll get back to you.'

It took Tandy less than fifteen minutes to do the business. 'All set,' she enthused. 'He'll be in The Mitre, just off the Mile End Road in Stepney, at nine.' Templeman was familiar with The Mitre, an authentic East End spit-and-sawdust pub in what used to be gangland territory, where the sadistic Kray brothers had ruled so ruthlessly.

'I'll go straight to the pub,' said Templeman.

'Do you want me there?' Tandy asked, hopefully.

Templeman mulled over this momentarily. 'I think so.'

'I'll meet you there, then.'

And that's how it was left.

Even if Rosselli hadn't been in the company of Tandy, Templeman would have recognized him immediately. The resemblance to the late Elvis Presley was uncanny, even with a three-day growth on his sagging cheeks, chin and neck. He wore a thick sweater that had been patched at the elbows with leather and repaired around the frayed hem with wool that didn't match. His fading jeans were so tight around the crotch that Templeman expected him to speak in a falsetto. A black leather zip-up jacket was hanging over the back of his chair. There was a half-drunk glass of bitter on a round table in front of him, while Tandy was nursing a gin and tonic. It wasn't until later that Templeman noticed the black cowboy boots.

Instead of a strangled squeak, Rosselli's husky, yet resonant, voice came from deep down in his boots. Templeman could imagine him hitting base notes with a pitch that came from both sole and soul, but having difficulty with up-scale demands, which could castrate.

Templeman had detoured to the table via the bar. Instead of shaking hands, they clinked glasses and saluted one another with glass. As Templeman sat opposite Rosselli, with Tandy between them, the impersonator quaffed feverishly as if in need of a booster shot.

'This is my local, but I've never sat near the door with my back to it since the day three heavies walked in, pulled out pieces, and used a poor old bastard on a bar stool for target practice.'

Templeman was sitting with his back to the door, but didn't flinch.

'What was the background to the mayhem?'

This was typical East End small talk.

'Who knows?' Rosselli shrugged. 'No one saw a thing. Forget about jogging, weight-watching and anti-cholesterol drugs, tight lips are the safest bet for a long life around here.'

'Were you here at the time?'

'I was having a pee. By the time I came back, everyone else was pissing themselves. I saw nothing, you understand?'

Templeman allowed the first wave of alcohol to hit Rosselli's brain before jettisoning the preamble.

'You know what this is all about?'

Rosselli's eyes shifted from Templeman to Tandy and back again, but not furtively.

'I read the papers and watch TV as much as anyone else. Anyhow, she's given an introductory spiel.' He cocked his head towards Tandy, whose eyes transmitted a succinct message to Templeman: *Don't worry, I've done nothing more than a warm-up act.*

'I want to talk about Harry Markham and the Elvis circuit.'

Rosselli finished his beer, smacked his lips, wiped dry his mouth with the sleeve of his sweater, and looked thirstily at Templeman.

'I'll get you a refill,' volunteered Tandy, taking the empty glass with her to the bar.

'A good-looker for a cop; where you find her?' asked Rosselli cheekily, smirking, the question reeking of innuendo.

'She's worked her way up,' said Templeman neutrally, aware that conflict would be counter-productive.

'And how!' Now Rosselli winked and pushed Templeman

lightly on the shoulder in what was meant as a gesture of male bonding and camaraderie.

Templeman resisted a show of recoiling and instead focused on the information he was seeking.

'It's my understanding that you and Markham had the same agent at one time?'

'Mind if I smoke?'

Templeman minded very much, but replied diplomatically, 'Not at all, go ahead.'

Rosselli clawed a flick lighter and a packet of Marlborough from his leather jacket. As he inhaled, sublime ecstasy washed over his face and his eyeballs rolled, as if he was high on an orgasm, his need for nicotine was so compulsive. By then, Tandy had rejoined them and Rosselli made rapid inroads into his second pint.

'What was the question?'

Without any irritability, Templeman repeated himself. At least Tandy wouldn't have to guess what Rosselli had been asked.

''Yeah, Abe did the business for both of us for awhile, that's true.'

'But you changed stables, as they say?'

'I split.'

'Was that because of Markham?'

'Good God, no!'

He wasn't very convincing.

'Why, then?'

Rosselli stroked his prickly chin reflectively.

'There comes a time when everyone should change his agent.' As he gulped more beer, he eyed the two detectives over the frothy rim of the glass. He could see that he wasn't fooling anyone. He put down his beer resolutely, drew long and hard on his Marlborough, then looked away. 'OK, I wasn't getting the work I thought I deserved. I had been doing very nicely.'

'Until Markham came along?' Templeman interjected.

'It wasn't just like that. We were both doing OK ... for a while.'

'Then he began getting the lion's share of engagements?'

'It wasn't a sudden thing. But I became suspicious.'

'*Suspicious*?'

'About Kline. I had a gut feeling he was pushing Harry at my expense.'

'And you resented that?'

'Sure I did. I was there first. Me and Harry were direct rivals – along with hundreds of others, of course. Kline shouldn't have taken on two Elvis impersonators if he couldn't stay impartial. That was my beef. That's all. Nothing else.'

'Did you tell Kline that?'

'Right to his face ... as close as we are now ... and more than once.'

'And?'

'He didn't care fuck.' Turning to Tandy, he added casually, 'Sorry, luv.'

'I've heard a lot worse,' said Tandy, her evanescent smile artificial.

'That I can believe,' Rosselli continued, more relaxed now. 'Anyhow, he denied he was giving Harry the big treatment while keeping me locked in the closet. He tried to sweet-talk me; agents are good at that; it's how they do business. Said I'd been in the game long enough to know that everyone had highs and lows, periods of being in demand and then out of favour.'

'Isn't that true?'

'To a point,' Rosselli accepted grudgingly. 'But I know I was better than Harry. I *am* better than Harry.'

The eyes of Templeman and Tandy instantly had Rosselli pierced as if they were polished and sharpened bayonets. If Rosselli had been impaled, he couldn't have experienced greater viscera penetration.

'You know what I meant,' he wriggled awkwardly. 'I meant no disrespect to the dead. But right up until his last breath, I reckon I was better value for money on stage.'

'This must have caused considerable tension and friction between yourself and Markham?'

Rosselli was shaking his head in denial before Templeman had even completed his question.

'Not at all. We hardly ever met. We were never on the same bill together. We weren't friends, so we never mixed socially.'

'You weren't friends, so there *was* enmity between you?' Tandy jumped in, causing Templeman to frown with concern.

'I didn't say that. You're verballing me. I thought *he'd* be playing the heavy, not you.' Rosselli stabbed a finger first at Templeman, then Tandy, who flushed.

'That wasn't my intention, believe me,' said Tandy, almost apologetically.

'We're not here to intimidate,' Templeman stressed amiably. 'Let's keep this civilized and constructive, shall we?'

Rosselli backed off, believing that Tandy had been rebuked, which was a deception. 'That's fine by me. I've nothing to hide or to be afraid of. Any differences of opinion I had were with Kline and always over business. Nothing personal. Not ever. My attitude to Harry was – "Good luck to you".'

Templeman continued to lead. 'So there was never a bust-up of any kind between you and Markham?'

'Never. We're peaceful people by nature. That's another respect in which we copy Elvis. Imitation is the sincerest form of flattery, right? We love Elvis and that's why we try so hard to be faithful to his image and memory. The highest paid Elvii are those who can deliver the whole package.'

'What's that?'

'The holy trinity of voice, looks and moves. I have it.'

'Did Harry?'

'Not in my view. Mind you, I only ever saw him in action once. Kline reckoned Harry had it and persuaded a lot of venue managers.'

'And that rankled with you?'

'*Rankled*! It pissed me off. I was raking it in, more than a grand a performance, until I was a silly boy. I've no doubt Kline told you all about that?'

Remaining impassive, Templeman said equably, 'Not a word. This is news to me. What did you do that was so *silly*?'

'Dammit! I should have kept my big trap shut. *This* stuff makes a fool of us all.' Rosselli held up his beer.

'Now you've started down this road, you might just as well finish,' Templeman coaxed him.

Rosselli had already resolved with himself to go on. 'Like most of us who are semi-pro, I did a bit of moonlighting as a cabbie on nights when I didn't have an engagement. One night I picked up a rat-arse drunk, who promptly puked all over my cab's leather upholstery, then tells me he has no money to pay his fare, let alone any compensation for the mess. I tipped him out in disgust.'

'You threw him out?'

'Yeah, headfirst. Wouldn't you have?'

'I'd have been sorely tempted,' Templeman admitted diplomatically, without committing himself.

Rosselli snorted. 'I was well within my rights. He was bang out of order. Trouble is, I lost my temper and blew it.'

'You hit him?'

'Fist first, then feet. I was real mad, I can tell you. There was a lot of stress in my life. My marriage was in freefall. I'd just separated from my wife and she was proving to be the worst of human leeches, after blood-money, trying to suck me dry. Anyhow, bang went my cabbie's licence. I also got charged with assault. I pleaded self-defence and lost. The bastard beak wasn't even listening.'

'What was the sentence?'

'A fine and community service. You know, I had to do the shopping for the housebound and take their pooches for a pee in the park.'

'When was this?'

'A year ago.'

'So you have a criminal record for violence?'

'I smacked a drunk around who'd trashed my cab. You call that violence? I call it violation by him.'

Not wanting to jeopardize the rapport, Templeman moved on. 'Since then you've had a lean time of it?'

'That's how it goes … in cycles, like crop rotation, one harvest every three years. My luck will change.'

'Now that Markham's off the circuit?' Tandy couldn't resist another contentious intervention.

Templeman watched for Rosselli's reflex reaction, rather than the public persona. It was a well-timed rapier thrust by Tandy and Templeman approved, while feigning to be vexed. Their interaction was as fluent as ever, with the chemistry unforced.

'What do you feed *her* on, raw meat?' There was now a glow of admiration in Rosselli's aside, before he went on without rancour, 'One less Elvii's not going to make much difference. Didn't Kline tell you how many there are in this world?'

'He did,' Templeman said blithely.

'No one would harm another Elvis out of jealous rivalry. It just wouldn't make sense. To make a difference, you'd have to go in for genocide, wiping out hundreds; no, thousands.'

'Unless it was personal.'

'Too far-fetched,' opined Rosselli. 'Despite the natural competitive edge, we're a family.' And then, as a mischievous afterthought, 'Of course, Elvis was a gun enthusiast, you know.'

Templeman's antennae pricked up. 'That's something else I've just learned.'

'He liked to shoot at TV sets, snakes – especially rattlers – chandeliers and cars.'

'*Cars!*' Templeman reacted.

Rosselli smiled knowingly. 'A car-park gun murder and Elvis's obsession with taking pot shots at cars is a rather tenuous connection, don't you think?'

'Perhaps,' Templeman conceded ruefully. 'What other trivia have you about the real Elvis that might, unknown to me, be of relevance?'

Now Rosselli's scarcely recognizable smile was patronizing. 'Oh, there's so much. I haven't a clue where to begin. He always carried his own cutlery with him and ate with it wherever he went, even if he was a guest in other people's homes; even in the White House, dining with the President of the United States of America. Out would come his knife and fork! But I doubt whether anyone shot Harry Markham because of his obsession with hygiene and bizarre eating habits, do you?'

'Do most Elvii have day jobs?'

'Almost all. You need a load of self-belief to go full-time trading in a false identity and that's the nature of this game. Major reasons for keeping the day job are a nagging wife or a nagging doubt, the former often being responsible for the latter.'

'You've told us about your broken marriage. Do you live alone?'

'Only when I have to.' A sly, fragile smile crept across Rosselli's florid face. 'There's no one special. I enjoy my new-found freedom and my own space. Since my marriage hit rocks, then the sea-bed, I've tried to avoid waking up alongside the same woman twice in succession. I prefer one-night stands. There are no emotional knots. You don't get stung. Neither do you have to make any effort. It suits my carousing lifestyle.'

Templeman was ready to close in. 'Were you alone the night Markham died?'

'I wondered how long it would be before you popped that one.' Rosselli's face was even more vulpine now.

'Well, what's the answer?'

'No, I wasn't alone. I was in bed in my flat with someone, but I can't tell you who.'

'Why not?'

Now Rosselli turned incongruously coy. 'Because I don't know her name nor where she lives. She was a bar pick-up, up West.'

'By *west*, you mean the West End?'

'What other is there?'

'Which bar?'

'I can't remember.'

'In which street?'

'Soho.'

'That's a district.'

'Old Compton Street, I think.'

'In that case, you'd have been only just around the corner from the Society nightclub.'

'But not after midnight. We were gone long before then.'

'How did you get home?'

'By cab.'

'Your own?'

'You must be joking! I'd had too much nectar to be driving. In fact, I was almost too bombed for shagging; limp in the limb. After much trial and error, I got it up once. After that, I flaked out and she was gone by morning, the way I like it.'

Rosselli was trying more shock tactics for Tandy's benefit, but she remained inscrutable.

'Was she blonde, brunette …?'

'Fake blonde. Very fake.'

'Age?'

'Past her prime, but still shaggable.'

'Any distinguishing features?'

'Only her hard as gun-metal, cash-register face.'

'Do you own a firearm?'

'No, never have.'

'Could Markham have done anything to so enrage another Elvii that he would be driven to commit murder?'

Rosselli took his time answering. When he did eventually reply, it was more expansive than Templeman had been prepared for.

'The last song Elvis sang in concert was "Can't Help Falling in Love". That's why so many of us finish with that number. Elvis earned well in excess of four billion bucks. Just imagine the value of the equivalent amount today. No imitator is ever going to get into that league, not even at the bottom. More than six hundred thousand Elvis worshippers make the pilgrimage to Graceland every year. Maybe Harry did something to desecrate the image of our saint in his eyes. We're a fanatical lot – friendly fanatical mostly – and possessive.'

'*Possessive*?' Templeman echoed.

'Yeah, sort of.'

'Let's hear it.'

'In a way we're a cult and you could say we're about owner-ship. We do tend to feel we own Elvis – body and soul. Mind you, we performers are different from ordinary followers. We just want to keep him alive. We *are* him on earth; you know, like the Pope is God's terrestrial lord of the manor, gamekeeper and spin doctor; the earthly trinity.'

'Have you a theory?'

'About what?'

'Why Markham was killed.'

Sensing he had come through the inquisition unscathed, Rosselli became emboldened.

'If I was you guys, I'd be looking at more conventional motives, like revenge, a pay-off. Maybe he was keeping bad company and he double-crossed someone. How about a jilted lover, or the husband of someone he was knocking off? Domestic conflict can get pretty rough these days. When couples split up, some of 'em would kill just for custody of the cat or pet rabbit. An even better bet, I'd say, is that he was mistaken for someone else. He was in the wrong place at the wrong time looking like the wrong man. How's that sound?'

'Very logical,' Templeman agreed. And then, 'Just how close was Markham to Kline?'

'What are you getting at?' An innate shrewdness possessed him.

Templeman refrained from rushing. 'I was just wondering whether there was something more than professionalism to their relationship.'

'You've got a dirty mind, Inspector, but it would answer quite a lot if you're right.'

'Steady on, I meant no more than to query whether or not they were friends who socialized outside of working hours … to the extent that Markham might stop over at Kline's home occasion-ally, perhaps when he had a London engagement.'

'I wouldn't know that, but you might well be on to something.'

'What exactly?'

'Something's occurred to me, because of what you've just said. I'm not going to be drawn any further tonight. I'll make some calls. If I get a fix on it, I'll get back to you, I promise. Have you a card?'

Like casino dealers, both detectives slid business cards, bearing their mobile numbers, across the table.

'Don't get too smart,' Tandy warned, her voice steady and articulate, her posture poised. 'Elvis mark one went out badly; Elvis mark two fared even worse. Heaven forbid what might happen to mark three.'

Rosselli's head rotated from one detective to the other, as if following a protracted tennis match. He couldn't read the shorthand and that troubled him.

Chapter Nine

After the meeting with Rosselli, Templeman and Tandy headed north-west across the city to a little Italian restaurant in Highgate Village. For most of the drive, Tandy was networking on the phone with other officers assigned to the same case. While Templeman was at the wheel, Tandy efficiently co-ordinated the different strands and fronts of the operation, from scene-of-crime hawk-eyes and plodding, uniformed door-knockers to the white-cloaked laboratory staff, known as the boffins.

'Nothing doing,' she said at last, by which time they were within sight of the Amalfi, which was known to take orders up until two in the morning for its faithful regulars.

Templeman dropped off Tandy at the unpretentious entrance and then maundered in search of a parking slot, eventually finding space further up the hill. When he reached the restaurant, Tandy was not only sitting at a table but already had in front of her a bottle of red wine, which she was pouring liberally into two slender-stemmed crystal glasses.

A Mediterranean-featured waiter in a freshly laundered white shirt and red bow-tie fussed around Templeman, who was an *habitué*, taking his overcoat, then insisting on showing him to the table, even though Tandy had already waved. Templeman and Tandy felt comfortable here among a cosmopolitan clientele. This was one of *their* haunts. It was a family-run, cosy little restaurant where they could afford to allow their defences to slip. The staff knew that the couple were Scotland Yard cops, but they never made reference to the fact, unless the subject was first broached by the detectives. They might well have read in the newspapers or heard on TV that Templeman was in charge of the murder that everyone in London was talking about, but no mention would be made of it, even if they overheard comments about the case. They had learned from flies on the wall how to behave.

When he was alone at the table with Tandy, Templeman made a call to 'Tiny Tim' Bone, an ex-con who had been his most reliable underworld informant for at least five years. During his free periods, when he wasn't in gaol, he was employed as a doorman-cum-bodyguard at a West End clip-joint that traded heavily in prostitution and drugs. His *associates* were connected to the Sicilians and American East Coast organizations. However, *omerta* wasn't a word within his vocabulary. In return for leniency whenever arrested on minor-to-medium charges, he was prepared to be Templeman's conduit with a large proportion of London's criminal activity.

"Ello.' Tim Bone was known as Tiny Tim because he was almost six feet, five inches tall and weighed seventeen stone *before* feast festivals, such as Christmas.

'Templeman,' Luke said, equally frugal with words.

'I don't fink I can 'elp you with this one.' Tiny Tim instinctively knew the reason for the call.

'Nothing on the jungle drums?'

'Not a dicky bird.'

'If it was a professional hit, there'd have to be some sort of footprint.' Templeman wasn't talking literally.

'Was it a pro 'it?'

'That's what I'm asking you.'

'And I'm telling you, the wires are dead on this one. No singin' whatsoever. It could be an out-of-towner. An import, even.'

'Transatlantic?'

'You knows 'ow it works better than I do, guv. Then there's always the possibility of an amateur first-timer. They fuck up for everybody.'

'If you hear anything, call me on this number. I'll see that you're looked after better than ever before.'

'I alwus said you was a real gent.'

Templeman almost disposed of his first glass of wine in one intake. 'That's better,' he murmured with visceral satisfaction.

Tandy watched him closely and covetously with a mixture of affection and mild amusement.

'Who was that you called – Tiny Tim?'

'Yep, but it was a waste of time.'

'Nothing on the grapevine?'

'Not a whisper, apparently, which is unusual if it was a hit. There's always something, even if it's wildly wrong. There's not much going on underground that Tiny Tim doesn't get to hear about.'

'Agreed.'

Kindred spirits clinked glasses, then fell into pensive silence as they pored over the menu with a sightless gaze, their focus elsewhere.

'To be honest, I'm not very hungry,' Templeman said desultorily, handing back the menu to a waiter who was poised ghost-like nearby to take their orders, without being intrusive.

'Me neither,' said Tandy, allowing her menu to be whisked away from her tendril-like fingers.

In the end they both settled for spaghetti bolognaise and garlic bread.

'Oh, and bring another bottle of wine, please,' said Templeman, trying not to sound officious.

The alcohol would give them a temporary lift before letting them down, finally dulling their brains as surely as switching off the lights, so they began to review the case as the first buzz of stimulation began to tweak their grey cells. Late-night working suppers gave them the chance to unwind and take an overview. Tandy was eager to hear all about Emma Kemsley. Templeman gave her the bullet-points. Tandy was transfixed.

'Do you believe her?' she asked incredulously.

By then the starter had arrived and they broke bread together, preoccupied, too engrossed in other matters to be conscious of anything other than Templeman's narrative.

'It's hard not to. There was an appalling, chilling fluency to it that was utterly compelling. What earthly reason had she to lie? She was doing herself no favours. Most people would have glossed over a past like hers when being quizzed by a complete stranger. By admitting her unbridled hatred of her brother, she must realize that we'll be putting a question mark against her name. In any case, we shouldn't have too much trouble verifying – or otherwise – most of her story. The obvious starting point is with criminal records and their mother's conviction. If that stands up, then we're more than halfway towards establishing her credibility, I'd say.'

Tandy finished munching her mouthful of garlic bread before responding.

'I think we should try to trace the mother.' She washed down the bread with the musky wine.

'That will be more difficult. She may not even be alive. She could have emigrated, or remarried, or done both. There's no telling what name she's going under, if not dead.'

Tandy ruminated over that as the main course was served. Spidery, animated shadows danced on the stone walls as if the marionettes of the red candles on each table.

'If she is anywhere to be found, maybe the corpse can lead us to her.'

Templeman followed her drift without any prompting. 'You mean Markham might have secretly kept in touch with his mother?'

'Wouldn't you think it highly probably if his sister has given you the truth? She was Daddy's girl. He was Mummy's boy. Sounds to me like Markham never had his umbilical cord cut.'

'My reading of the situation is that it was more revolting than that.'

Tandy became more intense as the glow in her veins from the wine helped her to warm to her reasoning.

'At Christmas and on birthdays, they'd have sent each other cards, I guarantee. Markham must have had an address book, with phone numbers. Although he and his sister were fostered, their mother would have had visiting and access rights.'

'Emma was adamant that her break from her mother was clean and final.'

'That was probably her choice. Perhaps the divide between them was too great for any form of reconciliation later, but the relationship between mother and son was very different.'

Templeman temporarily gave up trying to capture with his fork the recalcitrant, slippery spaghetti.

'This brings us full circle to the missing mobile,' he said. 'There are probably frequently used numbers in its memory; one of them could be his mother's.'

'Certainly the killer's number could be stored on micro-chip in his mobile. But if the mobile was lifted by the killer, why didn't he erase his number and return the phone to Markham' s pocket?'

'The time factor,' suggested Templeman. 'He wouldn't have known how much time he had before someone came along. The shots could have been heard, alerting passers-by. Someone could already have been mounting the stairs to see what was happening. Also, the killer wouldn't have reckoned on our latching on to this line so quickly, which still quite easily could be a false trail.

Markham may have simply lost his mobile; millions do every year. It may turn up some place with all its stored data intact.'

The cavernous restaurant had filled up and was throbbing to the resonant beat of good-natured bonhomie. All the other diners were too absorbed in their own cogent affairs to bother with the detectives' powwow.

Templeman had no stomach for his food and did little more than pick at it, his appetite was for other things.

'We must return to Bedford in the morning,' Templeman continued, planning ahead. 'Hopefully, we'll learn a lot more from Markham's documents.'

'*Documents*?'

'Any papers he kept – from his mobile phone bills to contracts and letters. You never know what leads there might be among his correspondence.'

'Do you think his widow will continue co-operating?'

'Why shouldn't she?'

'Human nature.'

'Pardon?'

'People can be funny about strangers going through the private belongings of a deceased loved one.'

'When a loved one's been murdered, that's very different. She should be raring to help all she can. There's also another reason for going back to Bedford.'

'To talk with Markham's GP?'

Templeman nodded. 'It's crucial we discover if Markham's cancer had been diagnosed. If it had—'

'We need to know if the bad news had been broken to Markham himself,' Tandy finished Templeman's sentence for him.

'And if so, had Markham told his wife?'

'If she did know, then that eliminates her from involvement in his death. No one privy to the fact he was dying would go to the trouble of killing him – or waste money hiring someone else to do the job – when God already had the matter in hand; when it was the Reaper's contract.'

That was enough food for thought for them and more to their taste at that moment than the spaghetti on their plates that was now almost cold.

'I also feel we should look more closely at Kline.' Tandy was thinking aloud.

'Go on.'

'Well, Mrs Markham seemed convinced that her husband stopped-over regularly at Kline's house. Kline was equally emphatic in his denial of that. So where *was* Markham on those nights? And why the cover story for his wife if he never did sleep at Kline's place?'

'There had to be another woman,' Templeman added it up for them both.

'Unless there was something going on between Kline and Markham, as intimated by Rosselli. Everything about Markham's public persona seems to have been a sham. The healthy, loving, loyal husband, faithful family man was nothing of the sort, if his sister is to be believed. There can be no doubts about his medical condition.'

'And Emma Kemsley's account of their childhood together will either stack-up or expose her as a fabulist.'

Templeman then summed up. 'If he had a secret lover, who is she? That's what we need to know. That has to head our agenda.'

Chapter Ten

While Tandy showered next morning, Templeman phoned his wife. Charley was still asleep and took the call on the bedside phone.

'What time is it?' she croaked drowsily, blinking, everything out of focus, including the alarm-clock beside her.

'Seven o'clock,' he replied like a speaking clock, knowing that Charley always had the alarm set for seven whenever he was away from home. On routine days, when there was no major investigation or dawn raids scheduled, he would be up by six.

At that very moment Charley's alarm buzzed and she aimed a fist at the 'off' button, hoping she would be on target and wouldn't break anything. Her blind aim was remarkably accurate.

'That's better,' she mumbled, her speech flavoured with overnight phlegm. She had rubbed away most of the rheum from her itching eyes and the clarity of the new dawn was something she, too, would now experience.

Templeman apprised her of his plans for the day ahead, which included being home 'sometime' that evening.

'I suppose you're running low on clean shirts and underwear,' she observed, shrew-like and with considerable feeling, a dig that Templeman eschewed.

'It could be late, but I hope there'll be time for us to talk some,' he said as casually as possible.

'Sounds ominous.'

Charley's comment was really a question, which Templeman avoided answering. Instead, he said, 'Are you in court today?'

'No. More case conferences. I should be home by seven ... unless.'

'*Unless?*'

'You know how it is; my days are as unpredictable as yours. I never know what's going to turn up from one minute to the next.'

Templeman heard Tandy emerging from the bathroom. 'I'll see you tonight, then – whenever.'

They hung up together.

Tandy was wearing a towel on her head like a turban. The rest of her was wrapped in a bathrobe as if she were mummified. Steam created an indelible impression of her emerging from a morning mist shrouded in an aura. Although there was no other woman detective in the whole of London more capable of taking care of herself in a tight spot, at that moment Tandy struck Templeman as so incongruously vulnerable, fragile and waif-like. A longing, starting in his soul and percolating down through all tissue, along every blood-surging canal and negotiating his viscera, teased the tumescence in his lower reaches. He yearned to embrace her, as if at an airport homecoming for a long-absent loved one, and to lead her tenderly back into the bedroom, where he would make love to her with saintly reverence, coupling with a spirit, a deity even, careful not to spoil the halo, which would serve to remind him of the sanctity of the sex between them.

'Was that Charley you were speaking to?'

The spell was broken. This was tantamount to the big tease, no less than a woman inviting a man into her bed, arousing him with foreplay, slipping a condom on his drooling manhood, guiding him to the gateway of the promised land, then leaving him high and dry with a 'Not tonight, thank you!' dismissal. The miracle of the male tumescence was surpassed by the speed of its deflation when the mental switch was turned off. Although he hadn't been sneaky, he felt like a pickpocket caught red-handed in the act of a grubby low-life crime. Tandy was well aware that he would be calling Charley, but she preferred not to be around when he did so. The duplicity of an affair was something she found tough enough to handle without adding to that baggage. She did worry a lot about the long-term impact of a guilt-complex. For a few minutes, however, all that guilt was transferred. Her lover was in the dock, condemned by his own hangdog face.

'I decided to get the call over early, before we hit the road.'

She approached him slowly, unfolding her arms. A sliver of damp, glistening flesh glowed through a gap in the bathrobe, tapering from shoulder to toe. The sash of the robe hadn't been fastened. She stopped about a foot from him. Barefooted, she seemed so petite and breakable, the top of her head barely reaching Templeman's shoulders. Yet this was the same woman who had kicked in doors, disarmed gunmen, and led raids on Russian Mafia dens in London. When she next spoke there was something almost skittish in the texture of her voice.

'There's no need to be so defensive. The trouble is, every time I'm reminded of Charley's existence in your life, I suffer spasms of insecurity. I realize that's irrational because you've always been married to Charley ever since we've known one another. It didn't matter at first. I didn't go into this expecting – or indeed hoping – for it to go as far as it has. It just happened, natural progression under its own kinetic energy. I hated myself at the beginning. I absolved myself with the belief that it couldn't have happened unless there were already cracks in your marriage. That was conjecture of convenience. For someone who has to deal in hard truths, it's amazing how susceptible I am to my own brainwashing. The problem is that kidology, like everything else, has a limited lifespan.'

She was very close now. Her sweet fragrance was intoxicating. There was a pleading sorrow within her meadow-green eyes. Her lips had parted and seemed to be speaking in muted messages. As he placed his hands on her shoulders, her robe opened a little further. A wet nipple became exposed and she made no attempt to return it undercover. Templeman, already weak at his knees, lowered his head, eyes closed, like a new-born baby gravitating by an instinctive navigational system to the fountain of gratification.

'Take me,' she said huskily, primitive desire thickening her throat.

Templeman's lips slipped from the nipple as he lifted Tandy off her feet and made towards the bedroom.

'No,' she protested, but more in explanation than admonishment.

'Here. Do it here. Primitive. Tribal.'

Their eyes became inextricably engaged, held firmly in an optical armlock. Templeman's breathing was short, as if he was asthmatic or had a weak heart. He was like a child on Christmas morning, unable to tear off the wrapping-paper fast enough from the biggest present of all.

What followed wasn't propelled by lust or love. Tandy's passion was fired and sustained by a subconscious demand for reassurance. Only when they were locked in love-making did she feel truly protected from the time-honoured uncertainties of an affair with a married man. Simone didn't doubt that Luke loved her. She fully accepted that there was much more to Luke's desire than fickle testosterone. Even so, his marriage lurked continuously in the background like an overshadowing iceberg threatening to shipwreck their relationship should it ever drift off course, albeit by the smallest degree. Sex with Luke was Simone's anchor; as much tethering as bonding. It was the adhesive that kept the package together at the seams and on all sides.

Templeman, who was half-dressed, didn't waste time removing Tandy's robe which by now was open all the way down the front. He popped a couple of buttons of his shirt as he tore it off. Simultaneously, Tandy unzipped his trousers, then sank to her knees as if in supplication at a pagan altar where pleasures of the flesh were worshipped and the wine came from the font of fornication. As she took the cup between her smouldering lips, so it overflowed.

'No! No! Not yet,' she groaned deliriously, but there was no stopping the tide now that it was in full flow.

In one acrobatic and balletic movement, choreographed with theatrical aplomb, Templeman raised Tandy from genuflection on to the kitchen table, sending crockery crashing. With his knees pressed into the table-top and Tandy spreadeagled beneath him, as if in sacrifice, Templeman entered her with all the savagery of a hunter going for the kill. He still had plenty to give and Tandy had room for it all, moaning for more, refusing to be satiated. She kissed his chest and the saltiness of his sweat carried the redolence of carnal nectar. There could be no quick sobering up from such intoxication.

'Stay in me,' she implored breathlessly. 'Don't vacate. Don't desert me.'

Templeman was numb to the excruciating pain in his knees, even though he was in danger of damaging his cartilages. Tandy's eyes were shut tight as her head throbbed to the rhythm of a hypnotic rhapsody; she was swimming – inside her body as well as in her head. Their juices mixed into a cohesive cocktail of contentment, but neither of them was completely fulfilled. There had to be more. The sequel between them was always better than the first edition because it lasted so much longer, with a controlled build up and Templeman having the power to pull back from the brink repeatedly until they were both ready to go to heaven in harmony. And that was the way it happened.

Together they cleared up the debris, crawling around the floor on all fours, laughing and fooling like a couple of kids at an infants' school.

'We'll stop for breakfast *en route*,' Templeman declared arbitrarily, suddenly catching sight of the wall-clock.

Tandy knew play-time was over.

It was Tandy's turn to drive. As she threaded their way through the work-bound traffic, Templeman undertook the networking on his mobile. He spoke with Commander Lilleyman, who was typically pugnacious and salivating for something 'tasty' with which to go public.

'Surely you have something upbeat by now for me to feed to the press vultures?' he grumbled.

'Yes, we're proceeding methodically, making steady progress, and we're optimistic of a successful outcome within a few weeks.'

'You call that sexy?'

'You didn't ask for sex, Commander, just an encouraging bulletin, or so I thought.'

Tandy gave him an odd sideways glance.

Templeman was bad for Lilleyman's ulcer.

'Where are you now?'

Templeman told him.

'Just get me a result.' Lilleyman always felt better for letting off steam.

Templeman was accustomed to the commander's histrionics and they washed over him without penetrating.

Tandy smirked knowingly.

It was several minutes before another word was spoken in the car. The cacophonous thump of heavy traffic – red double-decker buses, coaches and lorries – drowned all other sound, including incoming Heathrow-bound aircraft, which were enveloped in a swirling smokescreen of cloud. Vehicles, many of them traditional black London cabs, were kicking up muddy spray, inflicting a dirty, ice-cold shower on pedestrians. Fumes were trapped under the low atmospheric ceiling. Behind them, the River Thames resembled a gigantic oil slick that had sliced the city in two. The temperature had plummeted too low overnight for most Londoners merely to walk; they marched with their heads down and chins tucked tightly into their chests, taking advantage of minimal shelter from the smarting Siberian express wind. Lugubrious faces reflected the mood of the grey buildings and stonework. This was London very much off-colour. In a few weeks, the same melancholic scene would have metamorphosed into a sunny disposition as the painful labours of rebirth were over and new-born spring was celebrated. As miraculous as the season of lambing and flowering, the drab architecture of winter would come alive, shimmering in the heavenly spotlight. Heads would once again be held high, smiles sweeping away the city's frowns. The Thames would seduce with its serenity. Even the pollution would have a redolence that soothed the sinuses, rather than inflaming them. London would have regained its jaunty step. But that was around the seasonal corner and not yet in sight. For now, a north-easterly wind chanted through the leafless trees of suburbia as the bloated, drifting clouds started spitting on the city they seemed collectively to loathe.

Just before stopping for breakfast, Templeman briefed one of his detective constables. 'I want the name and address of Harry Markham's GP. Whoever he or she is, make sure I can have an appointment at about noon. Call Mrs Markham and say I'll be paying her a visit around two o'clock. The main reason I'm giving this call to you is so I avoid having to field questions from her about the purpose of my return. If she tackles you, then tell her the truth: you've no idea. Ignorance is a great ally of deception.'

The young detective agreed whole-heartedly without having any idea what Templeman was talking about.

Dr Ian Gregson was an affable GP, probably just the underside of fifty, Templeman surmised. He was one of the senior partners in a medical centre in the old part of town, near the river and no further than a five-minute walk from the Markhams' home.

'Your colleague explained that you wanted to discuss Mr Markham,' the doctor began. 'Bad business. Terrible. I'll give as much help as possible, naturally. I've had his medical records pulled for me. Now that he's dead, I'm not restricted by patient confidentiality considerations. Please be seated.'

He pulled up a couple of chairs solicitously so they were around his desk, on which there were family photographs – children with dogs and on ponies, and a handsome woman, presumably his wife, the detectives assumed correctly.

The doctor wore halfmoon-shaped spectacles resting nearer the end of his aquiline nose than the bridge. If he had been a patient, rather than the GP, he would have prescribed an immediate weight-reduction regime. His ruddy cheeks, slightly empurpled nose and mouth, and road maps of burst capillaries in his eyes, suggested that he might not be showing sufficient respect for his liver when it came to tippling. His full head of hair was a distinguished salt and black-pepper mixture, but his clothes were baggy and there was a carefree, unkempt country manner about him.

'How about a cup of tea or coffee? I'm sure I can get something organized for you.' His hospitality was unforced.

The detectives declined the offer graciously in unison.

'We don't want to detain you more than a few minutes,' said Templeman, as a way of disarming the doctor. 'Had Mr Markham been your patient for long?'

Dr Gregson thumbed through Markham's medical records and answered before he had finished his perusal.

'Must be ten years, minimum.'

'So he was well known to you?' Templeman led with the questions.

'Oh, yes ... the whole family.'

'So you're Mrs Markham's doctor, too?'

'And the children's, though they're not currently at home, of course.'

'What was the state of Mr Markham's health?' The question was posed without spin. When delivered, Templeman lowered his eyes, so that he was looking at the notebook in his lap. Conversely, Tandy's eyes, like movie cameras, were filming everything.

Gregson affected a cough on to the back of his hand, which had prominent veins resembling tramlines. 'He had been in excellent health.'

Templeman immediately picked up on *had been*. 'But not just prior to his death?'

The doctor laced his hairy fingers, then steepled them beneath his second, floppy chin. 'He came to me two years ago with plumbing problems. You know, waterworks. Getting up three or four times a night to urinate. Other times, he'd have to rush to the loo; just couldn't wait. Almost incontinent on occasions. Wet himself once or twice while on stage. Very embarrassing for him. He had all the symptoms of prostate problems, but ...'

'Yes?'

'I dismissed the notion at the outset. He was too young; far too young. Impossible. I thought he must have a chill or maybe a kidney or bladder infection. Accordingly, I prescribed antibiotics.'

'And?'

'He was back a couple of months later, complaining of being worse, having noticed blood in his urine. On hearing that, I wrote off to make an appointment for him at the hospital with a specialist. Unfortunately, he missed two appointments.'

'Why?'

'Singing engagements, out of town for the week, something like that. I was shocked by the result of the tests when finally he underwent them.' He coughed again on to his hand and cleared his throat. 'The verdict was that he had cancer. Because of the delay in the diagnosis, it had spread from the prostate to the bones. The primary could have been treated, quite possibly successfully, but not the secondary. It was terminal. You don't looked surprised, Inspector.'

'I'm not. I've already had the pathologist's report.'

'Ah, yes, of course.'

'Was Mr Markham given the bleak prognosis?'

'He was.'

'By you?'

'By me, yes. I considered it my moral duty to do so and not to pass the dirty buck to the hospital staff. I believe in total honesty with my patients, unless there's a very obvious reason why a lie is to their benefit.'

'How did he take it?'

'How would you expect, Inspector?'

'Badly.'

'That's an understatement. He wouldn't accept it. He demanded a recount, a second opinion, which I arranged for him. After that, he even went to someone in Harley Street for a third opinion. All the subsequent results confirmed the original diagnosis.'

'Did you see him after that?'

'Oh, yes, regularly. He seemed to have come to terms with his fate. He began asking the constructive questions I expect from a patient with a terminal condition as soon the situation has been accepted.'

'Such as?'

'How his condition would progress. Would he suffer? If so,

could the pain be controlled? Would he retain his mental facul-
ties? How long would he be able to continue working? And the
biggie: how long to live?'

'What were your answers?'

'That it's impossible to be precise about such matters. There
would inevitably be considerable pain, I told him truthfully, but
only in the latter stages, when he would be housebound and
opiates would give him extensive relief from his suffering. The
hardest of his questions to answer was the last one – how long
had he left? One can only ever give rough estimates. It's possible
to be many months out, even years. In his case, in view of the
speed it had developed, I couldn't envisage him surviving longer
than a year.'

'Is that what you told him?'

'No, I said between six and eighteen months.'

'When was that?'

'About eight months ago.'

'Was his family aware?'

'I stressed that his wife, at least, should be informed.'

'Why was that?'

'Because of the nursing that would be necessary in the final
stages. I did offer to have him admitted to a hospice if his wife
was unable to cope, but that wasn't an issue to address until
towards the end.'

Templeman remembered the bottle of whisky Markham had
been given at the nightclub and that led to a train of thought.

'Did he have a drink problem?'

Gregson turned over the last two or three pages of medical
notes.

'Not that he mentioned to me.'

'Would alcohol have helped him to overcome the pain?'

'In the short term, possibly. The respite would have been only
brief.'

'But sufficient to see him through a show?'

'Yes, that's feasible. Mind you, he would feel lousy an hour or
so after his last drink as its influence wore off. Alcohol would
react badly with his medication, especially the high-powered
painkillers.'

'How often would he have needed to take them?'

'About every four hours.'

No tablets had been found on Markham, nor in his car. How

could that be if the doctor was telling the truth, and quite clearly he was. It was all documented in the medical history and corroborated by the pathologist. Here was another irritating loose end, which might lead to the jackpot or, more likely, to yet another frustrating deadend.

The doctor became distant for a few seconds as he wrestled with a sentiment that demanded precise calculation if he was to avoid being misunderstood.

'I hope you will take this the way it's intended, Inspector,' he began cautiously.

'I'm sure I shall,' said Templeman, trying to make it easy for the doctor.

'What happened was a blessing. Not for a moment am I condoning murder, nor am I minimizing the enormity of the crime committed, but from a humanitarian viewpoint there is some satisfaction in knowing that the end was swift, that his death wasn't lingering, any fear would have been fleeting, and the pain was a long way from being unbearable. What I'm saying is that he was spared the final ravages of the disease.'

'I understand,' Templeman said sympathetically. He did, too.

The interview was over. Templeman stood. Tandy copied.

'I'm very grateful for your assistance,' said Templeman.

Gregson, also standing now, replied agreeably, 'If there's anything else ...'

'There is.' The interruption came from Tandy, making a belated contribution.

Templeman was at the door, leaving Gregson hovering by his desk and facing Tandy, who had become wan and tremulous.

'Has Mrs Markham been to see you since her husband was murdered?'

Gregson removed his glasses from his face and huffed on the lenses and cleaned them with a handkerchief, more in the motion of a mannerism than because he was having difficulty seeing. He was buying thinking-time. His features were less friendly.

'We are now in danger of trespassing on forbidden territory, Detective. As I stated at the outset, Mr Markham is dead and therefore I don't have the problem of patient confidentiality. Mrs Markham, however, is a patient of mine and very much alive. So, I do have a problem with patient confidentiality when it comes to her.'

'I'm not for a moment encouraging you to be indiscreet or

unethical,' Tandy argued, beads of unhealthy sweat strung like a string of pearls across her bloodless forehead. 'I simply enquired if you'd had a visit from Mrs Markham since her husband died.'

'Well, I suppose there's no harm in answering that,' the doctor said both reluctantly and uncomfortably. 'The answer is no, but to leave it at that would be unfair to you. She didn't come to me; I went to her.'

'When?' Tandy demanded politely.

'Late in the afternoon on the day she learned of her husband's death.'

'Had she sent for you?' Now it was Tandy's show.

'No. I went to see if I could do anything for her.'

'How was she?'

'Devastated, in shock, in denial. She still believed he'd be coming home.'

'Did you treat her?'

'No. I gave her a prescription for tranquillizers. However, I advised her not to trade the prescription for tablets unless it was absolutely necessary. Grief has to be purged naturally from the system. It's no use masking it, because you're merely putting back the monsoon season, not ridding it from the calendar.'

'Have you seen her since?'

'No.'

'Is she in good health?'

'I can't possibly answer that, to do so would be crossing the line I mentioned earlier.'

'How long were you with her on the day you prescribed tranquillizers?'

Gregson pulled a face to indicate that he was calculating.

'About half an hour.'

'In that time did she give any indication that she had knowledge of her husband's terminal condition?'

'No.' Gregson was struggling to keep up with the pace, unsure where Tandy was heading.

'If she had known, don't you think it's something she'd have asked you about?'

'Possibly.'

Gregson couldn't see the relevance.

'I'd have expected her to say something like, "I was counting on us having a few more months together".'

'Well, nothing like that was said.'

Tandy was preparing yet another supplementary question when she faltered and suddenly stretched out for support.

Gregson reacted much quicker than Templeman. The doctor was more experienced in recognizing the early warning signs of someone about to faint. Consequently, he was sufficiently swift into action to break Tandy's pitched fall.

Fifteen minutes later, Tandy was still unconscious and an ambulance was on the way.

Chapter Eleven

The Accident and Emergency registrar went to the waiting-room, where Templeman was ambulating aimlessly.

'How is she?' Templeman asked anxiously.

Dr Pauline Everson eschewed a straight answer. Instead, she said, 'We're still assessing her condition. It's important I have additional information.'

'Such as?'

'I think we should have this conversation in private,' she lowered her voice. 'There's a small unoccupied room off the A&E unit which we can use. Is that all right with you?'

'Of course. Lead the way.'

Everson, a diminutive blonde, was in her early thirties. The feature Templeman noticed most about her, however, was her lyrical speech, so soothing that it was laced with a hypnotic quality. He could imagine patients queuing and prepared to pay for a serving of her bedside charm. She marched with a ramrod straight back, her deportment that of a fashion model, though there was a fluidity to her movement that was more balletic than catwalk strut. Her dainty hands rested in the pouches of a white medical coat that was too long for her, completely covering her navy trousers and almost reaching her silent, rubbery shoes.

Everson's makeshift consulting-room was situated among a labyrinth of corridors which would have made most mazes easy to navigate by comparison. She closed the door purposefully and perched herself on the edge of a couch, conceding the only chair to Templeman. The room was hardly larger than a closet and the antiseptic smell was overpowering.

'How privy are you to Detective Sergeant Tandy's medical history?' the registrar began, businesslike. Her violet-blue eyes searched with a penetrating intensity.

'I'm not; in that respect I can't help you at all,' Templeman answered haplessly. 'But is she going to be OK?'

The registrar fingered the stethoscope hanging from her slender neck as if praying with a rosary. 'To be honest, I don't know.'

Such honesty, for which he had beseeched, jolted Templeman. 'Is she still unconscious?'

'I'm afraid so. I need information about her medical background *fast*. Who is her doctor?'

Templeman closed his eyes in despair. These questions exposed just how little he knew about the woman he loved. 'I can't tell you that, either. But those personal details will be on file at the Yard. It won't take long to have them made available to you.'

'Good; the sooner the better. Who's her next of kin?'

Templeman blanched again. 'She has parents, but I don't know where or how they can be contacted.' This was distressing. He felt like shouting, *Why ask me all the questions I can't answer when there's so much I could tell you about Simone?*

'You're simply work colleagues?' the doctor probed delicately, nothing barbed about her tone. She was trying to gauge just how circumspect she had to be with Templeman.

'We're more than that; much more.' Templeman was deflated and it showed. His head sagged on to his chest, his eyes clogged with cloudy emotion.

'I see,' said Everson, softening her approach, genuine sympathy finding expression on her small face. 'Perhaps you can help me, then, after all.'

'How?'

'Her collapse today was sudden, without warning, I understand?'

'Completely.'

'Had she experienced any fainting spells in the past few weeks?'

'No,' he replied peremptorily.

'And you're in a position to be that definite?'

This was a question that, perhaps wittingly, would test the depth of the relationship.

'I'm pretty certain, yes.'

'How about headaches?'

'Yes, now you mention it, yes; she's been complaining a great deal about headaches lately.'

'How often?'

'*How often*?' he repeated aloud. 'That's hard to say, but they've been quite regular.'

'Once or twice a week, daily, several times a day?'

'Daily just of late. I thought nothing of it; neither did she. I assumed it was down to pressure of work.'

'How's her vision been?' she continued briskly.

'*Vision*?'

'Has she said anything about her eyesight being blurred or experiencing reduced vision around the periphery?'

'No.'

'Does she have a healthy appetite? Has it changed noticeably in recent weeks?'

Templeman pondered momentarily before saying, 'She hasn't been eating much lately, but neither have I.'

'She's not diabetic?'

'No.'

'You're sure about that?'

'Sure sure.'

'But you wouldn't know if diabetes runs in her family?'

'That's something else that's never come up in conversation,' he said dismally.

'No matter. We'll check for it, simply to rule it out. Is she a migraine sufferer?'

'If she is, she's kept it a secret from me. I think she would have mentioned it, especially in recent weeks, when she's been having bouts of such bad headaches.'

The doctor nodded her acknowledgement of the logic of that. 'Now, as she collapsed, or just before, she didn't complain of severe pain anywhere, such as in the chest?'

'No, she was asking questions lucidly and then, suddenly, down she went. I had noticed how pale she'd become just before, but that was all.'

'Has she undergone a dramatic, unintentional weight loss in a short period of time?'

'I don't think she's lost any weight.'

'Have the two of you been working together regularly?'

'We're part of the same team, so, yes.'

'Have you noticed if she's been bumping into things, like tables or doorjambs, as if she hasn't seen them?'

Templeman delved into the archives of his brain for old film of their days of work and play together. The images were sharply defined and vivid, his recall truthful to the original scenarios, not distorted by cloying sentimentality or romantic editing.

'No, I can't remember anything like that,' he said at last.

'Fine!' The doctor didn't mean that at all as she slapped her knees, but it was a way of saying, *OK, I'm through.*

'What now?' Templeman asked, his concern etched in deep-running trenches on his forehead, the crow's claws at the corner of his weary eyes more marked than ever before.

'We go to work,' she answered professionally.

'May I see Simone?'

'Not possible,' Everson said authoritatively. 'I've already despatched her for a brain-scan. When she comes back, a lot of people are going to be fussing around and wanting a piece of her. By that I mean we'll be doing all kinds of tests and I'll have our top neurologist look at her. The best thing you can do is busy yourself with your job, keep yourself occupied over the next few hours, and call me later today.'

'When should you know something definite?'

'Hard to say. Give me a bell in three hours, but if anything happens in the meantime I'll get in touch with you; promise. Have you a number I can get you on any time?'

Templeman gave her a business card which bore his mobile details and wrote the name of Tandy's GP on the back.

'When you said, *if anything happens*, what did you mean?' His eyes were those of a hunted and haunted feral creature.

The registrar shrugged, trying to make light of her remark. 'I wasn't forewarning you of any particular imminent danger, so please don't read anything into it that wasn't intended. What I really meant was that if I have any news for you – positive or negative – I'll be in touch at the first opportunity.'

On that note, they shook hands and parted, Everson returning purposefully to A&E and Templeman maundering out of the hospital and into the unknown.

From the edge of white lace curtains – the symbiotic moats around the castles of suburbia and provincial Britain - Audrey Markham watched Templeman, head bowed, loping along the garden path towards the front door. His laborious stride was an accurate reflection of his disposition. He couldn't recollect ever before feeling so dispirited. Even when investigations had ground to a premature halt, he had never been crestfallen like this.

By the time he reached the porch, Mrs Markham was holding open the door.

'I'd given you up,' she greeted him reprovingly.

Only then did Templeman become conscious of the extent of disruption to his schedule. It was nearly four o'clock and he hadn't even noticed that it was almost dark.

'I'm sorry,' he said miserably, then gave a severely abridged version of the reason for his unpunctuality.

'Is she going to be all right?' Mrs Markham enquired, out of politeness more than genuine care, which was understandable: she had more than enough misfortune of her own, never mind taking other people's on board.

'I sincerely hope so,' said Templeman, anxious to drop the subject.

Before arriving at the lounge, Mrs Markham informed him, almost as a caution, 'My son and daughter are here. We're consoling one another. They're not only very upset, but also very angry – especially Richard – so I hope you'll tread very carefully.'

'I'll try not to add to their distress,' he pledged.

Richard Markham was a tall, gangling lad with a spotty, pallid face, untidy light-brown hair, angular features, a mean mouth curled up at the ends and sunken eyes. He was wearing an open-neck, country and western-style chequered shirt, faded blue jeans and fox-brown ankle boots. Several days' growth on his face and neck accentuated his untidy appearance. His handshake lacked both vigour and enthusiasm.

'So you're the economics wizard,' said Templeman, hoping to initiate a thaw.

'I'm reading economics at Cambridge, yes,' said Richard tartly.

'I went to the other place – Oxford,' said Templeman, determined to shoot down this upstart, despite the young man's tragic circumstances.

'What, Oxford University, you?' Richard's derision was unbridled.

'I read law. Walked away with a first.'

'So what the hell are you doing as a cop?' Richard's face was creased in contempt.

'I decided to catch sharks instead of trying to hoodwink juries into throwing them back into the ocean.'

'You could have been a prosecutor.'

'It's still not quite the same. Courtroom contests are similar to fencing or shadow-boxing; there's no thrill of the chase, of being one of the sniffer hounds in a pack, because that's already over.'

'Are you trying to tell us that we should be thankful that at least we have a *relatively* intelligent cop hunting my dad's killer?' Richard further taunted.

'I'm suggesting no such thing. You started this conversation. Any suggestions are all yours.'

'Are you going to catch my father's killer?'

'That's my intention.'

'How near are you to achieving that?'

'A little bit nearer than yesterday, that's all I can say.'

'The usual crap,' Richard sneered.

'There's no need for that Richard,' Mrs Markham rebuked her son, taking Templeman by the arm and steering him towards her daughter. 'This is Chelsea. You remember, I told you she's taking a year out before going to Durham to read English and history.'

Chelsea shook hands much more warmly. 'Don't take any notice of my brother, he's still a snotty-nosed kid who hasn't grown up,' she said apologetically.

'Thanks, Sis!' Richard seethed, before evacuating the room, slamming the door in a tantrum as he left.

Chelsea had an oval, friendly face that smiled even when she was frosty or crying inside. There was nothing of the severity of her mother or the spite of her brother in her. The profusion of puffiness around her candid eyes was evidence of the gravity of her grieving, but still her sadness couldn't completely subdue her bubbly, optimistic nature.

'Shall we sit down?' Chelsea suggested affably.

Mrs Markham breathed a sigh of relief as the tension evaporated into the ether.

The two women sat on the settee. Mrs Markham, dressed in a traditional black mourning suit, clasped her knees like a frightened flyer in an aircraft, white knuckles signalling her anxiety. She had used make-up as a cosmetic mask to paper over the external symptoms of grief and insomnia. The white powder and starkly contrasting lipstick had created the sad face of a clown. Conversely, her daughter, who wore no make-up, projected a subtle, inner radiance. Grieving suited her. Although making no overt concessions to bereavement – unlike her mother she wore casual clothes; jeans, loafers and a floppy, multi-coloured jumper – there was a chemistry of compassion dominant in her personality that combined with her free-spirited alter ego to generate something of an enigma, defying a definitive place in any one pigeon-hole.

'How are you coping?' he addressed the widow.

Mrs Markham took hold of her daughter's hand, as if clinging to a lifeline, when answering. 'Much better now that we're all together.'

'I'm glad, but what has prompted Richard's wrath?'

The explanation came from Chelsea. 'Suddenly he's the man of the house and he finds it scary. When you scratch off all the veneer and attitude, you see, Richard's a coward; a moral coward, I mean.'

'Chelsea! I do think you're being unfair,' Mrs Markham intervened protectively on behalf of her son.

'It's true, Mother. There's no point making out he's something he's not. He's weak, and what the inspector was treated to was all front; the burning-off of surplus testosterone.'

'I'm afraid crises bring out the best and worst in siblings,' Mrs Markham regretted.

'I'm a realist, Mother. There's no mileage in burying your head in sand. All that happens is you're blinded to what's going on around you.'

'I'm mother to you both, for God's sake! I'm proud of you both equally and I won't be compromised into taking sides. Now draw a line under it, please.'

'I didn't intend to ignite a family feud,' said Templeman, assuming the role of referee, seeking refuge in the middle ground.

'You have not started anything, you just walked into the middle of something,' Chelsea semi-explained.

'I'll try to be brief, then,' said Templeman, pleased for an excuse to raise the tempo and steer the interview back on track. 'When we spoke the other day, Mrs Markham, you made it clear that you and your husband had been looking optimistically towards the future.'

'Yes, that's right,' she agreed curiously.

'Were you aware that he'd been seeing his GP?'

'Yes, he was having problems with his waterworks. I was the one who made him go for a check-up, just to put both our minds at rest.'

'You didn't tell me about that, Mother,' said Chelsea, her demeanour accusing.

'There was nothing to tell. There was no point worrying you unnecessarily. It was nothing. He had all the tests and was declared in the clear. Nothing but a bladder infection.'

'Who told you that, Mrs Markham?'

'Harry did, of course.'

'Was he given medication?'

'Antibiotics. He completed the course. That was it. Over.'

'Did he stop getting up during the night to visit the bathroom?'

'Yes,' she said petulantly, in a way that challenged, *I dare you to call me a liar.*

'Are you telling me the truth, Mrs Markham?' Templeman pressed, lowering his voice rather than raising it.

'Of course I am. Why shouldn't I be?'

Chelsea was appraising her mother with darkling eyes, dimmed by a passing cloud in her mood that threatened to invoke a squallish backlash.

'Why don't you be honest, Mother?'

'What do you mean, Chelsea?'

Templeman's head was rotating between the two of them like a metronome, following the cryptic exchanges. 'How would you know about Daddy's nights? He was hardly ever home.'

'Stop it, Chelsea!'

'But it's true.'

'Not in front of a stranger.'

'Inspector,' Chelsea turned to Templeman, 'my father was doing so many out of town gigs that he seldom slept at home. And when he was at home, he had his own room, if you see what I mean?'

'Chelsea!' Mrs Markham broke down sobbing. 'How could you? How could you humiliate me like this? I've lost your father, my husband, now you're robbing me of my pride.'

Chelsea looped an arm around her mother's shoulder and produced a handkerchief as if a magician drawing a white rabbit from a hat.

Mrs Markham took the handkerchief and frantically tried to plug the leaks.

'If you are holding anything back, then the only person you're helping is your husband's killer,' Templeman prodded, as sympathetically as possible.

'It's easy for you to say that,' Audrey Markham sniffed. 'You're just passing through, part of a circus that comes to town, performs, then is gone, not caring what mess is left behind.'

'That's not true,' Templeman said firmly. 'The fact of the matter is that without the truth, I'm the one who's handcuffed.'

'He's right,' said Chelsea.

'Don't you think you've caused enough trouble for one day?' Mrs Markham rounded on her daughter again.

'Mrs Markham,' Templeman came between mother and daughter, 'your husband was dying of cancer – and he knew it. This has been confirmed his – and your – GP, Dr Gregson. The pathologist who performed the post-mortem also came to the same conclusion. You've heard of the saying on Death Row in American gaols of "dead man walking", well, that was your husband.'

Mrs Markham bent forward until her head was almost touching her knees, like a woman in prayer on a pew in church, then wept in silent pulses. In fact, Templeman wouldn't have known she was crying except for the spasms which she couldn't control. Chelsea did her utmost to console her mother, but was pushed away.

'Leave me alone. You're on his side.'

Chelsea looked appealingly at Templeman.

'There are no sides,' Templeman stated flatly. 'My task is simply to garner information, then to sew it all together into a coherent pattern. But with holes in the patchwork, there's a danger I'll come to the wrong conclusion and get the wrong person – or no one at all. Being judgemental isn't a part of my job.' Directing his attention towards Chelsea now, he said, 'Did you know your father was dying?'

'Good heavens, no!' she replied spontaneously. 'This is the first I've heard of it. Dad always appeared so robust and healthy. It seems absurd, but I take your word for it. We have to.' She glanced down at her mother's pulsating body. 'There's no mileage in running from reality. Richard couldn't have known, either.'

This intrigued Templeman.

'What makes you so certain?'

'Because he's never been able to keep a secret. He'd have been on the jungle drums within a minute of being told not to say anything to me.'

Mrs Markham had straightened up. Defiance dominated her bird-of-prey eyes. Her hawkish face resembled more of a tormented quarry than a persecuting predator. She gripped the soggy handkerchief in her lap, fidgeting relentlessly. 'Harry didn't share any of this with me,' she said resentfully, her voice hollow and haunting, as if rising from a grave. It had no cadence, no soul. 'I can only assume he was trying to spare me. That's probably why he stayed away so much; so I wouldn't see his pain and the tablets he had to take. He did it out of compassion; that was just like him, the fool.' More tears dripped on to her sallow cheeks and, angry with herself, she brushed them away rattishly with a sleeve. 'It's true he had been sleeping in another bedroom when he was home, but there was no rift between us. He said it was important he got an uninterrupted night's sleep and that wasn't possible in a double bed with the two of us. He said he got too hot and I was always restless. I was hurt, of course I was, but I accepted his reasons at face value. It seems to me now that he must have been in pain and didn't want me to witness any of his distress and disturbed nights.'

Chelsea raised her eyes to the ceiling, a gesture not missed by Templeman.

'Let me get this clear in my own mind, Mrs Markham, you're saying you didn't see your husband taking tablets in the last few months of his life and he didn't have medication about this house?'

'That's exactly what I'm saying, except for those antibiotics I told you about. Also from time to time he might have taken aspirin or paracetamol for a headache.'

'There are none of his tablets in the house currently?'

'Not to my knowledge.'

'You haven't disposed of any?'

'Most certainly not,' Mrs Markham said indignantly.

'Have you any objections to my taking a look for myself?'

'Be my guest.'

'You stay where you are and I'll show the inspector around,' Chelsea volunteered quickly, seizing the chance to be alone with Templeman.

As soon as the lounge was behind them and they were on the stairs, Chelsea said quietly, 'You mustn't take too much notice of Mum. Her memory is playing tricks on her. She's not deliberately trying to mislead you. She recollects things the way she wished they'd been, rather than how they really were. She referred to her pride and that's what it's all about, self-protection.'

The wide staircase was shaped in a dog's leg, leading to a horseshoe landing, fenced-in by a white balustrade. 'This is where Mum sleeps,' Chelsea announced, opening the door to the largest bedroom. 'It's south-facing and you get spectacular views of the river and the Embankment in summer. Not so enchanting this time of year, but still preferable to the northerly aspect. Sorry if I sound like an estate agent, desperate to sell the place, but I love it so.'

Templeman smiled benevolently as he crossed the room to the bay window. He peered out and nodded. 'I'll take your word for it,' he said blithely. Darkness had descended early. Winter still had a tight grip on the brush painting the scene. Amber lights did little to brighten the picture. 'Tell me, Chelsea, have you any doubts about your mother's ignorance over your father's health?' He was careful to couch the question diplomatically and to avoid any inference of wrong-doing.

'None whatsoever,' she replied, as spontaneously as a ricochet. 'When I said you shouldn't take too much notice of what she was saying, I was really talking about her relationship with Dad in recent months.' She paused to throw open the doors of the two ivory-coloured, walk-in wardrobes and pulled out the drawers of the matching dressing-table that shouldered three vanity mirrors. 'This will save you having to go to all the trouble of getting a search-warrant,' she said, trying to demonstrate that she was grown up and knew something of the law.

Templeman made no reply. The wardrobes contained nothing but women's clothes, while the drawers were stuffed with lingerie, jewellery and accessories. There was a bottle of tranquillizers on the dressing-table: Mrs Markham's name was on the label.

'Satisfied?' For the first time there was something provocative in Chelsea's tone.

Templeman looked around for bedside family photographs. There was none. 'Where's the bathroom?' he enquired pleasantly.

'It's *en suite*.' Chelsea pointed to a door next to the dressing-table.

'May I?' Templeman asked, assiduously avoiding taking anything for granted.

'Oh, please ...' Chelsea stood aside for Templeman to pass her.

The bathroom was white-tiled and spotless, equipped with a plunge bath, shower and sun-lamp. A standard cabinet was situated above the wash-basin, which was filled with female toiletries.

'Where did your father sleep?'

'I'll show you.'

They crossed the landing to a bedroom that was about three-quarters the size of Mrs Markham's. The furniture was much plainer and everything about the room was considerably more masculine.

'There's nothing here but clothing,' said Chelsea, 'but I'll allow you to confirm that for yourself. Everything else has been removed and given to our solicitor.'

'*Everything else*? What does that include?'

'Papers. Documents. Contracts. Bills. Credit-card accounts. All that kind of stuff. Mother can't be bothered with all that, not at a time like this. We threw it all into a dustbin-liner and took it to our solicitor.'

'Who's that?'

'Harvey Urwin, of Urwin, Wyatt and Watson. They're based in the High Street. The firm has always acted for us. They do everything from conveyancing to wills and company law, but don't touch criminal defence cases. Very staid, old-fashioned solicitors.'

Templeman noted the name before continuing, 'Which bathroom did your father use?'

'End of the landing, opposite my room and next to Richard's. There's nothing in there that'll interest you.'

She was right; just a couple of razors – 'one belongs to Richard,' said Chelsea, following Templeman's eyes – two bath-towels and some soap; that was all. No pills, no medicine.

'I appreciate your assistance,' Templeman said sincerely. 'You've made this much easier for me than it might have been.'

'We all want Dad's killer caught, but Mum is a very private person and Richard is very emotional.'

'So I noticed.'

Templeman waited, sensing that further elaboration would be forthcoming.

'Richard and Dad hadn't been close for years.'

'Why was that?'

'Oh, it was a silly territorial thing, I think. Two grown males always have problems co-existing under one roof, don't they?'

'According to legend,' Templeman agreed amiably.

'For Richard it was a teenage rebellion thing that just ran on. Now he's feeling guilty and very sorry for himself.'

'Why the guilt?'

'Because he hadn't made his peace with Dad; because he was denied the chance to make it all right and to say goodbye. I know it's irrational, but logic isn't much of a factor at times like this.'

Templeman acknowledged what she said and asked, 'Where will Richard have gone now?'

'To his room, where he'll be sulking. Best to leave him to snap out of it on his own.'

'I'll take your advice on that,' Templeman said convivially. 'When is it that you're going to university?'

'I've taken a year out. I had planned a few months of globe-trotting from next spring, but I think that's now destined for the back-burner. I'll stay at home now until going to Durham in September.'

'What career plans have you?'

'I'd like to teach.'

Templeman's thoughts were immediately transferred to Simone. Involuntarily, he checked his mobile to ensure that a network was displayed. No news was good news, he comforted himself.

'Very noble,' he said, without a trace of sarcasm. And then, 'Just for the record, where were you the night your father was shot dead?'

'In London.'

'Big place.'

'In bed.'

'On your own?'

'No.'

'I believe you share a flat with a girlfriend?'

'I have been. Whether that will continue now, I don't know. Probably not. Mum will need me here. My girlfriend's name is Lisa Lowen. We grew up together and went to the same school. She's training to be a nurse.'

'You're making me work hard for every crumb.'

'You're amusing me, Inspector. Why don't you question me about what you really want to know?'

'And what's that?'

'Ah! Now you're trying to entice me to ask myself – and answer – the questions you should be posing. Nice try.'

'How about helping me out?'

'You'd like to know who I was sleeping with, right?'

'Right! We've got there, eventually,' he teased her.

'We've got to the question, but not the answer. All I'm prepared to say is that I was with someone. Someone special. But it would be unfair of me to name names.'

'*Names*? Plural?' Templeman lifted his eyebrows, feigning shock.

'Wrong idea, Inspector. I'm an old-fashioned girl. Very singular. No swinging.'

'Were you at home in bed? By *home*, I mean your London flat.'

'Yes, I was. Fresh topic, please.'

'What was your relationship like with your father?'

'Very loving.' Her eyes misted over.

'When did you last speak with him?'

'*That* day.'

'On the phone?'

'Yes.'

'Did you call him?'

'No. He called me from his mobile in the afternoon.'

'How do you know he was using his mobile?'

'Because of the caller's number. It showed up on the screen of my mobile. I always like to know who's calling before I tune in.'

'What was the reason for the call?'

'Because I'm his daughter. Because he wanted to make sure I was OK, safe. Because he loved me and worried about me and cared. Why are you attempting to rubbish the most natural human behaviour?' Her steam was rising invisibly.

'There was no insinuation intended, I promise you,' Templeman said, anxious not to lose her trust. 'How did he seem?'

'Normal.'

'Did you ever get to see his shows?'

'Not for years. It was just a job. It wasn't as if he *really* was Elvis. He was a fake, an impostor. But a genuine fake, a very realistic imitation. He was a real dad, but not a real Elvis. Do the children of bus drivers go to watch their dads behind the wheel?'

'Possibly.'

'Once or twice, maybe, then it's boring. What he did wasn't so special to us; to me and Richard. I mean, we didn't go around cooing to our friends, "Hey, did you know we have an Elvi for a father?" That wouldn't have been cool. No one would have gasped and swooned. They might have asked what the hell an Elvi was and in which pond it could be found. We might have been given advice on how to get a life. Elvis isn't exactly cool to my generation. Dad appealed to those heavily into nostalgia. He made the earth move for people like that, but not for anyone under thirty.'

'Did you see a lot of him when you were a child?'

'No. He'd be away much of the time – like now.' A lump popped up into her throat and she had difficulty dissolving it. 'There I go again, talking about him in the present tense. It still hasn't fully kicked in; you know, the fact that he's no longer a player.' Emotion played havoc with her larynx. 'When I was little he'd sit me on his knee and sing to me – sometimes still strumming his guitar, sometimes without. If he was home, he'd always come into my room to kiss me goodnight before I went to sleep and make a little sign of the Cross with a finger on my forehead. "Jesus will see you safely through the night", he'd whisper. Richard was always jealous, of course.'

'Why do you say that?'

'Because it's true.'

'But what prompted it?'

'Oh, he felt left out, something like that.'

'And was he?'

'Of course not. It was all in his head. Dad loved him just as much as he did me, but you know how fathers dote over their young daughters; a well-documented phenomenon. For a while Richard couldn't handle it.'

'When was that?'

'Oh, I'm now talking about when I was, say, six to nine, and he'd have been nine through twelve.'

'How did his jealousy manifest itself?'

'He'd be spiteful to me when no one was looking and he'd get up to stupid attention-seeking stunts.'

Templeman absorbed all of that before returning to a delicate, thorny subject.

'It seems to me that your father must have been having an affair, something about which you more than hinted earlier, downstairs.'

Chelsea's embarrassed blush was more rose-pink than blood-red. 'A wife is always the last to find out. Isn't that what they say?' The question was a rhetorical one and more for explanation than answering. Then, with a resigned sigh, 'Yes, he was. Mum found out only a few months ago – long after everyone else either knew or guessed.'

'Did he confide in you?'

Suddenly Chelsea stiffened and hardened. 'I don't want to go into that. It's irrelevant now. There's no point in adding to Mum's pain.'

'Just how did your mother find out?'

'There's no great story to it, but I'm not here to dig dirt on my own family. Please have respect for that.'

'Very well, but are you prepared to give me the name of the other woman in confidence?'

'No, I'm not.'

'Despite what you say, it could be relevant. If she has a husband, for example, then jealousy could have been the motive.'

'I can't do it,' she said, without vacillation. 'I'm sorry. I think Mum and Dad were trying to sort it out, so it would be cruel of me to reopen the wounds. I've gone too far already.'

Mrs Markham was waiting for them at the foot of the stairs.

'Well, was your nose-around fruitful?'

'He wasn't snooping, Mother, and you know it,' Chelsea sprang to Templeman's defence.

'You were right, Mrs Markham, there was nothing for me to take away,' said Templeman, sidestepping a confrontation. 'Now I shall leave you in peace.'

'Until next time,' Mrs Markham quipped acidly.

'I hope next time I come calling it will be to let you know we've made an arrest.'

'On that occasion, you'll be very welcome,' Mrs Markham vowed.

Just as Mrs Markham was opening the front door, Templeman thought of something else.

'I almost forgot to ask you about your husband's biological mother.'

'What about her?'

'Is she still alive?'

'How should I know? Harry rarely mentioned her, as I explained to you on your first visit.'

'They never communicated, as far as you're aware?'

'No doubt about it; they never did. Anything else?'

'Not for now. Goodbye.'
The door was already clicking shut behind him.
And Templeman found himself out in the cold once again.

Chapter Twelve

Templeman had just heaved himself into the driving-seat of his car when his mobile went off. It was Pauline Everson.

Templeman held his breath.

'Are you near the hospital, Inspector?'

Templeman feared the worst. 'I can be there in ten minutes, driving legally; in seven minutes if I have to break all the rules of the road.'

'Do it the safe way,' the doctor recommended with a fruity chuckle. 'Simone is awake and asking for you.'

'I'm on my way.' His pulse jumped in his neck. A rush of adrenalin set his heart racing. His saliva had dried up, altering the texture of his voice, making it hoarse and unrefined.

Seven minutes later, following indiscriminate use of the accelerator, he was parking outside the hospital. Everson was waiting for him at the entrance to Accident and Emergency.

'No trophy for the record run,' she quipped, and then, 'she's been moved on to a surgical ward. She has a room to herself. I'll take you.'

They talked while on the hoof.

'What was the result of the brain scan?'

'That's what I need to discuss with you.' She stopped abruptly, her hands digging deeply into the pockets of her white gown, and threw back her head to look him directly in the eye. 'I suppose in your job you're used to giving it to people straight, Inspector, but can you take it?'

Templeman froze. 'Try me.' It was a banal response, generated more by his reflexes than anything cerebral; a self-protective cliché.

'The scan has thrown up the cause of her collapse. There's no way of softening the blow: she has a tumour.'

'A *tumour*? A brain *tumour*?' Templeman was pole-axed.

'I'm afraid so.'

'Are you certain? Is there any chance that you could be mistaken?'

'We, like you, Inspector, draw our conclusions from hard evidence. It's there in black and white, I'm afraid. The X-ray is conclusive proof. The culprit is caught red-handed on the job, still holding the smoking-gun, is your parlance, I believe?'

'The parlance of caricatures,' he corrected her, though not seriously interested in defending the image of his trade against outside snipers. 'What's the prognosis?'

They were standing at a bank of elevators. Porters were wheeling patients on stretchers to wards, operating theatres or the X-ray department. Some of the wheelchairs and trolleys were queuing for an elevator. Doctors and nurses stood huddled in little groups. Each group was a self-contained entity, an island, isolated from the mainland, deaf to the currents of conversation lapping their way.

'Too soon to say,' Everson answered the question truthfully. 'However ... but you mustn't hold me to this because the final verdict will come from Professor Geoffrey Crabtree, who is currently studying the results ... the first impression is that it's operable. Often there isn't anything that can be done because to operate would inevitably leave the patient a vegetable. However, when a brain tumour can be removed by surgery, the chance of a complete recovery is very good because malignant brain tumours are rare. Mostly they are benign.'

'How soon will you know if it's malignant or otherwise?'

'That's the catch; not until after surgery, when a biopsy can be carried out on tissue from the tumour.'

'How long will it take Professor Crabtree to come to a decision?'

'I'll have his assessment tomorrow morning.'

'And in the meantime?'

'We'll see that Simone is comfortable and free from pain.'

'If something can be done, how soon will the knife be necessary?'

'Pretty well immediately; the sooner the better.'

'And what if you cannot operate?'

'Let's put that aside until – and if – it becomes germane, shall we?'

'How much has Simone been told?'

'Nothing, apart from the fact that we're investigating. She's very confused and a little frightened, which is only natural. She has no recollection of where she was or what she was doing when she collapsed. That in itself is disorientating enough.'

'Will she know me?'

'Oh, yes, her long-term memory is fully intact, it would seem, and the rest should return within a few days.'

'She's bound to ask what's going on.'

'I'd be obliged if you'd lie for the time being. It's essential that any stress is kept to a minimum. Her blood-pressure's up and we must get that under control as a matter of urgency. The medication she's being given to rid her of pain is making her drowsy, so don't be worried if she slips in and out of sleep while you're with her. It won't mean that she's regressing into a coma.'

'How long can I have with her?'

'Not long. Ten or fifteen minutes, maximum.'

They took the next elevator to the third floor. Tandy's room was at the end of a long corridor. Two nurses, stationed on opposite sides of the bed, were stooping over the patient. One was adjusting a drip to Tandy's nose, while the other was injecting into a vein. Her eyes were closed and her face was porcelain white. Her breathing was shallow and evident only because of the imperceptible rhythmic rise and descent of the coverlet. Without a word, the nurses spirited themselves from the room, treating Templeman to a sympathetic smile as they exited.

'I'll leave you, then,' said Everson quietly. 'Don't forget, no more than fifteen minutes.'

Templeman pulled up a chair and sat close to Tandy's head, taking one of her hands in his. As he did so, her eyes struggled open, as if a weighty lid was being forced up. She smiled a very sleepy, content smile.

'I feel good, as if I'm floating,' she murmured. 'Like being drunk without having to pay for it. No hangover tomorrow, either, the nurses have guaranteed.'

Templeman was relieved most of all because Tandy obviously recognized him and was fully conscious of their relationship.

'How long have I been here, Luke? I've lost all appreciation of time.'

'Only a few hours.'

'How strange. I feel as if I've been here a fortnight, at least. What's the matter with me? No one will tell me anything. Were

we attacked? Did I take a blow to the head?' A big question mark
was emblazoned across her inquisitive face.

'Nothing like that. You fainted.'

'That all?'

'You were out for some time. That's why they're doing so
many tests.'

'What have they told *you*?'

Templeman hated himself for deceiving her, but had to accept
that it was probably for the best. 'Very little. There isn't much they
can say until they have the results. The most important thing is
that you rest and don't worry.'

'It's annoying me that I can't remember where we were when
I passed out. We *were* together, weren't we?'

'We were in Dr Gregson's surgery.'

'Gregson?' Her eyes clouded over.

'He's the Markhams' GP.'

'In Bedford?'

'That's right. That's where we still are.'

'I have a clear recollection of the drive from London, but
nothing else. Had we just arrived at Gregson's clinic?'

'No, we were just leaving.'

'Dammit! This is so frustrating.'

'Don't fret about it, everything will gradually come back to
you.'

'Who says?'

'The doctor.'

'I hope so. Being in limbo is so awful. I'm sure there's nothing
wrong with me. We've both been neglecting eating properly
lately. My blood sugar level was probably too low; I bet that's
what caused it. Syncope. I hope I'm not diabetic.'

Her eyelids drooped as her voice faded and failed her
completely. A serene smile was glued in place as she slipped into
sleep.

At first Templeman didn't feel the hand on his shoulder.
Neither had he heard Everson re-entering the room.

'Time's up,' the doctor announced kindly. 'It'll be several hours
before she wakes. The injection she was being given when we
came in will knock her out for a substantial period, which will
help with the pain management. What are your immediate
plans?'

'I suppose I'll have to return to London,' he said reluctantly.

'Call me in the morning, about ten, and I should have some news of Professor Crabtree's assessment. I don't foresee any dramatic change in her condition overnight, so no putting yourself on the rack, OK?'

'I'll try, Doc.'

'You do. Feel free to phone any time of the day or night to check on her.'

'I appreciate what you're doing.'

'I'm just doing my job, Inspector.'

'And that's all Simone was doing, doctor.'

The drive back to London was a solitary one for Templeman. He listened to Classic FM and occupied himself mulling over everything he had ingested from the Markham family and their GP. It had been such an eventful day that the storage space in his head was overflowing. In addition, he was overcome by a debilitating sense of engulfing desolation, as if the lone survivor of combat, abandoning his closest ally on the battlefield; camaraderie jilted. He reflected on Richard Markham's denial of the tragedy in which his family found itself embroiled and was confronted by his own parallel; the collapse of Simone and her subsequent diagnosis, all encapsulated in the blink of an eye within the context of a lifespan. It was all too much to compute in one day.

Charley called him just as he was entering his office at Scotland Yard. As he talked inconsequentially about 'not being too long', he loathed himself for what he regarded as the spiritual betrayal of Simone, who was lying fifty miles away on what could prove to be her deathbed and yet here he was indulging in domestic trivia with another woman, his wife. God, the duplicity of it all! He reviled himself all the more for his human foibles and lack of moral courage.

Commander 'Bulletbrain' Lilleyman had heard about Tandy being admitted to hospital and demanded an update, 'Now!'

Lilleyman was washing down a tablet with a glass of milk. 'Damned ulcer! It'll keep getting worse until this case is sorted. How much longer, for Christ's sake?'

'We're making good headway.'

'That's exactly what the captain of the *Titanic* told passengers dining at his table on his last night afloat. What's the matter with Tandy? Not pregnant, I hope?'

Templeman felt his fists clenching involuntarily, but he was able to hide his disgust and distress from his face. The last thing he wished to give the commander was the satisfaction of seeing that he had needled his inspector.

'They don't know what's the matter with her,' Templeman lied. This wasn't the time for an intimate conversation about the woman he loved with a man whose entire life was governed by targets, statistics and budgets.

'When will they know?'

Templeman shrugged. 'How long's a piece of string?'

'I'm the one with the questions, for fuck's sake!'

'I haven't an answer, sir.'

'You haven't an answer to another question, either, have you?'

'What's that?'

'Who the fuck killed Harry "Elvis" Markham?'

'I have suspects.'

This statement acted as a salve on Bulletbrain's ulcer, almost instantly palliating the burning in his considerable gut. 'Real or paper ones?'

'Real enough for starters.'

'Who are they?'

'Not now. Allow me to narrow the field first.'

'Don't fuck with me.'

'That's something I'd never do.'

The double entendre found its mark. The forest fire in Lilleyman's stomach was raging again.

After catching up with the rest of the day's developments from other senior members of his team, Templeman drove home, his thoughts far away, north of London.

'Hello, stranger.' Charley was padding around barefoot, heading from her study to the sitting-room. White flesh could be seen through the threadbare knees of her jeans as she curled up on the leather couch, with her feet tucked beneath her. She had fetched several thick files which she stacked beside her. The top three buttons of a white linen shirt were undone and the upper half of her unharnessed breasts was exposed. Her hair had been washed, but not blow-dried and it was still damp. A sweet redolence wafted from her, reminding Templeman of the days when he had been intoxicated by everything about her. All her beauty was inner, so the absence of make-up was immaterial. She was a free spirit and that was both her perfume and poison.

'Have you eaten?' she asked, without looking up.

'No, but I don't fancy anything.'

'I fixed you a tuna sandwich, just in case,' she said, now allowing her courtroom eyes to rise like searchlights from her homework. 'It's in the fridge. There are some cans of beer, too – or perhaps you've had your fill already?'

Templeman ignored the undercurrent. There was a more important issue to scrap over. Muted, he padded to the kitchen and cracked a can of cold beer. He decided on a glass, rather than sucking from the tin. If ever he quaffed from a can or bottle in the presence of Tandy, she always admonished him for promoting yob, jockstrap culture. More than ever he experienced a grumbling compulsion to be faithful to Tandy's expectations of him. Even in something so mundane and perfunctory as drinking beer, he was making a statement of loyalty to the other woman in his life, who might not have much left of her own.

With his overcoat, jacket and necktie carelessly removed, he purposefully rejoined Charley, who was highlighting sections of typed pages with a yellow marker. In the last few weeks she had started wearing glasses, but merely for reading and then only when she was at home or alone in her office at chambers. Despite all her front, she had been seduced by vanity as easily as a whore by the sight of silver. The gold-rimmed designer spectacles gave her a studious and slightly severe demeanour that could have been intimidating for many men. Not Templeman, of course. They had been naked together too often for either of them to feel threatened by the other's icebergs. She didn't look even when he flopped next to her on the settee.

'Which case are you preparing for?' Templeman opened the dialogue, trying to be disarming but deluding no one.

'Petrelli,' she answered flatly, eyes still down.

'That's what I want to have words about with you.'

'I think that would be unprofessional.'

'I'm not expecting you to breach any code of professional ethics.'

'I should hope not.' Now she removed her glasses, placed the document she was reading back on the pile, and finally gave Templeman her full attention. 'OK, let's have it.'

'Petrelli is a cop killer.'

'Carlos Petrelli is pleading not guilty to all charges. Until a jury decides otherwise, he's as innocent as we are.'

'Don't lecture and patronize me.'

'You do your job, Luke, and I'll do mine.'

This was hand-wringing time for Templeman. 'Let's stay calm,' he beseeched. A heated argument would be counter-productive, he was the first to acknowledge, but retaining his equanimity was no easy matter.

'I *am* calm,' Charley shouted.

'I'm not asking you to dump Petrelli; nor for your firm to turn its back on him.'

'What then?'

'Couldn't you pass?'

'*Pass*?'

'You belong to one of London's largest chambers. There must be a dozen other barristers capable of handling that rat's puny defence.' He contrived to keep emotive rhetoric to a minimum, but the challenge on his restraint was proving too much.

'You've got a bloody nerve! If I asked you to drop the Elvis case, giving it to that sidekick tart of yours, just to please me, what would you say?'

Charley had aimed beneath the belt and knew instantly that she had made a direct hit on her target of his soft underbelly. The *sidekick tart* poison dart had Templeman's head in a dizzy spin. The red mist descended with the speed and snap of a visor. His grimace of hate was a frightening spectacle and Charley was already taking evasive action as a fist appeared before her startled face with all the destructive potential of a fired projectile. Just in time Templeman unclenched his hand and allowed the intended blow to be parried. Nevertheless, its impetus was sufficient to unseat Charley and send her reeling off balance, landing indeco-rously on the floor.

'You bastard!' she raved. 'No man hits me and stays out of gaol – especially my husband.'

'I didn't hit you,' Templeman corrected her lamely.

'Only on a technicality, you didn't,' she provoked him further, by playing lawyer.

Templeman accepted resentfully that he had cocked-up big-time. Charley had needed the grit of a street-fighter to punch her way to the lofty pinnacle of a macho, clubbish profession from her working-class roots and she had no intention of rolling over just to pacify irrational, institutionalized prejudice. Someone with a more sybaritic upbringing and without a hunger for approval, plus a lust for the limelight in order to keep the darkness of her early struggles in the shadows, might have been more compliant.

'I'm sorry.'

'You will be.'

Pissed off, Templeman opined petulantly, 'Petrelli will go away forever, even with the sorcerer on his side.'

'If you're so sure of that, why the lobbying?'

Exasperated, Templeman retorted, 'This isn't going anywhere.'

'Wrong. It's going against *you*.'

Caressing his beer, Templeman took himself sullenly to bed in the spare room. His domestic life had taken a turn for the worse. Was it a watershed? Only in retrospect would that be answered. Sleep came to him slowly. None of the Markhams, nor Charley, figured in his dreams. There was only one star in his private nocturnal show and she was blind to the nature of her own drama.

For Templeman, the night, though short, seemed long, but above everything else it was harrowing.

Chapter Thirteen

Next morning, Templeman left home before Charley was awake. He headed straight for Bedford and stopped for breakfast on the way, exactly as he had done the previous morning with Tandy. As he savoured his first coffee of the day, so he liaised by phone with the most senior member of his team currently on duty. The intake of sugar was fuelling his brain and joined-up thinking was beginning to flow and take shape.

'There are still some very dark areas to this case,' commented Templeman. 'Number one: I'm convinced Markham was having an affair. Everything points to it. His family suspected it, even if it wasn't openly acknowledged. It's imperative we find the other woman before the trail goes cold. Number two: Markham's early background is still too sketchy for my liking. We have a vivid picture of his life up until his early teens, but after that, until his marriage, the best we have are a few cameo shots. His married years are quite well documented, but immediately prior to that there's a horrible vacuum. His time with foster parents is a blank.'

'We'll work on it from this end, then,' said Detective Sergeant Maurice Strange.

'Make these lines of inquiry your priority.'

'Will do. Are you planning to be out of town all day?'

'Out of town, but not out of touch. With luck, I'll be with you late afternoon.'

Neither of them had anything else, so the conversation died a natural death.

Harvey Urwin was a typical small-town solicitor. His father, Frank Urwin, had founded the firm forty years earlier. Frank had retired ten years ago when he was seventy, but he still shuffled into the office once a week and was listed on the official notepaper as a consultant, though no one had consulted him professionally since his eyesight began to fail him some three winters earlier. Harvey was a clone of his father in almost every respect. The march of progress, fast turning into a stampede, had been barricaded from these High Street premises.

Even the receptionist appeared to have been made-to-measure for this anachronistic firm. She had the face of a hawk and a bird-of-prey beak for a nose. Her wiry frame was shapeless and the younger secretaries dubbed her – behind her back, of course – 'Miss Lean'. The straight dress she was wearing underscored the fact that there was nothing about her figure to highlight.

'Do you have an appointment with Mr Urwin?' she demanded officiously.

'No, but—'

'Then he will not see you,' she interrupted him. 'You'll have to make an appointment in the regular manner through his secretary, preferably in writing, outlining—'

It was only then that 'Miss Lean' observed the ID badge being presented to her laser eyes.

'Oh, well, I suppose that makes a difference,' she said, making a grudging concession. 'Just wait there, will you.' This was neither a question nor a request, but an order. She had the falsetto voice of an army drill instructor who had just been booted in the balls.

While Templeman hovered the peasant-side of the divide – a high mahogany counter served as a bulwark – the receptionist spoke with Urwin's secretary from a dinosaur switchboard, the kind which had been replaced decades ago in most business premises by modern technology.

Templeman was left unattended for the next five minutes with only three-year-old magazines for company. Finally, a more friendly face made an appearance from the wings. Henrietta Sargent, personable and formidable, introduced herself as Mr Urwin's secretary.

'Mr Urwin's next client has cancelled, so I can take you straight up,' she offered, as articulate as she was decorous. Templeman gauged her age at about forty, though she could have been ten years older because it was evident that she cared for her appearance and was well preserved. Henrietta postured in the doorway to the inner sanctum, allowing Templeman to pass through the arch of her arm. The aroma of expensive perfume went to his head and was so overpowering that it made him momentarily giddy.

Harvey Urwin was tall and distinguished, with a ramrod military bearing. He was standing to attention behind his sturdy tank of a desk and approached Templeman affably. 'I'm sorry to have kept you hanging about downstairs,' he apologized unnecessarily and with a distinct absence of sincerity. His handshake was firm and Masonic. Meanwhile, his secretary was organizing a comfortable, leather-upholstered chair for the detective.

'Coffee? Tea?' Urwin enquired, affecting a searching frown, before depositing himself on the throne, a chief executive's swivel chair.

Templeman placed his coffee order with Henrietta before sitting to face Urwin, whose grey hair had been meticulously styled, swept back without a parting and waved at the front. His spectacles were brown and horn-rimmed, and his pinstriped suit was as sharply pressed as a commanding officer's uniform.

'I can speculate on the reason for your visit here,' said Urwin, threading his fingers, his elbows planted on his desk. 'In fact, I was anticipating you. When I say *you*, I mean a police officer from Scotland Yard, not necessarily you personally. Mr Markham was a client of mine. You're here to discuss his affairs, I assume?'

'Very astute, Mr Urwin,' said Templeman, suspecting correctly that Urwin would be susceptible to flattery.

'Only yesterday I was going through his file.'

'How well did you know Mr Markham?'

'Not very well at all. We never met socially. We didn't have anything in common.'

That was something Templeman found easy to believe. In fact, he was wondering why someone like 'Elvis' Markham had chosen such a staid, traditional firm as Urwin, Wyatt and Watson to handle his affairs. *Maybe they're all in a time-warp around here, the Markhams included,* he surmised to himself.

'I just drew up his will,' Urwin continued his ponderous explanation. He had pendulous and lugubrious features, which seemed a trifle manufactured, thought Templeman, as if the solicitor had a facsimile to follow fastidiously. 'Mr and Mrs Markham also came to me when they were buying their house. I did the conveyancing.'

'How often did you see Mr Markham?'

'No more than half-a-dozen times over a period of several years.'

'When did he make his will?'

'To be precise about that I'll need to refer to his file.'

Henrietta could not have chosen a more opportune moment to return with Templeman's coffee, and tea for her boss.

'Mr Markham's file,' Urwin requested civilly.

It took the secretary only a couple of minutes to find the relevant folder.

Urwin turned the pages methodically. 'Here we are. Yes, he made the first will seven years ago.'

'So he made more than one?'

'Oh, yes, three in all.'

'Were the differences substantial?'

'Let me refresh my memory.' Urwin began reading to himself. 'Yes, yes, now I remember. His first will, in essence, left everything to his wife. The second, drawn up three years ago, bequeathed a hundred thousand pounds to the Elvis Presley Foundation—'

'A hundred grand!' Templeman interposed. 'Where was that coming from?'

Urwin removed his spectacles, placed them perfunctorily on his blotting-pad and reclined, adopting a magisterial pose. 'Mr Markham was a man of means, Inspector. Weren't you aware of that?'

'I had no idea,' Templeman admitted, his pulse racing. 'It's not the impression his wife gave.'

'Maybe she wasn't privy to his financial affairs.'

'Just how much is he leaving, all told?'

'I'll come to that in a moment. I started to outline the second will. I think it best if I proceed chronologically.' He took a deep breath and returned his spectacles to the deeply indented bridge of his imperious nose. 'Now, as I was saying, in the second will the donation to the Elvis Presley Foundation was a defined amount. Like all three wills, it was relatively uncomplicated and the sort that could quite easily have been made without the involvement of a solicitor. All codicils were basically one-dimensional. His house was to go to his wife, plus fifty per cent of his estate and assets, the rest to be divided equally between his two children.'

'And the third?'

'The hundred thousand pounds donation was written out of it, the house continued to go to the widow, but after that similarity there were significant changes, though straightforward.'

Templeman was poised with pen and notebook.

'Half of the money and stocks were to be split three ways between Mrs Markham and the children. The other fifty per cent was to be paid to a Jennifer Roper, of Flat Sixteen, Chelsea Mansions, Dover Court, Fulham, London.'

'Who is Jennifer Roper?'

'No idea, Inspector. That's not the sort of question for me to ask. I simply take instructions.'

'Correct me if I'm wrong, but as the will now stands, this Roper woman will pick up three times more than any of Mr Markham's immediate family?'

'You are not wrong.'

'Did his family – his wife, for example – have a copy of the final will?'

'That would have been up to Mr Markham. We were most certainly not requested to furnish copies to other parties. There is, however, something else about which I should inform you.'

Templeman waited expectantly.

'Mr Markham had made an appointment to see me.'

'When?'

'He was due here the day he died.'

'Did he give an indication what he wanted to see you about?'

'Oh, yes, he wanted to make yet another will.'

'Did he give you advance details?'

'No, he simply explained to my secretary that it would be a codicillary meeting. Of course he didn't use the word *codicillary*, but that's how it was translated by Henrietta.'

'You didn't speak with him yourself?'

'No, my secretary runs my diary.'

'When was the appointment made?'

'Oh, about ten days in advance.'

'Was the state of Mr Markham's health ever an issue for discussion?'

'Good heavens, no! Why do you ask that?'

'No matter ... I started to ask earlier about his financial position ...'

'You did, indeed.'

'Just how much are his beneficiaries likely to inherit?'

Urwin rubbed his hands together in the familiar fashion of a miser. 'I'm not qualified to quote a value for the property.'

'I'm thinking more in terms of liquid assets.'

'Yes, I'm sure you are, Inspector.' Urwin flashed a fleeting, knowing smile that was rooted in smugness. 'As you'll appreciate, I cannot possibly be accurate about this. It'll probably be six months to a year before a settlement is made.'

'By *settlement*, you mean a division of the spoils?'

'Your profession has its own argot and so does mine, Inspector. I suggest we stick to our own. I have asked Mr Markham's accountant for the most recent set of accounts. Bank statements – current and savings – and all stock holdings will have to be forwarded to me within the next few days.'

'But I sense you have some estimate of the sum involved?'

Urwin took his time, like an accomplished orator who has learned to exploit the theatrical pause. 'After the Inland Revenue has taken its due, I shall be surprised if there isn't at least three million pounds in the kitty, excluding all property and possessions.'

'Did you say three million?' Templeman whistled as he doubted his own hearing.

'That's exactly what I said.'

'But ...' Templeman began a statement, not knowing where it was going, and so stopped. 'He was only an impersonator in the entertainment business, not a celebrity in his own right,' he began again.

'That was my understanding, too.'

'Had he benefited from any substantial legacies during his lifetime?'

'Not to my knowledge. As you're surely aware, he was brought up by foster parents. Maybe he did come into money that way. His banking history should shed light on how he came by his money.'

'You had no idea about the apparent extent of his wealth?'

'Only that he appeared, at one time, to be in a position to give away a hundred thousand pounds to a Presley foundation.'

'I'm staggered.'

'That's death for you, Inspector! It holds hidden surprises for us all.'

The hospital was only a few minutes' drive away.

A staff nurse was just emerging from Tandy's room as Templeman approached goose-necked and driven from the elevators.

'How is she today?' Templeman could hardly wait to ask.

'Sergeant Tandy had a fairly comfortable night,' the nurse replied in officious hospital jargon. 'Doctor Everson is on the main ward right now. I know she's keen to speak with you. I'll fetch her. Please wait.'

'Is it OK for me to go into Simone?'

The nurse vacillated awkwardly. 'I think possibly you should see the doctor first.'

Ominous, thought Templeman.

Everson had a disarming smile for Templeman. 'Come on, let's go to the same room where we spoke yesterday,' she said persuasively.

Nothing else was said until they had privacy.

'Old "Crabbers" – that's our name for Professor Crabtree – has studied all scan X-rays and other test data.'

'And?' Templeman was too impatient to wait for a pedestrian, chronological narrative to plod its full, sinuous course.

'Encouraging news. It's operable.'

'Thanks God for that!' Relief came out of him with all the drama of an exorcism.

'Don't go celebrating prematurely,' the doctor cautioned him. 'This is major surgery. It doesn't come any bigger. And as I warned you yesterday, even if the operation is a clinical success, we shall still have to await the outcome of the biopsy. Look on it as a race. These results have qualified Simone to take part; to go to the starting-post. That's all. There's still a long way to go from start to finish, with many hurdles in between.'

'What if it *is* malignant? Is there no hope?'

'Let's all pray that I don't have to give you an answer to that.'

'That *is* an answer.'

'As for now, you may visit Simone for a few minutes, but I'd appreciate it if you didn't talk "shop". I don't want her overworking her brain. It will only aggravate her condition and trigger more headaches.'

'Does she know the good news?'

'No, I was leaving that for you. It can be your gift ... of hope ... not of certainty, I'm afraid.'

'I'm grateful. How soon will she have to go under the knife?'

'As soon as practical. Probably tomorrow.'

'That soon!'

'Time, Inspector, is of the essence. In politics, it is said that a week is a lifetime. In medicine, the length of a life can often be determined by the action taken – or delayed – in a time-capsule of mere minutes or even seconds.'

Templeman nodded his understanding. 'How long will Simone have to remain here?'

'That'll be up to Crabbers, but I can tell you that even if all goes according to plan, she'll be sidelined for at least nine months.'

'That's a pregnancy!'

'I couldn't have put it better myself, Inspector. It's giving her a new life. Look on it as rebirth.'

Everson solicitously accompanied Templeman to Tandy's room. 'Don't forget what I told you. No longer than a few minutes and nothing to excite her,' the doctor reminded him.

Tandy was alone, her head swathed in bandage and padding, protecting her shaved head, which had already been prepared for surgery. There was no sign of life through the two spy-holes for her eyes and the slit for her mouth. But as the door clicked closed behind him, Tandy stirred. Her eyes fluttered and Templeman caught a glimpse of the desperate supplication within her soul.

'They still won't tell me anything,' she whispered, as Templeman held her hand and squatted on the side of the bed.

'They've given me that pleasure.'

Templeman could see enough of her eyes to read all the questions.

'It looks like you're going to be fine.'

Tandy was no one's fool. *Going to be fine*, made no impact; *looks like* did. 'You're telling me there's a doubt?' Her voice was sleepy, but not weak.

Templeman gave it to her straight; just the way he would on a doorstep to a stranger: *Your daughter is in hospital, desperately ill, but she has a fifty-fifty chance.* He felt her grip tighten. Fear froze in her eyes, then melted, dampening the bandage. Templeman wanted to cry with her, but that would have been self-indulgent and counter-productive for Tandy.

'How long has this been going on in my head, Luke?'

'Who knows? It doesn't matter; that's irrelevant. The future is the only thing for us to concentrate on.'

'When do they plan doing it?'

'Probably tomorrow.'

'Oh, God!'

'Less time to brood about it.'

'I'm frightened, Luke.'

'If you said you weren't, I wouldn't believe you.' Templeman had never seen her this vulnerable before. He resisted delivering a trite homily that would be an insult to her intelligence. She knew the score and the fact that the result was in the balance.

She squeezed his hand. 'You must have noticed something, Luke.'

Templeman didn't follow her drift and said as much.

'I must have been acting very strangely for some considerable time, showing symptoms of something very wrong.'

Templeman was shaking his head, the way he would in the witness-box in court, when refusing vehemently to accept a proposition put to him by a defending counsel. 'There was no warning I could see. True, you were complaining of headaches for a number of weeks, but not for a moment did I consider they were symptoms of anything serious. I put them down to work-related stress and being stretched; going too long without food. At worst, I thought you might be having mild migraine attacks. But that's all inconsequential now. How's the pain?'

'Blunted. Like a woodpecker that's been muzzled. It's banging away, vibrating inside my head, drilling like crazy, but its sharp beak is softened. Whatever they're giving me is great stuff. I'm getting fantastic trips! Round the clock I'm high as jet stream. This is the place for a fix, Luke! And it's all legal. No one gets busted in here.'

Tears meandered in rivulets down Templeman's cheeks. Tandy's stoicism and self-deprecating humour humbled him.

'Stop that, right now!' she pretended to castigate him. She was crying too now, but the tears had nowhere to run and were soaked up by the binding. 'Update me on the case. What's the latest?'

'Not allowed, I'm afraid. All talk about work has been outlawed. If I break my undertaking, I'll have my visitor's rights withdrawn. You wouldn't want to see me banned, would you?'

Templeman's efforts to introduce banter to lighten Tandy's load was only partially successful.

'Under all this wrapping, I'm frowning,' she said, again self-mocking. 'Why should our work be taboo?'

'Because you have to rest and free your head of all unnecessary input.'

'Surely you can relate it to me like a narrative? A detective story! It'll be therapeutic because it'll take my mind off everything else.'

'I mustn't, darling.'

'Just tell me this: are we getting closer?'

The *'we'* impacted immediately upon Templeman. It was a coded exploration. She was fishing for reassurance that they were still a team; that she was still on the team and hadn't been sidelined permanently. She peered into his eyes for the answers, having more faith in body language than words, which were so often woven into clever embroidery that made effective camouflage and hid the truth.

'We're making headway, but I'm not certain whether that's the same as getting closer. More avenues are opening up the whole time, but whether any of them lead to where we want ultimately to go ... well, quite frankly, I'm unsure. We still haven't progressed beyond the embryo.'

'Tell me about the new avenues.'

'There! I knew I shouldn't have conceded ground. I'll make a deal with you.'

'You know my feelings about plea-bargaining.' She faked a reproachful tone.

Templeman sensed the smile behind the mask. The old, honed telepathy between them was still intact.

'This is a non-negotiable *fait accompli*. I've got you at my mercy while you're down. As soon as the doc in charge says you're fit enough, we'll have a bedside case-conference. I'll open the books, metaphorically, for your inspection.'

'You'll pay for this, young man.'

'You make sure I do.'

Tandy didn't miss the message. 'I'm coming through this, have no fear about that.'

'But just to make that definite, I'll ask Detective Inspector Templeman to step outside, leaving you to rest,' said Everson, having slipped into the room unheard.

'I was just on my way out,' Templeman lied glibly, his smile engaging.

'Will you be here tomorrow for my big day?' Tandy's voice barely carried across the room.

Templeman looked to the doctor for guidance.

'I think you're going to be otherwise engaged for most of tomorrow, Simone,' Everson said delicately.

Tandy didn't want to let go of Templeman. Instead of releasing his hand, her grip tightened. Templeman knew exactly what she was thinking: *Is this the last time? The last goodbye?* They were his thoughts too.

'I'll call the hospital in the afternoon to see if I can visit in the evening,' he promised.

'You mean that?' Tandy pressed.

'You have my word.' He kissed her on the lips through the gap in the bandage, then had to break himself away, which was distressing for both of them.

Tandy waved weakly as Everson shooed Templeman out into the corridor. In return, he blew a farewell kiss. Tandy's languid wave would be the final picture of her in his mind until their apocalypse was over – one way or the other.

'There's no possibility of your seeing Simone tomorrow.'

'I realize that. I expect she did, too. I was just placating. What's the programme?'

'An eight a.m. kick-off. She'll be in theatre most of the day, as long as there are no complications.'

'And if there are?'

'Don't ask. She won't be in the recovery-room before five o'clock. After an hour or so there, she'll be transferred to intensive-care. The plan will be to keep her heavily sedated and just below the surface of consciousness for at least forty-eight hours following the operation. This will assist her recovery. If you visit and find her still unconscious, that will be because we're keeping her that way artificially. I'll arrange for old Crabbers to have a word with you sometime tomorrow evening. Will it be all right for him to call you on your mobile?'

'Please. Any time.'

'That's it, then.'

Templeman was about to pose another question when Everson stopped him.

'Don't. Hold fire until you're talking with Crabbers after the event. Only then will the prognosis have any worth. Until then, everything I said would have to be punctuated with ifs and buts.'

'You read my mind.'

'You're not the first anxious partner I've had to evaluate a case with.' She placed a hand sympathetically on his shoulder. 'There's absolutely nothing you can do here. Go away and busy yourself. She's in capable hands.'

'I feel so helpless.'

'And that's exactly what you are in this situation. Accept the fact. Fighting it is futile.'

'There ought to be people, within her family, I should be contacting, but I know so little about her relatives.'

'That's something I've already discussed with Simone. She's adamant that there's no one else she wants informed. She doesn't want to be alarming people; that's her decision and it has to be respected. In any case, it would seem that she's lost touch with most of her folk. You're her one and only port in a storm.'

'That's a lot to shoulder.'

'You'd better be up to it, Inspector!'

Chapter Fourteen

'Jennifer Roper?'

'That's what it says on the door.'

'May I come in?'

'That depends on who you are and what you want.'

Templeman proved who he was, but was invited inside before he had a chance to précis his reason for calling.

'You're not exactly an unexpected caller,' Jennifer Roper confessed conversationally, as they passed from the hall into a spacious L-shaped lounge.

'And you're the second person today to issue that sentiment,' remarked Templeman, hoping that she would latch on to this, but she didn't.

He allowed her to take his coat and to go through the standard preliminaries of offering tea, coffee 'or something stronger', while his eyes roved methodically.

'Is it *Mrs* Roper?' he enquired, on her return to the room from hanging up Templeman's coat and putting on the kettle.

'Just Jennifer will do,' she replied enigmatically, folding her legs beneath her shapely body – voluptuous even – on the soft leather sofa.

She was an artificial blonde with a friendly and not unattractive face. Although she had just been loafing about her third-floor apartment late in the afternoon, she was nevertheless smartly dressed in casuals. Her flesh-hugging trousers had been pressed with a permanent crease. She wore black tights, but had kicked off her fluffy Mickey Mouse slippers before settling on the sofa. The shape of her ample breasts was starkly outlined behind a pink silk blouse. If anyone had asked Templeman to guess her age, he would have hesitated, before plumping for thirty-eight; could be forty, though equally thirty-two or thirty-three were possible. Careful construction with make-up could cover a lot of wear and tear. Templeman suspected that quite a few hard-labour years were buried beneath that blood-red lipstick, eye-shadow and foundation cream. The harsh blonde façade was mellowed by her melting hazel eyes. Her figure was full and it suited her that way.

Whichever way Templeman looked, the décor was unremitting art deco. White rugs, black furniture – including dining-table and chairs on a raised level against the window – and black and white framed photographs of ballroom dancers, movie stars of the 1930s and 1940s, American gangsters during the days of prohibition and later political icons, such as John F. Kennedy (the assassination scene in Dallas), Bill Clinton (cuddling Monica 'Zippergate' Lewinsky) and Sir Winston Churchill (cigar-puffing among the rubble of the Blitz). Otherwise, all table-tops and surfaces were bare.

She followed his eyes and hoisted her left hand, twiddling her fingers. 'No rings, see. No help to you, is it?' Her voice was fruity with a tantalizing, husky undertone.

This was no emotional wreck. Whatever her connection with Harry Markham, she had not lost any sleep over his death, Templeman decided. What puffiness there was under her eyes wasn't the upshot of weeping.

'I'm here to talk about Harry Markham,' Templeman began.

'Of course you are.'

'Why do you say that?'

'Because it was inevitable that the trail would lead to my door eventually.'

'*Trail*?' Templeman's antennae pricked up yet again.

'Yes, you'd poke around asking questions, the way you people do, and sooner or later I was bound to come to your notice.'

'I only heard about you this morning.'

'My! You are a plodder, aren't you?'

God, she's cool! thought Templeman. 'Wouldn't you like to know where I was, and with whom, when your name was thrown into the ring?'

'Why don't you just go right ahead and enlighten me and let's dispense with the suspense.'

Refusing to have the interview structured for him and thus to forfeit immediately any psychological advantage, Templeman said instead, 'How well did you know Mr Markham?'

'We were lovers.' The answer was returned with the speed and spontaneity of a rebound. She eyeballed him defiantly, as if saying, *OK, now the ball's in your court. Wrongfooted, aren't you? I bet you weren't expecting an ace from my first serve.* 'I guess that counts as knowing someone reasonably well.'

Templeman maintained a visual hold. 'Since when?'

'I'm not one for dates,' she replied casually. 'I don't keep a diary. Diaries can be double-edged dangerous weapons, capable of wounding oneself as well as others.'

'When did the affair begin, approximately? A week ago? A month? A few months? A year?'

'Inspector, we had been together a long time.'

'*Together?*'

'I already said we were lovers. There's still a collection of his clothes in a wardrobe in the main bedroom. He lived here, Inspector.'

'He had a wife and family in Bedford.'

'A token wife.'

'Would you care to elaborate?'

'Why not. They hadn't lived as man and wife – physically and spiritually – for years.'

'He told you that?'

'Our pillow-talk covered history as well as biology.'

'And you believed him?'

'Inspector, I didn't need telling. He slept here more often than *there*. This was his oasis – his description, not mine.'

'Where did you first meet him?'

'In a nightclub.'

She answered every question as if she had been trained in the art of courtroom economy. She never expanded voluntarily. Everything had to be dredged out.

'Which nightclub?'

'Jack of Clubs.'

'What were the circumstances of that meeting?'

'He was the cabaret.'

'And you?'

'I was performing too.'

'In the show?'

'Not exactly. I was a hostess.' Her pugnacity not only blazed in her eyes but also smoked from her flaring nostrils.

Templeman made the mistake of allowing his face to be a truthful mirror of his mind.

'Do all pigs harbour prejudices as dirty as their habits?'

Templeman was jolted by the feral verbal assault that was enacted with a curious mixture of the spite of a baboon and the serenity of a saint.

'Pigs are very clean beasts. Only the criminal class use the porcine species as an insult for police.'

'And students.'

'*You* must have lost that excuse twenty or thirty years ago.'

'Ouch! Now who's the catty one?'

There had already been too much shadow-boxing, so Templeman curtailed the sparring. 'Nightclub hostesses are hookers, just like escorts and massage parlour tarts.'

'You know that from personal experience, do you?'

Templeman's testiness flared. 'Look, I haven't the time to fart around over semantics. Were you on the game when you first met Harry Markham?'

'Yes and no,' she said shamelessly, as if throwing down the gauntlet.

'What the hell does that mean?'

'It means I'd go to bed with only men I fancied.'

'For money?'

'But no amount of money would have bribed me into bed with anybody I disliked.'

'*No amount?*'

'You know what I mean.'

'So you were a hooker with principles.'

'I live my life my way. I have no wish to influence the morals of others. What gives you the right to be so judgemental? Are you yet another paragon of manhood?'

'I'm not judging. I'd simply appreciate straight, no-frills answers. No euphemisms. No riddles. No socio-mumbo jumbo. No crap.'

Jennifer fixed a kingsize filter cigarette, into a holder and lit it with a gold lighter. 'A present from Harry,' she said, tossing the lighter towards Templeman, who caught it one-handed and read the inscription: *All my love forever, H.*

'I'll fetch the coffees,' she said. She was gone no longer than a couple of minutes.

Templeman wasted no time picking up the thread. 'I'm afraid I'm going to have to press for more detail about your introductory meeting with Mr Markham.'

'Are you some kind of voyeur, Inspector?'

Templeman disregarded the incitement. 'Just how were you introduced? The mechanics, please.'

Jennifer idly, almost wistfully, watched smoke-rings climbing in curls through the air. 'He'd done his spot. About fifteen minutes later he appeared at a table in the restaurant towards the rear, not far from where we girls were sitting. We hostesses sat at a large, long, staff table at the back. If someone wanted one of us to join him at his table, the head waiter would take care of the introduction. If there was a group of men, perhaps enjoying a business party, or had been to a rugby match, for example, then maybe three or four girls from our "stable" would be assigned to them.'

'Did Harry ask for you specifically?'

'He did.'

'What then?'

'The usual stuff. We talked. We drank. We had a meal. He flirted.'

'You charged him?'

'There was a flat fee – a market price – for having a girl sit at a table with you, yes.'

'How much?'

'I can't remember now. It was nominal. It was more important, for the club, to encourage customers to splash out on champagne.'

'Did he proposition you?'

Jennifer, pained, looked to the ceiling for inspiration. 'I don't think it was as cold-blooded as that. It was more or less a case of our gravitating towards one another.'

'And to bed?'

'We slept together, yes.'

'It was a business transaction?'

'He paid me.'

'And the charge was negotiated in advance?'

'You're managing, deliberately, to make it sound very smutty and clinical, but there was respect from both sides and a certain dignity.'

'Where did the shagging take place?' Templeman laboured to ruffle her.

'We went to a hotel.'

'Not here, then?'

'I never *entertained* here.'

'When did you see him next?'

'The following night, at the Jack of Clubs. He'd been booked for a fortnight. He monopolized me for the duration.'

'Did you go to bed with him every night during the remainder of those two weeks?'

'I did.'

'For money still?'

'For less than the going rate, though.'

'He'd earned a discount?'

'You're not funny, Inspector.'

'When did the quantum leap occur in this rare relationship?'

'He asked for my phone number. I was happy for him to have it. He wanted to keep in touch. We got on well. I liked him beyond business. Whenever he had an engagement in town, he'd call me and we'd arrange to have dinner together.'

'At the Jack of Clubs?'

'No, I'd take the night off I'd catch his show and then we'd go on to a late-night West End restaurant.'

'Then shack-up together in a hotel?'

'My, my, you do have a way with words, Inspector! By then he was coming back here for the night.'

'But still paying for the pleasure?'

'No.' Still she neither flinched nor recoiled.

'How did you spend your nights when you weren't meeting him?'

'I went about my business as usual.'

'Whoring?'

'Hostessing.'

'When *exactly* did he move in with you?'

'Two or three years ago. I can't be *exact*.'

'Whose idea was it?'

'No one's idea. It was dictated by natural gravitation.'

'Did you continue working at the nightclub?'

'No.'

'What did you do for a living?'

'I didn't. I became a lady of leisure.'

'How was that funded?'

'You could say that Harry was my sponsor.'

'What's the monthly rent on this place?'

'A lot. If you really want to know, ask my landlord.'

'Where did the money come from?'

'I just told you – Harry.'

'He must have been earning big money.'

'Yes, he must have.' Her agreement was laced with truculence.

'Did he discuss his finances with you?'

'Never.'

'Surely you must have queried how he could afford such an outlay?'

'I wouldn't have been so rude or nosy. He was in showbiz.'

'He was on the periphery.'

'All kinds of money slosh around in that game.'

'As in yours.'

'If you're getting off by insulting me, please make the most of the moment.' Jennifer Roper could fence with the best.

'Did you know about his family?'

'I knew he was married, if that's what you mean?'

'That all?'

'What else is there to know?'

'Did he talk about the state of his marriage?'

'Hardly ever. The fact that he was with me was evidence enough of a failed home life.'

'You knew he had children?'

'I know he was the father of two adults. I wasn't robbing babies of milk or toddlers of a father figure.'

'Did he plan to leave his wife?'

'It was debated.'

'And?'

'He wanted to, but he feared the financial consequences.'

'What stance did you take?'

She wavered and lit another cigarette. The windmills of her mind were rotating at maximum velocity now. 'For a long time I took a neutral role. Look, I was happy with the arrangement as it was. He'd come here every night for a week or so and then I mightn't see him for a fortnight. That way our relationship was kept fresh. We had space. I've always found close relationships claustrophobic. I can't deal with being fenced in.'

'Did he share your view?'

'No, he was eager for us to become full-time domestic partners.'

Having teased out the background, Templeman now changed gear. 'Were you expecting him here the night he died?'

Jennifer stubbed out her half-smoked cigarette and began prowling the room like a big cat new to a cage.

'Yes, I was,' she admitted finally, coming to a halt at the window with her back to Templeman, so that he couldn't see the ambivalence etched on her contemplative, but unharried, face.

'What did you do when he failed to show?'

'I didn't know he wasn't here until I woke up in the morning.'

'How come?'

'I went to bed just after midnight. I slept soundly until after eight.'

'And then?'

'I assumed he'd changed his plans and had gone back to Bedford for some reason.'

'You weren't worried?'

'Not at all. Why should I have been? I didn't own him. He wasn't a scalp or trophy. I don't function that way. Things turn up unexpectedly in this life. Plans sometimes have to be changed at the last minute. We're not all programmed mice.'

Templeman resisted straying. 'Did you try to contact him?'

'I called his mobile.'

'And?' Templeman suppressed the significance of this from his face.

'I got the recording telling me it was impossible to make a connection and offering me the voicemail service.'

'Did you leave a message?'

'No. I was confident he'd call me as soon as it was convenient; as soon as he was ready to surface.'

'When did you learn of his murder?'

'That afternoon, on TV.'

'What was your reaction?'

'I was shocked, of course,' she said prosaically.

'Did you call the police?'

'Why should I have done that?'

'Because you could have enlightened us so much about his movements in his final hours. You could also have cleared up one mystery: where he would have been going from the car park.'

Jennifer wheeled from the window to face him, biting her lip, then averting her eyes.

'There's one thing you should know, Inspector.'

'Only *one* thing?'

Jennifer disregarded the gibe. 'I was in the process of ending the relationship.'

'Why was that?' Templeman did his best to block the rush of blood to his head.

'Because it had run its course. We'd begun to squabble every time we were together.'

'Over what?'

'Anything. Everything.'

'Was he aware you wanted to finish?'

'Oh, yes. I tried to do it gently, but that didn't work; it never does. Sadly, it always has to be brutal.'

'You've had plenty of experience of casting men adrift?'

Again she avoided being intimidated by another poison dart. 'I was doing what I felt I had to do.'

'How did he take it?'

'Badly. He pleaded with me. He even lobbied for the sympathy vote.'

Templeman's uncomprehending frown called for clarification.

'He told me he was dying of cancer, that he had only a few months to live and that I would inherit a lot of money if only I stuck with him to the bitter end.'

'You didn't believe him?'

'Of course I didn't. That was the moment I lost all respect for him. I told him he couldn't dupe me that easily; that he had no dignity, that he should start acting like a man, that what he was saying was a sickening insult to all those people who really were battling against cancer.'

'That must have wounded him severely.'

'He said I'd live to regret the hurt I'd caused. I retaliated by telling him to grow up and not to be so melodramatic.'

'But he *was* coming back here the night he died, wasn't he?'

'He was paying the rent. He had a moral right to be here. I'd made it clear that he wasn't to finance anything towards the flat from the end of this month. I agreed he could keep clothes here and stay over on occasions when he had singing engagements in town, until he made other arrangements. I wasn't entirely happy about the situation. The guillotine is always preferable to a drawn out, lingering death.'

'You don't look like the conventional woman in black, in mourning.'

'I'm not a hypocrite. It was over between us, as I said. Of

course I'm sorry he's dead, killed the way he was, but no tears of mine – or anyone else's, for that matter – will bring him back. A cliché, but true.'

'You still didn't consider calling the police?'

'Of course I *considered* it, but decided it wasn't such a good idea. I can't help you over his death, I really can't. Whatever happened that night is beyond my comprehension.'

'I take it that he slept here the previous night?'

'He did. We slept in separate bedrooms.'

'What did you talk about – before going to bed?'

'Nothing. When he returned from the club, I was asleep with the door to my room locked. I got up at about eight and went out at around ten. He hadn't risen by then. I didn't get home until eleven that dreadful night.'

'What were you doing all that time?'

Jennifer began ambulating, burning nervous energy. 'I was shopping in the West End. I treated myself to afternoon tea in Fortnum and Mason's.'

'You still have several hours remaining to account for.'

She stopped again at the window and folded her arms across her chest, before hurrying to seek refuge in yet another smoke-stack.

'I had a date.'

'There's another man in your life?'

'I'm not giving you his name.'

'I haven't asked for it.'

'I'm just warning you; don't bother asking because nothing, no amount of cajoling, will prise his identity from me.'

'Is this the reason you were finishing with Markham?'

'Partly'

'Is your new lover married?'

'*Lover* is your word, not mine.'

'But is he married?'

'He is.'

'Is the plan for him to move in with you?'

'There's no *plan*. It's all too early to say. What's more, it's none of your business. I don't want him being frightened off by you people.'

'Is that why you've kept quiet?'

'Among other things.'

'Did Markham know of this other man's existence in your life?'

'He had his suspicions. He kept asking me if there was anybody else.'

'What did you tell him?'

'No. I pretended there wasn't anyone else, but I don't think he believed me. There have always been men in my life, ever since I was sixteen or seventeen. It's the way I am. I'm not a man-eating temptress, but I like men. I've always preferred their company to women. That doesn't mean I'm always on the hunt for a new mate. I'm rarely responsible for engineering a liaison. It usually creeps up on me and unexpectedly gatecrashes my life.'

Templeman smiled archly, recognizing a woman who had been ambushed and mugged by circumstances beyond her management, before asking, with considerable inference, 'Were you here alone when Harry Markham was being shot?'

'I was.' Her look was that of a courtroom defendant locking eyes with the foreman of the jury, challenging, *I dare you to disbelieve me.*

'Who might have killed him?'

'It's beyond me.' She shook her head and sucked in more smoky pollution.

'Did he ever discuss his early life with you?'

'Never,' she replied emphatically.

'Did he treat you with respect at all times?'

She squinted, puzzled. 'What an odd question! What do you mean, exactly?'

'Well, did he ever abuse you?'

'Never. He wasn't like that. I had no complaints on that score.'

'On what *score* could you complain?'

'None. Nothing.'

It was time to turn the ratchet another notch. 'Had you any knowledge of his will?'

'Did he make one? If he had, it was never mentioned to me.'

'How about his financial position? Was that ever alluded to?'

'Not as such. I mean, I knew he had to be quite flush to fund this place for me, but we never talked about how much he was worth, if that's what you mean?'

'Did you expect to feature in his will?'

'I never gave it a thought.'

'He never showed you a copy of his will?'

'Never.'

'At any time did he ever comment upon what arrangements he

planned making for those people close to him in the event of his death?'

'We never had those kind of conversations. It's a morbid subject. He was always as full of life as I was. I can't imagine Harry dwelling on death. He would have seen that as being negative, not pragmatic. Death comes to those who anticipate it and prepare for it – that's the kind of sentiment I can just hear him expressing.'

'And you really understood him to be in good health?'

'He *was*, too, wasn't he?'

Templeman eschewed answering and instead posed another question of his own. 'Something we haven't so far recovered is his mobile and I'm wondering whether you can throw any light on that?'

'You mean he didn't have it on him?' Her astonishment was a reflex. 'It went everywhere with him. He wouldn't go in the bath without it.'

'Did you call him, by chance, on his mobile during the last twelve hours of his life?'

'No. The last time I spoke with Harry was around lunchtime and I called the land-line here from *my* mobile.'

'Did he sound normal?'

'He sounded sleepy. He hadn't been up long.'

'How long did you talk for?'

'It was brief. He pleaded with me to meet him for dinner before his show.'

'But you said no?'

'I said there was no point. It was over between us. Our relationship was a spent cartridge. No use sticking it back in the rifle; however many times the trigger was squeezed, it would never fire again.'

'Would it surprise you to know that you may inherit quite a large sum of money as a result of Markham's death?'

'I find that hard to believe.'

Before leaving, Templeman asked to have a look at whatever possessions there were of Markham's in the flat. Jennifer raised no objections, but she stayed closely at his side throughout his rummage, which produced nothing worth confiscating for analysis, not even tablets. But just before they shook hands, he made a note of her ex-directory and mobile numbers, 'Just in case I need to double check anything with you'.

He drove two blocks from the flat, pulled over and spoke with one of his desk-strapped team at base. After reciting the two phone numbers, plus name and address of the subscriber, he said, 'I want a printout of all calls made during the last month. The land-line account will be with BT; I think you'll find the mobile network is O_2.'

Templeman refrained from giving exposure to his thoughts, but if Tandy had been with him she would have known that he was confident that the records would reveal a call from Jennifer Roper to Markham's mobile on the night of the murder – before the one to which she had admitted.

You're thinking she lured him to his death – something like that – and that's why the killer had to steal Markham's mobile, because callers' numbers would be stored in its memory, Templeman could hear in his head Tandy's voice, which went on, *Conversely, she might have left a message – voicemail or text – and that would have to be destroyed. The killer wouldn't loiter around the body, messing with buttons, familiarizing himself with the mobile's functions. No, he would have taken it with him, away from the scene, pronto. Probably to dispose of it later. But disposal can also be dangerous. Once found, the DNA wizards can perform miracles these days. So perhaps the killer has hung on to it, vacillating, waiting to feel which way the wind is blowing. He spins a coin. Tails could be bad for him. Heads might be even worse.*

'You're absolutely right, Simone,' Templeman said aloud, gunning the engine, deriving a form of catharsis from the throaty roar of the engine and the punch of power in his lower back.

Chapter Fifteen

The foster parents of Harry Markham had been traced through Social Services records. Details were waiting for Templeman on his desk at Scotland Yard. He read the names and address aloud from the crisp, black and white computer printout: 'John and Chantel Grainger, of Churchill Manor, near Godalming, Surrey.' Several times he repeated to himself in a low voice, 'John Grainger ... John Grainger.' Could it possibly be *the* John Grainger? Purposefully, he plucked the latest edition of *Who's Who* from the rows of reference books leaning drunkenly along wall-shelves behind him. He thumbed through the high-quality, almost transparent pages until he came to the roll-call of names beginning with G. Eagerly, his index finger followed his hopeful eyes down the pages, slowing as he reached the first Gr....' Here we are,' he continued animatedly to himself.

There were several John Graingers listed, but none with a Godalming address. However, the one in which Templeman was most interested gave only the VIP's work address: the House of Commons, Westminster, London SW1, no less. He noted the date of birth. This John Grainger was seventy-one years old, the only son of a brigadier who had been decorated for bravery in the Second World War. On leaving Oxford, he had joined the Foreign Office, intending a diplomatic career. However, politics had been ambushing him for attention ever since his school debating society days and he entered parliament via a by-election in the rural, very Conservative South Downs constituency. Since then, his majority had risen steadily like heat at every General Election. During his political career, he had held a string of junior ministerial posts before being promoted to the Cabinet as Secretary of State for Trade and Industry. In the most recent Cabinet reshuffle by Prime Minister Winston Crompton, he had been rewarded with the prized Ministry of Defence portfolio. With Crompton approaching his seventy-sixth milestone, there had been much speculation in the media that he would be stepping down prior to the next General Election, probably at least eighteen months before the nation would go to the polls, giving his successor time to settle in and to seduce the electorate. Most insiders were agreed that only three names could seriously be considered for the shortlist. One of them was John Grainger, the least exciting of the trio, but the one with the 'safest pair of hands', gold-dust quality in these turbulent and volatile times. One political editor described him as 'stolid and predictable, but an attractive proposition for caretaker leader of his party because he comes without a ticking timebomb in his baggage; he is boringly untainted'. This encapsulated most people's opinion of John Grainger the politician. One of the more cryptic political sketch writers had credited him with being parliament's most skilled exponent of 'boring to the bone as well as the brain'. Grainger himself had once said that if he had remained a career diplomat, he would have been 'on a treadmill to eternity'. Of course, these facts were not to be found between the unbending covers of Who's Who.

Mostly Templeman was raiding the larder of his memory for non-perishable provisions, tasty titbits garnered over the years from newspapers and magazines. Was it possible that this powerful politician had been foster father to Harry Markham? He read carefully the rest of the substantial entry in Who's Who. Grainger had listed his recreations as 'theatre-going, reading war books, chess, classical concerts, shooting and fishing.' However, it was the family material that most captivated Templeman. The Graingers had two children; a son and a daughter; Henry and Charlotte. John Grainger had married his first wife, Chantel, in the House of Commons chapel. His first wife had died ten years ago and he had remarried. His current wife's name was Tiffany. She had been Tiffany Glendenning, the daughter of a Scottish landowner.

'Chantel!' Templeman echoed to himself, now conclusively matching in his own mind the Graingers who had fostered Markham with John Grainger, the Cabinet minister who was a frontrunner to become the next Prime Minister.

Superintendent Jock Stacey, of Special Branch, took Templeman's call. 'Of course I can confirm Grainger's address for you, but why do you want it?' Stacey said, bearish.

Templeman did his utmost to play it down. 'I think he and his wife could have fostered a kid who has ended up dead in early middle-age. I'm hoping they might be able to help me with piecing together the background picture.'

'I know what case you're working, Templeman. The *kid* you're talking about was that Presley prick, Markham, right?'

'Spot on.'

'Well, Grainger won't appreciate any involvement in that shit, he's a stuffy old sod.'

'Tough.' Intimidation was something to which Templeman was immune.

'Be it on your head. The address is Churchill Manor, on the Guildford Road, just outside Godalming.'

'Bingo!' exclaimed Templeman. And to himself, *We have a perfect match*!

'Your glee will be short-lived if you upset that humourless old fart. Beware.'

'Didn't his first wife used to be an actress?'

'Long ago. When you were in nappies. Only small-time. A few minor film roles, mostly nothing more than cameo roles. She did appear in the West End in a couple of long-running plays, but the parts were minor. She was a good-looker with zero talent. Best of luck.'

Commander Lilleyman had gone home grouchy at lunchtime suffering from the debilitating symptoms of full-blown flu, but he had left a pithy order for Templeman to call him at home the moment there was anything fruitful to report. The internal electronic message, which Templeman had called up on screen, informed him that Lilleyman would have his mobile 'active' at his bedside 'around the clock', awaiting the tonic that would propel him from his sick-bed. Lilleyman's communication had concluded on the sardonic note, 'I don't expect for one moment to be disturbed with news of a breakthrough, so the challenge is to prove me wrong for once in my life.'

The end-of-the-day team conference was a jaded and dispirited affair. Templeman was unable to concentrate on the agenda; his fragmented thoughts kept returning to Tandy, but he was indisposed to field questions about her condition. There is no more interactive and gregarious environment than that of the engine-room and think-tank of a murder hunt, and Templeman was feeling as incongruous as a silent order monk in a Stock Market bear-pit. As the *troops* migrated to the nearest pub,

Templeman sloped off forlornly for home, wondering whether Charley would be there and, if she was, would there be a rope of rapport left with which to string together a civil conversation.

Charley *was* at home and her rancour of the previous evening had receded.

'I ate out,' she greeted him affably enough. 'I haven't prepared you anything because instinct told me you'd be a no-show tonight. Why didn't you call?'

Templeman almost retorted, *You could always have called me,* but tact ruled. So, instead, he replied convivially, 'You know how it is. The day just flowed. Suddenly it was late and all I wanted to do was jump in the car and drive. Also, to be honest, I doubted whether you'd want to speak to me, certainly about anything as mundane as food.'

'I owe you an apology. I said some bitchy things yesterday and I'm sorry. You know how the stress builds up before a showcase trial, but I should have been more understanding about your pressures.' Contrition didn't sit easily with her, which made her effort all the more appealing. 'How did your day go? Are you near to making an arrest?' Sincerity suited her.

'Nowhere near,' Templeman answered sullenly.

Charley was in her nightdress and a pink silk housecoat. She was sitting at the dining-table with files splayed in front of her like playing cards dealt from a blackjack deck. All make-up had been removed and her raven hair was still damp from the shower she had taken half an hour earlier. Her black liquid eyes were now pools of patience. A perfume of affluence scented the air. Templeman had no doubt why he had fallen in love with this intellectual, imperious goddess. At moments like these, she was intoxicating. The memory of the first flutter in his heart all those years ago now blew through like a gust of grief as if he were at the graveside of a loved one, which, in a way, he was, of course. Her conciliatory mood unsettled him, introducing complications. Warfare can often be easier to handle than peace. While they were fighting, he was at ease with his conscience. He could excuse his infidelity and free himself from those demons of guilt that had a habit of storming the soul during sleep, inducing middle-of-the-night sweats. Subconsciously, he judged Charley's appeasement an underhand ruse designed to destabilize the situation, to shake his certainty and soften up his resolve.

Templeman tossed his overcoat over the back of the sofa and, hands nonchalantly in trouser pockets, ambled to the window. Below, cars drifted by as faintly as memories tiptoeing through his head. Millions of yellow street lights disappeared into infinity. In the distance, a Tube train, rattling fast above ground, trespassed through the back gardens of suburbia. A jet airliner blinked a cold greeting, like a giant eagle, with an eye-tic, swooping towards Heathrow. Hidden by the darkness was a riot of confusion. Babylon was perpetuated in every city. Some cities concealed it better than others. London made little effort.

'Bad day?' Charley enquired solicitously, following her husband with perceptive eyes, her interest sharpened.

Bad day? he intoned to himself. His gaze had become sightless. How could he possibly answer that question truthfully? There was no way he could say, *This has to be the worst day of my life. I may have said goodbye forever to the woman I was planning to leave you for. If Simone's lights go out, I shall be left in darkness for the rest of my life. I shall never be able to look you in the eye again. And if she makes it, I shall soon be walking away from you.* Instead, he said vaguely, 'Not altogether. I think I have a suspect.'

'That's good news, isn't it?' Charley humoured him, her eyes unsure now. 'Do you want to share it?'

Templeman hesitated, then decided it could be a catharsis. 'First I'll fix a drink.'

'You can bring me one too. G and T.'

While in the kitchen, Templeman clumsily prepared himself a crab sandwich, then plucked a beer from the fridge and poured Charley's gin and tonic over a bed of ice-cubes. Back in the lounge, he dropped himself lethargically on to the sofa, first having rid himself of his jacket and necktie. Charley joined him, saying she could 'do with a break from homework'.

They clinked glasses and saluted in the manner of old friends meeting for an after-work drink. Before taking a single bite of his sandwich, Templeman quaffed his beer as if it was needed for maintenance rather than social relaxation. Charley watched his intake with curiosity and concern, commenting, 'It really must have been a tough day.' Her smile was only a facsimile and hid something.

Templeman began regaling Charley with the highlights of the interview with Jennifer Roper. Charley didn't once interrupt. She was genuinely engrossed; gripped even. She listened as a lawyer, as if considering whether to represent in court the protagonist of the story.

There were a couple of intermissions while Templeman replenished the glasses.

'You're not suggesting this woman actually perpetrated the crime, are you?' Charley said earnestly, when Templeman came to the end of his narrative.

'No, but I'm thinking she might be guilty of *conspiring* to murder Markham.'

'With her new lover?'

'Reasonable, isn't it?'

'And rather obvious.'

'I don't believe she gave me anything like the complete truth.'

'And you read guilt into that?'

'She has the motive.'

'Which is?'

'She was going to be struck out of the will.'

'Have you any evidence of that?'

'It's a good bet that that's what Markham intended doing.'

'But this woman could never have imagined the kind of money she was in for.'

'You never know.'

'It sounds to me that she was very up front with you. She didn't try to gloss over the grot.'

'Maybe that was all part of the trick, the deception. Self-deprecation is perceived as openness. It can be the clever use of mirrors to refract.'

'If she *has* lied, you could be reading too much into it. You know what judges tell every jury at the start of their summing-up?'

'I'm sure you're going to refresh my memory.'

Charley didn't disappoint him.

'People lie for many reasons. It can be to protect other people. It may be to polish their own image and ego. It should never be assumed that it's a manifestation of guilt.'

'It can be a pretty good marker, though.'

'Only in conjunction with material, rather than circumstantial, evidence.'

'It's helpful to have a target.'

'*Target*?'

'A suspect, a scenario, a sketch, a crime synopsis. It helps to structure the investigation.'

'It can also be dangerous because the temptation is to bend the facts to make them fit. You know what it's like when you're doing a jigsaw and you're sure you have the right piece, but it just won't go in. What do you do? – you try to force it. That's the peril of having perceptions when conducting any inquiry. It's also human nature.'

'Are you warning me against being human?'

'No, I'm warning you of human foibles.'

And that is how they burned away the night. Templeman was content to drink and joust until he was punch-drunk. The mental wrestling was his therapeutic escapism, ring-fencing him from the reality of the showdown awaiting Tandy just over the threshold of the next dawn. This was how it must be during the last night on Death Row, he ruminated. *You make every second count. Why waste time sleeping when in just a few hours you'll have eternity for that?* He drank to forget Simone, but the more he consumed, the more he remembered. The booze resurrected more than it buried. When finally he tottered to bed, the executioner, old Crabbers, was waiting for him in a recurring nightmare, scalpel in one hand, axe in the other.

They slept together without sharing intimacy. In the sobering chill of morning, they continued to be courteous to each other, rather like survivors of a shipwreck who have taken to a lifeboat and have to make the effort to rub along in symbiotic survival. Neither had mentioned Carlos Petrelli and the impending trial, but it was there between them, as surely as the Iron Curtain that had divided Berlin into East and West Germany.

Professor Crabtree was 'unavailable' to speak with Templeman, but Dr Everson quickly came on the line, making excuses for her prima donna boss. 'Crabbers is always grumpy and reclusive just before a major op,' she explained blithely. 'It's a good sign. It means his nervous energy is getting to work on him. The bigger the challenge, the better he performs.'

'How's Simone?' he asked simply with tunnel vision.

'We kept her sedated overnight. We're in the final stages of preparing her for theatre.'

'It's going ahead, then?'

'As planned.'

'God, I'm nervous!'

'If you said you weren't, I wouldn't believe you.'

'Will you be with her?'

'I shall be assisting Crabbers throughout.'

'Get her through it, for me.'

'We'll get her through it for professional pride,' she vowed, with the primal force of a prophet.

Chapter Sixteen

John Grainger's Private Office was adamant. The Secretary of State had a full diary; impossible to unscramble. There was a Cabinet meeting at eleven, followed by a luncheon engagement at the US Embassy. In the afternoon, he was due to reply to a Private Notice Question in the House of Commons on the latest military developments in North Korea. From the Commons, he would be going to Chelsea Barracks for a farewell bash for a war-hero brigadier who was retiring. The evening would be taken up with briefings from his junior minister and other staff, and then on to the Guildhall for a black-tie dinner with the Lord Mayor and diplomats from around the world, all part of a package promoting world peace.

'I'm sorry, Inspector, but he hasn't a moment even to pause to breathe,' insisted Patricia Bowen, his Private Secretary, with a rasping voice to fit the prickly and prissy image projected.

'We all have our pressures,' Templeman said evenly, unrelenting.

'Perhaps you would care to leave a message for the Secretary of State?' she suggested stiffly, all starch and stuffy. 'If you give me a flavour of the subject, it might be possible for me to draw his attention to it within the next forty-eight hours.'

Big favour! thought Templeman. 'I don't think he'd thank you for cajoling a taster from me,' he cut her short, the warning, almost a threat, only thinly veiled. 'This is a very private matter. I have to see him today by appointment or without. Needless to say, I would prefer us to find a mutually amicable solution. However …' The unfinished sentence left nothing to the imagination.

There was a sharp intake of breath as Bowen struggled to compute the nuances of Templeman's trenchant intimidation. Eventually she tendered a statement, presented as a question. 'Are you sure you're not exceeding your limitations?' It's easy to be fearless when you have might on your side. Despite that, Bowen was a doughty opponent in her own right. She had filleted bigger fish than this one and had no intention of being bullied by someone she regarded disdainfully as small fry.

Templeman now knew exactly how this was going to be played. 'Ms Bowen, I am investigating a murder. I am empowered to do everything possible, within the law, to bring this case to court. I shall repeat myself: Mr Grainger would not appreciate your forcing me to elaborate to a third party. Now, what do you propose?'

The Private Secretary took her time answering. 'How long can you give me?' This wasn't surrender; this was negotiating from a position of strength; this was political horse-trading.

However, not for a second was Templeman being outsmarted, confident that he could sleep-walk through this *game*. Bowen's tactics were predictable, part of a format. 'I have to see him today.'

Her sigh was staged. 'I cannot make any promises. Leave me a number on which you can be contacted. I'll see what I can do.'

Templeman was in the corridor, outside his office, mugging the fraudulent drinks-machine that had pocketed his money without supplying the goods, when his mobile went off. It wasn't the hospital, *thank God*! That could only have been dire news. No, it was Grainger, in person. Templeman smiled to himself mischievously. The game was developing into a replay of hundreds of similar farces. Only the players changed.

'Thanks for getting in touch so quickly,' Templeman said icily, involuntarily glancing at his wristwatch, surprised that the government cabinet minister hadn't been more of a gambler with brinkmanship.

'What the hell's this talk about a murder, Templeman? And what can it possibly have to do with me? Didn't Patricia, my Private Secretary, tell you I have to be at the American Embassy in a few minutes for lunch?'

'You've just asked three questions. In which order would you like them answered?'

'Any order, but without the truculence, if you don't mind.' His manner was hectoring and superior, his voice over-groomed; too precise and studiously crafted.

'Have you been following the Harry Markham case?'

'That's a question, not an answer.'

Typical politician; all evasion and smokescreen, but he's already told me more than if he'd given a straight reply.

'It's my understanding you had a very close relationship with Mr Markham?'

There was a long silence, so protracted that Templeman had to enquire, 'Are you still there, Mr Grainger?'

'What information do you have, exactly? And what more are you expecting from me?'

'We did the usual checks into the victim's background; routine stuff, that's all. We discovered he'd been fostered as a child. Your name was there, in the system. Everything matched up. As for what I'm *expecting* from you, that's easy. Two words encapsulate it – unimpeded assistance.'

'What kind of *assistance*?' Now Grainger's speech was clipped and businesslike.

'An insight. You and your wife – your first wife – must have known the young Harry Markham better than most people.'

'That was an awfully long time ago.'

'Nevertheless, it might shed some valuable light on the darker shades of his past.'

'I doubt that very much.'

'I'm afraid I must insist on being the judge of that.'

Grainger telegraphed his irritation through sounds other than words, ensuring, for example, that Templeman could hear the tapping fingers. 'Can't we do this over the phone?'

'Not a chance.'

'This is ridiculous!' Grainger resorted to hectoring. 'Does it *really* have to be today?'

'Yes, *really*.'

Resignation came with unmistakable petulance. 'Very well. Come to the Palace of Westminster this afternoon. I'll meet you in the Central Lobby at four-thirty. I'll try to give you a few minutes before I leave for the cocktail party.' Each word had been molten and heavy.

'I'll be there.' Templeman contrived chirpiness.

Grainger killed the call in an act of wishful and willful castration.

The countdown to the next inevitable call had begun. *I'll give it half an hour*, Templeman estimated to himself. His guess undershot by fifteen minutes.

Commander Lilleyman sounded exactly the way he felt, angry

and unwell. 'Templeman!' His voice was as lacerating as a murderous cutlass.

'How are you feeling, sir?'

'Worse because of you, but I'm not calling to discuss my health. Damn you, man!'

'You sound rough.'

'Not as rough as you'll look, unless you've a fucking good explanation.'

'For what?'

'*For what*! For trying to embroil a senior member of the government – quite possibly the next Prime Minister – in a murder hotpotch.'

'I'm not *trying to embroil* Grainger, he *is* involved.'

'Says who? Are you mad?' Lilleyman began choking on phlegm, then spluttering, almost apoplectic. 'What the fuck do you fancy you're doing? I've just taken an ear-bashing from no less a personage than the Home Secretary, subjecting me to untold grief. He's also been leaning on the Commissioner. Leaning heavily.'

'Grainger has agreed to see me,' Templeman said starkly.

'That is not a meeting you'll be keeping, unless—' His voice, ragged with rage and soreness, deserted him.

'Unless I can make out a credible case for it, is that what you were going to say?'

'That's *exactly* what I was going to say,' Lilleyman croaked.

Without histrionics and with scrupulous impartiality, Templeman outlined his reasons for demanding the interview with Grainger, concluding, 'He could hold the key, without realizing it. We need every scrap of help we can muster. The Home Secretary will be the first to condemn us for not exploring every avenue if we don't solve this one. He won't make allowances and show gratitude for our keeping a colleague out of it. No, he'll kick butts. Especially *yours*.'

'You're right on that score,' Lilleyman granted grudgingly.

'Another thing: if I'd been the foster dad of someone murdered, I'd be in mourning, perhaps not to the extent of the biological father, but still the loss would be personal. Why didn't he contact us?'

'You know very well why not. Grow up!'

'What has he to fear?'

'Exposure, fool!'

'To what?' Templeman refused to be provoked.

'Murky publicity. Ruin by association. You're not *that* naïve.'

'To have a hand in the rearing of someone who was to pursue a career perpetuating the legend of Elvis surely would add the common touch and a human quality to an otherwise boring and pompous old sod.'

'You're talking sense and logic, which is dangerous in the world of politics. Grainger would be insulted to be beheld as a man of the people. He sees himself as a cut above that. He's trouble, let me warn you. He's after you, which means, if I back you, he'll be after me – via the Commissioner.'

'I have to be allowed to do my job unfettered.'

Lilleyman wheezed and coughed chestily. 'God, I feel ill! You'll be the death of me, Templeman. Nothing ever runs smoothly when you're part of it. There are always complications and conflicts. You're a maverick cowboy and there are a lot of people just waiting for you to fall out of the saddle.'

'Including you?'

'No comment. Listen I'm going to advise the Commissioner that your reasons for wishing to interview Grainger urgently *appear* valid. If you screw up, the Home Secretary will kick the Commissioner, he'll kick me, and I'll do everything to ensure you're kicked hardest of all.

'It has to be done.'

'Let it be on your head.'

Grainger kept Templeman waiting in the Central Lobby of the House of Commons for almost half an hour. Templeman immediately recognized the government minister from his TV appearances and newspaper photographs. Grainger had a military bearing and he approached at a marching pace, checking his wristwatch in a mannerism suggestive of a man in a hurry, for whom time was gold-dust. Not a single strand of Grainger's fastidiously manicured white hair was out of place. It had been cut short and styled close to his dome-shaped skull, with a meticulously straight parting on the left. His ruddy complexion looked artificial, as if induced by alcohol, probably lunchtime wine. His skin shone, as if polished. There was no mistaking that his dark suit had been made to measure, following his contours and girth like an outer layer of flesh, cleverly covering most of the portly evidence of the good life. Despite his age and sedentary lifestyle, he gave the impression of being relatively fit for his age and Templeman surmised that he probably worked out in a gym fairly regularly and maybe even jogged.

Grainger made no effort to be sociable and pretended not to notice Templeman's proffered hand.

'I'll give you ten minutes,' he announced tartly, glowering.

'That may not be enough,' Templeman railed.

'It's that or nothing.'

Templeman had no intention of allowing himself to be marginalized. 'If we don't get finished, I'll just have to come back another time, perhaps without an appointment. We could always do it at your home. I'll gladly come out to Godalming.'

Grainger's snake-eyes drilled straight through him. 'Follow me,' he snapped, spinning on his heels, amazingly agile for ageing bones. 'I've arranged to borrow a backbencher's office for a few minutes. He doesn't have a secretary or a researcher, so we shan't be disturbed. I'd much rather do this away from my own office and staff, for obvious reasons. This place is a hotbed of rumour, the world's largest manufacturing plant and distribution centre of gossip. I can do without any of that output.'

Templeman was already a couple of paces behind the strutting minister as they burrowed along cloistered corridors alongside cobbled courtyards within the Palace of Westminster, following the silent ghosts of political icons of history, such as Winston Churchill and Harold Macmillan. In single file they circumnavigated St Stephen's Yard, just as Big Ben boomed the hour of five, the crescendo of echoes reverberating like dropping bombs around Parliament Square. Darkness had already descended and the only light, like most other things in the capital, was synthetic. Traffic around the square was gridlocked. Homeward-bound commuters, like programmed laboratory moles, scuttled through the drizzle for the underground habitat of the Tube. Other pedestrians, heads bent against the unyielding breeze, joined the flood-tide migration over Westminster Bridge towards the South Bank and Waterloo railway station. Red double-decker buses hissed and burped as their hydraulics relaxed.

Grainger didn't even make a tentative contribution to conversation as they followed the flow through the underpass and up the escalator into Portcullis House and then rode a lift to a third-floor, functional office.

'I hope you're going to justify this intrusion on my valuable time,' Grainger said, tonelessly, adding to the ice, rather than initiating a thaw. His expression was portentous and granite-menacing.

'Your attitude surprises me, Minister.' *In for a penny, in for a pound*, Templeman recited to himself.

'What's that supposed to mean?' the MP growled, his rich voice losing much of its resonance and becoming more streetwise, pugnacious.

'I'll explain.'

'The sooner the better.'

'First, however, I must ask a question: how long were you foster father to Harry Markham?'

Grainger waved away the question, the way one would brush off a mosquito in the heat of mid-summer. 'I've already told you, it was a long, long time ago. I've no recollection.'

'Months or years?'

'You have access to the records.'

'It ran into years and my surprise is the result of your apparent indifference to the unfortunate fate of the man to whom you were the father-figure during many of his most impressionable and formative years.'

'You have a cheek!' Grainger fulminated, banging a fist on the desk, as if it was the Despatch Box in the House of Commons, his florid face reddening into an Hawaiian sunset. 'How dare you presume to know how I feel?'

Templeman shrugged disagreeably. 'It is strange, to say the least, that you didn't voluntarily come forward to pass on your intimate knowledge of Harry Markham's early life. You must appreciate the potential relevance.'

'I *appreciate* no such thing! How could there be a connection between his murder at his age with his boyhood?'

'Information cannot be dismissed as irrelevant until it has been evaluated.'

Grainger smirked derisively. 'So if we'd had him as a baby, you'd want to know how many times a day his nappies were changed, because that might have a bearing on his violent death years later, eh? Is that what you're seriously saying?'

'Frivolity does you no favours at a time like this. Even when you phoned, you were reluctant to assist me. Is there no grief in you?'

'You'll pay for this, Inspector!'

'With my life or my job?' Templeman said, slowly and with inference.

Grainger made a show of checking how long they had already been together. 'Your time is almost up and all you've done is fritter away your chance.' There was triumph in his scorn.

Templeman studied the senior politician like a pawnbroker valuing a potential customer's shoddy and over-rated heirloom.

'What can you tell me about Markham?' Templeman changed pace, pulling back from brinkmanship, encouraging his facial muscles to soften.

Grainger responded in kind, after a meaningful sigh. 'He was a handful. We did our best. He was different. I suppose that that was to be expected.'

'Do you mean he was *different* from your children?'

'Different from all of the family. I suppose what I'm trying to say is that he didn't really fit in. That sounds awful, I know, but it's the way it was.'

Diplomacy had opened up Grainger where dynamite had failed.

'You already had two children of your own. What made you go into fostering?'

'None of your damned business!' Grainger pinched his mean lips with a thumb and index-finger, an elbow riveted to the desk, supporting the weight of his upper body like a scaffolding upright. His pose was one of introspective, pained sincerity. 'Nevertheless, I'll tell you, although this isn't easy for me. I'm a Christian. I still go to church every Sunday. My first wife, the mother of my children, was also very religious. Like many politicians' wives, she devoted a great deal of time to voluntary work. She was drawn very much towards the needs of under-privileged children and those who had been damaged, especially emotionally. We realized how lucky we were; how lucky our children were. It was Chantel's idea that we should open up our home to the less fortunate, to children who were in care.'

'So Harry Markham wasn't the only child you fostered?'

'No, he wasn't. In all, we fostered four; at various times, of course. Only ever one at a time.'

'How did your own children get on with Harry?'

'No problems, especially Charlotte. You'd have never known they weren't brother and sister in the early days.'

'Were they about the same age?'

'Charlotte would have been a couple of years older. I suppose Harry was about thirteen when he came to us. He was the last child we fostered. We treated him exactly the same as our own – Henry and Charlotte. We dressed him in the same quality clothes as our children. We integrated him as best we could into our family.'

'Yet he didn't *fit* and was *difficult*.'

By now, Grainger had forgotten all about monitoring the march of time. The folds of flesh on his face creased in concentration and his reptilian eyes reflected his return journey into the aching past. 'Henry, who was a bit younger than Harry, was at Eton. Charlotte was a boarder at Roedean. We tried to get Harry into a private school locally as a day boy, but he failed the common entrance exam. I pulled a few strings, but it was hopeless. He interviewed badly. The head found him sullen and anti-social. Even if Harry had passed the entrance exam with flying colours, the head intimated that he would still not have offered him a place.'

'How much were you *au fait* with the reasons for Harry being taken from his parents?'

'We were told everything. Well, perhaps not *everything*, but enough. When you're fostering, it's essential to know as much as possible about what the child has been through. Harry was introduced to a life of luxury with us. The good life. Unfortunately, he was resentful.'

'Despite his *resentment*, as you explained it, he rubbed along amicably enough with Charlotte and Henry?'

'Very much so, early on.'

'That doesn't sound very much like rebellion.'

'To be honest, the problems seemed to arise mainly when I was around. He railed against discipline, especially when it came from a male.'

'A throw-back, perhaps, to his relationship with his own father?'

'More than likely, but who can tell. Still, it was hard to cope with. Even harder to live with. Many a time I threatened to give up on him and send him back to Social Services.'

'How did he take those threats?'

'I didn't make them to him, just to Chantel. Every time she prevailed upon me to give him another chance. And so it went on, recycled friction.'

'Did he have violent tendencies?'

'He got into a few scraps at school: he went to one of our local comprehensives. I wouldn't say he had *violent tendencies*. He could look after himself and was never bullied, to my knowledge.'

'Did you eventually give up on him?'

'No. He stayed with us until the bitter end … until he was seventeen or eighteen.'

'And then what?'

'He just took off.'

'Was there an incident, a watershed, a defining moment?'

'No, he just declared that he was leaving.'

'Did he say where he was going?'

'Not that I can recall.'

'Did anyone try to stop him?'

'Chantel tried to discover what his intentions were. He wasn't very forthcoming. He said something teenagerish like, "It's time I flew the nest. There's a great big world out there for me to conquer. Hold your breath, London, here comes Dick Whittington, Mark Two". Chantel asked me to have a word with him.'

'Did you?'

'I told her that if he wouldn't listen to her, there was no chance of his being counselled by me.'

'So you allowed him to walk out?'

'I was in no position to detain him against his will. In law, he was deemed old enough to be the architect of his own destiny, as you well know.'

'Was Charlotte at home then?'

'No, she'd already gone to Oxford, to read law.'

'Were Harry and your daughter still close?'

'No, they'd drifted apart. They had nothing left in common. Harry had become even more introverted and music-mad. We'd bought him a guitar for one Christmas – or it could have been a birthday – and he was really into that. He'd shut himself in his room for hours on end.'

'You've hardly mentioned Henry. What kind of relationship did he have with Harry?'

'None.'

Templeman sensed a change of rhythm 'Was that at your behest?'

Grainger slipped into the Honest Joe politician role. 'I don't deny taking positive action to discourage Henry from coming under Harry's influence. Henry was younger than Harry and was at a vulnerable age.'

'Your disapproval of Harry ran deep?'

Grainger eyed Templeman shrewdly. 'It wasn't that, so don't overplay your hand, Inspector. There was no great vendetta against Harry. After all, we didn't have to keep him. I'm not a snob, but you can't change one's birth and blood. Lineage is imposed upon us. It is not an option. Genes and human chemistry are beyond our control. They are a result of the luck – or otherwise – of the biological lottery. We are what we are to a large extent. No amount of social engineering can reconstruct the mechanism that shapes our character. Henry had his own friends; boys of his own kind, from Eton.'

'Did Harry have his own friends?'

'None that I'd allow in my house.'

'He was an outsider?'

'That was his choice.'

'How much supervision was there over him? You were in parliament, Henry and Charlotte were at boarding-school. Then Charlotte went away to university. Wasn't your wife in the theatre?'

Grainger's evanescent smile was patronizing. 'Chantel was a professional actress when I was introduced to her. She was a very attractive woman and was blessed with abundant talent. Unfortunately, luck proved elusive. After all, she married me!' Self-effacement didn't sit easily with him. 'Good looks and ability aren't sufficient to guarantee success in that fickle business. Most importantly, you need to be kissed by fate. Chantel had given up the stage long before we took on the responsibility of fostering children.'

'You say you knew the score about Harry's background: just *what* had you been told?'

'That he'd been abused by his mother and his father had died.'

Templeman was anxious not to telegraph the significance of his next question. 'You've talked candidly about the general problems you and your wife had with Harry, but was there anything explicit to her? You know, things happening while you were away?'

Intrigue was emblazoned all over Grainger's sanguine face. 'Now what are you getting at?'

'I'm fishing, with neither bait nor hook.'

'And without a catch, I'm afraid.'

There was momentary eye-contact, which was enough to alert Templeman, but this wasn't the occasion for speculative probing, he decided. 'Did he ever pine for his parents?'

'Not in my presence,' Grainger answered, glacial.

'He wasn't in touch with his mother?'

'She was out of the frame, out of the loop.'

'Would you have known if there had been clandestine meets?'

'Probably not. I was away so much, but my wife almost certainly would have briefed me about anything like that.'

Templeman leaned back to appraise the politician, as if measuring him for a coffin. 'Have you given much thought to Harry since his death?'

Grainger considered giving a political reply, but had sufficient sense to recognize a boomerang before throwing it. 'Charlotte and Henry called me when they heard the news. They were upset.'

'But not you?'

'Look, I wasn't the least surprised that he'd got into trouble, so stop trying to foist a guilt complex on me. I'm being frank with you. At least give me credit for that.'

'Harry is the victim, not the perpetrator, Mr Grainger.'

'I'm well aware of that and I can do without the preaching, but if you flirt with the *outré*, then you have to be prepared to be swallowed by it.'

'What evidence have you of his *outré* lifestyle, as you call it?'

'It was obvious,' he retorted petulantly.

'Does your son or daughter have a theory?'

'Of course not! How could they have?'

'There's nothing in his life, you're aware of, that might have caught up with him to bring about the fatal shooting?'

'He died in clubland and I should imagine that's where you'll find all your answers.' Grainger then pretended that he had just caught sight of his wristwatch and reacted as shocked as if he had been tapped on the shoulder by Death's appointments' clerk. With that, he gathered together his papers and shooed out Templeman in the unsophisticated manner of a farmer chasing off a trespasser from his land.

Only when Templeman was out in the cold, with the earth-shaking booms of Big Ben exaggerating the march of time, did the significance of the hour dawn on him. *I must call the hospital. Simone should be out of the theatre by now.* Then, with a weighty sigh, he added to himself: 'The moment of truth.'

Chapter Seventeen

The wait seemed interminable before Professor Crabtree finally came on the line.

'Crabtree!' the surgeon barked hoarsely, like a warlord woken by a middle-of-the-night call from a much lower-ranking officer.

Templeman was more amused than offended by Crabtree's unrefined bluffness. He started to explain himself, but long before he had completed his set-piece, the professor cut him short.

'*Yes, yes,* I know who you are and all that stuff, but what the devil do you want with me?' He was a caricature of his reputation, a ranting relic from a bygone age, when senior consultant surgeons lived in their own rarefied bubbles and recognized only the gods as their near equals.

'I'm calling about my partner, Simone Tandy.'

'I know that! Get to the point, man!'

'How is she?'

'As well as can be expected.' With that, he was about to hang up.

'Translate, please,' Templeman asked for more, as bold as Oliver Twist. 'What does it mean?'

'The job's done, that's what it means.'

'So the operation was a success?'

'My operations are always a success. It is the patients who sometimes fail me.'

If the professor had been within reach, Templeman feared he would have strangled him. As a more reasonable alternative, he beseeched, 'Is Simone going to be all right? That's all I want to know.'

'Who can say?'

'If you can't, then who the blazes can?'

'Absolutely nobody, true.'

'But it *was* a success?'

'Clinically, *yes.*'

This was proving harder for Templeman than interrogating the most evasive criminal suspect.

'So Simone is going to pull through?'

Crabtree sniffed dismissively. 'Clinical success and recovery aren't necessarily synonymous. I'm still awaiting the reports from the lab. on tests for malignancy; so much depends on that now.'

That was it, over and out, with all the bedside manner of a scorpion.

There was a message waiting on Templeman's desk for him to ring Commander Lilleyman at home 'immediately' and 'urgently'. In view of the serrated tone and tempo of the missive, Templeman first ambled to the canteen, socialized over another coffee, then caught up with the day's happenings among his team, and only then did he attend to the *urgent* and *immediate* matter.

'Took your time,' grumbled Lilleyman, sounding rougher and more ragged than ever.

'I was busy.'

'So I hear.'

'Nothing like a grapevine to sour the works.'

'Cut the prattle. You've had your sport with Grainger, now leave him alone.'

'That may not be possible.'

'Listen to me, Templeman, you make no further approach to Grainger without going through me, got that?'

'Even while you're on sick leave?'

'Even if I'm dead.'

'Now that really would be a pleasure, sir. Any realistic hope of my having to seek permission via a séance?'

'Fuck you!'

'Keep taking the medicine, sir.'

Templeman was just about to leave the Yard to join a group of his foot soldiers for a drink in an attempt to reinforce morale, when he took two calls in quick succession – the first on his mobile, the second on his desk phone.

'Darling, I have to be in Manchester first thing in the morning for a trial. It's not one of mine, but Joanne has gone down with flu at the last moment, so, rather than asking for a postponement, I'm stepping in. It's a guilty plea, so it's a straightforward mitigation job. It'll be over in a day. I'm driving up this evening and staying overnight, so that I'll be fresh for the ten a.m. kick-off.'

'Thanks for letting me know,' said Templeman, as if talking with one of his officers who was phoning to report sick.

Templeman wasn't fooled. He guessed that the Manchester case was fictitious and Charley would be getting laid, probably in a London hotel. And he cared not one jot.

Much more interesting was the second call – from Craig Dempsey, a ghost from the past.

Craig Dempsey hadn't mellowed with age. 'You're in the shit, Luke, I can tell,' he began as provocatively as ever, his way of being chummy. 'I've been following the Elvis case in the papers with interest. Reading between the lines, I'd say this could be your Waterloo.'

It was more than a year since they had spoken. On that occasion, Dempsey had been undertaking a little freelance ferreting on Templeman's behalf, bending – and breaking – a few rules and putting distance between the official cavalry and the cowboys, allowing Templeman plausible denial should the sub-contracted operation go up in smoke.

Templeman had been in charge of yet another murder case. Early leads had dried up and he was struggling, but there was still one rather tenuous line of inquiry eluding him. He needed access to a house, but magistrates turned down his application for a search-warrant on the grounds that his suspicions were too speculative and that he was merely on a trawl.

Templeman, not surprisingly, was pissed-off by the magistrates and, in knee-jerk petulance, recruited Dempsey's long-arm services. A few days later, the house that Templeman had wanted to search was burgled. Jewellery and documents were stolen, confusing the local police. Had the burglar primarily been after the gems or the papers? Which – if either – was the false trail? The break-in was clearly the work of a professional. No fingerprints or other clues had been left. Neither was there an obvious *modus operandi* to link the burglary with other similar crimes.

Six weeks later, all the jewellery was returned in a posted parcel, the name and address written in capital letters. The postmark was central London. No help. No documents, either.

Just one sentence in those documents, which just happened to fall into Templeman's hands, enabled him to solve the murder. Of course, those stolen papers were never produced in court and

Templeman would have denied ever having had them in his possession. What they had done for Templeman was confirm the motive and steer him in the right direction. It had been enough. Without that edge, though, as small as it was, a denouement would have foiled him.

'Where've you been all this time, Craig, doing porridge?'

'No such luck. No living off the state for me. I still have to earn an honest crust in order to live.'

'Since when?'

'You know me, I only ever poach for gamekeepers, Luke.'

'What can you do for me this time, old man?'

'*Old* only as in vintage! I think I know the point you're at, Luke.'

'Perhaps *you* know more than *I* do, Craig, old son!'

'You're faced with numerous choices. You've explored several attractive possibilities, but they've been deadends. They've simply led you up the proverbial garden path into a wasteland. Is that familiar to you?'

'I'd put it differently, but we wouldn't be so far apart. However, I don't believe you called me for an abstract debate.'

'Right again, Luke! What you're desperate for at the moment, I guarantee, is, in tabloid-speak, a vital breakthrough, something that will bring together all the different strands, making sense of the senseless.'

'And you can wave the magic wand and make it happen?'

'Maybe. You see, I've been working a case ...'

Templeman was overcome by a tingling sensation of *déjà vu*.

'Insurance fraud is fuelling today's black economy, you know that,' the veteran private eye continued, beginning to play his cards selectively, though not yet showing his hand. 'For three weeks now I've been on a big one. A roll. I won't bamboozle you with detail.'

'That's right, don't let facts spoil a good story.'

Dempsey ignored the sardonic aside. 'Suffice it to say that my sniffing has centred largely on Soho.'

'What part of Soho?'

'Certain companies. To do with films and their distribution.'

'Counterfeiting?'

'No matter. Those details are sideshows to why I called you.'

'Which is?'

'Not now. Meet me.'

'Where?'

'The old haunt.'

'When?'

An hour from now.'

'I'll be there.'

Dempsey filled a generous-sized burgundy leather club chair beside a roasting fire. He was rattling the rocks of ice in his whisky sour, encouraging his cocktail to hiss at him, as if he had a venomous snake held by the neck, except that this was his poison and he was about to enjoy its sharp bite. Shadows from the flickering flames danced on his fleshy face, ageing him more than age itself. He still shaved regularly, but he wondered why he bothered. Taking off the daily growth had become tantamount to scything through a rainforest; vegetation cut away at dawn had regrown by noon. He carried his baggage under his eyes in blue, swollen pouches. His thinning silver hair was swept back, but was as unruly as the life he had led. But when it came to his clothes, he had always been a natty dresser. Today was no exception. His navy-blue mohair suit had an expensive sheen to it and he could have shaved with the crease down his trousers. Spit and polish had been applied to his black shoes, a habit from his military days. His sky-blue shirt and polka-dot tie completed a concept of class he didn't deserve. Their manner was that of executives meeting to negotiate a deal.

A waiter didn't have to be summoned; one arrived like a genie out of a bottle. It was that sort of establishment.

'I'll have a whisky sour on the rocks, too,' said Templeman.

'Make that two,' chimed Dempsey, with a smoker's voice.

They sat opposite one another, a low, oblong mahogany table between them. They perched themselves on the edge of their chairs, their bodies arched over the table so that their words were one frog's leap from mouth to ear, enabling the volume to be kept down. Dempsey's paunch overlapped his waistband and Templeman couldn't help but contemplate how the bulky PI could so easily be mistaken for a Russian or German, a Muscovite or Berliner.

Dempsey downed his first whisky sour as if swallowing an oyster, allowing it to slip down in one gulp, travelling fast to the pit of his stomach, only to be deflected like a ricochet to his brain.

After the waiter had served from a silver tray the new order, including a bowl of peanuts, they clinked the chunky glasses in a time-honoured greeting ritual and then prepared for the sparring.

'This is the one you just *have* to solve, eh, Luke, my old son?'
His grin was spoilt by nicotine-stained teeth.

'I never look at a case that way. I always assume it will be
solved. There can never be any other approach, you know that.'

'But this one's special.'

'They're all *special*.'

'To the victim, of course; to the victim's family and the perpetrator, yes; but not always to the investigators.'

'*Always*, Craig, when I'm in charge.'

Dempsey's bloodshot, watery eyes were more roguish than sly.
'This is the one everyone's going to remember, the one books will
be written about and turned into movies. It has that one extra
dimension, the magic handle, and you know it, so don't play coy
and cool with me, old son.'

'So how can you help?'

Playtime over.

'I was telling you earlier about my current assignment. Well,
just the other day I came across some old footage of film.'

'What do you mean by *came across*?'

'That's sensitive information and on the need-to-know principle is immaterial.'

Templeman grinned knowingly. 'Says you. It was thieved, you
mean?'

'I mean it fell into my hands. During the last week or so, I've
been doing little but viewing hours of film, all of it steamy.'

'As in porn?'

'The whole gamut, from soft to hard. During the production of
this kind of stuff, the cameras tend not to major on faces; other
parts of the anatomy monopolize the close-up shots, though not
all. Faces are recognizable.'

A fresh breeze of anticipation swept over Templeman, awak-
ening eager anticipation, as if the wrapping-paper was being
ripped off a Christmas present.

'And you ID'd someone I should hear about?'

'*He* wouldn't have meant anything to me if his mug shot
hadn't been on TV and in the newspapers so much recently.'

'You have to be talking about Harry Markham?' Templeman
made an educated guess.

'You're not wrong.' A suffusion of sweat, had broken out like a
blister-pack of little white pills across Dempsey's forehead.

Templeman endured the histrionics stoically.

'There are two films in question. Both run for sixty-two minutes. They're professionally produced to a very high technical standard. We're not talking about home-made blue trash. Markham appears in them both, as one of the studs. He had what it takes, believe me.'

'There's no doubt about his identity?'

'None whatsoever. I froze several frames and compared them under a magnifying-glass. Now listen to this: the leading *lady* in both movies is the same woman. I also lifted a couple of stills of her because her face was vaguely familiar to an old film buff like me. I took the prints to a theatrical agent of long-standing to confirm my judgement, which he did without hesitation.'

'What's her name?' Templeman demanded impatiently.

'You're going to find this hard to believe.' Dempsey, like a professional storyteller, sustained the suspense.

Their glasses were empty. The ice was melting, leaving the two men without their rattles. A waiter, amazingly tuned into the drinking rhythms at each table, arrived as in response to telepathy.

'Two more, please,' said Templeman, his eyes not releasing Dempsey for a second from their adhesive hold.

Not until the waiter had completed his round-trip did the conversation recommence.

'OK, who is she?'

'Chantel Grainger. She was married to John Grainger, the Defence Secretary who could well be the next Prime Minister. Chantel Grainger died about ten years ago.'

'I know that.'

'Once she was on the brink of the big-time, but she never got beyond a couple of feature films, a string of forgettable cameo roles, and a handful of reasonable parts in the West End, but nothing more than a foot in the door.'

'Do you have the dates when these porno films were made?' Templeman brushed aside the CV.

'No, but Markham looks around twenty-five to thirty, so I guess they were shot a few years – maybe a couple – before Chantel's death.'

'Are there credits, naming the cast?'

'No credits. Those who take part in what we're discussing don't want to take credit for it. It's a gamble for them. Perhaps that gives them a thrill; like judges and politicians kerb-crawling in red-light districts, risking everything on the roll of the dice in the back of their car or up against an alley-wall. If you start thinking logically, you won't make any sense of it. Think irrationally and only then will you make headway.'

'What level of porn do we have here?'

'As hard as it gets.'

'Do you still have the films?'

'What do you think!' It wasn't a question. Dempsey patted the briefcase at his side, as if fondling a faithful pet.

'Originals or copies?'

'Originals – plus official copies.'

'I'm confused.'

'Copies are made for distribution. In other words, the copies in my possession aren't pirate versions.'

'I'll need the originals.'

Dempsey wavered. 'Maybe later, eh?'

'Now! The evidence you're holding could be crucial.'

'If it *is* evidence.'

'*You* obviously believe it is or you wouldn't have made the call and we wouldn't be getting mellow together. There's one thing I have to know for sure now: shall I be receiving stolen property?'

Dempsey drank some more as an emboldening measure. 'Do I get immunity?'

'I don't think you need worry about that.'

The rats of ambivalence gnawed inside his head. 'There's more to it than I've already told you; lots more.'

Templeman attracted a waiter. They communicated as if at an auction. A nod of the head placed a repeat order and a similar almost imperceptible response in return confirmed that the message had been received.

'Let's hear it *all*, then.'

Dempsey dug deep into his reserves of trust. 'I have documents.'

'What sort?'

'Company details.'

'Relating to the porn company?'

'Exactly.'

'How does that impinge on my investigation?'

'It's a private limited company.'

'Who are the directors?'

'That's what I was coming to. Brace yourself. Harry Markham was one; his wife is another.'

'His *wife*!'

'Oh, yes.'

'Who else?'

'One more; a Jennifer Roper. The name means nothing to me, but she's company secretary.'

Templeman remained implacable, his eyes mirrors of nothing except inscrutability.

'When was the company launched?'

'Twelve years ago.'

'You haven't given me its name yet.'

'EP Enterprises Limited.'

'EP standing for Elvis Presley, no doubt,' Templeman opined, his brain spinning. 'What's the address?'

'A basement in Dean Street, beneath a coffee shop. Just a couple of poky rooms and a closet toilet.'

'You've obviously been there.'

'Not by invitation!'

'No studio on the premises?'

'No, the movies couldn't have been made there.'

'What else have you?'

'What does it take to satisfy you?'

Templeman was distracted from answering by the arrival of the waiter. The Scotch was soothing and smoothed away the wrinkles of the night for both of them. They poured more of the nectar into their system. It had the effect of motor oil going into a car engine. Everything began to run a shade more effortlessly.

'I appreciate your coming to me, as always,' said Templeman, almost apologetically. 'I don't want you to think I'm ungrateful.'

Dempsey waved away the explanation as unnecessary. 'How will you protect me and yourself? I mean, how will you be able to explain this stuff without landing me in the shit?'

'I'll sort that if and when it becomes an issue.'

'I'm relying on you.'

'Have no fear. Now, anything else incriminating? Bank statements? Accounts?'

'Copies of contracts, one letter from a bank in the Cayman Islands, and another from an accountant.'

'What are the letters about?'

'The Cayman bank was confirming the safe depositing of two

hundred thousand US dollars into the account of EP Enterprises Limited, an electronic transfer transaction, apparently, from the US mainland. The accountant's letter was merely a reminder not to be late submitting the annual accounts at the end of the financial year.'

'And the contracts?'

'Usual ones for that sort of business; with performers and technicians.'

'How far back do the contracts go?'

'To the very beginning; the beginning of the company. Most of the older ones are photocopies. I doubt that the originals have been shredded. More likely, they've been deposited at a bank or with the company's accountant.'

'OK, Craig, you've obviously been a naughty boy, now tell me this: who commissioned you? Was it a private party, or an official agency, such as the Inland Revenue?'

'No comment.'

'OK, that helps to set down a marker. When can I take possession?'

'How about now? All you have to do is pick up my briefcase and leave. There's nothing else in it other than the goodies for you. I planned it this way so the handover would be uncomplicated; nothing on show.'

'You're a star, Craig.'

'Indeed, I am!'

It was not far off midnight before Templeman's working day was coming to an end. Much to his shame only then did his thoughts return to Tandy.

Chapter Eighteen

Templeman stayed up all night watching filth. He viewed both porn movies on his TV twice, from beginning to end. They neither disgusted nor aroused him. This was a purely clinical exercise, no more sexual than a male doctor performing an internal examination on a female patient.

From the first close-up, there was no doubt in his mind about the identities of the leading players. Hardest of all for him to compute, however, was the fact that the woman having sexual intercourse on screen – definitely not simulated – had been foster mother to the man screwing her. Occasionally he froze the frame, trying to estimate Chantel Grainger's age at the time the films were made. She had to be in her forties, he decided, but much of her camellia beauty had been preserved. Templeman knew as well as anyone that make-up artists could work miracles, achieving alchemy with impure human flesh, but there was something innate about Chantel's looks – a virginal innocence radiating from within, demonstrating just how wickedly deceitful nature could be.

The concentrated caffeine in black coffee helped to keep him awake. During the replays his mind turned to Markham's sister, whose account now assumed credibility. She claimed to have caught her brother and mother in coitus. Now Templeman wondered who had been the instigator of that incest. Harry had been only a boy, but he was no innocent and wouldn't have needed any cajoling. Had Markham and Chantel Grainger been sexually intimate while he was being fostered?

They must have, Templeman answered himself. *What part, if any, had John Grainger played in all of this? Had the Graingers become foster parents for the purpose of procuring a toyboy for Chantel? Had the Graingers, as a family, been dedicated to depravity on a grand scale? Was Markham blackmailing Grainger? If so, what stronger motive for a man to murder, especially a politician with the greatest prize of all within touching distance?*

There was a slight flaw to that scenario, however, which Templeman instantly recognized. Markham's wife, Audrey, was a director of EP Enterprises Limited, therefore she would have known all about the pornographic performances *starring* her husband and Chantel Grainger, surely? In that case, if John Grainger colluded in the murder in some way, what was the virtue in killing only Harry Markham? For all John Grainger knew, Audrey Markham and company secretary Jennifer Roper, Harry Markham's mistress, could have copies of the films.

Maybe they do. Other people, too. Quite a few people are required to shoot a movie, even this kind of obscenity. Another thing: if Craig could break in and get his hands on this stuff, it would have been a cinch for the kind of operatives John Grainger could have hired. Blackmail would also explain where Markham's apparent nest-egg came from. On the other hand, pornography has become a bank-rolling industry with a massive turnover worldwide. Countless sordid fortunes have been accrued from the underground celluloid flesh trade. Maybe the answer to Markham's wealth is that simple.

He examined the documents. They confirmed everything Dempsey had told him about directorships and bank accounts.

The first grey shafts of morning light took him by surprise. By the time he had showered, shaved and dressed, the hesitant birth of the new day had progressed into something more recognizable and well-formed. The lid of night had lifted completely and a cutting-edged easterly was blowing away most of the running cloud, allowing the sun a look in for a welcome change. Templeman was just preparing himself a light breakfast of more coffee, two rounds of buttered toast, marmalade and a couple of aspirins, when Doctor Everson called him.

'Non-malignant!' she proclaimed.

'No doubts?'

'None whatsoever.'

Templeman was on an adrenalin high that couldn't have been heightened even if he had been popping amphetamines all night, his sore eyes soothed by tears of relief and joy.

'When may I see her?'

'Tomorrow.'

'Not before?'

'Be patient for just a few more hours.'

'Kiss her for me.'

'Right away.'

'You're an angel, bless you!' he said, self-consciously, more cathartic than glib.

Only his eyes betrayed him as he appraised himself in the driver's mirror. Take away the eyes and no one would know that he was fighting sleep-deprivation. Kidology was a formidable antidote. He took his shades from the glove-compartment, steered them on to his wan face, and reappraised himself. That was better. *Fool myself, fool the world*! His whole life revolved around hidden truths.

As he headed for Bedford yet again, Templeman mentally mapped out the day ahead. He would *hit* Audrey Markham and Jennifer Roper unannounced. Exploiting the element of surprise would be paramount. The veracity of both women's testimonies was going to be severely tested and, for Templeman, it was imperative that they were given no time for preparation. As for John Grainger, Templeman would ponder that problem during the morning. Ideally, the same rules and tactics should be applied to all three, but Templeman resigned himself to having to finesse and compromise to a certain degree in respect of Grainger. Lilleyman would have to be counselled and consulted, of course. What a prospect! How sweet and smooth life would be without all the politics!

Chapter Nineteen

Audrey Markham was still in her nightdress, covered by a silk kimono. Surprise was frozen on her bland face and in her valium eyes, much to Templeman's pleasure.

'Oh, it's you!' she said, blanching; articulating the fact that this was a visit she had not been expecting.

As soon as they were settled in the lounge, Templeman opted for forthrightness. 'You left out a whole chunk of the story, why was that?'

Mrs Markham' s face reverted to a blank canvas. 'What are you talking about?' she asked querulously.

'Why didn't you mention the film-making company of which you're a director?'

Pink embarrassment rushed from her stem-like neck to her pinched cheeks and finally to her bulkhead forehead, as swiftly as spilt paint. Templeman had witnessed countless similar involuntary self-detonating implosions.

'Is it important?' Now her voice was spiked with a serrated mixture of petulance and defiance.

'You can do better than that, Mrs Markham,' he suggested derisively.

She trapped her hands vice-like between her knees, refusing to embrace Templeman's drilling eyes. 'It was Harry's company. He set it up. It was his baby. Nothing to do with me.'

'*Nothing to do with me!*' he intoned. 'You're a director, Mrs Markham.'

'Only nominal. I have two shares, just to help make it legal.'

'Why didn't you tell me this before?'

'What's its relevance? What does it have to do with Harry's death?'

'Maybe *everything*.'

'How do you figure out that?' she snapped, like a terrier.

'Because of the nature of the company's profile; its projects.' He was probing and prodding now, avoiding being too direct, giving her the opportunity to go wrong if she seized the chance to be evasive.

'What do you mean by that?'

'Come, come, Mrs Markham, you're not doing yourself any favours by protesting ignorance.' He needled her quite deliberately.

The hawk turned into a dove. 'I'm not playing games with you, Inspector. I really don't know what you're getting at.'

'Have you taken part in the making of any of the company's films?'

'No.'

'Never?'

'Never, no.' Now she accepted the invitation to meet his unyielding stare.

'What sort of films did you think your husband was making?'

'Films about Elvis. Films about the rock'n roll years. Nostalgia movies.'

'Did you view any of the finished products?'

'I don't think I ever did.'

'I find that hard to believe. Weren't you interested in *your* company's output?'

'How many times do I have to tell you it was Harry's company?'

'Didn't you ever talk about the productions, at night perhaps, in bed, when he hadn't a gig?'

'No. I left it to him. I'm not into nostalgia, not like some people, especially where pop music's concerned.'

'Yet that was your husband's life. If you didn't even have that in common ...'

'We had our family ... until recently.'

'OK, now let's turn to your relationship with Jennifer Roper.'

Mrs Markham didn't blink, something Templeman mentally filed away.

'How long have you known her?'

'I don't *know* her at all. We've never met.'

'Yet she's a fellow director.'

'She's the company secretary, a part-time accountant who's a competent bookkeeper.'

'That's what your husband told you?'

'Isn't it true?'

'You've never met her, not in all the years that the company has been in existence?'

'She was there only to make up the numbers. She had experience with the legal requirements of setting up a limited company.'

'What *experience*?'

'I'm not familiar with the details. Harry brought her on board. I have a recollection that he said she'd been recommended to him by someone in showbusiness, probably his agent. But that's ancient history. What's more, it was just a sideline, a side-show. It wasn't Harry's core business.'

'What did he say whenever you asked how the company was doing financially?'

'I never asked,' she answered stubbornly.

'Not ever?' Templeman said in disbelief.

'To be honest, I looked upon it as Harry's hobby. I didn't expect to hear anything more about it unless it was doing particularly well or badly.'

'You didn't anticipate any share of annual profits, if there were any?'

'Not at all. As I said, I took no part in it. I ran my own business as a hairdresser for a long time; that took up most of my time and interest.'

'Where were the films made?'

Mrs Markham's discomfiture didn't escape Templeman.

'I'm afraid that's something else I can't assist you with. You may find it hard to believe, but the operational side of that company was something we never discussed.'

'You're right, I do find it hard to believe. You must be aware that your husband had offices in London?'

'An office. One room, wasn't it? Just a base to provide the company with a mail-drop address.'

'It's slightly bigger than that, but not much, I grant you. So you've never been there?'

'Never.'

'Didn't it ever occur to you that at least some of your husband's income might have come from the film company?'

'Of course not!' she protested, as if such a proposition was utterly preposterous. 'The thought never crossed my mind. I'm trying to impress upon you that, for me, the company was medieval history. It wasn't a part of my life. It was established years ago as a toy for Harry and he played with it, not me, not the children. For all I knew and cared, it had lain dormant for years – or even wrapped up.'

'Without his telling you? After all, if there were debts or litigation against the company, you would be just as liable as your husband.'

'I never looked at it that way,' she said, brooding now.

The time had come to break cover and to up the tempo.

'Your husband was into pornography.' The delivery was direct. No fancy packaging, no frills, no cushion for a soft landing.

Mrs Markham looked up from her lap with a jolt as if stunned by an uppercut. Her eyes were those of someone made to see something against her will.

'Into *what*?'

Her incomprehension didn't appear a reflex to Templeman. Her expression was more that of someone unmasked. Well, that's how it seemed to Templeman, but was it he who now saw only what he wanted to see, he cautioned himself.

'The films your husband made were for the underground pornographic market.'

'You're kidding!'

Templeman sensed something superficial about Mrs Markham's responses. They lacked the ring of truth, but once again was that his wishful thinking?

'Where does this information come from?' she challenged him.

'I've seen two of the films myself.'

'But how can you be certain that Harry had anything to do with them?'

'Because he is *in them*, Mrs Markham.'

'*In them*,' she echoed, a vast pool of emptiness washing over not just her face but her entire being.

This did not strike Templeman as a camouflage. In fact, it was so genuine that Templeman experienced a pang of pity for her.

'He was the main player – if that's the right description – in both productions.'

Mrs Markham vacillated a moment before countering, 'Just what is your definition of porn, Inspector?'

'Not Snow White or Mary Poppins. This is not a debate about definition. The films your husband made and appeared in didn't straddle an arbitrary borderline. His movies were M-rated.'

'*M-rated?*'

'M for muck.'

'Who else was in them?' she asked intensely.

'Only one person that I can positively identify.'

'Is that *one person* Jennifer Roper?'

'Do you have some reason to believe that?'

'Only because of what you've been saying.'

'Well, it wasn't her.'

'Who then?'

'Does the name Chantel Grainger mean anything to you?'

Mrs Markham cocked her head sideways in intense delibera-
tion, her pebble-hard eyeballs momentarily disappearing into the
shells of her eyelids, wrinkles of concentration creasing her steep
forehead. 'No, I don't think so,' finally she replied slowly. 'Should
it?'

'Not unless you're something of a movie buff.'

'Which I'm not. You've come here denigrating my dead
husband, who has yet to be buried. In addition, you've made
serious insinuations about me.'

'Not so. I've asked questions about the extent of your involvement with a company of which you have been a director for many
years. And you are still a director, if my information is correct. If
I'm mistaken, now's your chance to remedy it.'

'Your questions – all of them – have been tantamount to accusations. Am I going to be allowed to judge for myself the so-called
pornography you've rejoiced in regaling me with?'

'Not yet.'

'And why not?'

'Because I don't think there's anything to be gained by it – at
this stage.'

'Shouldn't I be the judge of that?'

'Trust me, please.'

Audrey Markham was shaking her head vigorously. 'You've a
nerve!' She was regaining her composure and mental clarity.
'How did you come by the films?'

'I'm not in a position to disclose that.'

'Can't or won't.'

'Operational reasons,' he bluffed.

'*Operational reasons!*' she scoffed. 'How can I be sure they *even*
exist?'

'They exist, believe me.'

'No, I won't believe you, until I've witnessed them with my own eyes.'

'Belief will have to wait, then, I'm afraid. Do you own a gun, Mrs Markham?'

'Good God, no! What are you implying?'

'Have you ever fired a handgun?'

'Never. I wouldn't know how to. Are you suggesting I killed my Harry?'

'I'm giving you the opportunity to rule out the possibility.'

'That's something I don't have to prove.'

'And that's a wrong answer.'

'That's enough! From now on I shall not speak with you unless my solicitor is present. I shall be advised by him.'

'You were alone on the night of the murder, according to your statement.'

'I was and you know that, but I said no more questions.'

Templeman tried to squeeze out the last drop.

'There is no one who can verify the truth about your movements that night, correct?'

'There were no *movements*, now please go.'

'Are you prepared to make all your bank statements available to me?'

'No, I'm damned well not!'

Templeman pushed his luck.

'While I'm here, I should like to make another thorough search of your house.'

'Not without a search-warrant, you won't. Now leave, or I'll have you thrown out.'

'By whom?'

For a split second she hesitated then drew in breath sharply, before rasping, 'By my lawyer. You're upsetting me at a time when I'm most vulnerable. You're picking on me because you're failing in your job. Like most men, you're a bully at heart. Your previous politeness and urbanity were a sham and didn't fool me for one minute.'

'We'll talk again,' Templeman promised, heavy on innuendo, making his exit without further fuss.

Commander Lilleyman was back at his desk, though not yet fully recovered, something about which he was very quick to make Templeman aware, coughing on cue into the mouthpiece.

'You're not going to like this,' Templeman forewarned his bullish boss.

Lilleyman felt a relapse coming on already. 'Let's hear it. What have you done now?'

'Future tense, not past: I'm going to have to re-interview John Grainger.'

Templeman braced himself for the onset of apoplexy and didn't have to wait long.

'Let's just pretend I didn't hear that.' Lilleyman's temper was tethered only momentarily.

'One way or another, I intend to question the Defence Secretary a second time – today. It has become imperative.'

'Try that and I'll have you directing traffic in Parliament Square. Grainger will be in a position to piss on you from his office-window.'

'I'm advising you of my intentions out of courtesy,' Templeman tried a more oblique approach.

'If you know what's good for you right now, you'll drop all your *courtesy* into the nearest latrine and flush it down with one mighty jerk of the chain.'

Templeman faltered briefly as he conducted a referendum with himself on his next move. Without too much confidence in the outcome of his own counsel, he said, 'If anyone in the Shadow Cabinet *somehow* learned that we were involved in a cover-up for Grainger over such a serious criminal offence, it would be blown up into an international scandal by the press. Accusations would be made against us – *you* and the Commissioner – with the full protection of parliamentary privilege, so the newspapers wouldn't have to worry about being sued for libel. After that, there would have to be sacrifices to appease the press and the public's baying for blood. Heads would roll this end. Well, one head for sure ...'

'You wouldn't dare!' Lilleyman's voice had become as low and tremulous as a victim in a game of Russian roulette with the muzzle of a pistol pressed against his temple. Templeman had spun the chamber and now Lilleyman was questioning, none too confidently, the inspector's resolve to squeeze the trigger.

'I'm not saying *I* would do it, I'm hypothesizing.'

'You really think you can out-fox me, don't you?'

'I was going to suggest in view of your *reservations*, or hostility, I should show you what I have.'

'Before any new approach is made to Grainger, you mean?'

'Exactly. So you can evaluate for yourself the strength of it and make your own assessment.'

Lilleyman saw the trap.

'You're trying to pass the buck.'

'You keep reminding me that you're the boss, for which you're paid big bucks. And that's why the buck should stop with you.'

'Very funny,' Lilleyman said mirthlessly. 'I'll have a look at what you've got, but I'm making no promises.'

'That's fair.'

'This isn't about fairness, Templeman, but survival, and it's in your best own interests to be able to make that distinction.'

Chapter Twenty

Lilleyman, clearly uncomfortable with developments, fidgeted throughout Templeman's presentation.

Police mandarins were entrusted with implementing government policies. For the system to function efficiently, there had to be informal, as well as formal, dialogue. Hence, the top brass in the police didn't react favourably to anyone – or any faction – within their ranks creating tension between the law-makers and the law-enforcers. If Grainger and the Government were compromised and embarrassed publicly, even if justifiably, there would be a price to pay.

Despite his dapper appearance in smart uniform, gleaming silver buttons, starchy white shirt and polished shoes, in which he believed he could see the reflections of his past and the visions of his future, Lilleyman was more politician than policeman.

Templeman was the cop. Templeman cared only about solving cases, whereas Lilleyman was concerned more about *how* they were solved; method, transparency and public relations. Polishing the image was just as important to him as polishing his shoes. Political correctness had become the mantra; so, too, procedures and protocol. Every year annual clear-up rates were a sensitive issue. The government could help to massage figures that fell short of expectations or, conversely, it could be scathing and critical. Embroiling a government cabinet minister in a sleazy murder investigation wasn't the route of choice for fostering a harmonious working relationship with the country's executive. Therefore, Templeman's enthusiasm was countered by the commander's negativity.

After viewing in his office for ten minutes the first video, Lilleyman killed it with the remote-control. Swivelling in his chair to confront Templeman across the desk, he challenged, 'So?'

'Both films feature Harry Markham and Grainger's first wife, as I explained to you.'

'A woman who has been dried bones for many years.'

'That's not the point.'

'Just what *is* the point?'

'Markham was far wealthier than anyone could have imagined. It doesn't fit with his circumstances. He may have been blackmailing someone.'

'By *someone*, you mean Grainger?'

'It's a possibility.'

'Why?'

'You've just seen *why*.' Templeman allowed exasperation to fashion his expression.

'I've seen no such thing. Is John Grainger in either of the movies?'

'Not to my knowledge.'

'Is his current wife, or other members of his family?'

'No.'

'There you are, then! Nothing!'

'Grainger was in the government then, as now, when wife number one was romping naked in front of a movie camera and performing explicit sex acts for the black market. The money she earned would have been going into the family budget, perhaps funding holidays and new cars.'

'How do you know that?'

'I don't *know* ...'

'What you're embarking on is muck-raking speculation, a tacky trawl, the traditional fodder and function of the tabloids.'

'Grainger is in the running to become the next prime minister.'

'All the more reason why we should tread with extra care.'

'Something like this, fairly or unfairly, could scupper his chances.'

'Therefore we have to behave responsibly.'

'What I'm hinting at is that he, more than anybody, would have reason to suppress this stuff by paying up.'

'If he has been paying for so long, why now turn to murder, increasing the odds of downfall and a far greater penalty?'

'Possibly because the blackmailer was upping the ante due to Grainger's higher profile.'

'If that's the case, how come you have the films and not him?

By what means did you get them? What I'm really asking is would they be admissible in court as evidence?'

'I can't answer any of those questions.'

'Can't or won't?'

'A little of each.'

'Then we have nothing further to discuss.'

In trying to salvage something from this, Templeman attempted a limited explanation. 'I can only assume that someone else got to the films before the killer.'

'Or perhaps it was the killer who made them available to you.'

'I know that not to be true.'

'But could you prove it?'

'We're getting sidetracked here,' Templeman protested.

'Then let's get back on track and forget this brainstorm.' Heaving himself from his chair, Lilleyman extracted one of the films from the video and picked up the other from his desk. 'I'll take care of these,' he announced dogmatically, locking them in his safe, without enquiring if they were copies or originals. Templeman suspected that that was another matter over which Lilleyman preferred to remain ignorant.

'Perhaps Grainger was part of it,' said Templeman, still trying to rescue something from this débâcle.

'Now you really *are* shooting at shit.'

'So it's no go?'

'How astute! What deduction! One day, if you continue to show this sort of insight, you may even make a fucking detective.'

Templeman never took no for an answer. He would always find a way of negating a negative, either by guile or downright defiance. And although Lilleyman was a buffoon, he was no fool. He reckoned on Templeman defying him. Templeman was a maverick and knew no other way. Saying 'no' or 'don't do it' to him was equivalent to waving the red flag at a Conservative. But Lilleyman had covered his own butt. If all went up in smoke, the ashes would be Templeman's. Lilleyman, just like President Richard Nixon before him, recorded all his conversations. If necessary, he would be able to prove that Templeman had disobeyed a direct, unequivocal order. Consequently, the commander felt considerably better already. He had a soothing and settling feeling in his ulcer that this investigation was on a roll, but he also knew only too well the pitfalls of premature optimism. However, he also knew Templeman.

A dog with a bone, the commander was thinking.

While the one-word thought of Templeman at that precise moment was *bonehead.*

Chapter Twenty-one

As a consequence of his impasse with Lilleyman, Templeman changed the running order. Instead of hitting Grainger next, he first targeted Jennifer Roper, who, just like Audrey Markham, was totally unprepared for his visit.

'I thought I'd seen the last of you,' she said, ungraciously. She wasn't wearing any make-up and she looked older than her age, the mileage high for her years. Although half the day had gone, she had the appearance of not having been out of bed long. Night birds found it difficult to change their habits, even when their wings had been clipped.

'You don't smoke, do you?' she asked rhetorically, plucking the last Marlborough from a packet and igniting it with an ornamental table-lighter. She tossed the spent empty packet towards a wastepaper basket, missing her target. 'Always have been a bad judge,' she said, full of world-weary meaning.

They sat opposite one another, she on the newish, grey leather settee, he on a matching armchair. She had the eyes of a pickpocket; eyes that could hold your attention while her hands went to work unchecked. As she appraised him nonchalantly, so her mind was scampering. Templeman had a good idea what was going on in her head.

Her exterior calm was a cold front hiding the mental cyclone of activity behind it.

'Well, Inspector, have you caught Harry's killer? Is that why you're here?'

'No catch so far – and *that's* why I'm here.'

She managed a whimsical *touché* smile.

'Some loose ends to tie, is that it?'

'New developments would be a more accurate description.'

'I'm intrigued.'

This interplay was like an overture, or perhaps more cannibal tribal rites, before settling down to eating one another.

'I'm here to talk dirty.' Templeman stoked up the tempo just at the right moment. Everything was in the timing. Rhythm-change had to be dramatic if it was going to jolt and disorientate.

Roper's face was a picture of incredulity, utter disbelief. Boxing correspondents would have described her as pole-axed. Her smoky eyes had cleared. A wariness had overcome her. She was now a cautious cat, afraid of becoming the mouse. She was on her guard for the trap.

'Isn't this rather unprofessional?' That was the best she could manage in the circumstances.

'On the contrary. Trading in pornography is dirty business. That's what I'm here to talk about. As I said, I'm here to talk dirty. *Really* dirty.'

Roper uncrossed her legs and recrossed them the opposite way. She shifted uneasily on the settee, inhaled on her cigarette exaggeratedly and held the smoke too long in her mouth, until she began choking.

'Excuse me,' she apologized for nothing. And then, as she recovered, 'I think you're going to have to be a little more explicit.'

'*Explicit!*' Templeman pounced. 'Out of every word in the dictionary, what an apposite choice! If I'm wrong, please say so, but aren't you the company secretary of EP Enterprises Limited?'

Roper didn't even blink. They studied one another like a pair of undertakers clinically measuring up the other.

'Technically, yes.'

'You either are or you're not.'

'It's just a nominal appointment.'

'Which still bestows upon you legal obligations.'

'Which I undertook. It amounted to next to nothing. Now, explain the reference to pornography, if you don't mind.'

'What was the company's trading portfolio?'

'It was nothing more than Harry's plaything.'

'That doesn't answer my question.'

Still she remained unfazed. 'Harry had this dream of making feature films, documentary-style, about Presley and his contemporaries, cashing in on nostalgia, which is never out of fashion. It was going to be a sort of hobby, unless it really took off, when he would gradually gravitate from live gigs to movie-production.'

'Films were made?'

'So I understand.'

'Are you implying you took no part in their making?'

'I'm not *implying* anything. It's a fact.'

'What is?'

'That I was just a name on a piece of paper.'

'Where were the films made?'

'Out and about.'

'You can do better than that.'

'Unfortunately, for you, I can't.'

'Were they shot in studios, hotels, on location, in homes?'

'I don't have that information.'

'Why not?'

'I've told you why not, I was just—'

'*A name on a piece of paper,*' he completed her excuse for her.

'Mock me all you like, but it's the truth.'

'Where did he get his technicians from?'

'Beats me.'

'You must have frequently discussed the business.'

'Hardly ever. Certainly not recently. We were through, remember?'

'Even if you weren't taking an active role, surely you were interested in how it was coming along and what it was doing – if anything?'

'My understanding was that it had become a dormant company, being kept on the shelf, so to speak, for a rainy day.'

'Even so, yearly accounts had to be prepared and submitted.'

'Harry saw to that.'

'What about quarterly VAT returns?'

'Anything to do with admin. was down to Harry.'

'Shouldn't that be the responsibility of the company secretary?'

She sighed tiredly. 'In a regular trading company, obviously, but, as I've explained *ad nauseam*, EP Enterprises was different.'

'You mean it's not legit?'

'I mean no such thing. Please stop treating me like a fool and trying to trip me up the whole time. I just made up the numbers for purposes of legality.'

'How often did you go to the office?'

'*Office*! What office?'

'The company HQ in Soho.'

'That's just the registered address, isn't it?'

'You tell me.'

'I never went there. It was nothing more than an address to go on business notepaper, for credibility.'

'So everything was just for show, a fake – the premises, your position with the company and its very nature – is that *really* the best you can do?'

'You can rubbish me all day and night, but that's the way it is – and always was.'

'How much were you paid for your services?'

'I never received a penny. I didn't give a service.'

'You never asked Harry, at any time, how the company was doing and what his plans were?'

'Not for a long time, no.'

'And *he* never broached the subject?'

'Not in any big deal way; never.'

'You're surprised, then, that your lover not only made porn movies but also *starred* in them?'

Roper's mask of inscrutability remained unpenetrated. 'I'm astounded. What proof have you of that?'

'Plenty.'

'You can always find people who get a kick out of booting the dead.'

'I'm relying on my own eyes, not secondhand say-so.'

Roper leaned forward to stub out her cigarette in a heart-shaped, glass ashtray on the coffee table. She stayed in that crouched, cat-like pounce position as she said, 'So you've been poring over porn, have you, Inspector?'

'During most of last night, yes.'

'Did it turn you on?' Roper tossed back her head, the momentum of which propelled her into the squelchy upholstery, as if being sucked into a swamp.

'It was repellent,' Templeman said starkly.

'The police make good puritans until it's party time and then they're in the front row, with binoculars, of the bawdy striptease show.'

'That might be your personal experience, but it's not mine.'

Roper contrived a sardonic smirk.

'Doesn't it shock you to learn of the depravity of a man you have loved and lived with?'

'I haven't *learned* anything. I've heard a character-assassination, but you haven't shown me a thing to substantiate it. One man's obscenity can be another's religion. Are you really intent on desecrating the dead? I thought Harry was the victim. Now, just because you can't catch his killer, you make him the villain. You move the goalposts and change the rules. You even change the game. Typical cop ruse!'

Templeman had no intention of being deflected.

'You're sure the porno production business wasn't all your idea?'

'Piss off!'

'After all, the sex trade wouldn't have been anything new to you.'

'Smears come from people lacking substance.'

'Nice try, but you have lied to me.'

Roper searched for a fresh Marlborough packet, tore it open as if it was a bag of potato crisps, and shook out a cigarette, which she lit as tentatively as putting a flame to a fuse running to a gunpowder-keg.

'I assume you're going to elaborate on that.'

'The timetable of your affair with Harry Markham, as summarized by you, just doesn't stack up.'

Roper kept the cigarette between her lips longer than necessary, as if it was there for comfort, the way a baby works its mouth on a dummy.

'I was talking to you in good faith, from memory. I wasn't referring to a diary. I can't be precise about times and places when we made love over the years. I wasn't preparing to write a kiss-and-tell autobiography. I don't have a bookkeeper's mentality, another reason why I was a company secretary in name only.'

'You were not acting in good faith,' Templeman confronted her levelly and firmly.

Roper blew smoke in Templeman's face. 'Tell me about it.' Her street-fighter instincts surfaced in an ugliness that had physical expression and aggression.

'There have only ever been three directors of EP Enterprises Limited – Mr Markham, his wife and you.'

'So?'

'You have been a director since the day it was launched.'

'So?' she repeated herself, her eyes widening into satellite dishes, antennae twitching, searching for signals.

'Therefore, you must have known Mr Markham far longer than you made out when chronicling the history of your relationship with him.'

'So I truncated it into a précis.'

'By quite a few years. It wasn't a synopsis; it was a distortion: it was meant to mislead.'

'The way we met and how it developed and ended are a *faithful* record of the truth. Is that *all* this is about? Because you got only the expurgated version you feel cheated, is that it? You missed out on a cheap thrill, is that it?'

'Smokescreens won't help you,' warned Templeman, as Roper again exhaled heavily in his face.

'If there's one person in this room who needs help, it's not me.'

'Where were you on the night Mr Markham was shot dead?'

'I've told you that already – getting laid.'

'That's something we still have to corroborate.'

'What's been keeping you – too many private porn shows?'

'Do you have a handgun?'

'Up yours!'

'That's a no, I take it?'

'Grief, you're intuitive!'

'Mind if I look around?'

'At your leisure.'

Roper's spontaneous acquiescence gave Templeman little enthusiasm for a search that he sensed would be fruitless. Instead, he asked, 'Have you ever fired a gun?'

Roper began coughing on her derisive laugh. 'For God's sake!'

'Is that yes or no?'

'Of course it's no. What planet are you from? At most, I shoot verbal bullets. They damage without backfiring. Get me?'

'Got you.'

Roper sniggered 'You wish!'

'Once a whore, always a whore.'

'Now I *really* know you've lost the plot.'

Well played! thought Templeman, his secret admiration for her sincere but disguised. She had held her ground grittily and retained her dignity, scoring well with return of serve.

'Tie-break,' he mouthed under his breath as he rose to leave.

Chapter Twenty-two

Templeman didn't think twice about playing Russian roulette with his career.

One of John Grainger's political acolytes took the call. No, Mr Grainger wasn't in his office. Yes, he was around the Palace of Westminster, but where precisely was a mystery. Yes, he could be paged, but only in an emergency.

'This is urgent,' Templeman assured the factotum.

'That isn't necessarily the same as an *emergency*.'

Trust a politician to split hairs. 'I suggest if you value your job you'll get a message to your boss saying Detective Inspector Templeman called to say he will see him in the Central Lobby of the House of Commons at five p.m.,' he said arbitrarily.

'About what, Inspector?'

'About the past,' Templeman answered cryptically, before bailing out abruptly.

Templeman was gambling on Grainger's curiosity compelling him to turn up at 5 p.m., however much this would torpedo the Cabinet minister's schedule. His faith in his own insight into human psychology wasn't misplaced. Grainger was there ahead of him, looking at his wristwatch every few seconds, pacing, agitated, frustrated, fuming and yet seemingly powerless to free himself from the leash in Templeman's hands.

As soon as he saw Templeman, Grainger headed for him like a hunt-down and destroy missile.

'God, man, you've some explaining to do!' Grainger hissed, suppressed rage contorting his face.

'I don't recommend we talk where we can possibly be over-heard,' Templeman said evenly.

'I suggest we don't talk anywhere.'

'If I leave here without talking with you, I can't guarantee the outcome of these,' Templeman said slowly, patting his briefcase.

'Now what the hell are you prattling on about?'

'The films I have here. Commander Lilleyman has copies. I retain the originals.'

'*What films?*' Grainger demanded through bared teeth, his jaw as tight as a clenched fist.

'I really don't think you want this conversation here.'

'I thought it was plain enough I don't want a conversation with you *anywhere.*'

Central Lobby in the House of Commons, at peak periods, can resemble a railway station booking-hall.

'Very well,' said Templeman undeterred, 'I have films in which your first wife featured.'

Grainger blanched, like red wine being turned at a stir into white by some mysterious form of alchemy.

'So what? They are matters of public record, stored in cinematic archives and probably available to be hired in video rental shops. They may even appear on TV during the oldie re-runs season.'

'Not *these*. Not on mainstream TV. Maybe on the adult video channels in some hotels. Maybe in smutty cellar clubs of Soho.'

Their eyes locked in mutual understanding, without bonding. With one prick, Grainger had been popped; all the stuffing siphoned from him.

'Let's go to the Terrace.' This was said now almost as a plea, rather than an order.

Templeman acquiesced without comment. Grainger led the way, sagging mentally as well as physically.

They went down silent staircases of this Gothic fortress, insulated by history and age, followed by the sightless eyes of great statesmen, kings and queens, who had gone to the grave long ago but lived on in oil and canvas, framed in a manner commensurate with their social standing. On the lower floor, they passed the corridor to the Churchill dining-room, as stolid and traditional as its eponymous icon. The entrance to the Terrace at the foot of the staircase was guarded by a uniformed custodian sitting lugubriously at a desk.

The wind, sweeping up-river from the east, smacked them icily in the face the moment Grainger opened the door, but he wasn't put off. He threaded his way through the empty wooden tables to the far wall. Not surprisingly, in view of the weather, they had the Terrace to themselves. When Grainger stopped, he continued to face the river, which bubbled like a cauldron beneath him the other side of the grey-stone wall, the chop of the waves created by the relentless easterly. He kept his hands in his trouser pockets and wouldn't face Templeman, who gave up trying to brush his hair from his eyes.

'How did you get them?' Grainger asked bleakly, staring at a distant horizon, like an old sea captain looking nostalgically into his past from the shoreline.

'The films?'

'Yes, the films.'

'That's not important.'

'It could be to me.'

'Were you being blackmailed?' Templeman said, going his way, not Grainger's.

Grainger continued to peer eastwards down the Thames towards Westminster Bridge and Waterloo Bridge beyond in his mind's eye. Was this *his* Waterloo? Templeman wondered. There was no way of immediately telling, not while Grainger's eyes were hidden from him.

'*Blackmailed*,' Grainger repeated vacantly, as if in reverie.

'Yes, blackmail, Mr Grainger.'

The politician took his time, as would anyone at such a major crossroad. One step the wrong way and his career could be blown away in an instant.

Templeman shivered, but Grainger didn't feel the cold. He didn't even feel fear, which should have alarmed him more than anything.

'My lawyer ought to be hearing this.'

Templeman's question was answered.

'How long had you been paying Harry Markham?'

Grainger was only half-listening; perhaps by now only half-caring.

'I had nothing to do with his death, you know.'

Templeman hadn't been expecting a murder confession, so he wasn't the least distracted.

'Let's first deal with the blackmail.'

'How much of this is off the record and confidential?'

'If you are worried about something you say to me being leaked to the press, I give you my word it will not happen. However, this isn't a social call.'

Grainger understood the drill.

'Perhaps some background would help.'

Grainger was no longer in a hurry. He was anchored in depression, overwhelmed by a sense that he might now have gone as far as he was ever going. Suddenly he felt betrayed by the ambition that had seduced him. Fate, like a hooded bandit, had mugged him from the shadows, when least expected. Nevertheless, fool's paradise had given him much pleasure and considerable power, albeit perhaps ephemeral.

'In your own time,' Templeman invited.

'When we fostered Harry, he came to us with a history of sexual abuse.'

'So I gather.'

'It soon became apparent that his mother may not have been wholly to blame.'

'Meaning?'

'I can only describe his behaviour as sly, subversive and sexually predatory.'

'You didn't mention this before.'

Grainger didn't reply immediately.

'It would have needed elaborating upon. I hoped that wouldn't ever be necessary.' He paused awhile, gathering himself together before continuing, 'As you know, my wife, my first wife, was a very attractive woman. It was obvious to me after only a few days that Harry was looking at Chantel through the eyes of an admirer, rather than as a child to his guardian.'

'He was already in adolescence by then, surely?'

'Even so, there was something dark and sinister about him. He was very *knowing* for his age.'

Grainger again disappeared into himself and Templeman allowed him to stay there until ready to resurface.

'My wife had been unfaithful to me. Not just once, but several times. I didn't know for certain at the time, though I had my suspicions. They were just flings, blazes of passion that soon burned themselves out, like scrub fires do.'

Templeman noted the emphasis on the word *scrub*.

'You said, without equivocation, that your first wife had been unfaithful. How did that become confirmed?'

'Does it matter?'

'Obviously it did to you. It was you who introduced the subject.'

'True, very true,' Grainger agreed absently. 'I've no intention of going into too much detail over that. Suffice it to say, we had a rather uncompromising argument one night. It's on occasions like that when secrets are unleashed, fired like missiles with the intent of hurting the other. Such weapons invariably boomerang. Of course I was hurt, but in the long-term she was the more damaged, all of it self-inflicted. Anyhow, as a consequence, the physical side of our marriage went into chronic decline. Our children kept us together. I suppose Chantel's desire to foster was her way of handling her remorse, a sort of cleansing process, making amends.'

'It wasn't your idea?'

'I was busy enough. Chantel was the one with time on her hands.'

Grainger had turned to face Templeman, who read a coded message in the politician's lifeless eyes.

'Most nights in the week I wouldn't be home before midnight. There were also countless foreign trips on parliamentary business. It was only at weekends that I was truly at home.'

'What is the point you're making, Mr Grainger?'

'That Chantel had plenty of licence, lots of rope.'

'How trusting were you?'

'For a long time, very.'

'Did *you* cheat on *her*?'

'Is that pertinent?'

'Probably not.'

'For the record, I had a couple of mini-affairs with young researchers.'

'How *young*?'

'Not under-age, if that's what you're getting at. They were both in their twenties.'

'Did your wife find out?'

'Not from me.'

'From anyone else?'

'If she did, she never said so. It was Charlotte who first alerted me to Harry and ...' Grainger's sentence trickled away, picked up by the damp wind and carried off upstream. He began again, choosing his words as if plucking apples from a tree, being picky. 'We were talking one weekend. In the garden. Mid-summer. A Sunday. Early evening. The air still and perfumed. The sun sinking. Henry was spending the weekend away at a school friend's home. Chantel and Harry were indoors, watching some TV. Charlotte had left school and was preparing to go to university in the September. It must have been mid-August. We were just sauntering. I can remember it as if it happened only yesterday.' The wistfulness of his voice was reflected in his eyes. 'Harry had been to a party on the Saturday night. As we chatted, I asked why she hadn't gone as well, especially as the girl throwing the party was more her friend than Harry's.'

'What was her explanation?'

'Wasn't in the mood, but her eyes told me there was something more.'

'Did you find out what it was?'

'I probed gently.'

'And?'

'Harry had been making advances. She tried to make light of it, but it was obvious that it was bothering her.'

'Why should it have *bothered* her?'

'She looked on him as a brother; I told you that, I believe, when you were here before. It seemed like he wouldn't take no for an answer. Because of that, she was pleased she'd soon be leaving home for university; that troubled me. She also remarked that she didn't think her mother knew how to "handle" Harry. I was puzzled by that and asked what she meant.'

'What *did* she mean?'

'She was embarrassed. All she'd say was, "Be observant, Daddy. Grow up! Get switched on. Pick up the vibes. Get street-wise". It was like listening to a foreign language for me.'

'Was that the end of it?'

Grainger once more turned away from Templeman, turning from himself, as if trying to draw a line under his past, having brainwashed himself that at a point in middle-age he had been reborn and his previous life had been jettisoned, like a deciduous reptile shedding its skin, changing colour and character.

'We strolled back indoors in silence. I went to the lounge to fix myself a drink, a gin and tonic. The TV was still on, but neither Chantel nor Harry was in the room. Charlotte said she was going upstairs. I switched off the TV and prepared to read some more of the *Sunday Telegraph*. Next thing, I heard Charlotte running down the staircase, followed by Harry. The front door slammed and a few seconds later I saw them from a French window arguing in the middle of the lawn.'

'Could you hear anything of what was being said?'

'No.'

'How do you know, then, that they were arguing?'

'Body-language. Charlotte had her hands on her hips and she was leaning forward goose-necked, as if pecking. Harry was red-faced and shaking his head furiously, obviously denying something. In view of what Charlotte had just told me, about her reasons for not going to the party, I followed them outside. I wanted to know what was going on. When Harry saw me approaching, he scurried off.'

'Back to the house?'

'No, out of the grounds, into the road.'

'Did you discover what they were squabbling about?'

'Charlotte was still very upset. Her eyes were full of tears, but she wasn't crying. "If you really want to know, ask Mummy", she said, then ran off indoors. She locked herself in her room for the rest of the night.'

'Did you tackle your wife about it?'

'I did indeed. She shrugged it off as a "storm in a teacup", an irrational outburst of jealousy because she had shown Harry attention at Charlotte's expense. It was a clever reply. My wife had told a lie by telling the truth. In years to come, I was to spot many truth-lies in Parliament. I count that experience with my first wife as part of a very sharp learning-curve. I thought no more of it until one morning a couple of days later, when I was passing Henry's den. It was during the parliamentary recess, so I didn't have to be at Westminster. The door hadn't been closed properly and voices were raised.'

'*Voices*?'

'The first voice I heard was that of Charlotte. She was talking to Henry and I stopped.'

'To eavesdrop?'

Grainger continued to talk to the south bank of the river, so Templeman couldn't tell if he was blushing.

'As I said, the voices were raised and I couldn't avoid hearing what they were saying. Charlotte was in a trembling rage, her voice tremulous too. "Our mother's been messing with a kid, a kid we're meant to treat as a brother, as one of the family, and while Daddy and I were at home, out in the garden." I knew it was wrong to continue listening, but I couldn't help myself.'

'I'm sure I'd have behaved likewise. Did you hear more?'

'I'm afraid so. My wife had been leaving Harry's bedroom. Apparently, from what Charlotte was saying to Henry, Chantel was buttoning up her blouse and was flushed and flurried when they almost collided. Charlotte pushed past into Henry's bedroom.' Grainger ground to an emotional halt.

'And?' Templeman prodded him.

'Harry was zipping up his trousers.'

'Suggestive but far from conclusive.'

'Come on, Inspector!' said Grainger, spinning round on his heels.

'After overhearing that conversation, what did you do?'

'I was horrified.'

'That's how you felt, but what did you *do*?'

'Before doing anything, I poured myself a large drink and did some serious thinking. You, as a detective, know all about behaviour patterns and laws of probability, as opposed to those of possibility. Remember that I was aware of the reasons for Harry having been taken into care. I knew what had occurred between him and his biological mother. This was consistent with his track-record.'

'And was it consistent with your wife's track-record?'

'I've told you about our troubles.'

'Did your children know the full story of Harry's background?'

'Not the part to which you're alluding.'

'So Charlotte wasn't jumping to conclusions, making it fit preconceptions?'

'That's my point. So, fortified, I confronted Chantel.'

'Direct, without any preamble, without preparation?'

'I tried a few detours, skirting around the edges. She put on one of those outraged looks, saying something like, "What on earth are you suggesting, John? Not what I think, I hope". She played the wounded wife. She was a good actress, a wasted talent. However, the more she acted, the less convincing she became. She denied everything, of course. That's when I demanded Harry go.'

'Did she agree to that?'

'No. She accused me of being unfair. Said that further rejection would merely exacerbate his psychological problems and that I should make more allowances. It didn't wash with me.'

'Did you say that?'

'I did.'

'Was anything resolved?'

'She wept. When all else failed, she would always cry. I spoke with Harry the next day. I told him I wanted him to leave.'

'How did he take that?'

'He smirked and asked if that was also Chantel's wish.'

'What did you say to that?'

Like a chess player pondering his next move, Grainger focused on his position. Quickly he accepted that he was in too deep to retreat. Onwards was the only route open to him.

'I hit him.'

'Hard?'

'Hard enough. I slapped his face. Cut his lip. I lost control. It was his smirk that made me snap.'

'I can understand that, without condoning it. How did he take it?'

'Too well. His smirk became even broader. The fact that I had fallen for his provocation gave him satisfaction. He was winning, you see. He was manipulating me, everyone. That's what he was, a manipulator. I was angry with myself. I should have shown greater control.'

Templeman was beginning to see how Markham had developed his power-base, quite possibly involuntarily at the outset.

'From that day, he had a hold over you?'

'In the abstract, yes. He didn't push it. However, it was always there, like one's own shadow.'

'Is that when the blackmail began?'

'He never actually said, "If you don't give me this or that, I'll report you to the authorities and you can kiss goodbye to any political promotion". Everything was negotiated, by expression and attitude, in the manner of transferring an idea. Although quite subtle for someone his age, it was more the offspring of native cunning than of malice aforethought.'

'How did it manifest?'

'Oh, he'd say he needed something, or he wanted to go somewhere.'

'And you'd give in?'

Grainger sighed and relinquished a little more dignity. 'I could afford it, but it was the principle that rankled with me. It also caused resentment with Henry and Charlotte. I was saying no to them and yes to Harry, our fostered boy. They found the injustice and double-standard hard to deal with and rightly so.'

Templeman had no difficulty seeing how Markham had metamorphosed into a fully fledged and fluent blackmailer. He'd simply grown streetwise. The rest was freefall.

'When we talked first time, you told me that Harry had just taken off, basically: was that the truth?'

'More or less.'

'I detect an element of political fudging there,' said Templeman, wryly.

Grainger mustered a facsimile of a smile. 'We had our continuing difficulties. His stay with us had run its full course.'

'How long was it after that initial confrontation with your wife over Harry that he uprooted?'

Grainger's eyeballs rolled as he characterized concentration. 'It's many, many years ago.'

'Not *that* many.'

'In politics, a week is a lifetime.'

'We're talking about your family-life, Mr Grainger, not your job.'

'Just a matter of weeks, I think; maybe a few months. It brought things to a head.'

'Tell me about your relationship with your wife from that time.'

'Strained.'

'Did you fight?'

'Emotion provokes fights. That had gone.'

'When did your first wife die?'

'Several years afterwards.'

'After *what*?'

'What we're talking about.'

'I'm not familiar with the cause of her death. Help me out, please.'

Grainger first helped himself to a succession of deep breaths, then, 'She committed suicide.'

'How?'

'Is this really necessary, Inspector?' Grainger railed.

'Probably not. It's up to you.'

Grainger made a what-the-hell gesture, then, 'She jumped in front of a tube train.'

'Where?'

'Waterloo. She was supposedly coming up to town for a day's shopping in the West End.'

'And?'

'As I said, she stepped off the underground platform when the train emerged from the tunnel. The driver didn't have a chance;

that's what he told the inquest. He had only just started to brake when she flung herself in front of the train.'

'What time of day was that?'

'About nine in the morning. The platform was crammed with commuters.'

'Couldn't it have been an accident? Couldn't she have lost her balance? It's happened many times before. There's always a forward surge, like an incoming wave, as a train can be heard approaching.' Templeman refrained from articulating another possibility: *How do you know she wasn't pushed?*

'The driver had an unimpeded view. He was adamant that she dived. There were also a couple of witnesses on the platform. They saw her watching very intently for the train and she seemed agitated. She was standing very near the edge, beyond the painted warning line. The witnesses saw a man, who was directly behind Chantel, try to grab her, to claw her back, but she was gone. Forever.'

'Is that what *he* said, too?'

'He was never interviewed.'

'Why not?'

'He disappeared, like most of the people on that platform. A man in a hurry. The Northern Line was closed for several hours. Nothing he – nor anyone else, for that matter – could do for Chantel. The living got on with living; getting to work, making money and cursing yet another unscheduled hiccup on the capital's shambolic transport system.'

'Did your wife leave a suicide note?'

'Yes, she did. If she hadn't, I think the inquest jury would have returned an open verdict.'

'What did it say, the note?'

Grainger dropped his head. Being blessed with a reliable memory could be a painful asset.

'She'd had enough. She couldn't take any more. She wanted out. She hadn't anything left to live for. This was goodbye and good riddance.'

'Just a few lines?'

'Yes, just a few lines.'

Sleepwalker eyes had Grainger down a memory-lane studded with nails.

'Handwritten?'

'Handwritten, yes.'

'Verified as hers?'

'Scientifically, yes.'

'Dated?'

Grainger dithered. 'Not that I'm aware of.'

'Who found the note?'

'I did. That night, when I got home.'

'Where?'

'On my pillow.'

'When did you hand it to the police?'

'Then. An officer was with me. The police said it was important to search for a suicide note.'

'And you came across it quickly?'

'Within five or ten minutes of returning.'

'Where were you when your wife was hit by that Tube train?'

'I was around the House of Commons '

'MPs don't usually get there that early, do they?'

'I was preparing for a ten o'clock junior ministers' briefing. I'd stayed in town overnight.'

'Where? With whom?'

'What makes you think I stayed with someone?'

'I didn't. It was just a question. Now I think you probably did.'

'Even if I did, it's of no consequence. Let's not dwell on that, please.'

'Your wife's death must have been reported in the newspapers, yet I've no recollection of reading about it.'

'Her name wasn't released to the media for several days. By then, the actual incident was stale news. The inquest was covered by all the national newspapers, making a page lead in most of them, but it was all over in a day. I had many requests for interviews around that time, but I declined them all. I appealed to be allowed to grieve in peace and that wish was respected.'

'It must have been a particularly difficult time for your children?'

'For all of us, yes.'

'Did you notify Harry?'

'I had no idea where he was living. In any case, it had nothing to do with him. He was out of the family loop.'

'Did you blame him for your wife's death?'

'Partially. But he was only a boy … you know … when things happened that shouldn't. Chantel should have known better. She must have consented … or led … or whatever.…'

'So Harry didn't know about your wife's death?'

'I didn't say that. I said that *I* didn't contact *him*. A small piece appeared in the papers when she was named and before the inquest, which prompted the larger coverage. He read that and rang me. He wanted to come to the funeral. I advised him to stay away, that he wouldn't be welcome.'

'Did he comply?'

'Yes. But he sent flowers and a card.'

'What did he write on the card?'

Grainger bit his lip, then bit the bullet.

'Something about in loving remembrance of a very special relationship. The words *very special* were underscored.'

'That must have cut deep?'

'It certainly made me very angry … and sick.'

'Did your children see it?'

'They did. They were livid, of course. As discreetly as possible, I disconnected the card from the flowers, slipped it in my pocket and disposed of it later.'

'But that wasn't the end of Harry Markham in your life, was it, Mr Grainger?'

Grainger took a few steps along the Terrace, as if trying to walk away from his past and the baggage he had been carrying for so long. He shuddered more from the cool gusts of grief than the freshening wind.

'Unfortunately, it was not.'

'When did you next hear from him?'

Grainger worked his mouth and jaw as he contrived rumination.

'Not for several years. Then he called me out of the blue at the Commons and left a message with my Private Office.'

'Saying what?'

'Just that he wanted me to call him back.'

'Did you?'

'Of course not. I ignored him; forgot all about it – and him.'

'But he didn't go away?'

'No, he called a few more times and we went through repeat procedures. He would leave another message and I would disregard it.'

'But still he didn't give up?'

'He wrote to me, saying that the small film production company he ran was experiencing cash-flow difficulties and he wanted me to help him out. He stressed that it would be an investment and any injection of cash would be treated professionally.'

'He was offering to pay interest on any loan?'

'That was implied, though not directly stated. I binned the letter.'

'Was that letter sent to you at home or to your House of Commons office?'

'The House of Commons.'

'So it was opened and read by your secretary?'

'Correct. A fortnight later came the follow-up. He said he was sorry I hadn't seen fit to reply. His financial situation was becoming critical and he could see no other option but for him to sell his story to one of the mass circulation Sunday newspapers. He wrote something to the effect that he was sorry that he would be sullying Chantel's name and hoped none of the fall-out would damage me. It was a clear overture to blackmail, without actually committing himself to a crime. At the time, I didn't appreciate just how devilishly devious he was at such an orchestration.

'This time I did reply. I wrote a personal handwritten letter, expressing my regret at the contents of his note to me and warned him about the law of defamation. I had to be very careful. I had to avoid putting in writing anything that might suggest I had anything to hide or that I could have been privy to what – if anything – had occurred between Chantel and Harry. It would have been all too easy to incriminate myself innocently and inadvertently.'

'You didn't consider involving your solicitor?'

'I did *consider* it, yes; but dismissed the idea. I didn't want Harry to feel he was unnerving me. It was also my hope to keep the matter private. I could envisage how the gutter Press would treat it: poor boy seduced by rich MP's wife. They might even chance insinuating that I turned a blind eye to my wife having a toyboy on the side, a youth we had fostered and were obliged to provide with pastoral support and moral leadership. With my wife dead, there would be no way of defending any allegations against her. A few days later, I received a package at home through the post. It was a video, with a brief note from Harry, advising me to view.'

'Did you play it?'

'I'm human, so I couldn't resist.'

Grainger blanched, so much of his life and self-esteem haemorrhaging from him.

'I'm sure I don't have to tell you what I found myself watching.'

'How did he follow up?'

'With a phone message left on my answer-machine. He said I should meet him at the St Stephen's entrance to the Commons at noon on such and such a date and that I could have the pleasure of treating him to lunch in the Churchill dining-room.'

'Did you follow his instructions?'

'I did, to my lasting shame and folly.'

'It must have been an awkward lunch?'

'*Awkward*! It was awful. He wasted little time coming to the point.'

'Which was?'

'He needed an immediate infusion of ten thousand pounds to keep his company afloat. He insisted that this wasn't blackmail. He probably suspected I was tape-recording the conversation.'

'Were you?'

'No. Tapes can be double-edged swords. They record both sides of a conversation. Careless remarks can return to haunt even the victim. That was something I'd learned from an investigative journalist.'

'So you acquiesced?'

'I did. I wrote him a cheque there and then. I told him it was a one-off payment and I didn't want it paid back. Neither did I want any interest on it. I wanted him out of my life forever.'

'Not a chance after you'd coughed up.'

'It's easy to delude oneself, especially when you're hoping for a peaceful solution to a situation that threatens everything you've worked a lifetime for.'

'But it wasn't to be?'

'He was quiet for maybe a couple of months, then he was back again, making the point that no one would believe that I hadn't known about Chantel taking part in the movies with him. He even hinted that the police would become suspicious about Chantel's death and might start thinking it could have been foul play.'

Templeman refrained from mentioning that such a scenario had indeed crossed his own mind.

Instead, he said, 'From that moment, you were on the treadmill?'

'Hooked.'

'Did you make regular payments from then on?'

'No. I would wait for him to ask – to *demand*. The further I climbed the career-ladder, so the more secure was his black economy.'

'And you never contemplated turning off the tap?'

'Of course I *contemplated* it, but the nearer I came to the top, the less I fancied gambling with my future.'

'Harry Markham's death must have come as an immense relief to you?'

Grainger knew that denial would ring hollow. Conversely, ready acceptance of the proposition would be self-implicating. So he trod with the care of a man circumnavigating quicksand.

'I didn't shed tears, I'll go no further than that.'

'Over how many years were you paying him?'

'Several. I'd rather not count. I try not to think about it.'

'Does your current wife know about it?'

'No. Nothing. She'd be horrified. That was another reason why I paid up.'

'How much, in all, did he extract from you?'

'I never calculated. To have done so would have depressed me too much.'

'Two million?'

'That sounds an awful lot.'

'Could it have been that much?'

'I am not without such financial resources.'

'Even so, it must have made a big hole in your capital.'

'Over a period of time it wouldn't have been so noticeable.'

'How did you explain it away to your accountant?'

'The payments weren't regular nor for the same amount.'

'They still had to be accounted for.'

'Indeed, and they were. I always paid by cheque. The cheques were made payable to Harry's company. So I told my accountant the payments were investments.'

'You realize that you most certainly had more motive for murdering than anyone else?'

'Except for the killer,' Grainger said quickly. 'I was nowhere near Soho on the night Harry came face-to-face with his fate.'

'I accept that. I've never doubted that your alibi would be watertight.'

'You're hinting that you suspect I might have … what is the

term? ... paid someone to do it for me.'

'The term is a contract killer.'

'Where would I find such a person? I don't exactly mix in those kind of social circles. What's more, I'd be exposing myself to even greater blackmail potential.'

'You have logic on your side.'

Grainger wore the smile of a sky-diver whose parachute had opened at the last possible moment.

'What now, Inspector?'

'I continue.'

'Not with me, I trust?'

'I shall go whichever way the wind is blowing.'

Chapter Twenty-three

Next morning
It had been another night of sleep-deprivation for Templeman. Thoughts about the case had taken over his head, like illegal squatters, but there had been other intrusions, some welcome and others as unwanted as trespassers.

Simone was in and out of his head the entire night, even during the few hours of restless sleep. She was always a welcome visitor, day or night, even if she incited his insomnia. Conversely, Charley was an intruder with a distinctly disturbing influence.

Charley had spent another night away from home, without making contact or even leaving a message. Any day now, Templeman would be informed by text, on his mobile, that he was being divorced, he mused. Did he care? Not any more. After all, he was being seriously unfaithful and was planning for a future without Charley. It mattered not a jot now who had been first to stray; that was purely academic. They had both consummated their infidelity and Templeman was not one for seeking refuge in double standards. The acrimony wasn't over Charley abandoning his bed, but her refusal to vacate his head. Too often, when he wished only to think of Harry Markham or Simone Tandy, Charley would pop into his thoughts, just like a nuisance neighbour who kept calling to borrow something and then stayed to chat endlessly. Lilleyman, however, was the worst gatecrasher of them all. He would barge in throughout the night, his face always contorted in rage and his voice vinegary and dripping with derision.

Reverie dictated his driving to such an extent that he almost missed the Bedford turn-off on the M1. Twenty minutes later, he was at the hospital, where he was kept waiting for a similar length of time outside Simone's ward. Finally, Dr Everson appeared.

Templeman wondered whether her smile had moved since the last time he talked with her in person.

'I was anxious for us to have a few words before you saw Simone.' The change of tone in the doctor's voice would have been indiscernible even to anyone less perceptive.

'Why? Is there something wrong?' An aura of foreboding gathered around Templeman like a cyclone suddenly blowing up on the horizon, eclipsing the sun.

'Nothing to worry about.' Doctor Everson fiddled with the stethoscope hanging from her neck. 'It's just that ...'

'Yes?'

'Don't expect too much. Her memory will be hazy for a while yet. Whatever she says, just accept it. We don't want her confused or put under pressure.' Her look was beseeching.

'All I want is to see for myself that she's come through it.'

'I'm sure you mean that, but it can be difficult; that's why I'm preparing you. She is heavily bandaged around the head and she's still being drip-fed.'

'Will she be able to see me?'

'Oh, yes. The bandage doesn't cover her eyes, as before her operation.'

'Is she awake?'

'On and off. We're keeping the curtains drawn around her bed so that she's in her own little oasis. I hope you don't mind, but I'll stay with you at the bedside.'

The ward was sectioned into eight bays, Simone's bed was near the window in the first bay on the right, just inside the doors to the ward.

Doctor Everson parted the curtains around the bed just enough for them to squeeze through, as if they were entering a Bedouin tent.

Templeman hadn't known what to expect, but the sight of Simone swathed in bandages from the neck upwards and all the spaghetti network of tubes and machinery took away his breath. Some tubes were delivering life-sustaining fluids. Others were siphoning-off life-threatening toxins. The machines, silently macabre, measured everything from blood-pressure and heart-rhythm to brain-activity.

'Is she asleep?' Templeman whispered, as if he'd just tiptoed into a church during matins.

'I don't think so.' The answer came from a nurse, who quickly lifted herself from her bedside chair, smiling sympathetically as she brushed past Templeman and temporarily away from her sentinel post.

'You have a visitor,' the doctor announced silkily, bending over the bed.

Templeman could just make out Simone's lips mouthing soundlessly, 'A visitor? For me?'

'It's me, darling,' said Templeman, stepping forward eagerly, towering above Dr Everson. He was close enough to see the mist of bemusement in Simone's eyes; the vacant possession.

'Who are you?' This time there was enough sound to make lip-reading unnecessary.

'I'm Luke, darling.' Templeman felt stupid. He guessed that he must have *looked* stupid. His smile was artificial because he had nothing to smile about, but faking cheerfulness always seemed obligatory to hospital visitors. As he stooped to touch her limp hand, the fog in her eyes cleared, to be replaced by the clarity of fear. Both doctor and detective had witnessed such starkly defined terror many times before. Simone was running and recoiling, not physically because she could barely move, but inside she was fleeing from the unknown. Templeman was the unknown and because of his experience he knew immediately why the mental skids were under Simone.

'It's all right, don't get alarmed, there's nothing to be frightened about,' Dr Everson soothed, stepping between them, shielding Simone from her demon, simultaneously computing all the data from the high-tech equipment: blood-pressure soaring, pulse racing and brain-activity frenetic.

The doctor's glance over her shoulder at Templeman couldn't have been more telepathic. Politely but firmly, she said, 'I think you'd better step outside a moment.'

Crestfallen, Templeman did as entreated, fully aware that the full translation went something like, *Just get the hell out of her sight. Can't you see that, at a stroke, you're screwing up all our great work?*

As the nurse returned to Simone, so she shot Templeman a reproving look, making sure the curtains were drawn tightly behind her.

Templeman leaned on a window-sill, looking out forlornly towards the river meandering in the distance as it made its circuitous way out of town, a towpath on the far side and industrial sites monopolizing the foreground. A church spire and a few high-rise office blocks broke an otherwise low and repetitive brick-and-mortar skyline. The dominant colour was grey, the complexion of death and decay. The bathos of this moment wasn't lost on him. This was all wrong. He had come to celebrate with Simone, not to put a curse on her. A couple of rogue tears exposed his stoicism as fraudulent.

Ten minutes – a lifetime for Templeman – elapsed before Dr Everson joined him at the window.

'This was always a possibility,' she said, totally non-judgemental.

'Did you see her eyes?' he said, continuing to stare blankly into infinity.

'She was scared.'

'Yes, of me.'

'No, of herself.'

'She didn't recognize me. I was a stranger to her.'

'And that's what frightened her. Try putting yourself in her position. She spooked herself. You called her "darling" and, therefore, she knew the two of you must be close, but her memory was failing her. The chances are that everything will fall into place – in time, in trickles, and with patience.'

'I was shocked,' he explained regretfully.

'Of course you were. Now what I want you to do is go back in there.'

Disbelief filled his face. 'But ...'

'I've calmed and sedated her. Try to be relaxed about it. No pressure.'

'What the hell do I say?'

'How about: "Hello, I'm Luke, I do like your hairdo!" '

Templeman stayed with Simone for about twenty minutes. He did most of the talking, assiduously avoiding anything that encroached remotely on their personal relationship. In return, she made references to her earlier life, indicating little erasure to her distant memory.

'I'll see you sometime tomorrow,' he vowed, following Dr Everson's unspoken cue that advised, *That's enough, time's up*.

While walking him to the exit, the doctor said, 'It seems like everything's saved in memory until the very last few years. She remembers being a teacher and then joining the police force.'

'It's just me she's forgotten,' Templeman said plaintively.

'Feeling sorry for yourself?'

'No, feeling sorry for Simone.'

'Right answer.'

'How long will it take?'

'For everything to return?'

'Yes.'

'Maybe forever. Maybe by tomorrow. It's another lousy lottery. A single word or one mental picture could trigger the breakthrough, bringing back the forgotten in a flood.'

Templeman made good time on his return drive and was at his desk by noon. Three of the forest of yellow paper notes planted on the screen of his computer related to Lilleyman's demands for a 'chat', which Templeman translated into 'confrontation'.

Lilleyman's health had improved considerably in the few hours since his last clash with Templeman, though this could not be taken as an indication of an improved disposition.

'What's the latest on Tandy?' the commander began, more affably than Templeman could ever remember.

'Progressing, but slowly,' Templeman answered warily, not believing for a moment that Lilleyman was making a genuine enquiry about Simone's health. It could only be a stepping-stone towards his real objective.

'Such a shame. She was showing such promise.'

Lilleyman was already writing her off; that was the real drift.

'I won't keep you long,' Lilleyman continued congenially. 'Sit down, man, you're making the place untidy. That's better. Now, I note you've disobeyed me yet again.' Instead of playing king from his sumptuous throne behind the elaborate desk, he changed his style of showmanship and perched himself on the edge of the front of his desk with his legs dangling like those of a marionette.

'Grainger called you, then?'

'He was very complimentary about you.'

'I just did my job.'

'No, you did what you were instructed *not* to do.'

'Grainger's mixed up in it. Up to *here*.' Templeman raised his right hand to his eyes.

'In murder? Are you mad?'

'Mixed up in the investigation.'

'Only because *you've* mixed him into it. It could have gone horribly pear-shaped. I'm talking now about the porn factor.'

'I realize that.'

'You gambled with your career.'

'Not for the first time.'

Lilleyman remained benevolent. 'Luckily, for you, no serious damage appears to have been done. Nevertheless, that's a consequence of chance rather than sound judgement. I ought to suspend you, Templeman, without bothering to fart around with considering anything in mitigation. You know that, don't you?'

'I'm sure you could justify it to yourself.'

'And others. In fact, my initial inclination was to wash my hands of you, or at least to pull you from the case, when I heard about the blatant flouting of my authority.'

'What changed your mind?

'Not *what*, but *who*. Grainger dissuaded me. Quaintly, he's under the impression that you have talent; hidden maybe, but worth nursing, which demonstrated exactly why he's a politician. He knows nothing. The upshot is, you owe him one. A big one, I'd say.'

'I don't like the sound of that,' Templeman said querulously.

'You're a fool, Templeman,' Lilleyman continued, still without real rancour. 'With someone like Grainger in your camp you could go far, but you won't because you want to be at war with the whole fucking world the whole fucking time.'

'You misjudge me.' Templeman knew from experience that by keeping it simple in these encounters the target for the opposition was kept narrow.

'Like fuck I do! By the time you retire, you'll be as bitter as a lemon and as jaundiced as its skin. You'll have a gut bloated with regrets and a mutilated ego because, despite all your bullshit successes, you'll have fallen well short of your potential. In other words, you'll go to the grave with the epitaph, "A life of broken promises – to himself. Born with a silver spoon in his mouth and died having choked on it". Screwed by the F word – failure.'

'Is that why you sent for me? To tell me that?' Templeman still refrained from putting up his fists.

'No, I wanted words with you on two counts. Firstly, to let you know that, against my instinct, I won't be canning you. Not yet, anyhow. Secondly, I want an appraisal of where we stand. You've been ruffling a lot of feathers, but are we any nearer having a bird in the cage to show for it?'

'I think so.'

'That doesn't sound very confident to me. We *are* going to bottom-out this one, aren't we?'

'Rest assured.'

'Sorry, Templeman, I cannot *rest* and I feel far from *assured*.'

'We're teetering on the threshold.'

'Of what? A trapdoor through which to plunge and hang ourselves?'

Templeman's pained smile was an answer in itself. Then he added, 'We have the killer in the system.'

'Now that *is* interesting. Are you saying you've eliminated the possibility that it was either a random killing or a matter of mistaken identity?'

'I am.'

'Quite a leap of faith. I trust such confidence is based on something more material than just another one of your hunches?'

'Call it an empirical assessment.'

'So what we're left with is a shortlist?'

'I'd call it a *hotlist*, plus a few lively outsiders.'

'Ah! And does Grainger figure in your so-called *hotlist*?'

'Inevitably.'

'*Inevitably*! Only academically, I hope?'

'He was being blackmailed by the man who ends up murdered, for God's sake!' Templeman had had enough of this verbal ping-pong.

'About which he was open and upfront.'

'Only after being both confronted and cornered.'

'You made a deal with him, I gather?'

'I never make deals with suspects.'

'*Never*, Inspector?'

'Not without sanction from a higher authority.'

'Leave God out of this.'

'I was talking about you.'

'So was I!' Any irascibility was low-level.

'What *deal* am I supposed to have struck?'

'Everything you talked about with Grainger remains in-house, as protected as classified intelligence.'

'I don't call *that* cutting a deal. I guaranteed him no more than anyone else in a similar position. Until there's a court case in which that info becomes an item, it's confidential.'

'Crap! You leak just like every other porous pot and cop.'

'I know when and when not to.' Petulance flared then faded just as quickly.

Lilleyman pinched his pugnacious chin with thumb and forefinger, then eyed Templeman just like a cobra about to strike.

'You're a canny operator, Templeman. Who's your money on?' The snake, suddenly non-venomous, slithered back into the grass.

Templeman was slightly caught off-guard, having anticipated the usual mouthy pugilism, not cat-and-mouse capers.

'This isn't a game.'

'Sure it is. You're something of a toff, Templeman. You were sired into a horsy family, into the fast, racy life. You'd have a flutter on two flies. You're a gambling man; I told you that earlier. You gamble with your career, on horses, with women.'

'What does that mean?' Templeman finally allowed himself to be goaded.

'Nothing to get huffy and hot-headed about. I was just dropping a little pebble into a pond to see which way the ripples would go. And I saw.'

Templeman was now more annoyed with himself than with Lilleyman and it showed, pleasing the commander.

'So, as I was saying, who gets your vote?' Lilleyman exhibited the composure of a courtroom counsel who had a witness squirming.

'I'm more confident about the motive than of the identity of the perpetrator.'

'That's fascinating. Enlighten me. Share some of your infinite knowledge and insight.'

Templeman sidestepped the sarcasm. 'Everything's wrapped-up with Markham's sexuality.'

'That's rather murky and uncrystallized. Can't you be more specific?'

'No, but there was a dark thread of the *outré* streaking through his life, right from the earliest days.'

'Try speaking simple English, for God's sake, Templeman.'

'He was a philanderer, a rake.'

'You mean he had a hyperactive dick?'

'He was low-life sleaze.'

'Yet he had a comfortable home, good kids and a respectable wife.'

'On the surface. But there was a whole underbelly to his life that was very different from his public persona – and that's what I've been milking from people against their will, mostly. You know what suburbia's like.'

'Afraid not. You tell me, 0 wise one.'

'Their sewers smell of shit, the same as anywhere else.'

'What you're saying is that the solution lies within the body of Markham's life?'

'Just that, yes.'

'I hope you're right.'

Templeman was puzzled. 'Why's that?'

'Because it means the killing was a one-off and we don't have to worry about a second strike, then a third, and so on. A serial killer at loose in a city is bad for morale. Serial killers make communities nervous. No one gets any sleep.'

Lilleyman slipped from the table and maundered bovinely round behind his desk, signalling that he was about to bring the meeting to an abrupt close. He postured beside his chair and steepled the fingers of both hands on his desk in a contrived pose. Something was still niggling him.

'You've always thought this was a professional hit, haven't you?'

'I've always considered it more probable than possible, yes.'

'Wouldn't you have expected a whisper or two from the street by now?'

'Not necessarily these days. In the past, you could quickly narrow the job down to a few firms. There have always been a number of independents, but most of them were known to the underworld and us. Times have changed, I'm afraid. There's been a proliferation. The contract killing trade has become far more sophisticated. The import business is booming. The wealthy will hire an American professional, who flies in from Detroit, Miami or Chicago, does the business, and wings out the same day. No prints, of any kind, leading from hitman to hirer; no paper trail, like in the old days, either. Following the money is much harder than ever before. Payments are likely to be made electronically or in stocks.'

Lilleyman grunted his disapproval and disdain for the ways and wiles of the new world.

'Grainger wouldn't be associating with gangsters. Have you pondered that one? If you applied your mind to which of your suspects might have access to the criminal fraternity, you might well find yourself with a shortlist – sorry, *hotlist* – of just one.'

'Someone like Grainger would never deal direct with criminals, I agree, though it wouldn't be a first if he had.'

'No?'

'The late Lord Boothby, for example, was a soulmate of the murderous Kray brothers. Homosexuality was the common denominator. Sexual proclivities can bring together strange bedfellows. There has always been a courtship between politicians and sleaze.'

'All right, all right, you've made your point,' Lilleyman granted, becoming crabby. 'Just before you go, there's one other matter....' He began thrumming his fingers restively on his desk, but kept his head dipped. 'We had a case conference yesterday about Carlos Petrelli.'

Templeman fortified himself for the inevitable invective.

'From all accounts that wife of yours is proving to be a prize pisser. She's finding every way of stalling. Have you had words with her yet?'

'I tried.'

'And?'

'She closed down on me.'

'Nothing worse in my book than a man who can't handle his woman.'

'She's a professional, doing what she's paid for, the same as you and me. If the evidence stacks up, we'll get a conviction. She didn't graduate from Hogwarts; she's no wizard.'

'How come, then, she has the reputation of being a sorceress?'

'That's people being silly.'

'Silly or not, there's a growing lobby in this building who would rejoice if bad luck came her way.'

'That's irrational.'

'Wrong again. It's human. Think about it. Try talking some more with that witch of yours. If that fails, wait until she's asleep, then break her broomstick.'

'Talk is rigorously rationed in our household right now.'

Lilleyman was smirking as he looked up sharply. 'Messed up have you? Everyone knows you've been playing away from home. You didn't really think it would escape Charley's notice, did you? It'll cost you. And all for what? It hasn't done Tandy much good, has it? You could say all the shit's gone to her head.'

Lilleyman saw the intent in Templeman's blazing eyes.

'Go on, I dare you,' he taunted.

Templeman bridled his fury. 'You'll keep,' he said, with withering intensity.

Lilleyman was still laughing long after Templeman had slammed the door behind him.

Chapter Twenty-four

There was no logical reason why Templeman should have been startled by a phone call from his wife, but he was. Lilleyman's derision was still ringing in his ears as Charley competed for attention, quickly winning.

'I'll come straight to the point,' she began frostily. 'I want an unambiguous answer to one question: have you been sleeping with Simone Tandy?'

Templeman was halted in his tracks just as he was about to feed coins into a coffee-machine in a corridor.

'I don't think this is the time for this conversation,' he stammered, thrown into a mental spin.

Charley wasn't to be discouraged. She was pumped-up for this. Nothing was going to deter her from calling the shots.

'I had a phone call from a man who said he had information for me, about my personal life, that I should know about because I was married to a rat.'

'And you listened?'

'I accept human nature for what it is – and how it is. I don't attempt to put myself above or below it.'

'Look, can't we have this esoteric discussion later?'

'No, we can't. And, incidentally, there's nothing *esoteric* about asking my husband if he's been shagging away from home.' Boiling-point was only a couple of degrees away.

'Who was the phone call from?' This was a holding question, affording Templeman precious seconds with which to regain control of his brain-cells, which were in disarray.

'Don't mess with me, Luke. You know better than I do that those kind of tips are always anonymous.'

'And more often than not unreliable.'

'Not this one. The caller informed me that Tandy was in hospital in Bedford.' She paused for dramatic effect and didn't miss her husband's sharp intake of breath, as if he'd just been winded by a punch below the belt; a pulverizing delivery to the nether regions. 'So I called the hospital. I asked if a Simone Tandy was a patient there and I was put through to a ward. I made out I was calling on your behalf, enquiring about her condition. The nurse was suspicious. Do you know why?'

'I'm sure you're about to enlighten me,' Templeman said icily.

'You hadn't long left the hospital, you bastard!'

Templeman composed himself. 'Simone Tandy's my partner.'

'You bet!'

'Listen, Charley, I'm in a corridor at the Yard with lots of people milling around and staring.'

'All you have to do is give me a straight answer to my original question.'

The watershed had been reached. The timing was bad, but the Rubicon had been crossed and withdrawal or fudging weren't options.

'OK, the answer's yes.'

A woman detective in Templeman's team approached him and he shook his head, mouthing, *Not now*. She treated him to an odd look, before diverting towards the loo.

'Think it's funny, do you?'

'No, it's very serious, Charley.'

'Ah! The coded message. So it's more than a fling and trifling dalliance?'

'I'm afraid so.'

'You're not sorry at all. I'd rather you didn't come home tonight.'

'*You're* the one who's been staying away and keeping out of radar-range. Would you care to tell me where *you've* been shacking up and with whom?'

Charley sensed a counter-attack gathering pace. 'Stop trying to hide behind a smokescreen, but if you haven't the good grace to do the honourable thing voluntarily, I'll move out for a few days, while preparing for official action.'

'Don't worry, I'll go.'

They both recognized the finality of their valedictions. This was the outcome Templeman had been hoping to engineer, but now it had materialized, he found himself in an emotional vacuum, gasping for oxygen. On a cold-blooded level, he was giving up the woman with whom he had shared so much of his life for one who disowned him.

Nice one, Luke! he ridiculed himself, as he took the initial steps into an unknown future.

The woman detective, who had approached Templeman in the corridor, caught up with him a few minutes later.

'A report's just in from the Bedford police that Audrey Markham's put her house on the market,' said Laura Mannings, her Essex voice tinged with restrained excitement.

'Since when?'

'Since yesterday.'

'Thanks.'

'Do you want me to follow up or will you?'

He was about to say, *Leave it with me*, but changed his mind, recognizing the need to have the confidence in his officers to delegate. 'You have a crack at it, Laura.'

'Will do,' she said positively, rewarding him with a thank-you smile.

Just before noon, Jennifer Roper entered the office of Sunshine Living in the Bayswater Road, Queensway. Sunshine Living specialized in selling and renting villas and apartments overseas, particularly in the Mediterranean regions.

'I'm looking to buy,' she announced to one of the salesmen. She exuded attitude, her designer shades pushed up like ski-goggles on to her forehead and her wishy-washy blue jeans tucked inside russet cowboy boots. She had applied vivid make-up skilfully and she wore a white, buttoned blouse, one size too small, a ruse that helped to promote her dramatic contours. By allowing her hair to go its own way, she projected insouciance and a free spirit.

'Which country?' the young salesman enquired pleasantly.

'Cyprus.'

'Villa or apartment?'

'Villa.'

'In town or out?'

'Outskirts preferably. A short drive to shops and restaurants.'

'I get the picture.'

'Perhaps near Paphos. That would be ideal. I'm familiar with that part.'

'One last question—'

'There isn't one,' she jumped in.

'I beg your pardon?'

'I was pre-empting the question. You were going to ask the price range, weren't you?'

'As a matter of fact, yes, I was.'

'And as I said, there isn't one. Cost is immaterial.'

'Right, madam, we're in business!'

Around the same time, a woman in Nottingham was boarding a train for London. She had bought a first-class day return ticket. Less than two hours later, she had arrived at London St Pancras station, courtesy of Midlands Mainline.

On arrival, she transferred to a taxi, giving the driver an address in Gray's Inn Road, the Holborn end. While in the back of the black cab, she applied powder to her nose and cheeks, then appraised herself in the tiny round mirror of her compact. She was a handsome woman and she knew it. The years hadn't ravaged her the way they had most of her contemporaries. Although life had been neither easy nor kind, her eyes hadn't been dulled by disillusionment and her skin lied favourably about her age. She wasn't an old woman by any means, but neither was she a newcomer to middle-age. The time had been reached when there was more behind her than in front; more to look back on than to run after.

She replenished her mouth with glossy lipstick, plucked a few overgrown eyebrows, added a subtle framework to the eyes, masked the network of fine purple veins at the end of her dinky nose and tidied her carefully sculpted brunette hair. In seconds, with female magic, ten years on the clock were wound back.

The offices of Kirk, Calder and Lynch were standard for solicitors' premises within London's square mile of the legal holy land. Although not part of the cloistered inns of courts, they bore all the features of such hallowed, wig and gown, bookworm establishments.

Cecil Calder was a jolly, 55-year-old with a florid complexion and a figure shaped by long lunches. His silver hair suited him and blended with his dapper attire. His smile was a satisfied one, but not a reflection of self-satisfaction, and his handshake was as firm as his commitment to his clients.

He offered tea or coffee perfunctorily. She declined graciously.

'I made this appointment because I wanted a few points clarified face-to-face,' she began, businesslike, which Calder appreciated.

'I'm glad you did,' said Calder affably, his fingers and treating her to one of his every-minute-is-more-money-in-my-bank smiles.

'Firstly, I want reassurance about the legitimacy of the will. Can it be challenged?'

'It can be challenged; oh, yes. Anything can be challenged. But you began by mentioning the legitimacy of the will. Let me assure you that anything drawn up by this firm, and especially by me, will be legally watertight. As binding as Faust's contract with the Devil.'

'Isn't that a contradiction?'

'Not at all.'

She was confused. 'All right, what are the chances of that happening in my case?'

'I'd say it's inevitable.'

'*Inevitable?*'

'Others will demand the testing of the legitimacy of the will. Reverse positions and ask yourself if you would.'

'How long will it take to resolve?'

Calder allowed his eyeballs to disappear beneath their hooded lids to give physical expression to rumination.

'A couple of years maybe.'

'Two years! As long as that?' Her face reflected an equal mixture of disquiet and disbelief.

'We could always try to cut a deal.'

'What sort of *deal*?' She became wary.

Calder bent across his desk, using a fleshy fist as a prop for his flabby chin.

'As soon as the will's been proved, we could offer to settle for fifty per cent of the equity.'

'But why should *I* make such an offer?'

'To have done with it. You have to accept that his widow will have a rightful claim.'

'Even though she's not included? Even though she's been written out?'

'Included or not, she's entitled.'

'I'm not minded to relinquish fifty per cent without a fight.'

'On that score, I strongly recommend you be advised by me.'

'That's what you're paid for.'

'And you ignore that fact at your peril. Legal Costs are a major consideration. If the other side is prepared to settle out of court, but you don't accept and press on, then lose, all costs will land on your doorstep. It will be your tab.'

'You mean I'd have to pay *her* legal bill?'

'In its entirety. You could be talking about a quarter of a million pounds. Going to court in civil litigation is a lottery. It's never worth the wager if it can possibly be avoided.'

'Will *she* be aware of that?'

'If her solicitor is worth his crust, he'll be imparting the same advice as I'm now giving you.'

'If I agree to settle for half of my *entitlement*, could that be hustled through?'

'Nothing can be rushed in law. However, it would be expedited much quicker than if it has to be sorted head to-head in court.'

'Have you contacted the other side? Do they know of the existence of this recent will, cancelling all others?'

'No, but they will do within half an hour of this meeting.'

'I shall wait to be advised by you.'

'Do you wish me to begin horse-trading?'

'What have I to lose?'

'More than a million pounds.'

'My God! Put that starkly, you really are testing my trust in you.'

'Perhaps you'd like more time to think about it?'

'No, go ahead.'

'Sure?'

'No, but any action at this stage won't be irreversible, will it?'

'That's right. I'm planning an overture, not a finale.'

'Press on, then.'

After shaking hands, Cecil Calder escorted his client out of his office and saw her on her way with a cheery wave.

Susan Harper, Harry's biological mother, was still shaking as she went in search of a place for some late lunch.

Chapter Twenty-five

That evening, John Grainger drove with his wife six miles from their home to the Boatman Inn, one of their favourite haunts. The Boatman, more than a hundred years old and totally unspoilt, was located on the bank of a sleepy stretch of river at an idyllic spot with a copse on one side and a village cricket pitch on the other. Coltish horses ran freely and friskily behind the pub in fields squared-off with ranch fencing. The pub, hidden from a sinuous lane by high hedges, attracted a catholic clientele from near and far, especially in summer. But during the week at this time of year there were no crowds.

There was something about Grainger's manner that made his wife ask, 'Anything bothering you, John?'

'No, should there be?' he answered tetchily.

'It`s just that you seem on edge and remote. It was a lovely idea of yours for us to get out, have a simple pub meal and unwind. We haven't done this sort of spontaneous thing for ages, but it doesn't seem to be relaxing you.'

Stiffly, he ordered two large gin and tonics and carried the drinks to a corner table next to a window. Tiffany followed him, the distance between them spiritually more than a mile; more than it had ever been.

They chatted about the children, preliminary plans for a holiday in Hawaii, and a couple of charity launches. However, a woman's intuition forewarned Tiffany that there was more to their togetherness at the pub that evening than an escape from life in a goldfish bowl.

John Grainger waited for the gin to hit his head before introducing the main item on his agenda.

'What would you say if I decided to bow out of politics?'

Folding her arms, Tiffany said solicitously, 'OK. John, what's all this about?'

'You haven't answered *my* question.'

'I can't believe what I'm hearing. Politics is your life.'

'You're my life.'

'Not true, John.' Tiffany was shaking her head. 'I married you knowing that I would always be in second place to your career.' She held up a hand. 'Don't interrupt. I've never minded being your second love. Your ruthless yet sanitized ambition was part of your attraction. Ambition has always been an agreeable feature in urbane men for me. I've always tried to support you in everything you've done.'

'You have. And I couldn't have done it without you.'

'That's not true, but thanks anyhow. Several times you've asked me how I'd feel about being the prime minister's wife. And I said it would make me very happy if it meant that you were fulfilling your ultimate goal in life. Ever since we first met, I've known that your sights were set on the top prize.'

'Has it been that obvious?'

'To me? of course it has. Probably to most other people too; certainly at Westminster. So, you see, John, I return to my question, what's this all about?'

'For the first time in my life I'm beginning to have self-doubts.'

'Why? There's no more accomplished, all-round performer in the House of Commons. You haven't put a foot wrong since your first election victory. You haven't become *too* aligned to any particular lobby or pressure group. Nor have you allowed yourself to become marginalized by an issue. You've very cleverly marketed yourself as a safe pair of hands; the first choice of most Conservative supporters and the alternative choice of the rest. Your moment cannot be far off now. The door to your dreams has been unlocked and is ajar and now all that's required is the final push. And here you are talking about turning away from it, leaving the grand prize for someone else to pick up by default.'

John drank fast. 'There has been a development that might change everything,' he said cryptically.

'What kind of *development*?'

John turned sideways to gaze out of the window, ready to look anywhere except into his wife's eyes.

'I've been trying to protect you from this.'

'I'm not a child.'

'But it's unfair that this should burden you. It shouldn't be your cross. It's outside our time-frame.'

Tiffany put a hand across the table in a touch of tenderness and physical bonding.

'Has this anything to do with Harry Markham?'

If it was possible to be in a state of rigor mortis while still very much alive, then John Grainger was a perfect specimen of a living stiff.

'How do you know about Harry Markham?' His face was as bloodless as a cadaver.

'I read the newspapers.'

'I mean how do you know about Markham and *me*?'

'Because we've met.'

'How?'

'He came to our house.'

'When?'

'Several weeks ago; a few months.'

'Why didn't you tell me about this … at the time?'

'No need. I handled it myself perfectly adequately.'

'What did he want?'

'To drive a wedge between us.'

'How much did he tell you?'

'A lot, but how much was the truth, I've no idea. Neither do I care. I knew you'd fostered children with Chantel. He said you threw him out on to the streets; that you were insanely jealous of the motherly love Chantel was showering on him and that you chose to misconstrue it because of your envy and warped mind.'

'You listened to this?'

'*Listened* is hardly the word. I said to him, "I'll give you twenty minutes, then I want you out".'

'You should have called me. I'd have had him out in twenty seconds.'

'You wouldn't have; you were in the Commons.'

'Why, then, didn't you send for the police?'

'He wasn't attacking or threatening me.'

'He was harassing you.'

'Well, I didn't,' she said, shrewish.

'I'm so angry.'

'You're wasting nervous energy on a dead man. He told me about a film company he claimed to be running and the roles Chantel was supposed to have played in the productions. He wanted to give me a demonstration on our video.'

'My God!'

'It's all right, that's when I showed him the door.'

'And not before time!'

'He expected me to be giving you earache and that's one reason I kept his visit to myself. If he wanted mind games, then I was determined to prove that he was no match for me. He wanted me to go one way, so I jumped the other.'

'And that was the last you heard or saw of him?'

'Oh, yes, he knew better than to mess with me after our little get-to-know-one-another session. I intended to shock him and I think I did.'

'How?'

'I simply warned if he went to any newspaper with his lurid story to hurt you, or if he repeated to anyone else what he'd just told me, and I heard about it, I'd kill him.'

'You said *what*?'

'I said I'd kill him.'

Chapter Twenty-six

Templeman spent half an hour at Tandy's bedside and, following instructions to the letter, refrained from putting Simone under any pressure. They talked about the weather, hospital food, TV and all things anodyne, such as the racing stables run by Templeman's parents and sister. He made no attempt to kiss her – not even on the cheek or forehead – and kept his emotions on a tight rein.

As he was leaving, Simone said soulfully, 'Thank you for coming. I really enjoyed your company. I can understand why we got on so well. Are you going to return tomorrow?'

'Do you want me to?'

'That's a leading question.'

'Be led, then.'

Simone laughed in the abandoned way Templeman remembered.

'Please visit me tomorrow if you can. Tell me more about your family. Their way of life in the country sounds idyllic.'

'It's hard work, a real sweat, but, yes, they enjoy it. Perhaps you'd like to stay there for a few days while you're recuperating?'

Had he gone too far, too fast? He held his breath.

'I'll think about it. We'll have to see how things progress, won't we?'

'See you tomorrow, then.'

He took a chance and blew her a kiss from the door. She mustered a weak wave in return that, in the circumstances, was tantamount to a smouldering embrace and a caress. Everything was relative, Templeman reminded himself.

All mobile phones had to be switched off in the hospital. Templeman had complied with the rules. As he reactivated his Nokia while crossing the car-park, so a text message flashed on the screen.

'maj devel … call me …dc mannings'

Templeman did as entreated.

'You're going to love this,' Laura Mannings began.

That kind of introduction was usually an overture to news that would be anathema to him. Every muscle in his body tightened.

'The solicitor of Widow Markham left a message this afternoon,' Mannings continued. 'Not with me or you'd have heard about it before now.'

Dump the excuses. Just give me the details.

'Harry Markham made a new will shortly before his death, but not with his country, family solicitor – not with the old boy who drew up the original. And this is the bit you're going to drool over.'

Templeman was *drooling* already.

'Nothing goes to the wife. Nothing goes to Jennifer Roper. Nothing goes to his kids.'

'Who then?'

'Everything goes to his mother – Susan Harper.'

Chapter Twenty-seven

Templeman checked into the Travel Inn near the London Eye and Westminster Bridge, on the South Bank, facing Big Ben and the Palace of Westminster. He was asleep by ten. No sweet dreams, but no nightmares, either. In other words, a night of breaking even. That had to count as a winning night; a rare victory over the demons.

After catching up on office chores between seven and nine the next morning, Templeman called Harvey Urwin, who had been solicitor to the Markham family in Bedford.

Urwin, as punctilious as ever, refused to discuss Harry Markham's affairs until he had checked Templeman's status. So it was around 9.30 before Templeman was able to put his first question.

'Is it true that there is another will, made by Mr Markham after the one in your possession?'

'It is true that there is a claim of the existence of another will that would outdate the one in my safekeeping, should it be authenticated.'

'Are you suggesting it's a forgery?'

'Not at all. I have to see it before I can form an opinion. Even if it is genuine, there are many other considerations.'

'Such as?'

'The state of Mr Markham's mind when it was drawn up and signed, for example.'

'When we talked before, you intimated that he was contemplating making changes to the will that you have on file.'

'More than *intimated*, he was coming to see me.'

'But details hadn't been conveyed to you in advance?'

'They had not, as I have said all along.'

'Having made a will with you and having hinted, or whatever, at injecting codicils – or a complete rewrite – why should he have then gone to another solicitor, without even advising you?'

'Why indeed!'

'No ideas?'

'None whatsoever.'

'Did this Mr Calder – I believe that's his name?'

'It is.'

'Did he contact you by phone?'

'He did.'

'Can you tell me exactly what he said?'

'Not *exactly*, no. He said he had called to apprise me of the existence of a will, made by Mr Harry Markham, that rendered obsolete the one under our roof.'

'So Mr Markham must have told him that he'd made an earlier will with you?'

'Presumably, though that did not come up in our rather brief conversation.'

'At what point did you become aware that the new beneficiary was to be Markham's mother?'

Urwin's artificial cough was a lawyer's device for slowing down proceedings while he counselled himself. 'I said to him that Mrs Markham would be shocked. I wanted to protect her, especially at a time like this. So I asked him if she remained the sole beneficiary – or at least the major one. That is when I learned that she had been totally excluded in favour of another woman.'

'But you didn't know at that stage that the other woman was the deceased's mother?'

'No, Mr Calder just mentioned a name that meant nothing to me.'

'And that name was Susan Harper?'

'Correct.'

'Did you pursue that?' This was tantamount to milking a cow. There was no resistance, but it was hard work.

'I did. I asked about the connection between the deceased and the proposed new beneficiary.'

'And that's when you learned that Mrs Harper was Harry Markham's mother?'

'*Allegedly* his mother.'

'Have you reason for doubt?'

'There is always reason and room for doubt until it has been eliminated.'

'Have you alerted your client, Audrey Markham?'

'I did so by phone. It was not news, I decided, that should be imparted by an impersonal missive.'

'How did she take it?'

'She's in denial.'

'I believe you left a message for me?'

'Yes, immediately after putting down the phone, following my conversation with Mrs Markham.'

'Did you call me on the instigation of Mrs Markham?'

'No, it was my decision entirely, though I did forewarn her of my intention. I considered the information germane to your inquiries.'

'I'm grateful to you. What will be your course of action now, Mr Urwin?'

The solicitor changed gear into didactic, legal mode. 'That will depend entirely on my client's instructions.'

'What will be your advice?'

Urwin's brain skipped a beat, then he said, evasively, 'My advice will be in my client's best interest.'

'So you'll be contesting?'

'Certainly we won't be accepting this rabbit-out-of-the-hat on face value.'

'When there are further developments your end, I'd appreciate a tip-off.'

'I shall take any *lawful* measures to protect my client's interests. Now, Inspector, may *I* ask *you* a question?'

'Of course, though that's not to say it will be answered.'

'What are you going to do with this information?'

'As soon as I hang up, I'm going to pay Mr Calder a visit.'

Templeman could almost hear Urwin's brain cells grinding.

'Perhaps you could do *me* a favour.'

'If it's at all possible.' *I owe him one.*

'I'd be grateful for a call after you've spoken with Mr Calder. I'm keen to learn more about Susan Harper and the circumstances surrounding the surprise, last-minute will.'

'Me, too.'

Calder received Templeman into his office with bumptious bonhomie.

'I have no problem with telling you everything,' he began sonorously, as soon as they were settled with tea and biscuits.

'There's no great mystery. Mr Markham came to me on word-of-mouth recommendation:'

'Whose?'

'I don't consider that pertinent.'

'You just promised to tell me *everything*.'

'Everything of relevance, yes.'

'I'll be the arbiter of *relevance*, if you don't mind.'

'Oh, I do *mind*, but, to be honest, I don't even know who gave him my name.'

'That's a cop-out.'

Calder nibbled a biscuit noisily as a diversion. 'I really don't know how we came to get off on the wrong foot, Inspector.'

'Oh, but I do! However, let's progress. When did Mr Markham first come to you?'

'He came only the once and that was exactly three weeks to the day before his death. He had made an appointment a few days earlier via my secretary.'

'Please talk me through your meeting with him.'

'Well, he explained to me that he had a terminal medical condition and it had started to advance rather rapidly and that he wanted to make a final will, rescinding all others.'

'Did you ask him about his previous will?'

'I did. He gave me the name of the solicitors with whom it had been sworn and deposited. I questioned him gently as to his reason for coming to me, rather than to the solicitor he'd dealt with before.'

'And?'

'His earlier will had been made with his family solicitor and he didn't want the embarrassment of having to face a grilling as to why he was abandoning his wife, in terms of inheritance. A *grilling* was an exaggeration of what might have transpired. I'm sure Mr Urwin's probing would have been oblique, though he'd have been duty-bound to advise Mr Markham, the same as I did, that his wife would have every right to mount a challenge.'

'You say you saw him only the once.'

Calder's forehead creased into a frown. 'And that is so.'

'Isn't it customary to draw up a will and then have it signed and witnessed on another occasion?'

'That is the normal procedure, yes, but Mr Markham was a man in a hurry; short of time; though he didn't look particularly ill.'

'Did he mention his mother?'

'Not at all.'

'He gave no indication whether or not they were in regular touch with one another?'

'He didn't volunteer anything along those lines.'

'Did he indicate how soon he expected to die?'

'Yes, he said he had only months to live.'

'How would you describe the state of his mind?'

'If you're wondering if he was unbalanced, forget it. He was very rational and self-possessed. He had clearly given thought to what he was about to do and there was nothing more to be discussed.'

'May I take a copy of the will?'

'I anticipated that request; I have a photocopy here for you.'

Calder slid open the top drawer of his desk and withdrew a manuscript-sized brown envelope.

'I'm obliged,' said Templeman, taking the envelope before the solicitor had a chance to reconsider his prompt compliance.

'One last thing I need from you....' Templeman continued optimistically.

'If I possibly can.'

'Mrs Harper's address?'

'Ah! Yes, of course. That is with my secretary. She'll give it to you on your way out.'

Templeman had never been shown the door more politely.

Chapter Twenty-eight

Susan Harper welcomed Templeman as if he was her own son, returned unwanted by the Reaper.

'You really must let me get you some lunch. You've come so far.'

And when Templeman declined, she pressed, 'How about a sandwich?'

'No, nothing, really. I stopped for a snack at a service station on the M1.'

'You'll at least allow me to make you a drink?'

'Thank you, but no.'

Susan Harper appeared genuinely disappointed that her offer of hospitality was being spurned.

'Oh, well, I suppose you have a heavy workload and you're in a hurry to get back to London,' she said, almost in a monologue. 'To be honest, I was expecting to hear from you long before now.'

'I had no idea if you were even still alive.'

'Good heaven's! I'm not that ancient.'

Templeman wasn't going to be drawn into frivolity. 'We knew nothing of your remarriage. We've been following the trails of Mrs Markhams all over the world, but, of course, they all led to deadends. Now I know why.'

She treated him to a motherly smile as she postured opposite, long legs crossed and her head cocked, as if appraising him with trifling amusement.

'Several times I had the urge to contact you.'

'Why didn't you?'

'My husband, Tom, begged me not to.'

'Why should he do that?'

'Because of the past. *My* past. He was afraid old skeletons would be dragged out of the cupboard, that we'd be hounded by press photographers and reporters. Exposed. Outed. '

He was probably right, too, thought Templeman.

'Since remarrying, I've lived quietly here in the suburbs of Nottingham. It's a delightful part of the country, as you can see. We're only a few miles from Sherwood Forest, fabled Robin Hood territory. We're quite active socially in the community. Tom's anxious we shouldn't take risks with our way of life; our quality of life. After all, nothing can bring back Harry.'

'No, but perhaps you can help us to catch his killer.'

'*Me*? How on earth can I do that? What do I know?'

'You can throw light on parts of his life that no one else can.'

'That was a long, long time ago.'

'Seeds grow – and not always straight.'

'I'm no good at riddles, Inspector.'

'A distant event or relationship could have been a precursor to the crime in the Soho car park.'

'I can't help you there. There was bad blood between Harry and his father, but he died fairly soon after ...'

'The scandal,' Templeman helped her out.

'The vendetta.' She preferred her own waspish interpretation.

'What about Emma, Harry's sister, your daughter?'

'What about her?' There was poison in her eyes and bile garnishing her words.

'I've interviewed her. She hasn't a decent word to say about you or Harry.'

'I bet she hasn't, the lying viper.'

'She's your flesh and blood, just as much as was Harry.' Templeman played the umbilical cord and womb card.

'I won't have those two mentioned in the same breath. She lied and lied and lied. She was at the root of all our troubles.'

'Are you persisting, all these years on, in denying that incest occurred?'

'All that stuff is history. I don't want old wounds reopened. This is just what Tom hoped to avoid. We don't want to have to move, but we'll have no option if all that old muck is raked up. We're not rich, but we're comfortably off.'

The cue was too good a gift to be scorned.

'But you will be rich if Harry's last will and testament is upheld.'

Susan Harper shrugged, as if nothing more than the photo-finish of a minor horserace was at stake.

'That is something for the future, I'm reliably informed.'

'Harry's wife had no idea that you and he were in contact.'

'Is that what *she* told you?'

Templeman nodded. 'Obviously she was wrong.'

'*Obviously!*' Her expansive output was suddenly curtailed.

'Harry and Emma went to foster homes. You were denied access. You weren't even permitted to know where they were living. How did you learn of Harry's whereabouts?'

'Do you object to my smoking?'

'It's your home.'

Mrs Harper shook a kingsize filter tip from a Camel pack on a magazine table beside the sofa. She lit the cigarette with a chunky silver lighter that doubled as a paperweight, then watched it burn. Her darkling eyes followed the smoke-rings all the way to the patterned ceiling. If there was any message in those signals, it floated way over Templeman's head.

'It didn't take me long to find Harry.'

'How?'

After an early release from prison, I had to report to a parole officer.'

'So?'

'He was liaising with social services and child welfare officers.'

'So?'

'He knew where my kids had gone. Correction, he was in a position to *find out* where they had gone.'

'Why would he imperil his career for a stranger?'

'What makes you presume we remained strangers?'

Now she exhaled smoke-cloud directly into Templeman's face. Her expression and attitude were choreographed with triumph and innuendo.

'How long did it take you to seduce him?'

'Inspector, you disappoint me. I took you for a cerebral man. Seduction was unnecessary. I merely raised expectations.'

'Let's keep this to basics. You led him on?'

'No, no, everything was in his own head. He wanted to believe that he was on a joyride to the bedroom, but all the signposts were ambiguous. He chose to interpret them to suit the spirit of the satyr, himself.'

'It was just a game to you?'

'No *game*, Inspector. You insult me and my son. I was plotting a reunion. I was being machiavellian as only a mother knows how. I worked at it and won. To hell with those who would damn me.'

'After you got what you wanted, you dumped him?'

'You're forgetting, he was my parole officer. I was in no position to break off with him. I simply kept control, until I was free. There was nothing he could do for revenge because he had broken the law. I had him well and truly in a vice and he knew it. And I didn't let go until I was good and ready.'

'How did you get in touch with Harry without his foster parents finding out?'

'I followed him to school for several days. I observed his routine. I noted who his friends were. Finally, I gave one of his friends a letter in a sealed envelope to give him. I made it clear in the letter that Harry should only contact me if it really was his wish.'

'And he did?'

'The very next day. We never lost contact again.'

'Did you meet regularly?'

'Not *regularly*, but frequently.'

'Was the relationship what one would expect between mother and son?'

'How sensitively structured! I thought police officers were more blunt than that.'

'I'm trying to be cerebral for you.'

'*Touché*! Nothing illegal ever occurred between us after I came out of prison. Whenever we met or parted, we'd kiss each other on the cheek, just like other mums and sons.'

'When did you remarry?'

'Sixteen years ago.'

'Are you still married?'

'I am.'

'Happily?'

'Not unhappily.'

'Did your husband ever meet Harry?'

'Just a couple of times, when we managed to catch his show.'

'But he knew all about Harry?'

'I'm not sure what you mean, but I talked to him about Harry early in our marriage, mainly about his singing, his club act.'

'Did you talk about your daughter?'

'To my husband?' Her question was rhetorical. 'God, no! I'd disowned Emma long ago.'

'So you never tried to trace her?'

'If she was in Hell, it would be too decent for her.'

'That's a very harsh thing to say about your own child.'

262 BULLET FOR AN ENCORE

'Emma's evil. She destroyed my marriage and got me gaoled. Most of all, she was responsible for my being separated from Harry.'

'Is your husband employed?'

'He's a security officer with a bio-tech laboratory, Eco Research Institute of Third Generation Technology. When I first met Tom, he was in the navy; a sergeant in the Royal Marines. He saw action in terrorist hot spots all over the world.'

'Where is he right now?'

'At work.'

'Does he know you have a prison record?'

'He does. After he asked me to marry him, I sat him down and gave him a one-hour resumé of my life. Chapter and verse. My version, of course.'

'Did you tell him why you were gaoled?'

'I told him what I was convicted of.'

'But claimed you were innocent of the charge, is that it?'

'There was no guilt attached to anything I'd done.'

'Not in *your* eyes, maybe, but I'm not here to be judgemental.'

'Sweet Jesus, you're not!' she erupted sarcastically. 'Listen, Tom wasn't concerned with my past. He was already married when we started dating, but his had been a loveless marriage and that was all I needed to know. I didn't ask for any run-of-play, blow-by-blow commentary about his failures and failings. I'm a pragmatist. So's Tom. The past is dead, so the only sensible thing to do is bury it. We looked to the future.'

'How frequently did you see Harry?'

'No more than twice a year after his marriage, when he had a family of his own.'

'They were clandestine trysts?'

'*Tryst* has a certain connotation that's not applicable. We would rendezvous; we didn't have *trysts*.'

'Didn't you go to his shows?'

'He was never famous. He did a nightclub cabaret. I saw him a couple of times with Tom, as I told you. He was good, but it was the same performance each time. Presley was dead, so there couldn't be any new songs of his to add to the repertoire, now could there?'

'When did you last see your son?'

The tempo of the questioning went up a couple of notches. Susan Harper kept pace with the change of rhythm.

'About a month before his death.' The answer came only after some fancy mental arithmetic.

'Where?'

'Right here. He was working one of the city's nightclubs for a week.'

'Was your husband here, when Harry visited the last time?'

'No, he was at work. Tom does days. Harry came one afternoon.'

'Did you know in advance that he was coming?'

'He rang me the day before. That would have been a Sunday. We chatted on the phone for about ten minutes. I said he could stay with us, but he'd already booked a room in a small hotel for the week. I don't think he fancied being drawn into talking about old times with Tom.'

'That I can understand.'

Her smile was withering. 'When Harry came, we talked for about two hours. That's all we did – talk.'

'Did he tell you he was dying, or did you know that already?'

'He broke it to me that afternoon. I didn't believe him at first. For a couple of days I was in denial. I hugged him. I sobbed. I didn't sleep for several nights. I wanted to catch his show, to be near him, to watch over him, to see him doing what he loved most one last time. But he implored me to stay away, saying that it would make it easier for him. I said he should seek a second opinion from a top specialist, but he'd already been down that road.'

'Did his marital family, particularly his wife, know he had been communicating with you?'

'He always said not. It was our little secret all those years. I preferred it that way. So did he.'

'Did that excite you?'

'I suppose it did, in a way; I'd be lying to say otherwise.'

'When you saw him the last time, a month or so before his death, did he mention his will?'

'No, it never featured in any of our conversations.' Templeman ignored her answer and instead looked for the truth in her body language. *She's lying.*

'I was shattered, in shock, over what I'd heard. Harry appeared so fit. It was too big a thing for me to absorb all at once. For me to have raised the subject of his will and money at a time like that would have been obscene.'

'I asked if *he* mentioned the will.'

'Well, he didn't!'

Too prickly by half, too defensive, too much of a blood-rush to the head. A lie-detector would be in spasm.

'I took it for granted that his wife and kids would be getting everything. When I say *everything*, I had no idea he had much to leave, apart from his property.'

'So you were shocked to learn that you were coming into a fortune?'

'It still hasn't sunk in. I can't believe Harry made that sort of money, but it can't compensate for what I've lost. I'd happily give it all away to have Harry back, even for just a few hours.'

'Didn't it ever occur to you to get in touch with the police?'

'What was the point?'

'The *point* is that you could have assisted more than anyone with recreating his early life.'

'What possible bearing could that have on his violent end?'

'One never knows.'

'It's unthinkable. Yet, as a mother, there's a portion of me – a small portion admittedly – that holds no grudge against Harry's killer.'

'I think I understand what you're saying, but I'd like to hear it articulated by you.'

'Harry was facing a painful end. He was spared that, so I suppose, in a way, there's a part of me that owes the killer a debt of gratitude.'

'Where were you that night?'

'The night Harry was shot?'

Templeman nodded and watched.

'You're not seriously thinking…. Look, even if I hated Harry, I couldn't have harmed him. How could you logically imagine that anyone – never mind his own mother – who knew he was dying would bother to kill him?'

Templeman remained implacable. 'You haven't answered me. Where were you?'

'I was here, at home.'

'Alone?'

'No, with Tom.'

'All evening, all night?'

'Not all evening, but we were together in bed when it happened.' She bit her lip and turned away. 'Tom had been out in the evening, but he had to be up early for work next morning.'

'Where had he been?'

'Ask him. He's old and big enough to speak for himself. But he was here, in this house, one hundred and fifty miles from London, when ...' Emotion drained the rest of the sentence from her.

'How do you feel about inheriting everything from your son when he has children of his own and a wife?'

'It was his wish,' she snapped petulantly, eyeballing Templeman as if he had just questioned the legitimacy of her origins. 'It's not as if she is going to end up with nothing. She'll do all right out of it, even though Harry didn't want her to have a penny. You know how the law is.' Every word was now individually dunked in derision.

'I know next to nothing about civil law.'

'A little is more than enough to be familiar with a widow's rights, apparently,' she commented with vinegary sharpness.

'Even though Harry was terminally ill, I'm sure you would still like to see his killer arrested, tried and convicted.'

'Of course I would.'

'What does a mother's instinct tell you? Was he shot by mistake? By that I mean were the bullets meant for someone else? Was it a random killing; a crime for kicks? Was professional jealousy the motive? Or was it an act of revenge, or passion-related crime? Lastly, was he shot for money, by someone who wasn't aware that he had changed his will but had reason to believe he was about to? What's your gut instinct?'

'It could only have been a nutter,' she replied spontaneously. 'I'm the first to admit that Harry was a bit of a rogue....'

'*Rogue*?' Templeman pounced.

'Yes, you know, something of a Jack the Lad, but there was no real evil in him. As a boy, he was a rascal, a lovable rascal, but never a lout or hooligan. The Elvis fraternity is just one big international family.'

'How do *you* know that?'

'Harry was always talking about the camaraderie. So, you see, it had to be either the work of a maniac or a case of mistaken identity, and I favour the former.'

Templeman allowed Mrs Harper to surmise for a further ten minutes, then thanked her for her co-operation and promised to call again within a few days.

'You'll always be welcome,' she said coolly. 'But next time you must come for afternoon tea.'

'I'll keep you to the warm welcome,' he said, as a veiled fore-warning.

If she doesn't win her pocket money playing poker, she's missing out on a lucrative sideline, thought Templeman. *Such reckless sang-froid!*

Chapter Twenty-nine

Templeman briefed his team at Scotland Yard from his mobile. He had pulled up around the corner from the Harpers' home.

'I want a complete rundown on a Nottingham couple – Tom and Susan Harper,' he instructed briskly. After giving the address, he continued, 'Enlist the help of the Nottinghamshire police. Find out everything you can. The local police might know things that don't get officially recorded.'

His next call was to Cecil Calder.

'One question I forgot to ask you, Mr Calder: when Mr Markham made his will at your office, did he happen to say if his mother was aware of his intended generosity towards her?'

'That *was* something that surfaced in conversation. I'm not sure exactly how it arose, but he did mention that he had talked it over with his mother at length and in detail.'

'You're certain of that?'

'Absolutely. Is that important?'

'No, no, just a minor point,' Templeman lied glibly.

Susan Harper had been ambulating in her lounge ever since Templeman's departure and only stopped when the phone rang.

'Oh, hello, Mr Calder, you have some news already?'

'Not yet from Mr Urwin, though I have been in touch. Naturally, he was surprised, to put it mildly. Mrs Markham, he assured me, would be even more surprised. He has to consult and take instructions, then we shall proceed accordingly. However, the reason for my ringing you is that I've just had a phone call from Detective Inspector Templeman.'

'What did *he* want?' Her voice hardened. So, too, her body.

'He had just one innocuous question for me. Well, I think it was *innocuous*.'

'What was it?'

'He simply wanted to know if you knew before your son's death that he had changed his will in your favour.'

'What did you tell him?'

'The truth, of course; that your son confided in me that he'd cleared it with you.'

'Shit!'

'Pardon?'

'I swore.'

'Have you a problem with what I told the inspector?'

'Nothing I can't handle. Harry might have given you the impression that I was privy to all his plans towards the end, but his will wasn't something he discussed with me. It may have been his intention, but he never got around to it. Obviously he was reckoning on a few more months before it became a crucial issue. It's a piddling discrepancy, but thanks for alerting me.'

On the drive back to London, Templeman detoured to Bedford, spending a precious half-hour with Tandy. He bought flowers and a box of milk chocolates in the hospital shop before going to the ward, where, still resembling the upper part of an Egyptian mummy, Tandy greeted him with smiling eyes, as bright as headlights switched on to beam, set deep in the swath of bandage.

'Simone can have the bouquet, we'll look after the chocs,' joked a friendly nurse, taking away the flowers to put in water and pretending to hide the chocolate-box inside her uniform.

'They're great fun here,' said Tandy. 'Nothing's too much trouble for them. They make me feel that my fight is very personal to them; that if I lose, then it'll be their loss as well as mine.'

'And *mine*,' said Templeman.

'You're a very strong person, Luke. I feel your strength running through me. I know we have an affinity, though I've still to rediscover how it was forged. That could be exciting; you know, falling for you all over again. In the meantime, I feel so comfortable with you that we could be brother and sister.'

Seeing the crestfallen look on Templeman's face, Tandy proffered a hand for him to take tenderly, a reflex that marked a watershed in the rehabilitation of their relationship. Templeman could feel his heart kicking his ribs like an incarcerated beast trying to break the bars of its cage.

'Where've you been today, Luke? What have you been doing? Tell me a story.'

After listening to Templeman's edited account of his day in Nottingham, Tandy said drowsily, 'Follow the money is a maxim that will rarely let you down. That's what someone once instilled in me.'

'That *someone* was me.'

The bandages concealed Tandy's attractive blush.

As Templeman was preparing to leave, Tandy pinched his hand, then implored, 'I want you to give me your word you won't come tomorrow.'

Templeman stiffened, 'Why's that?' The hurt in his voice tickled Tandy.

'Because I'm having my bandages taken off. I don't want you seeing me bald. The raw scar and stitches will also be unsightly.'

'Don't you worry, we'll have a natty cap for you to wear,' giggled a passing nurse.

'Just give me a day to get used to it,' said Tandy, with gentle firmness. 'Please.'

'I'll see you the day after. OK?'

'OK.'

Templeman exited the hospital reciting to himself, *Follow the money. Think conventional. Dodge the smokescreen and sideshows. Who stands to gain? Who's the big winner? Only one person – Mother Macbeth.*

Chapter Thirty

Instead of stopping another night in the hotel, Templeman cut across country westward from Bedford, phoning ahead to his parents to ensure that his old room was available.

'Will Charley be with you?' his mother enquired, which seemed to Templeman like two questions in one.

'No, just me.'

His mother seemed to have parted with a whole load of baggage by the time she next spoke.

'I'll have your bed made up for you.'

That evening, Templeman, his sister and parents tucked into a stew and dumplings dinner in the farmhouse kitchen. Hilda, the housekeeper-cum-cook, had prepared the meal. In Templeman's memory, Hilda had been there since before time began for him.

'This is especially for you, Master Luke,' said Hilda, ladling the bubbling stew into bowls from a cast-iron cauldron that had been brought to the boil on a black kitchen range. Despite Templeman's age, Hilda still treated him as the restless child, Master Luke, who ran as free and wild as he rode horseback. 'This will do you more good than a dozen feasts on all that fancy food in them big city bistros. Get this down you and it won't matter if you don't eat again 'till Christmas. Isn't that right, Mr T?'

Hilda had always called Templeman's father Mr T since her first day of employment with the family.

'You're right there, Hilda,' George Templeman confirmed, adding, 'as ever.'

Gracing the wood-panelled walls were the framed photographs of the best horses Mr T had ever trained. Riding tack, including polished silver stirrups and brass mouth-bits, was hanging from the ceiling-beams. The house had been added to over the years until it had become a sprawling mansion, a mixture of ancient and modern. The racing-stable staff lived in a purpose-built accommodation block on the estate, about a quarter of a mile from the big house, while the head lad and his wife occupied a newish cottage next to the stable-yard and horse-boxes. London was only an hour and a half away by car and yet, whenever Templeman was here, for him there was a sense of being on another planet, free of pollution, where although time didn't stand still, it went at its own unhurried pace, not pushed by the clock of civilization gone mad. This was the real world. His other existence was an offshoot of Hollywood; celluloid crap; polluted and perishable.

'Well, Son, how's the big case coming along?' his father oiled the homecoming conversation.

'Slowly.'

'We've all been following it. The papers seem to think you're stumped and met your match this time,' observed Grace – otherwise known as Mrs T – a doughty woman in a floppy jumper, tweed skirt and lace-up shoes, almost as clumsy as Dutch clogs.

'What do they know?' Hilda quipped scornfully. She had returned to top up the bowls from which the family were eating their dinner.

'Less than nothing if the crime reporters are no more knowledgeable than the racing correspondents,' griped George.

The blood was thick with blind loyalty here. Templeman had almost forgotten what home ground advantage felt like because he always seemed to be playing away these days. Now that he was back on his turf, he was lapping up the therapeutic merits of local hero-worship.

'I'm getting there,' Templeman said decisively.

'That's good enough for me,' declared his father. 'I'd wager my last pound on Luke outsmarting that lot.'

That lot embraced much more than the killer of Harry Markham and the entire criminal fraternity; all townies were suspect in this household.

'Anything else to tell us?' said his mother with a parent's nose for domestic bad odours.

All eyes fell on Luke, as if he were in the dock at the Old Bailey and had just been asked how he pleaded.

'Charley and I have separated.' It came out like vomit; there was no means of keeping it inside any longer, but the foul aftertaste lingered.

'I thought as much!' his mother chimed, almost with relief.

'Not before time!' commented Hilda, on her way to the kitchen.

'That was uncalled for,' Mr T remarked reprovingly.

'True, though!' Hilda had the last word, which had become a long-standing tradition.

'You know you can stay here as long as you like,' said Templeman's mother, wistfully.

The moment was suddenly right for him to introduce Tandy to his family vicariously.

'I think this would be the place for her to recuperate.'

'I'll build her up with some good country cooking,' said Hilda, who had returned from the kitchen with an apple crumble and custard dessert for everyone.

'But is she a country girl?' asked Mrs T.

'Not by your criteria, Mother.'

Her sniff translated into, *Not another mistake, I hope.*

That night, Templeman slept sounder than he had for months. The demons had found other heads to torment. He was up by five o'clock, when Hilda was already lighting fires and making coffee. The aroma of the coffee beans served as a wake-up call to his sluggish metabolism. His first drink of the day slipped down like nectar. The others surfaced at six. His father and sister Rachel stuck to their routines of riding out with the first string before having breakfast. His mother, who would man the office in the stable-yard from 7.30, ate with her son, who made tracks before seven.

By nine o'clock, a dossier was beginning to build up on the Harpers. Nottinghamshire police had e-mailed a negative report. Criminal records had nothing stored on Tom Harper, and his wife seemed to have been clean since her release from prison some twenty years ago. However, mid-morning Templeman took a call from Nottingham city police.

'I hope I'm not wasting your time,' began the civilian employee. 'We're not investigating the Harpers, but Mr Harper *reported* a crime recently.'

'What sort of crime?'

'His car, a Vauxhall Astra, was broken into.'

'Anything stolen?'

'A camera, a wallet with two credit cards, driving licence and twenty pounds in cash, a mobile phone and chequebook.'

'Have they been recovered?'

'Apparently not.'

'What was the date of the break-in and theft?'

'I'll have to get back to you on that, if you think it's of use.'

'I'd be obliged. You never know.'

Half an hour later, Templeman had the date of the car crime in Nottingham city centre. It had occurred on the day after Markham was murdered.

Chapter Thirty-one

The phone companies had their records available late in the afternoon of the same day that Templeman learned of the vehicle offence reported by Tom Harper.

As soon as the different sets of records had been e-mailed to him, Templeman printed out several hard copies. Sitting at his desk, with a coffee in a Styrofoam cup at his side to give him a re-charge as his caffeine level dropped, he scrolled through the various lists.

Two hours later, Templeman had written these facts on his yellow jotter pad:

Two calls had been made from Susan Harper's cell phone to Harry Markham's mobile on the crucial night of the murder – one about three hours before the shots were fired and the second just a few minutes before the shooting. She had also used her cell phone to call her husband at about midnight on that fateful night. Although those irrefutable items had set Templeman's pulse fluttering, he was even more inspired by something else: calls had been made on Tom Harper's mobile every day since the murder – yet he had made a report to the police that it had been stolen from his car on the day after Markham's death.

Ripples of excitement percolated through the team as the ramifications began to crystallize. There were only two plausible possibilities, and the fact that the mobile was used after it was allegedly stolen almost certainly meant that the service provider hadn't been informed. Why not? *We answer that question and we have the killer*, Templeman speculated to himself.

Commander 'Bulletbrain' Lilleyman agreed to a case-conference with Templeman at 7 p.m., which, to begin with, was almost as formal as an audience with the Pope. Within minutes, however, Bulletbrain was assuming the hands-on role of a fugleman.

'This is just the breakthrough I was counting on and I believe our patience may well be paying off,' he enthused, leaping from his chair as if he had just sat on a bumble bee. 'Be careful, though, not to overplay your hand. You have to wind-in this catch very adroitly. There are still many ways they could swim free. I take it you'll be returning to Nottingham in the morning?'

'First thing.'

'Will you pull them in?'

'There are advantages for and against. On balance, I think I favour the softly-softly, let-them-simmer approach. That way, all options are kept open. And they have the chance to panic and do something silly.'

'That gets my vote. Do it by increments. But by the book. No cutting corners. The ratchet traps the rat.'

'I'll remember that,' said Templeman, instantly forgetting it.

As Templeman reached the door to leave Lilleyman's office, the commander said, as a contrived afterthought, 'I hear you and that wife of yours have separated.'

'Your sources are almost as reliable as mine.'

'You might now find you have some friends again in this building.'

'She's still going to be defending Petrelli.'

'Most people here are mature enough to cope with shysters. But a cop who's married to one is something else.'

'You mean I'm suddenly clean.'

'No, you've suddenly won probation, I'd say – and no more.'

After a short night in his inexpensive London hotel, Templeman headed north long before daybreak and was at the Harpers' modest, suburban home by 7.30.

Susan Harper was in her satin housecoat when she opened the front door. Jumpy surprise registered in her groggy eyes.

'Inspector! A second visit so soon! Is it me or this city you've fallen for?'

Templeman was impressed by the rapid recovery of her composure.

'The truth is that I wanted to catch your husband before he set out for work.'

'*Catch* my husband! That sounds ominous.'

Templeman was determined not to permit his professionalism to be compromised.

'This shouldn't take long, depending on the answers. May I come in?'

'Oh, of course, how rude of me; you must think I'm very anti-social.'

'I'm not here to socialize; I must make that clear,' he said stuffily.

Her giggle belied her age. 'Goodness, you are keen this morning. We'll go into the lounge. I hope this won't involve Tom for too long. His shift starts at eight today. You're lucky he was still here. Often he begins at seven. He hates being made late. His obsession with punctuality is a throwback to his armed service days.'

As soon as Templeman was seated, Susan Harper excused herself, saying, 'I'll just go fetch Tom.' She closed the door behind her so that Templeman wouldn't overhear the whispered conversation upstairs.

It was more than five minutes before Tom Harper entered the room confidently, his wife close behind. He wore dark uniform trousers and a freshly laundered white shirt with a starched collar. His tie was funereal black. He approached Templeman with a hand extended, ready to squeeze flesh; his handshake bone-crunching.

'Susan tells me you're here this time to talk with *me*. I'm intrigued.'

I bet you are. 'I'm actually here to put questions to you both.'

'How long do you anticipate this taking?' Tom Harper made a point with an exaggerated glance at his ostentatious wristwatch.

'I'll try not to make you late for work.'

They all sat. This time Templeman wasn't offered the hospitality he'd been promised. The Harpers sat alongside one another on a settee opposite Templeman, who was in an armchair beside a wood-carved fireplace. Tom Harper perched on the edge, while his wife reclined. He laced his fingers in his lap, every muscle in his body taut and twitching, while she was as relaxed as a tourist sunbathing on a desert island.

'You must understand that in cases such as this—'

'You're talking about Harry now?' Tom Harper interrupted, his voice gravelly, as if distorted by years of barking orders or abusing his throat by smoking excessively.

'Harry Markham, yes. In murder investigations, we make all sorts of inquiries about all sorts of people, mostly as a process of elimination.'

'Surely you can't be treating Harry's own mother as a suspect?' Tom Harper looked first to his wife and then to Templeman.

'Mr Harper, on the day after Harry Markham died you reported to the police that your car had been broken into.'

Tom Harper cracked his knuckles. Susan Harper's antennae pricked up.

'My car was broken into, yes. I couldn't confirm the date without checking.'

'I'd have thought the murder of your stepson would be an unforgettable marker.'

'I never considered Harry my stepson. You shouldn't read anything into that, other than the fact that there was no relationship because we only ever met twice; very briefly both times. Since the murder, everything has become blurred, as if we've been continually crashing through time zones.'

'Even though he was nothing to you?'

'He was *everything* to Susan. She is *everything* to me. Therefore I share her distress just as much as her moments of joy.'

'Among the items you reported stolen was a mobile phone,' Templeman plodded on routinely.

'So?'

'That mobile is still missing, I believe?'

'And everything else that was pinched with it.'

Tom Harper still retained much of his military bearing, even though he was clearly out of condition. The nicotine stains on his fingers were evidence of his smoking habit. He still boasted a full head of hair, though it had turned the colour of high quality, stainless steel; not a dark hue to be seen anywhere. His face bore the tread of rubber that had covered many rough miles and he looked at the world through what Templeman would have described as 'fair weather eyes', which would swing between happy and hostile according to prevailing conditions. The climate in the Harpers' house was deteriorating by the minute.

'However ...' – Templeman played the theatrical pause – 'the records from your network company show that you have been using your mobile regularly ever since reporting it stolen.'

Susan Harper coughed up phlegm, then tremulously pulled a packet of cigarettes from her housecoat pocket. Flustered, her husband leaned across to help himself to one. The lighter was nearby and Tom waited for his wife to pass on the flame.

Meanwhile, Templeman was counting the missed beats: one, two, three, four, five, six ...

'Like many people, I own two mobiles,' Tom Harper finally

replied, a smug grin stretching the smarting, recently shaved skin. 'Or should I say I *owned* two. Hopefully, you people will get my other one back for me.'

Templeman wasn't ready to allow any slack into the tension. 'How is it that there's no trace of a second account with any of the network companies, Mr Harper?'

'That's because my second one, the lost one, is programmed for pay-as-you-go use. There's no billing. I just buy a card. You know the way it works, Inspector; you purchase air time. It's an effective way of avoiding running up big bills. That's why I needed to report it missing only to the police.'

'Tom is very thrifty,' Susan Harper joined in, conspicuously satisfied with her husband's fancy mouthwork. 'He's good for me. I don't have lasting relationships with money. Tom manages our finances.'

'May I see your mobile, Mr Harper?'

''Course you may. I've got it with me now.' He removed his cell phone from a waistband-pouch and handed it cockily to Templeman.

'An Ericcson,' Templeman observed, turning it over. 'Pleased with it?'

'No complaints. Had it three years.'

'When did you buy your other?'

Tom Harper ruminated at length before answering cautiously, 'It must have been more than a year ago.'

'Where did you get it from?'

Tom Harper turned to his wife for help, but she just shrugged, before saying, 'Does it *really* matter? I mean, what the hell can this possibly have to do with Harry?'

'I must say I'm equally mystified, but I'd hate you to get the impression that I'm not taking this seriously.' Tom Harper followed the thread.

'The significance of *my* questions and *your* answers may become apparent only with the passage of time.' Templeman employed stilted language as an irritant.

'As far as I can recall, I bought it in the city centre from one of the many dealers. There are more mobile phone shops these days than pubs.'

'How did you pay?'

'With money – not chickens, not eggs.' Mr Harper's exasperation wasn't feigned.

'Cash, cheque or credit card?'

'Cash.'

'How much?'

'I couldn't begin to even hazard a guess.'

'What's the make?'

'You already have that information from the Nottingham police.'

'I'd like to hear it from you.'

'A Nokia.' His sigh said it all.

'You bought your second mobile about two years after your first, which you still have and with which, in your own words, you have "no complaints". Why, then, didn't you purchase another Ericcson?'

'Because I wanted a change. Because I liked the look of that particular model. Because, even at my age, I like to keep up with fashion in some things.'

'What particular feature do you like about it most?'

'Everything.'

'You've had it a year – at least – you say, so you must be able to describe to me its unique characteristics, which I can then verify with the country's main distributor.'

'Why are you being so officious, Inspector?'

'No offence intended. I'm simply trying to get things sorted in your head because that's the only way they'll be straightened in mine.'

Tom Harper threw up his arms in mock surrender. 'Look, it's a mobile with all the usual tricks in its repertoire.'

'You wouldn't describe a Rolls Royce as just a car, now would you?'

'So what? I don't follow.'

'You'd rave about what it does for you.'

'But there's nothing to *rave* about. The stolen mobile is bog standard. I can text people. They can text me. It has voicemail, a phone book for my favourite numbers and a moderate memory.'

'*Bog standard*! If that's true, then why did you buy it when you already had one that's at least bog standard?' said Templeman, toying with the Ericcson.

'Because that's my fucking business!' Tom Harper fumed, clawing back the Ericcson.

'You're baiting him, Inspector,' Susan Harper complained.

'Not so. I'm merely testing the veracity of your husband's story.'

'It's not a *story*,' Tom Harper balked.

'When did you last use the lost phone?'

'I can't remember,' Tom Harper retorted petulantly.

'But you said you used it frequently.'

'Reasonably so,' Mr Harper said cautiously, mentally sniffing around for a trap.

'Therefore your fingerprints will be all over it?'

Susan Harper straightened, a nerve in her roseate neck pulsating. A light suffusion of sweat crept across her husband's face like an incoming tide and he cursed himself for being unable to control his glands.

'I guess so,' Tom Harper answered ruefully.

'Unless the thief has wiped everything clean, of course,' Susan Harper came to her husband's rescue. 'But we won't know that until you people do what you're paid for by us taxpayers and start catching and locking up these anti-social menaces. I'm here grieving the loss of a son and instead of hunting his killer, you're pestering us with puerile questions about my husband's mobile phones. It's surreal! No, it's obscene, not to mention barmy.'

'Here! Here!' Tom Harper intoned, like a laddish backbench MP in a parliamentary debate.

'Well, I won't keep you much longer *this time*. I just have a couple of questions for *you* now, Mrs Harper.'

'Let's hear them, then,' she said combatively.

'You also have a mobile phone?'

'I do.' She stuck out her chin, as if saying: *Come on, have a crack at me. You should know by now that I'm more than a match for you, young man. If not, you'll just have to learn the hard way.*

'You made three calls from it on the night of Harry's murder.'

'You've been snooping on me, too, have you?'

'Making inquiries.'

'If I made three calls, I made three calls. What are they to do with you? Tell me about them. You're the one who appears to have all the answers as well as all the questions.'

'Two were to your son. The other was to your husband.'

'Is that a crime?'

'No, but it could indicate one.'

'Oh, really, you're too much!'

'Mrs Harper, what was the nature of those calls?'

'They were personal. Mother to son. Nothing to do with you. Subject closed. OK?'

'I thought you were anxious for us to find your son's killer.'

'So I am, but your stupid-arse questions to us are only delaying, not helping, with that.'

'You were the last person to speak with your son, Mrs Harper.'

'How can you possibly know that?'

'Your second call to him was made just minutes before he was shot. A very brief call indeed. What was that about?'

She began stammering. 'It was a follow-up to the earlier call.'

'In the early hours of the morning?'

'I couldn't sleep and I knew Harry would be up because he was working in Soho.'

'What was so urgent at that hour that wouldn't wait until the next day?'

'It was to do with his condition. I wanted him to give up singing, which I feared would hasten his decline. I wanted him to go to the United States to consult specialists there. They are so much more scientifically advanced.'

'But the second call was so short you couldn't possibly have had time to talk about anything like that.'

'That's true. He was walking to his car from the nightclub. It was a freezing night. He said he'd call me back.'

'Did he?'

'No.'

'Did you try phoning him again?'

'No, I dropped off to sleep.'

'You were in bed?'

'I was.'

'Why didn't you make the calls on your land line?'

'Because of being upstairs. It's easier on the mobile, even though I do have an ordinary bedside phone. With a cordless phone, you can walk about, from room to room, while talking.'

'One final query for you, Mrs Harper: you told me that your son had made no mention to you about making a new will in your favour.'

'That's the truth.'

'Yet according to Mr Calder, the solicitor who drew up the will, Harry assured him you knew all about it.'

'Mr Calder must be mistaken,' she insisted, her attitude intransigent. 'It could be that Harry meant he intended telling me, but he didn't get around to it before ...'

'That it, then?' said Tom Harper, eager to conclude this ordeal. He stood up, preparing to lead the way to the front door.

'Oh, Mr Harper, I almost forgot: where were *you* on the night your stepson was murdered?'

'I was out.'

'I gather that, but where?'

'I'd gone for a few drinks ... I think.'

'Not locally, because the call your wife made to you was long distance.'

'Oh, yes, that's right, I'm confusing nights,' he claimed with a hangdog expression. 'I'd gone to Oxford to see a football match. I remember now because I was under the weather that day from a really bad cold and Susan tried to dissuade me from going, saying I'd end up with pneumonia. But it was a very big FA Cup replay for Nottingham Forest against Oxford United. I'm a life-long Forest fan and I can tell you everything about that game.'

'Did you go with anyone?'

'No, I was alone. Is that suspicious, Inspector?'

'You drove to Oxford after work, did you?'

'That's precisely what I did.'

'And you were at work the next morning?'

'I was. Why don't you ask my boss.'

'That will be taken care of in due course. After the football match, you drove home?'

'I did.'

'Getting indoors at what time?'

'About twelve-thirty to one o'clock.'

'So you'd have been indoors when your wife made that second call to Harry?'

'I suppose I must have been, but I didn't hear or see anything of it.'

'How come?'

'I stayed downstairs awhile, preparing myself a sandwich and a drink.'

'Then you went to bed?'

'Soon afterwards, yes.'

'Was your wife asleep by then?'

'I think so.'

'You say you've always been a Nottingham Forest supporter.'

'Well, ever since moving to Nottingham.'

'Your team won *that* night, I believe?'

'In style, we did.'

'As a matter of trivial interest, who did Nottingham Forest play last Saturday and what was the outcome? That should be dead easy for a *lifelong fan*.'

After much bluster and bluff from Tom Harper and excruciating embarrassment from his wife, Templeman said with considerable overtone, 'Whatever the score, it certainly wasn't a good result for you, Mr. Harper.'

Then he left.

Chapter Thirty-two

Commander Lilleyman listened to Templeman's account of his interviews with the Harpers. Unusually for Lilleyman, he made few interruptions. Only when Templeman had finished, did he ask for an opinion.

'It's them,' Templeman said, peremptorily.

'In it together?'

'Up to their necks. They had to be.'

'Motive?'

'Money.'

'Hard to believe. Doesn't add up. Fails your own litmus test of logic you're always so keen to lecture others about. It would appear that Mrs Harper knew her son was on the way out of this world, so we're back to that old conundrum in this case: why kill him and risk going to gaol for life and missing out on the loot and luxury that's only months away? There's one helluva black hole in our case – *your* case – and just how do you propose filling it with credibility?'

'Not easily,' Templeman admitted, scratching his head. 'There's something missing.'

'For once we're in total agreement!'

'At least we now know who did it. That means the inquiry takes on tunnel vision. We have the solution to the equation. The task is to demonstrate how the answer was achieved.'

'Has Tom Harper a licence for a gun?'

'No.'

'Are you planning to apply for a search-warrant?'

'That has to be one of the next thematic steps.'

'He'll have disposed of the weapon,' Lilleyman predicted negatively.

'We might come across something else incriminating; cordite on clothing, for example; you never know your luck without giving it a shot.'

'If only there'd been CCTV cameras in the car park,' Lilleyman lamented.

'If there had been, another venue would have been chosen. The outcome would have been the same.'

'Maybe,' Lilleyman accepted. 'As an ex-marine who saw combat against terrorists, Tom Harper would be at home handling a gun.'

Templeman grunted his agreement.

'But this is all implausible supposition because of the motive problem,' Lilleyman droned on. 'That's where we have to concentrate. Unless we can fathom that, any circumstantial case is destined to fail. The CPS will throw it out with the bath water. They won't allow us within sight nor sound of a court with what we have – and especially what we haven't.'

Templeman wasn't hearing anything he didn't know already, but confrontation would have been counter-productive. He was anxious to keep Lilleyman on side.

'I think I'll apply today for a search-warrant and hit the Harpers' house before the cock crows tomorrow,' said Templeman thoughtfully, structuring his strategy as he went along. 'I'll stay away. My presence might prove too provocative. I'll leave that mission to a couple of the lads.'

'How's Tandy?'

Templeman was taken by surprise, but Lilleyman seemed genuinely solicitous, so Templeman gave a considered reply.

'She's improving. There's some memory loss, but surgery has been a clinical success. Now it's down to old Father Time to complete the healing.'

'Shame she's not around. She'd be ideal to lead the house-search. You could rely on her not to miss anything, while keeping the couple as content as anyone could reasonably expect.'

'We're all missing her.'

'Especially *you*?'

Lilleyman's eyes bored into Templeman as if he were the suspect.

'*Especially* me, yes.'

'Oh, well, that's life,' said Lilleyman emptily, slapping his sides cavalier-fashion, then bovinely circumnavigating his desk; an ageing cowboy confined to the stable, just itching to be about to ride out with the posse. 'Will you have the Harpers arrested immediately after the search?'

'What's your take on that?' *Make it look as if I really value his opinion.*

'It would help to turn the screw. Yes, do it. Have them driven here in two cars. Stick them in separate interview-rooms. Caution them. Question them in forensic detail, going over old ground, looking for discrepancies, however minute. Tape-record every burp and fart. It'll be worth it, if only for show.'

'They'll demand that solicitors be present. It'll be the end of any goodwill and voluntary co-operation.'

'So be it. Sounds to me you wouldn't get beyond their front door again without a search-warrant.'

'True.'

'I suggest you also leave the interviewing to others, so the circuit is broken.'

'That's my thinking too. I can deploy my time better elsewhere.'

'Such as?'

'I reckon the time's come for me to revisit Widow Markham's solicitor in Bedford.'

'Sounds about right to me. Go for it.'

Chapter Thirty-three

Harvey Urwin was delighted to see Templeman.

'I welcome the opportunity to speak with you frankly, Inspector, and, I trust, off the record.'

Templeman avoided committing himself, but thanked the solicitor for seeing him at such short notice.

The preamble of pleasantries was truncated when Templeman said, 'News of Harry Markham's final will, drawn-up and lodged elsewhere, must have come as a shock to his widow.'

'The poor woman's mortified,' said Urwin, settling at his desk. 'Mind you, it came as no less a shock to me, although, of course, my involvement isn't personal. The whole thing is all very fishy. Speaking confidentially, and I wouldn't like this repeated outside these four walls, I think it stinks.'

'You suspect some form of corruption?' asked Templeman, from the chair reserved for clients.

Urwin was uncomfortable with the boldness of this question. It wasn't small town solicitor-speak, so he answered the question as if it had been posed the way one of his peers might have constructed it.

'The whole thing's very irregular. In all my dealings with Mr Markham, his mother was never mentioned – certainly not as a potential beneficiary. This is the proverbial bolt out of the blue.'

'But he was intending to change his will, wasn't he? That was something he had discussed with you and he had already made an appointment.'

'Exactly! That's my very point. He was coming to *me* to make the codicils he had decided upon. There was no reason to go elsewhere. You have highlighted the cause for concern. You have strengthened the reason for suspicion.'

'Perhaps he might have felt embarrassed about making such a

dramatic and fundamental change with the solicitor who knew his wife and children. Might that not be an explanation?'

'I'm a professional, Inspector,' Urwin reacted indignantly.

'I'm not questioning *your* professionalism, but *his*. Just looking at the timetable of events over the wills, it would seem that he made the appointment with you – the one he couldn't keep because by then he was already dead – after he'd revoked his original will, by swearing a completely new one with Mr Calder.'

As Urwin ruminated, so his eyes were fixed on a static spider clinging to the ceiling, before rejoining, 'That's a fascinating point which I'd overlooked. In other words, he could have been coming to me to abrogate the will that his mother and Mr Calder are claiming was his last wish for the disposition of his estate.'

'But why should he suddenly be chopping and changing?'

'Why indeed! Maybe it was a symptom of his illness. Yes, yes, that's something I shall certainly to have look into. It may give us grounds for challenging the state of his mind.'

'Are you yet in possession of a hard copy of the will from Mr Calder?'

'Only a photocopy. I plan to have forensic experts inspect the original.'

'As far as you can tell, superficially, does it seem in order?'

'All I have to go on is the signature, which *superficially* bears a strong resemblance to the one for Mr Markham which we have on file.'

'Has Mr Calder proposed a compromise?'

'He has.'

'He intimated to me, Mr Urwin, that he would be advising his client to accept half of her son's estate and to forego the other fifty per cent to avoid much of it being soaked up by litigation fees.'

'We're now in danger of breaching client confidentiality,' Urwin said guardedly. 'However, while refraining from either confirming or denying the specifics of those details, I can say that an outline proposal has been received, without prejudice, of course.'

'How will you be responding?'

'I shall be thanking Mr Calder for his letter and noting the contents therein.'

'Is Mrs Markham likely to go for it?'

'First and foremost the validity of this rogue will has to be subjected to robust examination. If it is authenticated, we shall have to take advice from learned counsel. Knowing Mrs Markham the way I do, I can't see her yielding easily.'

'She might lose everything.'

'In her present frame of mind, I think she believes she's *already* lost everything. She might well adopt a "plague on both our houses" stance.'

'Mr Markham's offshore holdings are becoming clearer, but I also believe there's a substantial life insurance policy that will form part of the settlement.'

'The pay-out will be a *substantial* figure, but the insurance company still has to calculate the exact amount. The minimum is two hundred thousand pounds, but the policy is with profits, so, over the years, the settlement figure has snowballed. There are also special clauses.'

'*Special* in what way?'

'The payment for accidental death, for example, is considerably higher than for death by natural causes.'

'Are there any exclusions?'

'Yes; anything HIV-related, anything connected with the abuse of drugs or alcohol; death as a result of participating in dangerous sports, such as mountaineering, sky-diving or stalking sharks. Unnatural acts, like self-mutilation practices or masochism. Oh, and the common one, suicide.'

'Is it a joint policy with Mrs Markham?'

'No.'

'So the insurance policy is a component of Mr Markham's overall estate?'

'A sizeable slice of the cake, yes.'

'To be part of the disbursements?'

'That's right.'

'Wouldn't the proceeds from a life insurance policy normally automatically go to the next of kin?'

'*Normally* and *automatically*, yes, unless stipulated otherwise.'

'And that stipulation exists in the controversial will held by Mr Calder?'

'So it seems.'

'Has Mrs Markham talked to you about selling her house?'

Urwin frowned and pushed his glasses back on to the bridge of his nose.

'No, but I doubt that she would do so until a sale was agreed and she was ready for me to negotiate the contract. I haven't heard anything about her planning to sell, but I could understand her doing so. If I was in her position, I think I'd want to uproot and replant myself where I was unknown, making a fresh start.'

'She's entitled to sell, is she?'

'The mortgage is in their joint names. On the death of one, the other assumes one hundred per cent ownership. So the answer to your question is yes. Whatever else goes, she keeps the house.'

Templeman departed Urwin's office with a copy of Harry Markham's life insurance policy and a much clearer idea of the motive behind his murder.

Chapter Thirty-four

The search of the Harpers' home produced no gun; no surprise there. Clothing was confiscated for forensic tests, all of which proved negative. Tom and Susan Harper were then driven in separate cars to Scotland Yard, where they were placed in different interview rooms.

Templeman assigned four detectives to question the Harpers. These detectives split into teams of two. The interviews were conducted simultaneously, lasting two hours. Each interviewing team comprised a male and female detective – a Ms Nice and a Mr Nasty – working from a script of set questions, most of which Templeman had asked previously.

Templeman was amazed that neither Tom nor Susan Harper demanded the presence of a lawyer. Throughout the renewed interrogation, neither of them deviated from the answers they had given Templeman. Late that afternoon, they were driven home, this time in the same car.

'This is the last time you talk to us without a solicitor present,' Tom Harper decreed, when told they were being released. 'I've lost a day's work. I have to explain where I've been and why. You didn't even allow me to call in with an excuse. For all I know, I might lose my job. If I do, I'll sue for compensation, you see if I don't.'

The detectives remained sphinx-like and impervious, refusing to be incited into verbal retaliation. They had learned from their mentor, Templeman.

'Come on, you're wasting your breath on these goons,' said Susan Harper, resorting to insults. 'They're just echoes of their master's voice. And we all know who the master is, don't we?'

Meanwhile, Templeman was at Tandy's bedside, animatedly updating her on his meeting the previous day with Audrey Markham's solicitor, Harvey Urwin.

'From within hours of the shooting, we – that's you and me – had decided that the victim's missing mobile phone could be the key that would unlock the door to the dénouement.'

'We did?'

'Harry Markham wouldn't be caught dead without his mobile, yet he was. His mobile went everywhere with him, because it was his business lifeline. He couldn't afford to miss a call from his agent at any time of the day or night. When he was found shortly after the shooting, nothing of real value appeared to have been taken.'

'But his mobile had gone.'

'You remember?'

'No, I'm just following it through with you. The cell phone must have had a significance.'

'A recorded message or last call; something like that.'

'You've found out about the last call, without the help of the phone.'

'The Harpers didn't reckon on our latching on to the importance of what was *missing* from the crime-scene rather than what was *there*.'

'Is this something we discussed in the café?'

Templeman blinked and did a double take, his face a vacuous blank, as if there wasn't a single light switched on inside his head.

'The café?' he intoned, mystified.

'A photo clip just popped into my head of a café. I'm in it with you, Luke. We're at a table. It's dark outside and cold. Icy, snowy – that sort of weather. It's not a smart place, more a greasy spoon. What does it mean, Luke? Somehow it seems connected.'

'To what?'

'To us, to the investigation.'

Templeman gave his brains a shake, hoping for some sensible fall-out. Then it came to him like a spiritual revelation, just the way it had to Tandy.

'From the scene of the shooting, before the body had even been removed, we went to the café you've just described in Chinatown. That was at the beginning of the investigation.'

'I didn't believe the doctors when they said everything would probably come back to me in fragments. I never thought it would. I believed they were just kidding me along. I feared there'd always be a hole in my memory. Like a hole in my head. Oh, Luke! You know what this means. This is rebirth.'

'What is going on here?' a nurse enquired curiously.

After being told, the nurse scurried off for the doctors and the celebrations began. There couldn't have been more excitement and happiness if a syndicate from the ward had just won the National Lottery jackpot.

That evening, while still feeling high, Templeman called Craig Dempsey.

'I've a job for you.'

'A toughie?'

'For you, a cinch.'

'It can't be legal or you'd do it yourself.'

'Not so much illegal as unethical.'

They arranged a meet for eight o'clock that evening in the Prince of Wales pub, not far from Waterloo station and the Old Vic theatre. The pub was one of the last remaining buildings in a block that had been almost entirely demolished for new office developments. It was a pub typical of the freshened-up neighbourhood; flower baskets hanging outside, a fresh coat of maroon paint, framed photographs of old London on the inside walls, two tarted-up bars – not much space in either of them – and a jolly landlady pulling pints of tepid ale. Buster Edwards, one of the notorious Great Train Robbery gang, had been a habitué in the days when it was an infamous gangland haunt. Now it was a lunchtime watering-hole for nearby office staff, while in the evenings it was frequented by theatre-goers and some of the dwindling number of residents still living in the regenerated area just south of Waterloo Bridge.

By chance, Templeman and Dempsey arrived almost together. Dempsey was dressed smartly – his trademark – while Templeman had put on jeans, a heavy-woven pullover and sneakers.

'Working the streets again?' said Dempsey; his way of saying, *You look a scruff.*

'I'm unwinding.'

'I thought this was business.'

'It's business with an old friend.'

'*Friend*! Wow! You must want something real bad.'

Templeman bought the drinks. It was an unusually mild and humid evening for the time of year, so they both ordered pints of draught lager and sat outside at one of the two pavement tables, although it was virtually dark.

Dempsey put his glass to his lips and didn't remove it until he'd downed at least half a pint, then wiped his mouth with the back of a hand.

'That's good,' he said.

Templeman was still fingering the frosty outside of his glass. He was having a drink to mix business with pleasure, not because he needed an alcoholic fix.

'OK, who do you want killed?' Bleak humour was part of Dempsey's social survival kit.

'Take out your notebook.'

'Yes, sir. Anything you say, sir.' Dempsey threw a playful salute.

'Two names for you to write down. Tom Harper. Susan Harper. Married. Live in a Nottingham suburb. I'll tell you where in a moment. I want to know everything they say to one another over the next few days.'

'From when?'

'The day after tomorrow.' Templeman then spelt out the address.

Dempsey knew exactly why Templeman wasn't writing anything himself. This way, there would be no evidence of Templeman's involvement should anything go wrong; no paper trail.

'Sorry to raise the sordid subject, but this could be quite expensive.'

'You'll be paid according to results.'

'From the Yard's special fund?'

'You know I'm not going to answer that.'

'I'm not wired.'

'Of course you're not. Because you're not stupid. If you ever were wired for a meet with me, you'd never work again. Nowhere. There's no question of your losing out financially. You won't be short-changed, I'll see to that.'

'Do the Harpers have a daily routine?'

'He goes to work – eight a.m. latest. She doesn't work.'

'How smart is she?'

'Above average.'

'Pity. Any dog?'

'No dog; not even a pussy or budgie.'

'Burglar alarm?'

'Yes, but it could be a dummy. Don't count on that, though.'

'You're talking to an old pro, Luke.'

'That's precisely why you're the man for the job.'

'If only flattery could be spent! Any special requirements?'

'Just make it clean.'

Dempsey assumed that he was being drawn into the Markham investigation, but he didn't ask. It was unimportant. It would make no difference to the way he went about his assignment. Often it was better not to know too much. Detachment allowed for a clinical, dispassionate approach. If Dempsey messed up, he was alone; left for the wolves. Templeman wouldn't bail him out. They were the rules of engagement, understood by both parties and not worthy of mention.

'How do you want delivery?'

'By hand.'

'How soon?'

'Four days should give you long enough. If you don't have the goods by then, you never will.'

'If I'm to meet that deadline, you'll have to do your own transcribing.'

'I'd prefer it that way on this occasion. Just hand over the tapes. And don't keep copies.'

'You'll never know if I do. That's *your* risk, which is a lot less than mine.'

On that note of mutual respect and co-existence, they drank up and parted.

Chapter Thirty-five

Thirty-six hours later, Templeman received a terse phone message from Dempsey.

'All set. We're ready to go on air.'

'I'll let you know when to shut up shop and pull out,' said Templeman.

'I'll wait to hear.'

Telling the key players in his team no more than that he would be 'out of town for most of the day', Templeman made his way by motorway to Nottingham, where Susan Harper started to close her front door in his face.

'This won't take a minute,' Templeman began.

'It won't take one second.'

Only Templeman's foot prevented the door from closing completely.

'There's something I have to tell you.'

'Tell it to my solicitor.'

'I haven't a single question to ask you, Mrs Harper. You don't have to say a word.'

'Don't worry, I won't.'

'All I'm asking is that you listen to me for five minutes.'

'You said it wouldn't take a minute. Now it's five. More deception!'

'This is for your benefit.'

'Like the proverbial hole in the head! Have you made an arrest?'

'No, but I soon shall.'

Grudgingly, she relented. 'Five minutes, no more.'

'A deal.'

He was in.

'I'm doing this only to avoid gossip among the neighbours,' said Mrs Harper, emphasizing that she hadn't weakened.

'Neither do I want you untidying my doorstep. If you're here longer than five minutes while Tom's at work, tongues will start wagging. The neighbours will think I've got myself a toyboy.'

'I'm flattered.'

'Don't be.'

'Can't we go into the lounge?'

They were standing just inside the front door and Templeman wasn't sure how much of the house Dempsey had been able to bug.

'Why?'

'Because you ought to be sitting for what I have to say to you.'

'I don't want you making yourself comfortable. Overstep the mark once and I'm on the phone to my solicitor and you're out of the door.'

'It's your castle.'

'And don't you forget it.'

Templeman manoeuvred himself towards the lounge. Mrs Harper compromised just to get rid of him as quickly as possible.

'No sitting down, mind you.'

Templeman positioned himself centrally, confident that this would have been the first room for Dempsey to target.

'I'll come straight to the point.'

'I wish you would.'

Templeman took a deep breath, then, 'I know that your husband fired the shots that killed your son. I know also that you were central to the conspiracy – pivotal, in fact – and are equally guilty.'

'Get out!' Blood rushed to her head like an oil strike.

They were measuring up to one another in the middle of the room, not more than a couple of feet apart; pugilist and pacifist.

'I promised I wasn't going to ask you any questions and that still stands. You don't have to say a word. Just listen to me for a few more minutes and I'll be gone.'

Despite having ordered him out, Mrs Harper made no attempt to enforce her demand. Templeman was a shrewd judge of human nature. He knew that she would have to hear him out. Ambivalence was a riveting, immobilizing emotion.

'I understand why you did it,' he continued.

'You don't know anything.' She had turned to stone.

'It wasn't for greed; it wasn't to get your hands on his money: it was for the love of Harry – at his own behest.'

Now Mrs Harper began shaking as if in a car being driven at high speed over cobblestones and her eyes were overflowing with fear rather than fury.

'The pain must have started to become unbearable for your son, with the medication no longer providing him with relief. I'm guessing a bit here ...'

'The whole thing's fantasy, the rambling of a half-wit.' She spoke without conviction.

'He was drinking heavily because alcohol, combined with morphine, gave him a number of hours respite each day from the pain. He was reaching the end of his tether and was ready to put himself out of misery, but there was one snag. His life insurance policy excluded suicide. What I'm not sure about is at what stage he decided to leave you everything and when he first put the proposition to you. I suppose you'd have a good case for contending that what you did was motivated by a mother's mercy. You may well say that you would have done it anyway, even without the inducement of financial gain.'

Mrs Harper began biting her lip to prevent herself from speaking.

'There must have been an awful lot of soul-searching. I wonder just how much persuading Tom needed. He would have known more than most people how to come by a weapon and how to use it. In your call to Tom that night, you no doubt reminded him to take Harry's mobile after killing him – because you were afraid of what might be stored in the cell–phone's memory. It's only fairly recently that I realized the mobile phone stolen from your husband's car, the day after the shooting, was Harry's not Tom's. If that phone should turn up with your husband's other stolen items, then the game would be well and truly up.'

'Is that it?'

'I said I wouldn't delay you longer than a few minutes.'

'You've come all those miles for that absurd little speech?'

'I leave you with the thought that you're living on borrowed time in a fool's paradise.'

'And I'll leave you with the thought that I won't be losing any sleep over it. I'll show you out.'

'I know the way by now.'

'Nevertheless, I want the pleasure of seeing you off the premises; kicking you out. If Tom was here, he'd be booting you on to the pavement.'

Despite her aggressive language, everything else about her, especially her eyes, was in panicky flight.

As Templeman walked unhurriedly to his car, he could sense Susan Harper's eyes burning into the back of his skull. Quite deliberately, he avoided giving her the consolation of a furtive backwards glance over his shoulder.

Two hundreds yards along the road, as he steered his car around a wide arc bend, he passed a white TV rental van with heavily tinted windscreen and front door-windows. There were no windows on the rear doors or along the flanks. The driver's cab appeared to be empty, though Templeman couldn't be certain of that because of the dark tint and he was encouraged that Dempsey was already in place with his equipment. He had instantly recognized the bogus company name on the van. *About time he splashed out on new livery.*

Templeman drove out of Bedford towards the nearest south-bound entrance to the M1 and pulled into the first lay-by to call Dempsey.

'Are you rolling?' Templeman said.

'I got you loud and clear when you were in there.'

'I was sure you'd have the lounge fixed.'

'The whole place has been turned into a recording studio. You'll even have the sound effects of every time they take a leak.' And then, 'Is it really true?'

'What?'

'What you said to her.'

'We'll soon find out. You'll be the first to hear. Keep tuned in. The critical time will be early this evening, when her husband returns from work.'

'I'll keep my fingers crossed for you.'

'I'd rather not have to rely on luck and superstition, but thanks anyhow.'

Chapter Thirty-six

Forty-eight hours later, Scotland Yard's pool of electronic wizards were busily transcribing the batch of tapes dumped on them by Templeman.

When Dempsey had handed over the consignment to Templeman at Scratchwood service station, just north of London on the M1, he said, 'Bingo! A jackpot return at the first hit.'

Of course Templeman was ebullient and bullish, but he had to hear the succulent self-immolation for himself. The transcriptions would put him in possession of a printout of all dialogue from inside the bugged rooms of the Harpers' home during the period of Dempsey's electronic surveillance. He would avidly devour every word, using a yellow highlighter to illuminate the dynamic passages. Then he would listen to the tapes himself, matching the spoken words to the hard copy printouts, double-checking the accuracy.

It was a further twenty-four hours before the bundle of transcripts landed on Templeman's desk. He began reading immediately and didn't have to wait long for that familiar blood-rush to the head that came with every new conquest.

Woman's voice (WV): Thank God you're home!

Man's voice (MV): What's up? You look terrible. Are you ill?

WV: No, but we have to talk.

MV: That's what we're doing, aren't we? You look as if you've seen a ghost.

WV: I feel as if I have, too. That bastard detective's been back pestering me.

MV: Which one?

WV: The detective inspector … from Scotland Yard.

MV: Templeman?

WV: That's him.

MV: *You didn't let him in, for God's sake?*

WV: *Only for five minutes.*

MV: *You, what!*

WV: *He wasn't here to ask questions.*

MV: *I don't care. You know what our solicitor said. You know what we agreed.*

WV: *He knows, Tom!*

MV: *What do you mean, 'He knows'?*

WV: *He knows it all; well, near enough. Most of it.*

MV: *God, what's going on?*

WV: *He came to gloat. I just listened. He even knows why … the reason.*

MV: *He's guessing. He has to be guessing. How can he possibly know? Just think about it. If he had a shred of evidence, he'd be charging us. What did he say?*

WV: *We did it for Harry. Harry wanted putting out of his misery, but if he did it himself the life insurance policy would be invalid. It was Harry's way of getting round it; of beating the system.*

MV: *(long pause): He hasn't the gun.*

WV: *Can you be sure of that?*

MV: *Susan, if he had the gun, he'd have us. What's more, he can't prove I wasn't at the football match.*

WV: *You can't prove you were there.*

MV: *I don't have to. We don't have to prove a damned thing. They got zilch from the search of this house.*

WV: *We haven't been told that.*

MV: *Which means there was nothing to question us about. Templeman's visit, while I was at work, is just a cowardly attempt to unnerve you. He knows if he'd come while I was here, I'd have bounced him down the road. He sees you as the weak link.*

WV: *I gave him nothing.* (big sigh) *Harry's mobile worries me. If they find that …*

MV: *They hardly ever find stuff nicked from cars.*

WV: *But if they do … He thinks I spoke with Harry just before he was shot. He doesn't know that I couldn't connect, so I sent him a text.*

MV: *Why did you do that? You've never explained that.*

WV: *I had my reasons. It doesn't matter now. If only you'd got rid of the mobile straight away.*

MV: *You know exactly why I didn't. I needed time to check on everything stored in its memory and to delete it. Dumping it in a* hurry could have been more dangerous than holding on to it for a couple of days. We were just unlucky. There seemed no immediate threat. No trail to Nottingham. We agreed that it made sense for me to return to London after a week or so to dispose of it there, so the police wouldn't widen their hunt. This is no time for recriminations.

WV: I wish now you'd never reported it stolen.

MV: That wasn't an option; you know exactly why I had to. I had to report the credit cards stolen to avoid the thief running up thousands of pounds-worth of debt on my account and so I could get replacement plastic.

WV: You didn't have to mention the phone.

MV: And what then if all the other stuff was recovered in one cache? The police would want to know why I hadn't listed the phone as missing. And if it was traced to Harry, we wouldn't be able to talk our way out of that one. It was a choice between two evils, but I think I chose the less dangerous one.

WV: I don't see any difference. We're scuppered if that phone turns up. What can you say?

MV: I can say I've never seen it before. I can say it's similar to mine, but that's all. My fingerprints won't be on it.

WV: But what would it be doing with your other stolen property?

MV: Stolen property gets traded around in the underworld. It would prove nothing.

WV: My text message and other stored material will establish it was Harry's.

MV: So what? They still have to physically, forensically tie it to me and they can't. Never will. We have to keep our balls; that's all. Just for a little longer. Then we're home and dry. They can guess all they like, but they can't prove shit.

WV: I'm nervous.

MV: That's his game. That's why he came here today – to rattle you. Now he stands back, counting on our doing something daft.

WV: Such as?

MV: Such as squabbling and falling out. We have to be strong or else he divides and conquers.

WV (pause): You're right, but it still doesn't make it any easier.

MV: No harm was done.

WV: I wish we could go away until everything's settled.

MV: That's out of the question. For a start, we can't afford it. I can't give up my job. How would we survive? More importantly, it would look bad; as if we were running away.

WV: *That's exactly what I feel like doing.*

MV: *But we mustn't. We must stand firm.*

WV: *I think we should instruct Mr Calder to settle with Audrey on the best terms possible and with the least hassle. Just get it done with. Then we can take a long holiday. Maybe a cruise.*

MV: *We can even think about selling up and moving abroad. But we must avoid giving the impression of being in too much of a hurry. Let's just distance ourselves from it and leave everything to Mr Calder. We're going to be like goldfish in a bowl for the next few weeks.*

WV: *I'm hating it, Tom; every minute of it.*

MV: *We mustn't crack now, with the end in sight. We knew the score. We decided the stakes were worth it. Now we have to see it through.*

WV: *It's all very well for you. You've had military training. You've been in combat. Having your life on the line is nothing new to you, but it is to me. It's scary.*

MV: *That's why you should let me take the strain.*

WV: *Easier said than done.*

MV: *Have faith. Take a back seat. As I said, we're almost there.*

WV: *But where is there?*

MV: *The end of the road.*

WV: *Which end, though? Ours or Templeman's?*

Templeman turned the pages, until he came upon another section that warranted highlighting.

(*Bedroom*)

WV: *I know I'm not going to be able to sleep. I'll have to make an appointment tomorrow with my doctor and get her to prescribe me something.*

MV: *Anything that'll help you get through this.*

WV: *You still think we did the right thing, don't you?'*

MV: *I know we did. We can't keep going over and over this.*

WV: *No one would ever believe us that it wasn't for the money.*

MV: *That's their problem, not ours.*

WV: *Everything we did was for him. It was Harry's wish.*

MV: *Stop torturing yourself.*

WV: *Harry's resting in peace, but it's important for me also to find some of that peace.*

MV: *What you have done goes way beyond any mother's call of duty.*

WV: *And what about you, Tom? What did you do it for? Me? Harry? Or the money?*

MV: *We have to stop this, Susan, or we're going to tear ourselves apart.*

WV: *You haven't answered me.*

MV: *You came first in my thoughts, as always. I didn't know Harry, but I knew how much he meant to you, so it's all mixed up.'*

WV: *And how about the money?*

MV: *(long delay): I'd be lying if I made out it wasn't a consideration. For me, it was part of the trade.*

WV: *Trade?*

MV: *It offset risks.*

WV: *But you wouldn't have done it for money alone?*

MV: *Of course not.*

WV: *Because that would have been cold-blooded murder. What I went along with was mercy killing that coincidentally gave us a financial return.*

MV: *Leave it now, Susan. What's done is done. You have no reason to reproach yourself. I burned the jacket and shirt I was wearing that night and I also disposed of Harry's drugs, which were in his car, so nearly all weaknesses have been eliminated.*

WV: *Say no more. I'll try reading myself to sleep.*

During the next two days, Templeman and his officers listened to the tapes to verify the accuracy of the transcriptions. As soon as that had been completed, he called Dempsey.

'A couple of questions.'

'Is that all? I must have done even better than I thought.'

'Is all the hardware out?'

'Yes. All removed.'

'Now the important question.'

'I'm ahead of you, Luke. Did I do something really naughty? Did I break the law?'

'Well, did you?'

'I didn't even pick up a parking fine.'

'No forced entry?'

'I used my tongue, not a jemmy. I talked my way in. Twice. Nothing but old-fashioned con.'

'Keep the method to yourself. I just need the reassurance that you didn't commit a crime on the premises.'

'You have that assurance.'

'You're an artist.'

'In that case, when will you be showing your gratitude with something I can spend?'

'Give me a couple of days and I'll have a brown envelope ready for you.'

'Make it a fat one.'

'It'll be fair.'

'I'll be the judge of that.'

They had run out of banter.

Lilleyman's over-active gastric juices were scalding his stomach-lining. He was popping antacid pills like ducks being fed crumbs in the lake of a popular park. He dissolved more gut-salves in water and swallowed two headache tablets with the fizzing mixture. *Why is it that Templeman always does this to me? No one else, just Templeman. He is my one and only allergy; the bane of my life. Results are no longer everything: how they are achieved counts for much more. But that's something Templeman will never understand. Doesn't WANT to understand, more like. He's never been a team player; never will be. If only I could get him transferred…. But he does have a habit of delivering. He helps the Met's image, which rubs off on me, but it comes at a price. Is it a price we can afford nowadays?*

Lilleyman's reverie was broken by the appearance in his office of Templeman.

'Nice of you to spare me the time,' the commander said sarcastically, thundering past Templeman to slam the door.

'Shall I sit?'

'Stand on your fucking head for all I care.'

Templeman sat. 'You sound upset.'

'*Upset!*' Lilleyman was apoplectic. 'I came to work today with one stomach ulcer. A stomach ulcer with which I've co-habited for several years. Some days we rub along fine. Other days we fight like cat and dog. But we've always had a sort of mutual understanding. We have established accepted parameters. I know when I've overstepped the mark. Equally, my ulcer knows when it's gone too far and I declare chemical warfare on it with an attack of medication that keeps it quiet for a day or two. Today, however, I find it has spawned a whole family of siblings, all hungrily gnawing at every centimetre of tissue of my raw gut. And through some perverse form of biological alchemy the little bastards have transmuted into rattlesnakes.'

'Has this anything to do with me, sir?'

'Everything!' Lilleyman had returned behind his desk, but he was far too restless to sit. His jacket was slung over the back of his chair and he was massaging his dilated stomach through his white shirt.

'I thought *that little lot* would have made you happy.' Templeman pointed to the box of tape-recordings and transcripts.

Lilleyman stopped wearing his carpet thin.

'*Happy*! Just what have you been up to *this time*, Inspector?'

'Harvesting information.'

'How?'

'That came to me from a source.'

'Out of the blue, eh? Just like *that*!' Lilleyman snapped his fingers as he leaned menacingly across his desk. 'A late delivery by Father Christmas, was it?'

'Someone happened to be undertaking surveillance on the Harpers. Matrimonial snooping.'

'Just *happened*! Bullshit! And who might that *someone* be?'

'One of my most reliable contacts.'

'Working without your instigation?'

'Working independently, yes.'

'You're being slippery as usual and not answering my question.'

'No crime was committed.'

'How do you know that?'

'That's my understanding.'

'*Understanding*! How long have you been a police officer, Inspector?'

'It feels like forever.'

'This is entrapment, man! No trial judge would allow any of this to be presented to a jury. In fact, it would never get as far as court. The CPS has had its fingers burned too many times lately. The CPS will say "No, no, no" all down the line. I can see the hand of your old crony Craig Dempsey, in this.'

'No comment.'

'You put him up to it, right?'

'Have you listened to the tapes? The Harpers did it, beyond all doubt now. We've got it there.'

'You've got fuck all because it's not usable currency.'

'These tapes represent the best confession one could ever have.'

'Except, as I said, they have no value. They can't be used.' Lilleyman had come off the boil. The chemical raid on his ulcer had brought relief.

'Can't we try it on the CPS? Get a second opinion. See what they say. They may come up with a formula for getting into court with this. After all, that's their job. At the very least they might make suggestions.'

'They'd make suggestions, all right; no doubt about that. They'll suggest both of us consider new careers.' With his elbows smearing the patina of his desk, Lilleyman threaded his fingers against his resolute chin, posing as both savant and patrician. 'The problem would come in court when the defence demanded details about how these tapes came into our possession. You wouldn't be allowed to be vague about it there as you can with me. You'd be pressed relentlessly. The judge would order you to answer or be held in contempt. That alone would put you at odds with the jury. Dempsey would have to go into the box. There'd be no way of keeping him out of it. If we didn't call him, the prosecution would most certainly subpoena him.'

'I couldn't allow that.'

'You wouldn't have any say in the matter. Those legal jackals would pick him to pieces. We'd be crucified. You'd be back in uniform. I'd be living prematurely off a pension – if I was lucky. Got the picture? We had a similar discussion over the Grainger material. Don't you ever learn?'

'We could always claim the tapes were sent anonymously. That way, we would keep my man out of it.'

'Are you prepared to commit perjury? Think hard before you answer, because if you say yes, then you'll raise doubts with me about every testimony you've ever given in court.'

Sanctimonious old hypocrite! Bulletbrain would be the first in line for perjury if it would save his skin or boost his promotion credentials. Such thoughts were not for airing in this company. 'I'd better give you the answer you want to hear, then. No, I won't commit perjury.'

'Right, that's settled then.'

'So we grind to a standstill.'

'No, *you* keep pissing in the wind because you never know which way it's going to blow. Find the weapon and link it to Tom Harper. Find Harry Markham's stolen mobile and tie it to the Harpers. Just try being a conventional detective for once in your lifetime. You might be pleasantly surprised by what you accomplish. Stop watching so much TV. Get back to basics. Let's have the Harpers watched and followed around-the-clock. Push them to the edge by remote control. Maybe one of them will break. It wouldn't be the first time that villains fell out. You can tell from the tapes that the wife is already wobbling. Time's on our side. They have to be lucky every day for the rest of their lives. We have to get lucky only once. One mistake by them and we're in.'

Templeman went to take the tapes and paperwork from Lilleyman's desk.

'No, leave this little lot with me,' Lilleyman said firmly.

'That's final then.'

'As *final* as final ever gets.'

Templeman couldn't allow his disappointment to infect the rest of the team, so he made a brave effort to be upbeat, but the other detectives working the investigation sensed his frustration. Without asking, they were able to make an educated guess at Bulletbrain's reaction to the tapes. Meanwhile, Templeman acted on the commander's orders for a day and night vigil on the Harpers. Accordingly, he drew up a roster of three eight-hour shifts a day. Two detectives were assigned to each shift. One of the early morning pair would follow Tom Harper to work, while the other remained in a car outside the house. A member of the middle watch would tail Tom Harper home, which might include a stop at a pub or a supermarket. As soon as the couple were indoors for the evening, the graveyard shift pair would take over, staying together in their car, just watching lights go on and off, listening to music, reading paperbacks, exchanging gossip, regaling one another with jokes and keeping up caffeine levels from flasks of coffee. The routine would be broken only if the Harpers went out. Murder work could be as monotonous as any other.

The police in Nottinghamshire went out of their way to help Templeman who was as forthcoming with information as prudence would allow him. Out of courtesy, he tipped off the Nottinghamshire chief constable about the watching brief on his turf. It was essential for protocol to be upheld if goodwill was to be reciprocated. The chief then initiated his own plan. Targeting vehicle break-ins was one of his pet priorities. Now he had a persuasive argument for drafting officers from all over his county into an elite cadre for a purge on some of the worst anti-social parasites in the community. Combined with this offensive, he offered a one-month amnesty. In that period, any goods that had been stolen from vehicles – no matter how long ago – could be handed in anonymously to any police station in the county and the case would be closed without a prosecution. Simultaneously, the addresses of known offenders in this category of crime were raided in what had been suitably named 'Operation Take-Back'.

Tandy had been discharged from the hospital and was recuperating in the Wiltshire countryside at the stables of Templeman's parents. She would rise late – not until gone ten – and it would be nearer eleven before she was ready for breakfast, by which time Hilda was already preparing a cooked lunch for the others. The morning ritual also included set-piece dialogue. Tandy would go to get herself some cereal in the kitchen and Hilda would berate her, 'No you don't, my girl! You sit yourself at the table and I'll see to the food in this house. That's the way things are. Now, how about a couple of eggs, sausage and bacon?'

'No thanks, Hilda, just cereal, please.'

'What about some nice warm toast, *real* butter and home-made marmalade?'

'Tempting, but I'm not going to give in to your sales patter.'

'No wonder you city folk never have no colour nor beef on the bone. Tea?'

'No, coffee as ever, please.'

'Just like Master Luke. Ever since he left for London, he's done nothing but drink coffee instead of tea. Treachery, I call it. Drinking tea is a British tradition. If we don't drink it, who will? The poor tea-growers of Ceylon will starve.'

'Ceylon no longer exists.'

'It jolly well does in this house, my girl, and don't you forget it!'

She would walk in the fields and sit by a stream, either daydreaming or reading. Templeman had given up hotel-living and would join her at night, mostly quite late. Hilda, with her old-fashioned mores, didn't really approve of Tandy sharing a bed with 'Master Luke' while he was still married to someone else, but she overcame the prejudice by persuading herself that it was apt retribution and comeuppance for unsuitable Charley. There had been no watershed moment when Tandy had declared her readiness to renew the relationship from the point it had reached before the hiatus. Her acceptance of the past as the way to her future had been seamless.

On the Sunday after Lilleyman had rubbished the Harper tapes, Templeman said to Tandy as they maundered hand-in-hand in the country, 'The trouble with Bulletbrain is he can't differentiate between entrapment and invasion of privacy.'

'Doesn't *want* to understand,' said Tandy.

'There was no entrapment. There was no *agent provocateur*. The Harpers weren't set up. No one lured them on or put them up to anything. Dempsey simply planted mechanical flies on their walls – or wherever. Everything gathered was self-inspired by the Harpers.'

'I can see the argument, though, that entry was gained under false pretences,' said Tandy, siding with the devil's advocate.

'Catching killers isn't a game of cricket. It's not about sportsmanship. Our spies, for example, don't go around wearing badges saying who they are. We have to be as cunning and devious as the enemy.'

'In an ideal world.'

'No, Simone, in an ideal world we wouldn't be needed.'

They drifted on, for once not strapped to the wheel of time and deadlines.

Chapter Thirty-seven

The amnesty in Nottinghamshire proved fruitful. In the first few days, the handing in of stolen property had been a mere trickle throughout the county. But as word spread through the underworld about the truce, more petty villains and their 'fences' took the opportunity to unload gear they couldn't shift on the black market. After three weeks, mountains were stockpiling in police stations. Low-ranking officers who had been assigned to sort the items and to compile an inventory weren't so charmed by their chief as was Templeman.

A check of the crime-report data in Nottinghamshire since Markham was gunned down revealed that someone had tried to use Tom Harper's credit cards separately at two stores in Nottingham city centre. Each time the swipe machine had come up with the message, 'Authorization denied. Retain card and return to company.'

Local detectives interviewed the shop assistants who had been presented with the stolen cards as payment. Both described the customer as in his thirties, tallish and bulky, with dark bushy hair. His face 'resembled a boxer's', said one. There was a tattoo across the back of one of his hands, but neither shop assistant could remember what it said. He wore faded jeans and a black woollen jumper. His accent was more 'Londonish' than East Midlands.

It was in the electrical department of an all-purpose store that he had first tried to pass off one of the thieved cards for a CD player. In the second store, he was after a sheepskin coat.

All these personal details of the suspect were fed into Nottinghamshire's own police computer, which came up with five names of known professional thieves whose MO was breaking into vehicles and who matched the description. Only one of them, however, had a tattoo on the back of a hand. His name was Jason Boon, aged thirty-three, who already had five convictions and had served three prison sentences. He lived in a flat near the canal and castle with a prostitute, Ann Grimes. Both were registered drug addicts. Ann, a mother of two daughters who were in care, plied her trade to finance both their illegal habits. Jason stole to top-up their heroin supply. The tattoo on his right-hand read, 'The King'.

There was no escaping the Presley connection, even when it was purely coincidental.

A squad from the special cadre raided the Boon/Grimes flat at 5 a.m., exactly a month after the launch of the chief constable's initiative. Both Boon and Grimes were comatose. It was to be another two or three hours before they surfaced from their drugs-induced stupor. In the meantime, the detectives uncovered an Aladdin's cave of stolen property – everything from car tools to radios and cassette players. And in a sack under the bed were more than forty mobile phones.

Templeman was told of the find just before noon that same day and within minutes he was setting a new record on the road from London to Nottingham.

Of the forty-plus cell phones, sixteen were Nokias. These were put aside for Templeman. The batteries in all of them were flat, so recharging them was Templeman's first mundane task. With that accomplished, he worked through the illegal stockpile methodically. Number eleven almost stopped his heart. The favourite numbers stored in its memory confirmed instantly that this had belonged to Harry Markham. The long search was over. Journey's end was in sight. The last text message was still retained for Templeman to read with wide eyes agog.

'Don't go to your car. Tom's waiting there. This is the night. Don't go through with it, my love. Think again. There must be another way. Please, please. I wanted to say this earlier. Call me. Let me know you received this in time. That you changed your mind.'

Templeman stayed overnight in Nottingham, where he was joined by four of his team from London. Next morning, on the stroke of six, they arrested the Harpers. Once again the couple were driven to London in separate cars. Neither would now answer questions without a lawyer being present. Susan Harper asked for Calder. Tom Harper, as cocky as ever, said he would use a pin to pick one from Yellow Pages. 'I'm so obviously innocent a Boy Scout would have me out of here in under an hour.'

When Lilleyman was apprised of developments by Templeman, he enthused, 'What did I tell you? Didn't I say orthodoxy would pay off?'

Templeman conducted both interviews, starting with Tom Harper, while his wife was held in a secure room, though not a cell, two doors along from Templeman's office. The interview-room on the ground-floor was spartan: one table, four hard, wooden chairs, a tape-recorder and four glasses of water. That was it. Templeman and a male detective constable sat with their backs to the door. Tom Harper and his solicitor, Patrick Flaherty, sat opposite. Templeman went through the formalities, then started recording. The first questions were nothing more than an extension of the opening formality; confirming name, address, occupation, age and marital status.

'I have to tell you, Mr Harper, that Harry Markham's missing mobile phone has come to light,' said Templeman. Business had begun.

Tom Harper hadn't been allowed to shave and his mood was as dark as his chin.

'Good for you,' he said, in response to Templeman's bland statement.

Flaherty, who specialized in criminal defence work, shot his client a reproachful sideways glance. In a brief meeting with Tom Harper before this interview began, he advised his client that economy with words had to be the mantra. Harper had breached this charter with his first utterance.

Templeman hauled his black briefcase from the floor, between himself and the detective constable, on to the table, and snapped it open. He took a transparent bag and latex gloves from the brief-case. Before doing anything else, he pulled on the gloves, then opened the bag and produced the Nokia phone, holding it up to Harper's face.

'I don't want you to touch it, but have you seen this before, Mr Harper?'

'How should I know? It's just a mobile. Just like millions of others. What's so special about it?'

Flaherty, who looked and sounded the part, was already realizing that he had wasted his expensive breath on Tom Harper.

'This was Harry Markham's,' Templeman stated flatly.

'So?' Harper was slumped in his chair, arms folded, and resentful.

'We have established that this was stolen from your car.'

Before Harper had a chance to say anything, Flaherty quickly whispered in his client's ear, 'Hold your tongue. You haven't been asked a question. Don't make it easy for him. Remember the guidelines.'

Templeman smiled knowingly, having heard every word. 'Can you explain how Harry Markham's phone came to be in your car?'

Flaherty and Harper again conferred. Flaherty then spoke, his voice brushed with a faint lyrical Irish brogue. 'My client has already told you that he doesn't recognize the phone you have showed him. You'll have to do better than this, Inspector, if you wish our further co-operation.'

'This phone was found on the premises of a thief in Nottingham. He has admitted that he broke into Mr Harper's car and stole a number of items, including this phone.'

Flaherty, portly and middle-aged with thinning, grey hair, placed a restraining hand on Harper's shoulder. 'And how did the thief know it was my client's car?'

'We described the car to him, where it had been parked, date and time.'

'Has this thief previous convictions?' Flaherty continued, adjusting his rimless glasses.

'He has.'

'So why should he be believed?'

'He has nothing to gain by lying.'

'Except perhaps a deal, an exemption from prosecution if he testifies according to your script. We've all read about the amnesty in Nottinghamshire.'

'There has been no deal with this thief. He did not hand in his stolen goods. He was caught in a bust.'

'Were the other items my client reported stolen recovered with the phone?'

'No.'

'Isn't that strange?'

'Not at all. The thief attempted to use the credit cards, but a stop had already been placed on them and they were kept by the stores and returned to the issuing companies, where they were destroyed.'

'And the wallet and cash?'

'We wouldn't expect to recover anything like that. The money would have been spent within hours.'

'On drugs, do you suppose?'

Templeman had never before come up against Flaherty, but already he had a grudging respect for him.

'What makes you say that, Mr Flaherty?'

'Because stealing to fund the purchase of drugs is the most common motive for this category of crime. Surely I don't need to tell you that, Inspector?'

'We are talking about a drug-user, yes,' Templeman admitted ruefully.

'Then how on earth can you place any reliance on his memory?'

Harper wore the jittery grin of a man reading about a plane crash in which all passengers perished; a plane for which he had a ticket but had missed the flight by some quirk of fate.

'His memory won't be an issue,' Templeman said categorically, then to Harper, 'So you have never had this phone in your possession, Mr Harper?'

'He didn't say that,' Flaherty stepped in, unbuttoning the tight-fitting jacket of his pinstripe suit in a gesture that suggested combat was hotting up. 'He said there was nothing to distinguish the phone from millions of others.'

'Except that it was Harry Markham's. That much we can prove. It also has a text message retained that can be traced to Mrs Harper's mobile. She is already on record as having made that call.'

Flaherty's liquid eyes became flooded with high-octane challenge. 'When my client was here last time to help with inquiries, it is my understanding that he willingly allowed you to take fingerprint samples for the purpose of eliminating him from suspicion. Are his prints on that phone?'

'No.'

'There you are, then!' boomed Flaherty flamboyantly, arms held high. 'What are we all doing here when we could be out enjoying the sunshine?'

Tom Harper drank from his glass and then shook his head, as if saying, *What buffoons! What amateurs!*

'We certainly don't need to be here much longer,' Templeman conceded, alarming Flaherty.

Harper relaxed, but not the lawyer, who was alert to all the psychological nuances of interrogation. Something wasn't quite right. Flaherty suspected a concealed trap. Templeman wasn't trying hard enough, as if there was something he was holding back.

'Mr Harper, if this phone, which we know to have been Mr Markham's, can be linked with you, then you realize the seriousness of your position?'

'But you can't. If you could tie it to me, I'd be the first to throw up my hands in surrender.'

Flaherty frowned and flinched.

'Can I go now?' Harper asked in the tone of a demand.

'Not just yet,' said Templeman, taking away Harper's unfinished glass of water. 'We still have some unfinished business. We'll leave you and Mr Flaherty together for a while. Doubtless you'll have matters to discuss.'

After giving orders to keep Tom Harper locked up, Templeman headed for the forensic laboratory with the glass of water from which Harper had drunk.

Succinctly, Templeman explained what he was looking for: a DNA match between anything on the mobile phone in the plastic bag and the person who had just been drinking from the glass; hopefully a poisoned chalice.

The Harpers were kept on ice while the tests were carried out in the laboratory by the science detectives, who worked through the night.

Just before nine o'clock the next morning, Templeman was visited in his office by Professor Carl Tennyson, head of the crime DNA bank. An academic in looks but one of the boys to those who really knew him, Tennyson moseyed in as if just killing time, rather than closing a case that was destined to make Templeman a household name for at least five minutes.

With hands in the pockets of his threadbare tweed jacket, he remarked casually, 'Your suspect wouldn't have a cold by any chance, would he?' He pulled out a pipe and banged it on the edge of Templeman's desk. He was tall and stooped, with an imperious, intimidating air that was all contrived. In stature, he probably fitted most people's image of Sherlock Holmes. He was nicknamed 'The Don' – with a university don in mind and not a Mafia godfather – but in the pub he was the narrator of more ribald stories than anyone.

'*A cold?*' Templeman echoed, scratching his head, puzzled. 'Why do you ask?'

'Because we have a DNA match from dried spittle on the mobile and saliva from the rim of the glass. Your man must have sneezed while holding the mobile at some point. That's why I wondered if he had a cold.'

Suddenly everything fell into place. 'He hasn't a cold now, but he did have one at the time of the crime.'

'Well, that's it, then. Now you can have the pleasure of telling him he's just caught another cold.'

'The mother of all colds, I'd say, Carl!' And then, 'No room for doubt?'

Tennyson's look was withering.

'OK, Carl, when shall I have your report?'

'Soon as. Not before. Ciao.'

Tennyson hadn't even closed the door behind him when Templeman took a call from Flaherty.

'What time can I come to collect my client, Inspector?'

'You beat me to the draw. I was just about to phone you. I suggest you come immediately. You won't be leaving with anyone, however. I'm just preparing to charge Tom and Susan Harper with murder. You're invited to the party.'

Chapter Thirty-eight

Tom Harper was haunted by his earlier challenge to Templeman regarding Harry Markham's stolen mobile, *If you could tie me to it, I'd be the first to throw up my hands in surrender.*

Flaharty now advised his client to 'cut his losses' and 'say nothing', reserving his defence.

True to character, Tom Harper believed he knew better than the expert.

'It wasn't my idea. I didn't want to hurt anyone. There was no malice involved. Susan begged me to do it for Harry's sake, to save him from any more suffering. I was to be a sort of blessing in disguise. The whole thing was dreamed up by Harry himself. It was nothing more than assisted suicide. OK, that's still illegal in this country, but it's nothing like murder. He didn't want to know when it was going to happen. He wanted it to be totally unexpected; "A gift from heaven", he called it.'

'You were also helping to defraud an insurance company,' Templeman said equably.

'They can afford it. In a few months, they'd still have been shelling out when Harry died from his cancer. How can I be blamed for releasing someone from pain?'

'Where did you get the gun?'

'From someone I knew from my military days. Someone who trades in surplus army stock. The revolver came from Bosnia, I believe.'

'Give me a name.'

'I couldn't do that. He never knew what I wanted it for; no questions asked, no explanations given. You know the drill.'

'How was the gun smuggled into this country?'

'How should I know? That was *his* business. Probably in the back of a lorry, among a consignment of apples or bananas, along with all the other stuff. He's bringing in that sort of gear all the time through little ports like Poole in Dorset.'

'What did you do with the firearm?'

'Threw it in a river from a bridge on the M1 on the way back to Nottingham. Now I wish I'd done the same with that wretched mobile.'

'On the same night that you shot Mr Markham?'

'The same night that I did him a favour, yes.'

'Which bridge, which river?'

'I think it's in Leicestershire. I'm not sure which one it is.'

'But you could take me to it?'

'I could, but I won't.'

'We'll find it easily enough.'

They did, too.

Templeman was finished with Tom Harper.

Susan Harper was more canny than her husband. She followed Calder's advice and would say no more than, 'I tried to stop it happening. You have the evidence of that in the text message I sent. I had been talked into something I didn't really agree with, but I wasn't thinking straight at the time. I simply wanted what was best for Harry. I tried to save Harry. By then I'd opted out of the plot in my own conscience. I don't intend to say anything else until my trial.'

Harvey Urwin was able to assure Audrey Markham that her husband's last will would now be declared null and void.

'The law precludes, where it can be prevented, anyone bene-fiting financially from a crime, so Mrs Harper will not reap anything – except what she richly deserves, which is a long future in gaol,' said the country solicitor in the most trenchant tone he'd ever used. He liked the sound of it, too, and promised himself a few more similar offerings in the future.

Meanwhile, Jennifer Roper, Harry Markham's erstwhile mistress, had no choice but to accept that she had been duped. Nothing of Harry's was likely to be coming to her without a marathon legal battle, trying to establish common-law wife status; a forlorn hope. Accordingly, ambitious plans to emigrate to sunnier and warmer climes had to be shelved, until she could give birth to a new scam. She also had to live with the knowledge that, unwittingly, she had denied Harry his last chance to be saved from the bullet. It was her call that he had answered on his way to the Soho car park from the nightclub. He was going to her place that night and he switched off his mobile immediately after speaking to her … and just a few seconds before his mother sent the text.

A fortnight after the Harpers had been charged, the front page splash of all national newspapers – broadsheets as well as the tabloids – was the announcement by John Grainger that he was resigning from his cabinet post, with immediate effect, and wouldn't be seeking re-election to Parliament at the next General Election. He gave a desire to spend more time with his family and 'failing health' as the reason for his decision. Columnists speculated feverishly about Grainger's *real* reason for standing down just as he was on the threshold of fulfilling his life's ambition. They were all shooting way off target.

Templeman was taking a well-earned two-week vacation and was out walking with Tandy when Lilleyman shattered the serenity from afar.

'I've good and bad news for you,' the commander began, clearly hardly able to contain himself. 'The good news is that your wife has dropped herself at the last minute from the Carlos Petrelli defence team, we've just heard. The bad news is that she's ditched Petrelli in order to concentrate on defending Susan Harper. I'd say that's pretty personal, wouldn't you?' There was unfettered glee in his voice.

'Thanks for the tip-off, sir,' said Templeman, his voice bereft of appreciation.

'I thought you'd rather hear it from me than read it tomorrow in the papers. Enjoy the rest of your holiday.'

'Lesson number one when on holiday is switch off your mobile, the umbilical cord to the wide body of people who can encroach on your leisure time, and bury it in a bedroom drawer for the duration,' said Tandy, snuggling up to him.

'No, that's lesson number two,' he said, taking Tandy in his arms and demonstrating lesson number one.